Praise for

PATRICIA WILSON

The Summer of Secrets

ABOUT THE AUTHOR

Patricia Wilson was born in Liverpool. She retired early to Greece, where she now lives in the village of Paradissi in Rhodes. She was first inspired to write when she unearthed a rusted machine gun in her garden – one used in the events that unfolded during World War II on the island of Crete.

www.pmwilson.net
@pmwilson_author

Also by Patricia Wilson:

Island of Secrets
Villa of Secrets
Secrets of Santorini
Greek Island Escape
Summer in Greece

Patricia Wilson

The Summer of Secrets

ZAFFRE

First published in the UK in 2022 by
ZAFFRE
An imprint of Bonnier Books UK
4th Floor, Victoria House, Bloomsbury Square, London, England, WC1B 4DA
Owned by Bonnier Books
Sveavägen 56, Stockholm, Sweden

A CIP catalogue record for this book is
available from the British Library.

ISBN: 978-1-83877-901-6

Also available as an ebook and an audiobook

1 3 5 7 9 10 8 6 4 2

Typeset by IDSUK (Data Connection) Ltd
Printed and bound in Great Britain by Clays Ltd, Elcograf S.p.A.

Zaffre is an imprint of Bonnier Books UK
www.bonnierbooks.co.uk

For my darling husband, Berty.

Go back to Castellorizo,
gaze at the iridescent sea,
and find your soul.

The Scent of Summer

Honeysuckle, jasmine and sweet frangipani,
Rose petals, lemon blossom and pine.
I'll mix you a perfume, a scent to entrap him,
Bewitching, yes, simply divine.

Wear it when you pass the man of your dreams,
He who sets your heart on fire.
With a dab of my scent, in every right place
His attention will turn to desire.

But beware, fair maiden, once that spell is cast,
Understand, only you he'll adore.
Once he's tasted your scent, he will never relent
No matter how much you implore.

He'll come to your bed, in the darkest of hours,
You'll think him a dream of the night.
With his hand on your breast, he'll submit to your nest,
You'll become his divine Aphrodite.

So, Goddess, consider the risks that you face
If you capture the man you hold dear.
Be ready to lose all the others you love,
For the sake of that one Buccaneer.

Patricia Wilson

PROLOGUE
BABA

Castellorizo, Greece, 1948

'OUT! OUT!' THE MIDWIFE YELLED, slapping the young soldier around the head.

He staggered outside, passing Mamá and María on the way. Babá rolled up with a backgammon board and the neighbours provided a small table and two chairs.

'It's time you learned to play *tavli*, young man,' Babá said sitting in the same spot as he had twenty-two years earlier, on the day of the earthquake. He glanced at the sky, then the ground, then at the soldier. Remembering his brother, the flamboyant Uncle Kuríllos, Babá looked towards heaven once more and crossed himself.

'Are you all right?' the soldier asked. 'You look a little peculiar.'

Babá blinked. 'What do they call it, *déjà vu*? I was sitting right here on this spot, playing *tavli* with my brother, while Mamá lay inside there giving birth.' He nodded at the door. 'That was the exact moment when our lives were changed forever.'

The soldier glanced around, then stared at the ground apprehensively. 'What happened?'

'María's the best one to answer that question, I was preoccupied the events indoors. Couldn't even keep my mind on the game. Me and my brother had been up all night, waiting, playing *tavli*.' He shook his head and sighed. 'If only I'd known what lay ahead . . .'

CHAPTER 1
MARIA

Castellorizo, Greece, 1926

THE VILLAGE WAS UNUSUALLY QUIET that morning, holding its breath, waiting. With a length of old clothesline, eleven-year-old María skipped towards the *plateía*, the village square and home. After a night with her two old grandmothers in the next bay, she could not wait to see if she had a baby brother or sister.

People passing through the *plateía* glanced at the neat, Venetian-style house where two men sat at a small, round, table outside the door. Everyone waited for the father's yell of delight when his wife gave him a son.

From the back of the village, Mimi appeared in her long sooty clothes, black headscarf and spotless white apron. She led the blacksmith's mule loaded with olive wood for the furnace. The beast's hooves clattered on the cobbles. Mimi peered at the house, then threw an enquiring glance at a neighbour who swept outside her own home. The woman shook her head. Mimi studied the two tired souls then called María as she skipped by.

'*Ela!* María, I've a cheese and spinach pie and a bottle of water for the men. Come to the smithy and collect them.'

'Yes, Kyría Mimi.' María headed over to her father and uncle and interrupted their game of *tavli* with news of breakfast. They looked up from the backgammon board and smiled wearily.

* * *

A slight breeze fanned the Greek village of Megisti, the only village on the island of Castellorizo. Fingers of golden sunlight shimmered into back alleys and through open doorways. The iridescent turquoise water was flat as glass, vividly reflecting the brightly painted fishing boats.

'*Kaliméra*, Kyría Ioánna.' Good morning, Mrs Joanna, María cried as she passed the old woman at the end of the row of houses. At dawn each morning, Kyría Ioánna tugged on a lanyard to raise the Greek flag. The octogenarian stood with her chin jutting defiantly and feet glued to her own precious plot of earth. This act of blatant defiance was punishable by a term in prison, enforced by the occupying Italians.

'This is forbidden, take it down,' a soldier, new to the island, ordered.

She cupped her hand around her ear and squeaked at him, 'Aye? What's that? Speak up, young man! Can't you speak Greek? Where are you from?'

'Where's your husband? He must take that flag down!'

'Eh? My husband, you say? My husband has gone to God. He was shot by the Italians in the Great War!' Overcome by loud and hysterical crying, she beat her chest, pointing at the soldier and directing her voice at the sky. 'You hear that, Adoni? He asks me where you are. I told him, Heaven. Where his sort put you all those years ago, leaving me a widow with six children and eighteen grandchildren!' Then, throwing herself against the soldier's chest, she continued to screech and dribble against the front of his uniform. 'Oh my dear God, tell me – what will I do in my old age without my Adoni?'

After the Italian had removed the Greek flag himself, Kyría Ioánna stared after him with narrow eyes. She would simply hoist another the next morning and repeat the performance.

Eventually, much to everyone's glee, the new soldier would ignore her and the flag. She would be left in peace until a new recruit arrived on the island and the whole pantomime would start again.

María passed a small boy who shouldered his home-made wooden gun and marched boldly back and forth outside his family's charming, balconied house.

'Good morning, Sergeant Niko,' María called. The child stopped, stood to attention and saluted María. She returned the courtesy, then chuckled as she continued.

All the island's beautiful young women over the age of seventeen were married with at least one toddler. They took pride in procreating as many children as possible, determined to spread the noble spirit and intrinsic beauty unique to the Castellorizo gene.

'Castellorizo is ours!' adults cried at special occasions, raising their wine glasses and staring out over the sparkling sea. 'Our people may travel the globe and settle at the other end of the earth, but their souls remain here awaiting their return.'

* * *

'If you win another game, I might have to kill you myself,' said Bartholomeus Konstantinidis, Babá for short. Uncle Kuríllos threw the dice. Double six; he was destined to win.

'Don't worry, at least you're lucky in love,' Kuríllos muttered. The men's eyes met, Babá's full of sympathy while his brother's displayed an unspeakable sadness. The *tavli* session had started when Babá's wife went into labour at midnight. Apart from the mayor, Babá had the largest belly on the island, proving the wealth of the Konstantinidis family. He wore a short black beard that was so neat it appeared to be painted on and a black,

4

tasselled kerchief casually wrapped around his polished pate like a napkin around a boiled egg. His black shirt and beige jodhpurs were the traditional clothes of fierce warriors that lived in the Cretan mountain villages of Anogia and Zoniana – where his grandfather came from.

Keeping Babá company was his younger brother, long-haired Uncle Kuríllos wearing his signature tan-leather gilet with a deep money pocket on the inside. Under his waistcoat, this skinny, big-hearted rebel wore colourful embroidered braces from Switzerland and a fine woollen vest from Albania. His striped, baggy breeches came from Turkey and his soft black leather boots were a gift from Babá, made for him by an expert cobbler in the high, snow-capped mountains of Crete. Seldom seen without a smile on his tanned face, Uncle Kuríllos smoked his customary cigarillo. Slung on the back of his sea-grass and olive-wood chair was his *baglama*, a three-stringed, spoon-like lute. Famed for his expertise with this traditional Turkish-Greek instrument, he only played when he was too drunk to walk, or too sad to speak. Nobody ever asked about the source of his sadness for fear of seeing tears on his face.

*　*　*

María, Babá's only child, returned from the blacksmith's with the cheese and spinach pie and set it on the table next to the *tavli* board. She loved her uncle fiercely and could listen to his tales for hours.

'Will you tell me how you lost your eye, Uncle?' she asked, standing close to his chair and running her finger over his redundant eyelid.

Kuríllos, a colourful character with one eye, had the other stitched closed in a permanent wink that suited his mischievous persona. His smile widened and displayed even, tobacco-stained teeth. He patted his thigh and she scrambled onto his lap and flung her arms around his neck. He laughed. 'How many times have I told you, María, one hundred . . . two hundred?'

'I know, lots of times, Uncle, but it's such a good story. I'm afraid if you stop telling me, you'll forget how it goes.'

He looked across at Babá and laughed again. 'All right then . . . I lost my eye while fishing – dynamiting for grouper near the blue grotto cave.' He nodded and squinted through his good eye. 'Unfortunately, due to some very delicious whisky that I drank with your father at Manoli's christening the night before, I had a painful head. Because of this, I misjudged the distance. The boat lurched at precisely the wrong moment and *boom!* The stick of explosive bounced off the cliff face as it detonated. A flying shard of flint, spinning like fury, headed straight for my face and though I ducked, it whipped my eye out and hurled it into the sea.'

As he cried, '*Boom!*' he suddenly jigged his knee, throwing her off balance so she almost fell. She squealed and clung to him and he and Babá forgot their tiredness and laughed.

'Go on, go on!' María cried, knowing the story so well. 'About the grouper . . .'

'Well, yes. I hope that grouper ate my eye!' Kuríllos yelled in mock anger, shaking his fist towards the sea. 'Because if I ever catch the *maláka poutána* I'll eat both of his!'

María's eyes popped, thrilled to hear such bad language every time he repeated the story. Uncle Kuríllos also had a limp, which no one was to ever mention.

Kuríllos threw his dice across the *tavli* board. 'It had better be a boy after waiting all this time,' he muttered at his brother. 'And after all those silver *tamatas* we hung under the icon of the Blessed Virgin.'

6

'Of course it'll be a boy. Even the Mother of God knows how important that is. Imagine if *she'd* had a girl, what then? Anyway, the Blessed Virgin couldn't ignore the weight of so much silver.'

Babá and Uncle Kuríllos had made each effigy larger and more detailed than the last. Both men were clearly convinced they could bribe the Mother of God with precious metal and a prayer.

A loud groan came from indoors. Inside, midwife Dorothéa attended to Mamá who lay on a beautiful multicoloured quilt on the low table in the centre of the room.

The men turned to stare at the doorway, then at each other. María scrambled off her uncle's knee and took her father's hand. 'Oh, I hope it's a girl, Babá,' she said.

'No, no, I have a beautiful girl already, don't I? The baby has to be a boy, María.'

'What will you call him?' Kuríllos asked.

'*Yeorgo.*' George. He smiled. 'After our father, of course.'

'I wish Mamá would hurry up,' María said. 'It's not much fun waiting, is it?'

'Why don't you go and sit with your grandmothers?' Babá suggested. 'Then we can finish our game of *tavli.*'

* * *

María skipped across the square, a few metres from the island's magnificent harbour. Under a broad-leafed rubber tree, she saw the two ancient grandmothers sitting shoulder to shoulder on a low wall. Mikró Yiayá and Megáli Yiayá, Little Grandmother and Big Grandmother.

'Hello, my María,' they cried together.

María grinned, climbed onto the wall beside them and kicked her heels against the hewn grey stones. Glancing sideways at her grandmothers, one wizened and bent as a dried twig, the

7

other, round and pillowing as risen dough. Identically dressed in their widow's weeds they crocheted and prayed, only pausing to admire the broad shoulders of Simonos the fisherman, as he pulled his cart into the square.

Simonos, fond of the two old dears, doffed his cap and called, 'Good morning, ladies,' in a gesture of respect. 'You're both looking beautiful today!'

They laughed, remembering his grandfather and wishing they were sixteen again, but soon calmed down and returned to their crocheting and supplications.

'Blessed Virgin, have mercy,' Mikró Yiayá whispered. 'We are martyrs to our granddaughter's dowry chest.'

María laughed, delighted to see the fine lace that would one day belong to her.

Megáli Yiayá added, 'Give us a grandson today, so we can toss these blistering crochet hooks and abandon the bridal fabrics, once we've finished María's wedding linens.'

'Lord, hear our prayers,' they said together. María copied them when they crossed themselves three times. The old women turned their attention back to the role of white silk lace that would trim María's marital bed linen and table runners in five years' time.

* * *

A peal of bells rang out from the church, marking nine o'clock. 'Almost there,' midwife Dorothéa muttered. 'Two big pushes and your baby will be born, Mamá.' Everyone called María's mother Mamá, though her full name was Mamárita.

The baby knew nothing but the safety of Mamá's watery womb. Although that abode had become cramped of late, the infant was reluctant to leave. Elbows and knees dug in. Tiny fists hung on with determination that would stay with the child into its adult life and beyond. However, nature was a powerful mother and no force for an unborn baby to deal with.

*　*　*

María scrambled back onto her uncle's knee as another powerful groan resonated from indoors. The men paused the boardgame to listen for an infant's cry. Babá's fist clasped the dice and hovered over the *tavli* board. He met his brother's gaze, offering yet another silent prayer for a boy.

CHAPTER 2
MARIA

Castellorizo, Greece, 1926

THE DAY OF MAMA'S CONFINEMENT was also the eve of Orthodox, All Saints Sunday.

'Come and collect wild flowers,' women called to their neighbours. 'We're going to decorate the churches.' Housewives hurried about their work, making time to polish inside the chapels and the magnificent cathedral of Saint George of the Well on the harbour. The air was unusually still, laden with the scent of blossom and beeswax.

A sickening *boom!* jolted everyone into a state of terror and a sudden sense of danger infused the atmosphere. Backs straightened, eyes widened, senses were electrified. Mothers glanced around urgently for their children, finding themselves inexplicably afraid. Dogs cowered and slid under tables or chairs. Cats hunched their backs, fur on end, tails a startled exclamation mark. Birds took to the air and flocked towards Turkish shores.

'What in the name of God was that?' Babá yelled. 'Too loud to be someone fishing with dynamite.' He turned towards the harbour where sailors leapt off their boats and peered at the horizon. María screamed, thrown from her uncle's knee by a jolt that jarred the whole island. Instantly, the two men understood.

'Earthquake!' Kuríllos shouted above the gathering roar. 'A big one. Get away from the buildings!'

All Satan's malice hurled itself at the tiny island of only five square miles.

'Run to the centre of the *plateía*, María,' her uncle ordered, pulling her to her feet. 'Hurry! Tell your grandmothers to get away from the tree, it may fall on them. We'll bring Mamá just now.'

The ground rippled and heaved. A riderless horse bolted towards the sea, its eyes bulging and nostrils flared in terror. The first of many buildings crashed to the ground.

The air filled with terrified shrieks and billowing dust tumbled around María. She felt a sudden need to vomit and clasped her hands over her mouth. She raced towards her grandmothers as grit rained over her head. The old women trembled and whimpered, unable to move. María pulled on their hands, yelling above the racket, 'Come away from the tree! Come away!'

A terrific scream eclipsed the roar of more demolition. The grandmothers hugged each other, staring around with wide, fearful eyes.

'It's the end of the world,' Mikró Yiayá muttered, her face white with terror.

Megáli Yiayá, becoming calm, took Mikró Yiayá into her arms. 'Then let's step into heaven together, old woman. Don't be afraid.'

The rubber tree's metre-wide trunk rocked, its roots wriggling like great serpents as they lifted through the earth, breaking the retaining wall apart. María grabbed their hands and pulled them to the centre of the square, just as the tree crashed to the ground.

Church bells clanged a violent and discordant tune as campaniles plunged to the pavement and their high towers collapsed.

11

The old women fell to their knees, bending their bodies over María to protect her.

* * *

'We have to get Mamá out of there!' Babá shouted at his brother.

With no thought for their own safety, the men staggered over churning earth and ripped down the curtain. As they lurched into the room, they grabbed the corners of Mamá's quilt, then lunged towards the door. Mamá, arms hooked under her knees and bearing down, bashed her head on the edge of the table in the process. The midwife threw a tablecloth over Mamá's legs to achieve a modicum of modesty. Violent tremors continued to build, surging upward, causing both men to lose their balance but not their determination.

'Head for the centre of the square!' Babá yelled as they dragged Mamá through the doorway. He glanced back to see ornamental plates, a crucifix, several precious icons and the black mummified head of a giant swordfish that Uncle Kuríllos caught twenty years back, all swinging wildly before they crashed down from the walls. Wide fissures raced up opposite sides of the room, cracking their beautiful home into two halves. Although terrified and peppered by masonry grit, the men continued to pull Mamá towards safety.

As they left the building, a shaft of daylight pierced the fractured roof. Sparks flew off dust motes like bolts of static through the house and a pool of light illuminated the low, round table. Just outside the door, terracotta roof-tiles smashed around them like plates on *bouzouki* night, miraculously missing Mamá. The two men managed to crawl clear of the building. Onward, they dragged the blanket and the birthing mother, preoccupied with her penultimate contraction, towards the centre of the *plateía* where she would be safe from falling masonry.

The midwife, who had hurriedly gathered her things, was miraculously still on her feet and stepped safely through the doorway. However, before Dorothéa had taken one step away from the crumbling house, the huge balcony dropped from the first floor, leaving no sign of her existence.

Everyone in the densely populated village headed for the *plateía*. Tall venetian buildings disintegrated with a roar, spewing rubble and roof-tiles into the air then raining it all down without discrimination. The earth undulated as if seen through the eyes of a drunken fool, then snapped open in random and unexpected places.

Some buildings and even dogs and old people were swallowed whole into the bowels of the earth, never to be seen again. Old man Alakos, a disciple of the church, miraculously survived by scrambling frantically out of a chasm before it closed again, catching the toe of his boot and pulling it clean off his foot. After, he sat right next to the crevasse, hugging his knees to his chin and staring at his bare foot, quietly crying. An unrecognisable man, covered head to toe in white dust, gave him a glass of *tsipouro,* the alcoholic cure-all, then placed a blanket around his trembling, bony shoulders.

The priest, with a raised crucifix in one hand, made crosses in the air. 'Surely it was an angel, sent by God to comfort the righteous. Pray, my children, and you shall be delivered!'

Through the stench of hell's sulphur and smoke, the terrified people of Castellorizo whimpered supplications as they crawled, staggered, or lurched out of their elegant homes. In the centre of the square, they dropped to their knees around María's birthing mother.

Mice, lizards and geckos bolted from their nooks and crannies and raced along the streets. Cats shot up the trunks of ancient bougainvillea or grapevine, hissing and spitting from the upper branches. In the harbour, boats tipped and tilted to such extreme angles, some took on more water than they could deal with and sank. Larger vessels rocked violently, their stout wooden masts clashed together and fell in splintered heaps under furled sails. The island lifted three feet above sea level, then fell back slightly off kilter so that many buildings sloped and wobbled dangerously. All this happened on Saturday, 26 June 1926.

Sofía entered the world as the bedlam paused for a second and mayhem took a breath. Her baby cry resonated with gusto, heard by everyone, delivering the hope of survival to all. Mamá, exhausted, put her knees together and sighed and from that moment, the quake began to subside.

*　*　*

Aftershocks continued for three days. At the first sign, everyone rushed out of their houses. The few buildings that still stood had shifted so that window-glass splintered under pressure, doors hung open from frames that were out of kilter and cracks like canyons gaped down the length of stone walls. The entire front of the Filosofos family home fell forward, like a slice cut from a loaf, leaving the family inside unharmed but totally exposed and terrified.

Boulders bounced down the mountain as Satan played skittles with the remaining homes. The hilltop reservoir cracked open and spilt the last of the island's water. Some people had their own water *depósito*, built below their homes, but these cisterns now lay buried under tons of rubble. Everyone shared what they could, but those with families, understandably, were reluctant to part with more than a thirst-quenching drop. The next rain would not come until October.

'Send a pigeon to Rhodes,' the mayor ordered. 'Tell them to send a tanker of water and tents for the homeless.'

Everyone hoped the water-schooner would arrive the next day. Meanwhile, men dragged their rowboats, laden with all the pots they could carry, into the sea. They rowed across to the nearby Turkish mainland, hoping wells on their farmland there had not collapsed in the quake.

Suspicious islanders hinted the earthquake might be an omen connected to the baby. Others claimed it was Sofía's birth that had stopped the seismic activity and those supporters bestowed blessings upon the infant.

'May all her children be male and all her goats and chickens be female.'

Babá, disappointed by the birth of a useless girl after everything else, stared up at the small church, miraculously unharmed by the quake.

'You'd think after all that silver, the Blessed Virgin would have given us a boy,' he said to his brother.

'I think perhaps She hasn't noticed our gifts, or perhaps She simply doesn't want them,' Kuríllos said. 'Perhaps She was offended by them – being so graphic and all. Too late now, isn't it? You think we should remove them? I think it would be the decent thing to do.'

Twenty minutes later, Babá's eyes narrowed as he kept lookout by the chapel door. Unobserved, his brother slipped inside, quickly unhooked the silver *tamata*s and slipped them into his deep money pocket. He then faced the Virgin and crossed himself three times in respect. The reclaimed *tamatas* were not exactly stolen from the Virgin, they rationalised. After all, the Mother of God had not done her job, the baby was a girl. Clearly, Holy Mary had not accepted their votive offerings – the men were perfectly justified to reclaim their silver.

'You know when we melt the pendants down,' Uncle Kuríllos said, 'I want to keep the largest *tamata*.'

'What for?' Babá asked staring at the explicit relief carefully hammered into the silver.

'It's such a beautiful work of art,' Kuríllos said. 'I want to thread it onto a shoelace and wear it as a medallion around my neck.' He grinned mischievously. 'Bound to impress the ladies, isn't it?'

'Our mother won't approve and besides, people might think it's a sign you're a eunuch,' Babá said. 'Anyway, if the Virgin recognises it, she might turn you into one just for spite.'

Horrified at the thought, Kuríllos threw it into the melting pot. The pendant wilted, along with the others, in the heat of the blacksmith's furnace. The silver ingot paid for several bottles of the best whisky, providing some consolation for spawning a useless girl.

* * *

'Babá, the doctor insists that Mamá has three days off. Will you help me light the stills?' She tugged her father's hand.

'Do you think we can manage without your mother?'

'I've helped so many times, I'm sure we can manage, Babá.'

Their family business, their own distilled precious oils, was famous all over the Mediterranean and, more recently, over Northern Europe. Secret recipes, concentrated liquids so rich and mysterious that they transported the wearer into a dreamlike mood. Inhaling the exotic, often deeply floral, scents brought a special kind of euphoria. Some induced peace, others a profound sense of happiness, intense contentment, or joy. And then there was love, or more precisely, desire. Such was the power of these oily elixirs, that only the smallest drop was infused into each batch of perfume.

There were darker brews too. Hedonistic, musky aromas so overpowering they sent a man's blood rushing, while his heart pounded lustfully, helpless to fight instincts that had driven the male of every species since time immemorial. Those who dared to inhale the dark and spicy precious oils submitted their body and soul, without question, to Eros, the god of lust.

Patchouli, gardenia, cinnamon, peppermint, aniseed and a hundred more ingredients came from further afield. The family also extracted oils from locally grown produce, honeysuckle, jasmine, rosemary, frangipani, myrtle and sage. Lavender and rose came from Bulgaria, Holland, or Turkey. Bergamot arrived from Italy and sandalwood came all the way from Australia.

Great Parisian fashion houses bought the bulk of the family's secret blends. Greatly diluted, they added these tinctures to their own exotic concoctions. The commodity giants sold their rich and enticing perfumes in expensive cut-glass bottles. Fancy labels carried famous French brand names, with no mention of the women of Castellorizo.

CHAPTER 3
OLIVIA

Brighton, England, present day

I'M THINKING OF MUMMY AS I reach for the black umbrella on top of the wardrobe – in my mind she's always Mummy – though I say Mum in company as anyone would. She always called me Sweetheart.

Mummy died peacefully in hospital after a short illness, five days ago.

My grief arrives in waves so strong I feel swept away and out of control. At other times I'm numb; then, unexpectedly, sorrow steamrollers me. The dark, sad place that now sits in my heart was once filled with my mother's love. I fear the pain will never lessen. Every time I look into the mirror, she gazes back at me. Her olive skin, wide brown eyes and a thick mane of dark hair. Unmistakably Greek. I want her back so fiercely it hurts.

I unfurl the funeral brolly cautiously to stop dust falling out. It has lain undisturbed since Granny Sofía passed away in 2016. Mummy's cremation will take place after a short service in the chapel of rest, at eleven o'clock. I peer out of the window at blustering clouds. Perhaps if I'd persuaded her to go to the doctor sooner . . . gone with her . . . been more supportive? I'm horrified that I can't remember the last time I hugged her.

Oh, Mummy!

Water thunders into the tub, steam billowing. I sprinkle a drop of lavender oil into the bath and inhale the scent, hoping it will calm me. The phone rings, drawing my attention away from the delicate perfume.

'Good morning, Olivia. Hope it's not too early for you?'

Yeorgos Konstantinidis is known by everyone as Uncle George. In fact, he's my great-uncle, but I simply call him Uncle. He's a retired history teacher who has lived and worked in England for many years. I smile at the image of him in my mind: crinkly grey hair, still thick despite his eighty-something years. Brown, heavily lashed eyes that scrutinise everything and store special images to duplicate onto future canvases. A willowy frame softly weathered by the storms of life. His long-fingered hands, restless for the artist's paintbrush, or ready to dash urgent lines and curves onto paper before they vanish from his mind. Although I hardly know him, I feel as though we've been friends forever.

'Of course it's not too early, Uncle. How are you on this sad day?' Back in the bathroom, I turn off the taps.

'A bit creaky and in the misery-dumps of course, but good enough. Chin up, my dear girl. Tomorrow will be a little easier. May I invite you for lunch at my hotel after the cremation service?'

To be honest, I just want to mope, but I guess he does too. Having lunch together will fill part of the day and the night will be long enough for contemplation. 'That's very kind, Uncle, I'd love to.'

'Perfect. Will you come back with me once we're finished at the chapel? I'll take the liberty of pre-ordering so we don't have to hang about. They do this marvellous light lunch of smoked salmon and poached eggs on thick slices of avocado, followed by a fresh raspberry meringue and ice cream.'

'You had me at smoked salmon.' I try to inject a smile into my voice, but suspect it isn't coming through too well. I long to curl up on Mummy's bed and cry.

'We can take a stroll along the pier after, if you like, Olivia?'

He's being nice, trying to take my mind away from my mother's death. Suddenly, I realise tears are rolling down my face. 'Must go, bath's running. I'll pick you up around nine fifteen.'

* * *

After a lovely lunch that I really didn't want, I stroll along the pier with Uncle. We bump elbows a couple of times, before I loop my arm into his. He smiles softly; I feel comfortable in his company.

'Would you like a look in at Mum's flat, as we're here? See if there's anything you want for a keepsake before you go back to Norfolk?' Another urge to cry explodes in my chest. I turn away and blow my nose.

He pats my arm. 'It will get easier,' he says. 'Yes, I really would like to see the old place again if you're up to it. It was my home, too, until your mum got married and your father moved in.'

'Really? I didn't know. I hardly remember my father.'

After a sigh, he appears to be in deep thought.

'I was only a child when he took his life,' I remind him. 'I always believed he'd died in his sleep. One of my school friends told me, years later, what had happened. She'd heard her mother telling somebody. A length of hose fixed to the exhaust pipe and pushed in through the car window.' I sigh, thinking how sad Mum must have been. 'Odd, really, as he couldn't even drive. I found Mum crying one night when I got into bed with her, but apart from that, it seemed he wasn't greatly missed. Isn't that awful?'

Uncle lowers his eyes and nods. 'Yes, very sad, but not wasted. He was a good father, I believe. How old were you?'

'Seven. Seven's my unlucky number. The last time I saw you was seven years ago, you know?' He shakes his head. 'Yes, you came to my wedding. I've just got my divorce through after seven years of marriage. Mum died on the seventh of July too.'

'No, I saw you at Sofía's funeral, after your wedding, I think,' he says.

'Oh, goodness, you're right.' I smile, feeling he's broken the hex. 'After Daddy died, Granny Sofía stepped into his shoes and I loved her very much. Homework, bath time, school runs and so on became such fun, an adventure while Mum worked. She talked to me like an equal, not a little girl. I remember having wonderful times with her. Granny Sofía was lovely, wasn't she?'

'She was. You never met my other sister, María. She was incredibly beautiful. Certainly, the most beautiful young woman on the island – before the fire, of course – but Sofía was always my favourite.'

'Fire? What fire?'

Uncle is deep in thought and doesn't hear me. He rests his arms on the railings and peers out over Brighton's shore. 'Yes, I'd really like to see the flat.'

* * *

We stroll back to the car, talking about our working lives. 'What are you doing right now?' my great-uncle asks.

'I'm a freelance copy-editor and also the author of a reasonably successful Greek cookery book,' I tell him. 'I have a decent following of foodies on social media.'

'What's it called, this book of yours?'

I turn and grin at him. 'It's called: *Smashing Plates*, with the subtitle *Flavours of the Greek Islands*. It was a pleasure to produce and even more of a pleasure to recipe test. What a way to earn a living, eating! My long-term plan is to write a series: Greek food with a splash of posh.'

I drive in the direction of Brighton Marina and park on the sea front at Madeira Drive. We link arms and walk through the underpass that leads to the private gardens of Lewes Crescent. The Grade I-listed building has a white façade and glossy black wrought-iron railings.

'Magnificent, isn't it?' he mutters, gazing up at the building.

My grandmother, Sofía, had bought the top-floor apartment outright when she came from her Greek island. Even then, around seventy years ago, it must have cost a fortune. I wonder how simple people from a distant Mediterranean island could afford such a thing? Why they left Greece is another mystery. A taboo subject in our house. I don't know the whole story and remind myself to quiz Uncle about it.

Once inside, he heads for the window and stares out over the gardens, to the sea beyond. 'I love this place. What will you do with it, Olivia – move back in?' he asks, sounding a little breathless.

I shake my head, taking two china mugs from the cupboard and filling the kettle as I speak. 'The service charges are too high for me.' Through no fault of my own, I lost my job recently. 'Like I said, I'm working freelance right now, but the pay isn't great. I'll let the flat. The going rate will cover my mortgage in Hove.' His eyebrows shoot up so I explain. 'I have a small two-up two-down I bought with Andrew when we married. It became mine as part of the divorce settlement.' I keep my voice light, trying to hide my bitterness on this sad day.

Something catches his eye on the windowsill as he turns. He reaches behind the heavy drape and picks it up. 'Well, goodness me,' he cries, peering at the old black-and-white photograph of two children. 'I'd forgotten about this. It's the earthquake girls!'

I frown and smile at the same time. Mummy had explained the picture was Granny Sofía when she was four years old and her older sister, María, at fifteen. María wears a flamboyant costume, which probably weighed more than she did and would account for the serious look on her beautiful face.

'Is that the local costume María's wearing?'

'It's her wedding dress.'

I gawp at him. 'But she's a child!'

He shakes his head. 'Fifteen was the age when all the girls married – well, not Sofía, but that's another story.'

'What happened to María? Granny Sofía would never talk about her. Mum warned me not to pry, said it would upset her too much, so I didn't. When I was younger, I imagined María died in some tragic accident, too horrible for Granny to speak about.'

'I'll tell you one day, but not just now. Too difficult, you see, especially today.' Uncle stares at the picture for a long time. He says, 'Tell me I can I have first refusal on the flat. I've always loved this place – it still feels like home and the photograph confirms that I belong here.'

I blink at him. 'To tell the truth, that would be amazing. It would solve most of my problems, but would it be right for you? These flats have become terribly expensive, Uncle.'

'I'm not exactly a poor pensioner, you know. We'll see the estate agent together and ask about the charges.'

'You'll be shocked.'

'It's not a problem.'

'Let's agree to a fifty per cent reduction for family?'

'Too much. How about twenty per cent?'

'You drive a hard bargain, Uncle. Twenty-five per cent off the rent and I'll throw in the furniture?'

'Done!' He turns and offers his slender hand, warm and dry in mine. We smile as we shake, both knowing Granny Sofía and Mummy would approve. The misery of the day lifts for a moment. Now I need to think about booking flights – to scatter my mother's ashes over the sea, on the tiny Greek island of Castellorizo.

CHAPTER 4
MARIA

Castellorizo, Greece, 1926

AFTER THE EARTHQUAKE, THE WORLD held its breath. The detritus of a destroyed community floated over the harbour. They recovered the midwife's body, then laid her to rest in the cemetery. Shattered planks – once brightly painted fishing boats – undulated gently on the dissipating wake of a grey patrol boat. Italian soldiers swarmed onto the island of Castellorizo like brown ants, small and fragile individually – formidable on mass. The soldiers erected rows of cream conical tents on every piece of flat ground, to the relief of homeless families.

'They look like sow's brassières,' María claimed, pointing at two straight rows of six tents. She giggled hysterically, too young to appreciate the seriousness of the situation.

From across the channel, the benevolent Turks sent food, blankets and more water. The summer heat rose. Everyone's discomfort made the wide-open spaces of Australia seem appealing. The broad-shouldered local men were adept at both sheep-shearing and sailing and, according to letters from friends, there were plenty of jobs awaiting hard workers. The few who still had a house standing started packing their possessions.

* * *

Mamá sat with her back against the trunk of the fallen rubber tree and took baby Sofía to her breast.

'When I get married I'm going to have a hundred babies, Mamá,' María said.

Her mother laughed. 'You might change your mind after the first half dozen, María.' She stroked her daughter's long curly hair. 'How are the men getting on?'

'I'm going to the grandmothers' house to see if they can sleep there. They say they'll kill a chicken for dinner but they need help to catch it. Then I'm running errands for Babá and Uncle.'

She kissed her mother and the baby, then went to the grandmothers' house in the bay of Mandraki, a short walk over the peninsula's brow.

*　*　*

After tidying her grandmothers' small house, María returned to her father.

'Their back wall has the most damage. The lining-stones have slipped, Babá, breaking a chair and a few ornaments. Part of the ceiling has fallen too. But the outside's all right.'

Trunks of sturdy pine stretched from wall to wall above the one-room house. Across these lay closely packed bamboo which supported dried grass, then a half-metre layer of wet clay that had baked hard, protecting the grandmothers from blazing summer sun and winter rains.

'It doesn't sound too bad. Can you see the sky from inside, María?'

'No, luckily, only one patch of old bamboo collapsed. I've cleared the mess and dumped it outside. I'm sure you'll be able to fix it in a few hours with Uncle's help.'

'Good. Much as I love them, I don't want to listen to them snoring in the distillery all night.'

María giggled. 'Is that where we'll sleep, in the distillery?'

'Exactly. Your uncle's acquired half a dozen water cans. We've cleared our house pump, so we'll fill the containers and take them up there as soon as we can borrow Mimi's mule. Tonight, we'll all sleep on sacks of myrtle leaves in the distillery.'

The long, rectangular building sat behind a row of pine trees at the back of the village. The elevated position meant it had an amazing view of the harbour. It housed three gigantic copper stills and all the equipment for making their famed precious oils.

Everyone was thirsty. Babá and Uncle Kuríllos pumped a little water up from the *depósito*, under our house for anyone with a cup. Word got around and soon a queue of desperately thirsty people reached across the square and down to the harbour.

A group of young Turks came to help. One, Mustafa, was the son of a merchant who traded with the people of Castellorizo and owned the most magnificent schooner that was anchored in the harbour.

Young Mustafa, a big, strong boy of sixteen, worked furiously at the head of a chain gang shifting rocks and rubble all through the night. The handsome youngster, liked by everyone, had rowed across the mile-wide strait between the Greek island of Castellorizo and the Turkish village of Kaş on the mainland. After eighteen hours of hard labour, he was both physically and emotionally drained.

Babá saw Mustafa stagger away from the rescue party and realised the boy was on the point of collapse. He caught sight of María carrying the family's possessions to her grandmothers' stone house.

'*Ela*, María *mou*.' Hey, María mine, Babá called. 'Leave that for a moment and take this jug of water to the young Turk with his head in his hands.' He gave her an enamel jug that had survived with hardly a dint.

María hurried over to the boy. 'Here, my father sent this,' she said, touching his shoulder and feeling embarrassed when he looked up, though she didn't understand why. She wasn't usually shy.

He smiled at her, which made her blink rapidly and feel slightly unbalanced. From his streaked face, it was clear he'd been upset. Quickly, she took the hanky from her apron pocket, dipped it into the water and wiped his cheeks.

'That's better,' she said, matter-of-factly, feeling more at home being bossy. 'Now get some water inside you and you'll feel all right.'

He smiled wearily. 'What's your name, little one?'

'I am María Konstantinidis.'

'Ah, Konstantinidis, the perfume people?'

'Well, not exactly just now. My mother had a baby yesterday, just as the earthquake ended. Anyway, it's not perfume we make, it's the precious oil that's used in perfume.'

'I know, my father and I take it to sell in Europe. I am Mustafa. My father has the three-masted schooner, the merchant sailing ship *Barak*. You must have seen it in the harbour. How old are you?'

'María!' Babá called.

'Almost twelve. Look, I have to go. Will you take the jug back when you're finished? My father's the one dishing out water to that long queue.'

He nodded, eyes sparkling. 'I'll thank your father for his kindness.'

* * *

Two months passed before Mustafa and his father were back on the island of Castellorizo with a cargo of charcoal and oranges from Crete. Mustafa searched for María around the harbour, afraid she had been promised already, in which case she would be hidden away until her wedding day. A girl with such beauty was surely betrothed on her twelfth birthday to be married at fifteen, as was the Greek custom. Why hadn't he asked her father when he had the chance?

Then he spotted her coming out of the bakery wearing the white headscarf of the virgin girls. 'Hey, you there, princess. Take me to you father!' he called.

María laughed. 'I'm not a princess!'

She took his breath away. 'Do you remember me?'

She nodded, cheeks burning as she peered, shyly, from under long lashes. 'My father's helping Mamá in the distillery.'

'I see, then perhaps we can walk there together?'

'Why do you want to see him?'

'I have come to do business.'

'It's usually your father,' she said as they walked up the steep narrow road between hurriedly rebuilt houses.

'I'm learning my father's trade, as I believe you are learning yours. Do you have a favourite precious oil, María?'

He wanted to take her hand as they walked but it was too soon and she was still too young. It would be improper to touch her. His father and her father had to make a betrothal contract and the dowry money must be agreed before he could even touch her hand.

29

María smiled at the Turkish merchant. 'You are right. I am learning to make the precious oil.' Feeling he understood her, she confessed a secret. 'I want to mix a new perfume, although I haven't managed to find exactly the right combination of oils yet. I'll keep trying until I perfect the recipe.'

María's heart raced, excited to recall her dream of a scent that made people love each other. An elixir that brought an end to all conflict. She wanted to tell him about it, but he'd think she was mad, so she said nothing.

'How old did you say you were?'

'I'm twelve, Mr Mustafa.' María blushed again, lowering her gaze, intrigued and flattered by the attention of this handsome buccaneer. He made her heart race so much, she dared not look him in the eye. Anyway, since donning the white scarf a month ago, she was forbidden to look any man in the eye, that was a fact.

She smiled shyly, liking the way he spoke to her, as if she were more than just a child. She glanced his way and correctly guessed his age to be sixteen. Oh, how he made her heart race! Then, quite suddenly, she was afraid for no reason that she could say. She turned back and called, 'I have to go. Goodbye, Mr Mustafa!'

With her heart pounding and a fire burning in her cheeks, she hurried back to her grandmothers' dwelling on the chicken plot.

* * *

Over the next months, the Castellorizo people continued to rebuild their houses and life steadily returned to normal. Babá and Uncle Kuríllos loaded stones from their destroyed home on the square into a barrow and pushed them up the hill to rebuild against the front of the family's distillery. A door was knocked into the back wall, so the women didn't have to go outside to enter the distillery.

The two grandmothers, too old for physical labour or child-minding, finished María's linen and started crocheting for the day that little Sofía would be married off. The men had made baby Sofía's dowry chest from the best olive wood on the island.

CHAPTER 5
OLIVIA

Brighton, England, present day

Two weeks after Mummy's funeral, I stride into Brighton with the tickets for Greece in my bag. I plan to collect Granny Sofía's ashes which are still in Mummy's attic. The urns should stand side by side as the two women had in life. We'll soon be on our way to their homeland – a charming lump of rock that can't even decide on its own name. Castellorizo or Kastellorizo or Megisti? The birthplace of my mother, Granny Sofía and Uncle.

My uncle once told me I have hundreds of relations from Castellorizo living in Australia too. My mother, Tsambika, or Sammy as everyone in Brighton called her, wasn't interested in discussing her roots or relations. 'No good comes from digging up the past, thank you,' she would say. 'Best leave it dead and buried, where it belongs.'

Uncle lets me into the apartment and kisses my cheeks. 'My dear girl, you don't know how delighted I am to see you,' he exclaims, his eyes crinkling in a most charming way. He turns towards the window. 'Come and look at the light on the water today. It's simply poetic.' He raises his hand, gesturing the view. 'Coming from Castellorizo, I simply must see the sea. Brighton's promenade is special, isn't it, darling girl?'

'You've settled in then?' I ask.

'I certainly have. The architecture and the pier, the Pavilion, the gardens, the museums, all together it's the most captivating city. I'm not sure you know this, but I lived with Sofía for a while, after I'd heard about your grandfather's death. I was very happy here. Your mother was a beautiful child and I loved her very much.'

'What made you leave?'

'I moved to the Broads when your mother got married.' He shakes his head sadly. 'I wanted to stay, but there really wasn't room for us all. There was a bit of a rift, you know?'

'A rift? You mean you fell out over something?'

'Sad, isn't it? A silly squabble between me and Sofía. I can't even remember what it was about now. If we hadn't been so overcrowded, it wouldn't have happened. Your parents in one room, you and Sofía in another and me in the third.' He shrugs and sighs. 'We were all too proud to take the first step towards reconciliation, until she fell ill.'

'I'm sorry.'

He smiles softly. 'I've been absolutely everywhere this week – alone, of course – retracing the walks I took with your grandmother so many years ago.' Sadness flickers across his face before he smiles again and pulls a chair out from the round oak table at the window. 'I'll just make the tea. Here, help yourself to cake. It's home-made parkin and I have some wonderful Irish butter to spread on it.' He is thoroughly pleased with himself.

'Uncle, I have a surprise for you.' I try to contain my childish grin. 'Close your eyes and hold out your hands. No peeping now.' He stares for a moment, then does as asked, his thin eyelids twitchy, like he is trying to see through them. I place the tickets in his hands. 'OK, you can look.'

His face is a picture.

'Oh, goodness, is this what I think?'

'Certainly is. Two weeks in Greece. Rhodes and Castellorizo, to be precise.'

For a moment, he stares, disbelievingly, then he swallows hard. 'So kind of you, Olivia. I'm really touched. Thank you for organising these precious tickets. How much do I owe you, darling girl?'

'Absolutely nothing. This is my treat, paid for by the advertising fees I saved on the flat. No ...' I lift my hand when his mouth opens. 'No protesting. Let's go to Castellorizo, deal with the ashes and have a lovely holiday, all right?'

His sparkling eyes tell me he's too emotional for words. I give this dear sweet man a hug.

* * *

Teetering on top of the ladder, I rummage in Mum's small attic for Granny Sofía's ashes.

'It's so musty up here!' I call to Uncle who's surrounded by boxes and sacks at the bottom of the steps. 'Ha! I can see the urn.'

'I'm worried you might fall, Olivia.'

'I'm fine, there's something in front of the urn, a box of some kind ... no, it's an old photograph album. Here, can you take it?' I grasp on the trapdoor frame and gingerly pass the book down, though it's so heavy it starts slipping through my fingers. 'Quick, I'm going to drop it!'

Relieved of the album, I stretch for the urn. 'I've nearly got it.' I just get my fingertips to it but can't get a grip. 'This is nuts. I just need another six inches.' I'm on tiptoes, reaching, when the ladder wobbles. I squeal, Uncle drops the album and grabs a rung to steady it. I spread my elbows so at least I'll be hanging by my armpits rather than crashing down to the floor if the ladder tips. 'Oh, God! That was close.' My heart's hammering.

'Olivia, leave it, I'll get the caretaker.'

'It's OK, I have it. I'll just pull it to the edge. Gosh, it's heavy. Come on, Granny Sofía, you're going back to Castellorizo.'

CHAPTER 6
MARIA

Castellorizo, Greece, 1929

SOFIA'S EARLIEST MEMORY WAS THE day María married Mustafa. 'Mamá, I think my sister is so beautiful they will make her the queen of everywhere!' She clapped her hands and twirled in the dress Mamá had made for the occasion. Moments later, too dizzy, she plopped onto her bottom and cried, 'Wheee!'

The wedding took place on María's fifteenth birthday, as was the island's custom. Mamá gazed upon her daughter in her bridal costume and dabbed her eyes. 'Never have I seen such a wonderful sight,' she whispered. 'I want you to know that I have no worries about my daughter marrying a Turk. Mustafa comes from a good family in Kaş. It's where my own family – your great-grandmother – came from too.'

'I didn't know that,' María said.

Mamá nodded. 'The carpet belt, where rugs have been woven by talented Greek women for many generations. Oh my, such craftmanship, such colours, such detail. When Megáli Yiayá came over, she brought her loom with her, but she's too old to work it now.'

'It seems a shame that it isn't used, Mamá.'

'But we're too busy with the distillery. Perhaps when Sofía is older, I'll teach her the basics. Turn around now, let me check you over before we lead the procession to the church.' Mamá's face sang with pride and love as she studied her precious daughter in the extravagant wedding clothes.

María turned, showing every part of the ornate Castellorizo costume. First, she had slipped into the long cotton shirt, held closed by the flamboyant silver brooches. The size and weight of these five ornate *boúkles* symbolised the family's wealth. Over this, she wore a dazzling silk kaftan, open to the waist so that the brooches were on display. Then, knee-length baggy trousers bound low over the hips with a wide silk sash. Over all this, the great coat, made of heavy wine-coloured velvet, richly embroidered, with a lining and wide trim of mink. A pillbox hat, scarf and long-fringed lace shawl finished the outfit.

'Oh, my child, you look so beautiful!' Then Mamá cried with alarm. 'Shoes! Where're the shoes!'

'They're too small, Mamá, I'm afraid I'll tear them.'

'Never mind that, we'll wet them, then they'll stretch to fit. Hurry, Mimi is at the door with the mule. Babá and his brother must tie the dowry chest to its back. If they're drunk already I'll flay them alive!' She turned to her youngest child. 'Sofía, go and look outside and see if your father is there.'

Half an hour later, the bridal procession left the distillery house to a boisterous, four-gun salute, arranged by Uncle Kuríllos and executed by the somewhat tipsy local Italian garrison. All the soldiers were, of course, invited to the wedding. In fact, everyone on the island had an invitation. With great merriment, they lined the street from the distillery down to the magnificent church of Saint George on the harbour. Well wishes and applause rang out as the Konstantinidis family passed.

Leading the procession was Uncle Kuríllos playing his *baglama*, accompanied by Philipo on his Cretan three-stringed lyra and Ilias blowing his *tsambouna*, the goatskin bagpipe. They made a fine uproarious racket together. Behind the musicians, the best man led the mule decked out in white crocheted shawls and a string of multicoloured tassels over its eyes. Roped to its back was the magnificent dowry chest with the lid flung open and the delicate linens on display for the groom's mother to inspect.

Behind the mule walked the bride and her parents and Sofía holding her mother's hand. The two grandmothers, too proud to use a walking stick, followed with Simonos the fisherman. As the old women clung to his muscular arms, they shared a secret smile, remembering his grandfather. The mayor followed and then the townspeople in order of importance, with everyone else tagging on at the end.

They approached the church. Someone threw dynamite into the harbour sending a plume of water up with a frightful bang. Men and boys grinned, while women squealed and crossed themselves.

'There, there, don't worry,' Simonos cried, throwing his arms around the two grandmothers and pulling them against his chest. 'I'll look after you. There's no need to be afraid.'

The two grandmothers, with their faces pressed against his chest, looked as though they might die of pleasure.

Pomegranates were hurled to the floor, splitting open and shedding their seed. This would ensure a fruitful family with lots of children; and older women spat gently at the bride to ward off the devil.

All through this, the musicians kept up their playing and the guests continued to shout well wishes and congratulations. Then the church bells tolled. The mule was handed over to the groom's mother, who headed the enormous and colourful

Turkish family from across the strait. Every man wore a red fez with a long black tassel and the Turkish women wore beautiful silk scarves draped over their hair.

Silence fell as Mustafa's mother inspected the needlework and, after a tense few seconds, she gave a hardly perceptible nod to Babá. Everyone smiled with relief and Babá, seeming half a metre taller, took his daughter's hand and led her to Mustafa's family. There, he placed María's hand in that of Mustafa's, giving her away.

The people of Castellorizo went crazy, shaking hands with each other and applauding the wedding party. Mamá spat three times on the church step, to warn the devil to stay away and then the entire island's population tried to cram itself into the cathedral.

* * *

Usually, the bride would live with the groom's family. Because the middle floor of the distillery house was built with María and her future husband in mind, Mustafa was happy to move over to Castellorizo and live with María's family. Besides, already a competent sailor, the Turk was now learning the rudiments of trading and therefore would be away for months at a time.

Mustafa's first child, a girl, was born on María's sixteenth birthday.

'What a wonderful gift you give me, María,' Mustafa cried, utterly delighted. 'I know she will be as beautiful as you.'

María, exhausted after thirteen hours of labour, smiled, grateful that it was over.

'We shall call her Ayeleen. It's a Turkish name meaning light around the moon.'

Mustafa loved his first baby and cradled her in his big arms whenever María would allow it. To celebrate her birth and him becoming a father, he asked Kuríllos to photograph him holding his daughter.

CHAPTER 7
OLIVIA

Brighton, England, present day

'There's something very charming, very human, about seeing a big man with a newborn in his arms, don't you think, Uncle? Look at this photograph.'

After easing the picture off the page, I turn it over. 'The writing's not quite the same as before. The letters are smaller and I'm not even sure it's the Greek alphabet.' I touch the words with the tip of my finger. 'I wonder if Mustafa himself wrote it. Would the baby be Ayeleen, do you think?'

I hand Uncle the picture of a huge, square-jawed young man with thick, dark hair holding a tiny naked baby. Together, Uncle and I have drawn up the family tree and with the aid of the ancient photo album, we put faces to names.

'Yes, you are absolutely right. This is Mustafa and Ayeleen – look at the date, 1930,' he says.

Mustafa wears a mix of east and west clothing: suit trousers with a few pleats to the waistband, a white button-fronted collarless shirt and a flamboyant, embroidered waistcoat. On his head is a fez with a long black tassel.

'Are there any pictures of my grandfather, Jamie Peters? I never knew him, of course, but Granny Sofía had a wedding photograph in her bedroom. The silver was completely worn away from the sides of the frame, she had picked it up so many times through her long life.' I smile, remembering how I wasn't allowed to touch it. 'Jamie was in his British uniform and Granny was in her traditional Castellorizo outfit. A great crowd stood on a quayside in front of a beautiful wooden galleon. I know he died a few years after the Second World War and dear Granny Sofía died in 2016. That's the extent of my family history knowledge, Uncle. So, I only know the Granny Sofía I grew up with.'

Uncle holds another photograph and sighs. 'By all accounts, it really was an unusual start to a relationship,' he says. 'Jamie was a British soldier whom your grandmother knocked unconscious when she whacked him over the head with a shovel.'

'I doubt there'll be a photo of the event, then?' I say, intrigued.

He chuckles. 'No, but luckily, it was a family tradition to write the provenance on the back of each picture, so we shall learn a lot from this album.'

'You're kidding!'

'Look for yourself.' He plucks another picture from the album and turns it over. 'Date, place, people, it's all written on the back.'

* * *

I'm confident now that through this ancient album my family history will be revealed. I am bound to discover what split the family, although I can't imagine the secrets that divided my ancestors. I only know they must have been profound. Odd to think that all through my curious teenage years, the answers to my questions were just above my head in the attic.

Almost every afternoon for a month, I walk along Brighton's promenade to see Uncle and listen to the stories behind another page of historical photographs. We carefully transfer each picture from the disintegrating album to the new one. Each episode adds to the excitement of our upcoming holiday.

'Have you noticed that nobody smiles?' I say. 'I find them fascinating, Uncle – and look at the beautiful scalloped margins of cream. I've never seen photos like these before. They're so special.'

'Ah, you know in the early days, they had to keep very still for the exposure time. The later photographs were taken by Uncle Kuríllos on his instamatic. Mustafa bought him the Kodak not long after they came out. The big Turk was the most generous man I ever knew and he seemed to have a knack for knowing what gifts would really please people. The new-fangled camera was all the rage then and Kuríllos was the envy of the island. He loved it.'

Uncle lifts a few pages, then seems to change his mind and goes back to the beginning. 'I had a little peek, before you came. Simply couldn't resist, dear girl. This is a marvellous historical record of your ancestry. I'm impatient for you to know everything. As an ex-history teacher, one couldn't want a more detailed visual account.'

'Will you translate the writing on the backs, please?' I study the Greek letters, written with a nibbed pen, that have faded to light brown. It seems so romantic to record the lives of people as they live them. I have a little notebook and number each photo, then record the translation as Uncle provides it. They start in 1925, according to the captions.

'Look at these bi-winged sea planes and the majestic, tall-masted schooners in the small harbour.' I blink at the postcard-size picture. 'So many fishing boats and there's a battleship to remind us that the photograph was only taken seven years after the end of the Great War. Just fascinating!'

'They say Castellorizo was a rich and prosperous island in the days between the wars. However, I can't imagine how they made money before tourism, especially as they say there were 9,000 people living there with no agriculture or industry – apart from the distillery, of course. Thanks to selective memories, facts are distorted, so this album is a superb record of the island.'

'Look at this photo – is it a baptism?' A naked baby girl held by a finely regaled priest. 'It's dated 1926 but what else does it say, Uncle?'

'You're right about the baptism, it's Sofía's. Here's another photo of the same harbour, also 1926. Look at the ruined houses and this one showing a hundred or more white conical tents. They say the Italian soldiers put them up the day after the earthquake. But again, this was before I was born.'

'So the earthquake occurred on the very day Sofía was born?'

Uncle nods. 'By all accounts, it destroyed almost every house on the island. The army brought the tents from Rhodes – look . . .' He points to another photo. 'María described it to me when I was a child. As a youngster, they say María was one for the drama and I believe she started this album.'

'María? Your oldest sister?'

'Exactly, she was only eleven when it happened.' He snorts, staring at the picture. 'María had more children than anyone I've ever known. Sixteen, all together.'

'You're kidding! Sixteen children? How come I don't know anything about María? What happened to her family?' He's silent, staring through me, lost in the past. I let him dream for a minute, wondering what's going on in his mind, then I bring him back to now. 'Uncle? Granny Sofía would never talk about her past, or the family history. She kept it all a big secret. I don't know about María.'

44

He closes his eyes and makes a slight nod. 'Ah, now that's a story and a half. I'll tell you about it when we're in Castellorizo, but you must know it's a tale that spans over ninety years. The point is, it's all here in the photographs – well, most of it, anyway.'

'Why wouldn't Granny Sofía or Mummy tell me?'

He sighs. 'Love, shame, hurt and heartbreak. That just about covers it.'

After a silent moment, he pulls out a big white handkerchief and blows his nose.

* * *

When the mood takes Uncle, he speaks about his little Greek island with great urgency, as if a time-bomb fuse hisses and sizzles towards an explosion. I do some research on Google and discover that although 9,000 people once lived on the tiny island, today, most people have never heard of the place. I get the impression that's how many Castellorizons would like to keep it. A few tourists go there, but once they return home at the end of October, most of the locals leave too.

'Where do they go for the winter?' I ask Uncle.

'The second, third and fourth generation Castellorizons return to Australia for their summer. I believe less than a hundred locals stay on the island all year, these days. Most go to the larger island of Rhodes and enjoy the comforts of a more cosmopolitan existence and a livelier Christmas and New Year. But even Rhodes is only a small place. To put it into perspective, although Rhodes is the fifth largest Greek island, the whole island has less than half the population of Brighton.'

'Will you tell me why you left?'

'Castellorizo?' I nod. 'Nobody leaves Castellorizo,' he says. 'They go away for a while. They take a ferry or plane to somewhere else, sometimes for many years, sometimes to the other side of the world. However, their spirit stays behind, sitting at the edge of the harbour staring at the turquoise water waiting for their return. In those four-in-the-morning moments, when you realise you're awake but don't know why, that's when a person's mind goes back to Castellorizo, gazes over the iridescent sea and reunites with its soul for a while.'

'How romantic. But I don't understand. Do all those who left feel the same? Are they all longing to return to their motherland? And when you talk about Castellorizo, I sense there's a wound – some terrible secret – but am I mistaken? Am I just being melodramatic?'

He stares at the floor, slides his hand across his mouth and shakes his head. 'You're right, but I can't talk about it, not yet. I don't know if I will ever be able to say what happened. If only I could . . . purge myself of the whole event, then perhaps I could find my own peace.'

His voice resonates with deep sadness, as if trapped by some terrible event of the past. My heart breaks for him. I wonder if Sofía also had this great sadness inside her. Suddenly, I realise how little I know about other people; even my own mother, or my husband. I miss Andrew now the anger has subsided, but catching him out made me realise I didn't really know him either.

Uncle sighs deeply again, breaking my thoughts. 'Anyway, it's no good me telling you anything until you've seen the island for yourself, tasted its food, eaten its cake, smelled its perfume and met its people. If I try to describe the beauty and tragedy of Castellorizo or relate its terrible history or explain why its uniqueness must be saved, you'll just think I'm a sentimental old fool and say, *How could all that happen to an island of less than five square miles?* I mean – what's that in your modern measurements?'

'Eleven or twelve square kilometres?'

'Exactly. There are things connected to that lump of rock that even I find hard to believe and, don't forget, I was there.'

'Can't you tell me anything?' I glance into his eyes and see they are tear-drenched and dangerously close to spilling over. I have to stop questioning him. He lifts a hand, spreads it over his face and stands perfectly still for a moment. I wonder what visions or memories he is trying to block.

'I found such love there. The kind of love that perhaps only touches one in a million. We were united in everything.' He flaps his hand, as if to shoo the memories or the subject away.

After a moment, he lowers his hand and smiles, his eyes sparkling, distant, then he comes back to now. 'All right,' he says softly. 'I can see you're not going to give up. I'll share a few facts with you.' He sighs. History is still the love of his life and Uncle is clearly in his element talking about it. 'Today, it's estimated that over 50,000 Australians claim some familial link to Castellorizo.'

'Fifty thousand people, from five square miles – you're kidding me.' I laugh at the ludicrous idea, but see his eyes narrow and know he is serious.

'In its heyday, Castellorizo supported almost 10,000 Greeks.'

'How big, did you say?'

He grins, grey eyes bright with pride. 'You heard!'

After contemplating for a moment he continues. 'Olivia, have you looked through this album already?'

47

'Not at all. I've not had a spare moment really.'

'I haven't set foot in my homeland for more than half a century and now, I'm too old to tackle the pilgrimage alone. Just the thought of returning to Castellorizo warms my bones. Thank you for the tickets, they mean a lot.' He closes his eyes and smiles. 'I'll sip an ouzo with my friends on the quayside one last time and watch fishermen gut the biggest fish in the area, the beautiful Bonito.'

'What is that?'

The eighty-four-year-old smiles wistfully and tugs on an imaginary fishing rod. 'Twenty kilos of fighting muscle caught for the restaurants. *Lakerda* the Greeks call it, though some sell it as fresh tuna. The bones and innards are tossed into the water, a treat for the local turtles.'

'Turtles?'

His grin widens showing strong, even teeth. Delighted he's managed to shock me, he continues.

'Yes, huge turtles, over a metre long; seals too and every once in a while, dolphins.' His eyes sparkle and a flush of excitement brightens his cheeks. 'I can take you around the island in my caïque.' He nods at one of his acrylics hanging near the window. 'I wonder if my little boat's still in good shape. It was my father's, you know. Babá and Uncle Kuríllos built it before I was born.'

Uncle's personal possessions returned from Norfolk with him. Around the walls hang several of his paintings, most are of his traditional Greek fishing boat with its lucky eye painted on the prow to ward off the devil.

'Would you like one of my paintings, dear girl? Here – take this one home with you, a gift from your great-uncle. I've painted it so many times. Usually it's moored outside my friend's taverna.'

He lifts the painting down with such reverence and I understand it is a great part of his dream: to sit in his boat again. He pops it into a Tesco bag and thrusts it towards me. 'Please . . .' he says when I murmur protests. 'I paint at least one every year, but am running out of room now. Perhaps it's an omen.'

'An omen?' I blink at him, hoping he isn't going to say what I fear.

'Well, who knows? Perhaps I'll take you fishing in *Sofía-María* one of these days. We'll catch the biggest bonito of all. The boat's named after my sisters, of course. Sofía loved fishing and she was good too. María was always busy with her babies – so many babies it's a wonder she remembered all their names! One was simply called the Baby for the first two years of its life, because nobody could decide what to call it.'

I meet his eyes and see a lonely old gentleman with many stories, but nobody left to tell them to. He's lived the last chapter of his life and is now writing the metaphorical epilogue.

'You're wondering why I'm still painting them?' he asks. 'It's not the pictures that please me, but the memories of Castellorizo that come back while I paint.' He looks right through me, visits that distant place and time, then returns to now. 'Yes, it's essential we go, Olivia, and we must fish. I haven't been fishing since . . .' He sighs, worn out by his own active imagination. With his eyes closed, he rocks content-edly in his chair. 'I was with my sister, Sofía. I remember it so well. Sitting in the brightly coloured wooden boat, bobbing about on a warm, crystal sea.'

'Ca-ee-kee,' I practise the Greek word for this sturdy wooden vessel, knowing I'll want to go out in it.

* * *

49

Three weeks before departure, I find Uncle grey-faced, staring out of his bay window at a rain-flattened sea. He clutches his arm and mutters apologies for not being too hospitable. 'Chest pains,' he says as my fear rises. 'I wasn't doing anything energetic, just writing the answers to your questions. Unfortunately, I got a little upset, remembering it all.'

Two hours later, I sit in a chair beside my lovely uncle. He peers at me from his hospital bed having just completed a series of medical tests. His hand is smooth and warm in mine.

'I swear if they take any more blood, my arm will be empty,' he jokes. Screens and monitors behind his bed squeak and blip a language only known to medical science. My uncle's voice sounds dry and his eyes are weary. 'A mild heart attack, they say. Blocked artery, so they're going to fit a stent. I'm so sorry, Olivia, but it's no flying for ten days. The specialist said, taking my age into account, it will be safer to wait two or even three weeks before I take a holiday abroad.'

'I'll postpone the tickets, put them back a couple of weeks, you'll be fine by then, Uncle.'

'No, go without me. I'll be with you in spirit,' he whispers, gently squeezing my hand as his lids slide down over dull, life-tired eyes. 'It will mean so much to me. There's no time to waste. Tell them about me. Listen to their stories.' His eyes flash open and he gazes at the ceiling for a moment. 'In Sofía's sewing stool is a white linen table runner made by one of your great-great-grandmothers. It was part of Sofía's dowry linen. Take it to Castellorizo and give it in to Eleni's taverna. Eleni's mother and Sofía were good friends and I believe she would want her to have it.' He pauses thoughtfully.

'You know, things happened there – things you can't imagine. Keep a journal so you don't forget anything, dear girl. Come back to me with video messages from my old friends, Demetriou, Stamatou and Chalkitis. We were the gang of four, chasing girls and annoying the Italians when we were boys, but we lost touch. So, take plenty of photographs and please go without me. Give me something to look forward to . . . something to live for.'

*　*　*

The past fortnight has flown by without a moment to spare. Uncle grows stronger each day, but is still not able to leave with me. If I hadn't kept pushing him to tell me the secrets that divided our family, would he have had that heart attack? I promise myself I'll never pressure him again.

'A few more tests they say, but I'm well on the mend, Olivia,' he assures me when I pay a final visit. 'Don't forget to take that table runner for Eleni.'

CHAPTER 8
SOFIA

Castellorizo, Greece, 1937

AFTER ELEVEN YEARS OF SEWING and crocheting, the two grandmothers finished the last and most grand piece of linen for Sofía's dowry chest. A crocheted table runner with pointed ends and panels of intricate detail.

'At last it's complete,' Mikró Yiayá squeaked. 'We can throw out the crochet hooks and straighten our fingers.'

'No, we have to start on María's child's linen, God have mercy! As if we haven't done enough. What's her name?'

'Ayeleen.'

'Ay?' Megáli Yiayá yelled.

'Aye-leen! Deaf ears, her name's Ayeleen!'

'No need to shout. Why don't we talk María into selling her child to the convent, then we won't need to make all the dowry linen.' Her plump cheeks jigged as she tried to quieten her laughter.

'You wicked old crow. Because there's half a dozen girls after Ayeleen, so we don't stand a chance.'

'I'll never get to play the piano. I've always wanted to learn. I can see myself playing all the favourite tunes and people singing and dancing in the street. It's my dream.'

'First I've heard. Apart from your great age, what's stopping you?'

'No piano.'

*   *   *

Mamá tied the white scarf of the virgin girls around Sofía's head to hide every strand of her glossy dark hair. She had begun her first bleed the day before, at the tender age of eleven.

'You are a woman now, Sofía, this means you may not scramble onto the knees of Babá or Uncle Kuríllos or fling your arms around their necks the way you do. Your dowry chest is ready, so from now on, you must behave like a lady and beware of men until you are safely married. Do you understand?'

Sofía thought about her two most favourite people and felt herself punished for something of which she was innocent. She pulled off the scarf and held it in her lap. 'Mamá, this isn't fair, they're my father and uncle!'

'Don't answer me back, child.' Mamá took the girl in her arms. 'And don't get so upset. When you're old and ugly – with wild bushy eyebrows and a moustache – your sons and cousins will hug you and kiss your cheeks with great affection. Until then, you must hide your irresistible beauty away for the sake of those you love.'

Sofía didn't want to be old and ugly; she intended to stay as she was now and to kiss her father's cheeks and snuggle in her uncle's lap to listen to his wild stories until she fell asleep.

Mamá, a woman of great beauty in her time but now faded and tired, picked up a hairbrush and ran it through her daughter's mane. 'Listen, Sofía. We women have terrific power that you don't understand. This impact that we have on men is dangerous and until you learn to control it, we must keep you hidden away for your own safety. When men lay eyes on your glossy tresses, or see the beauty in your enchanting eyes, their own bodies will cause them unbearable pain and discomfort. You will steal their sleep without even knowing it and they will slowly go crazy with the desire to be with you.

'For your own sake, keep yourself hidden. Everyone knows if a man loses control, then you will be blamed for flaunting your irresistible charms.' She knotted the symbolic white kerchief around her daughter's head again. 'You will not speak to any adult male apart from your father and uncle, nor will you look any man in the eye, for even a glance. Just the sound of your voice could be deemed too alluring for a weak man to resist.'

Sofía nodded although she wasn't sure what her mother was saying, only that it was important. Mamá's shoulders dropped and the anguish left her for a moment.

'I love you, Mamá. Please don't worry about me,' Sofía said and then smiled as her mother's eyes welled and she hugged her tightly. Sofía knew that from now on, the only time she would appear at public occasions was at religious services and, even then, the married women would circle around her.

* * *

To the pride and joy of everyone in the family, especially Mustafa, María went on to have a baby every year, the first seven of whom were girls and now she had another on the way. This kept Mamá, Sofía and Ayeleen busy, taking care of infants and toddlers, while the adult men worked the distillery from dawn to dusk. Then a real miracle happened, Mamá found herself pregnant too.

Down at the *kafenio*, Babá and Uncle Kuríllos discussed the situation over coffee and a game of *tavli*. 'Shall we make the *tamatas* again?' Kuríllos asked. 'I can start buying silver to melt down.'

Babá peered at the *tavli* board and decided he stood a chance of winning the game. 'No, I've decided the child will probably be a girl.' He blew on the dice in his fist and rolled them across the board. 'We have to face it, we're unlucky like that. How many useless girls has María got now, seven? Eight?'

Kuríllos grinned and lit his cigarillo. 'Mustafa doesn't mind at all. He says every child is a gift from Allah.'

* * *

The months passed quickly and soon the family were in the front yard, awaiting the arrival of María and Sofía's sibling. After each groan from Mamá, everyone looked up. Eventually, a baby's cry rang out. The two men turned their eyes to heaven and chanted, 'Dear God, please make this one a boy!'

On the stroke of six, on that hot September evening, Babá rushed out of the house with his third child. He raised the naked baby above his head and bellowed across the town with such voice, some said they heard him a mile away, across the sea, in Turkey.

'God blessed me; I have a son!'

Women who were walking to the bakery stopped and smiled at each other. 'At last, the man with two daughters and seven granddaughters now has his own boy!'

The priest, Papas Luke, arrived and shook Babá's hand. 'I must talk to you about the christening; it is better to have it sooner than usual. Germany is itching to make war with some-body. Countries are already picking sides. There's talk of serious conflict in Europe within the next few years unless there are drastic changes of leadership. Who will Greece side with?'

'More importantly, who will Italy side with?' Kuríllos asked. 'I can't see how it will affect us here. Nevertheless . . . only God knows what will happen.'

'Will you have a coffee, Papas?' Babá asked.

'I will, thank you. Do you have a name for the infant?'

Babá nodded. 'He will be baptised with his grandfather's name, *Yeorgos*, George!'

'At the big church – Saint George of the Well?' the priest asked, nodding towards the magnificent cathedral on the harbour's edge. 'Best to be sure, with so many churches in honour of our venerable dragon slayer.'

'Saint George of the Well it is.'

* * *

The years passed and Sofía grew into a teenager. On 17 September, all the Sofías in Greece celebrated their Name Day. Fourteen-year-old Sofía's friends came around to wish her, '*Kronia polla!*' Big year! Her former schoolfriends were betrothed now, some of the older ones already married with a child. On seeing the tired resignation of those young mothers Sofía was not motivated to join their ranks. There were more than enough children in the Konstantinidis family already.

Her loved ones brought little gifts they had made to mark the occasion. A cotton bobbin with four nails knocked in for French knitting, from María. A new crochet hook and silks from her grandmothers. From her parents, a wooden clamp for Sofía to press her wild flowers, instead of using a rock on a piece of wood. The most marvellous gift of all came from Uncle Kuríllos. A fountain pen with three spare nibs, a bottle of ink and a leather-bound notebook. She no longer had to write her history book in pencil.

Sofía broke all the rules when she rushed up to her uncle, flung her arms around his neck and kissed his cheeks. 'It's the most wonderful present ever, Uncle. Thank you!'

'You have some film left in that Kodak of yours?' Babá asked his brother. 'It's time for a family photo. Let's get everyone outside.'

* * *

Teenager Sofía could not sit still. She helped María, now twenty-three and currently pregnant with her eighth child.

'Why doesn't anyone want to marry me, María?'

'You're wrong, my sister. They all want you. The problem is you are too good for them. You have a passion for perfume and history, you're an expert carpet weaver and you speak three languages when most can hardly write their own names. So be proud and be patient. The right man will come along.'

'I'm going to die a spinster,' Sofía cried in dismay.

'You're so stubborn!' María said. 'Let me remind you: you're in the process of writing a Greek history book, in Greek, using the Greek alphabet, which is absolutely forbidden by that mad Italian fascist, Benito Mussolini, on penalty of death. So, what do you do? You hide it under your mattress. Who would think of looking there? Your threat to come back as a ghost and haunt him will not stop you getting shot. You're a rebel, Sofía, and the boys sense it. They all want a wife who'll do as she's told.'

'I can't change,' Sofía said with tears in her eyes. 'I've tried, but I just can't.'

María slid her arms around her beloved sister and gave her a hug. 'Nobody would want you to, we all love you just the way you are and one day the right man will come along and you will fall madly in love. So don't be hasty to marry the wrong one now.'

* * *

'Sofía, take these hens to the bakery and stick them in the oven once the bread's finished,' Mamá said, making use of the town's free oven. The day was too hot to light the house-fire to cook. 'The pot's not heavy and they're all plucked and trussed. They'll flavour the roots and rice that will fill our bellies tonight.'

Sofía trapsed down the hill to the square, wondering about the sudden shortage of food. Just as she struggled to keep a grip on the pot and open the bakery door, it flew open and a tall, elegant woman blocked her way.

'Ah, sorry, let me help,' the woman said in Italian, holding the door open.

'Thank you,' Sofía replied, going in and placing the pot on the counter as the smell of yeast filled her senses. To her surprise, the woman followed her back into the shop.

'Young lady, do you go to school here?' Sofía nodded. The woman held out a slender hand. 'Then let me introduce myself; I am Anastasia, your new teacher.'

Sofía practised her first handshake and experienced a rite of passage into the adult world.

'Pleased to meet you, I'm Sofía,' she said, suddenly horrified to realise she'd spoken Greek to the stranger. She momentarily placed her hand over her mouth, then quickly repeated herself in Italian while a blush burned her cheeks.

The teacher bent forward and whispered in Greek, 'Don't worry, I prefer Greek too.' Then she stood tall and winked, her wide smile promising mischief and affection.

The red-faced baker shoved Sofía's chickens into his empty brick oven. 'This is the girl I was telling you about,' he said to the teacher. 'Her family own the distillery where they make precious oil for overseas.'

The teacher smiled. 'Precious oil . . . how interesting.'

* * *

58

Later, they all ate chicken-flavoured rice while Uncle Kuríllos repeated the town gossip.

'They say the new teacher's a woman of Greek-Italian descent and a further anomaly is she's both a spinster and very beautiful.'

Babá, first to finish, helped himself to more rice. 'Listen, we know from ancient times that only men are wise enough to hold the position of *teacher*.' He paused with his fork halfway to his mouth. 'Even I, with my great wisdom, am not intelligent enough to be a *teacher*.'

Mamá squinted at him but kept her thoughts to herself.

Kuríllos said, 'Anyway, teaching girls to read and write is dangerous enough, but imagine if they learned mathematics, politics or medicine. Before you know it, they'd think they're as intelligent as men. Then we'd have nothing but trouble!'

'Absolutely,' Babá agreed. 'She must have bribed someone, or been the crazy daughter of an important person in Rhodes. Imagine the embarrassment of having a self-opinionated spinster with ideas of grandeur in the family. They'd remove her to a distant island and there's no further Greek island than Castellorizo.'

Kuríllos nodded. 'If she had any brains, she'd know a woman's purpose is to satisfy her husband in bed—' At this, Babá grinned and Mamá's eyes narrowed. She threw another venomous glance at her husband and shifted the chicken and rice out of his reach. Kuríllos continued, '—feed him well, keep the house neat and give him as many male children as possible.'

María glanced at Sofía and then rolled her eyes in disgust.

* * *

Sofía, inspired by the day's events, lay in bed that night, dreaming about her idol, the teacher, determined to follow Anastasia into the teaching profession. The next morning, she wasted no time in broadcasting her intention to instruct other girls to read and write and learn mathematics.

'But who will help María with her children?' Mamá asked.

'Who will make the precious oil for Mustafa to sell to the French?' Babá asked.

'Who will finish weaving your glorious rug?' María asked.

'Who will help Mamá with the cleaning and washing and cooking?' Uncle Kuríllos asked.

'You see? This is what happens when you give useless girls big ideas,' Babá stated.

In despair, Mamá shook her head at Sofía and said, 'The fact is, you're so useless, child, nobody can survive without you.'

Sofía said, 'I love you, Mamá,' and then smiled at everyone.

* * *

Sofía also loved the building that was their family home. The house consisted of three floors. Mamá, Babá, Sofía and baby George slept on the attic floor. María, Mustafa and the three youngest children slept on the first floor. On the landing of the first floor was an ornate iron hand pump that brought water to the house from the cistern up the mountain. Ayeleen and her younger sister, Rosa and all the other children slept on the ground floor, which had the traditional wall-to-wall bed over an assortment of cupboards. Filling the back of the room was a mezzanine, built for when the boys were older. Under this indoor balcony, against the far wall, hung a vertical carpet loom and Sofía's three-metre-wide carpet that was nearing completion.

'You're doing a wonderful job,' María said as Sofía tied off another row of tufts. 'I was having a look at the pattern – you've got the whole family in there.'

'Thanks, but it's not all my work you know, Mamá and Mikró Yiayá started it when the loom hung in the distillery, before I was born.'

The stout adjoining door behind the carpet linked the house to the distillery where the precious oil was produced.

CHAPTER 9
OLIVIA

Rhodes, Greece, present day

MY CASE IS PACKED AND I'm ready for my journey to Greece tomorrow. I can't leave without saying goodbye to Uncle so I walk hurriedly into Brighton. Although he arrived home from hospital a couple of days ago, I know he still feels fragile. A street vendor outside the station catches my attention. I stop to admire her blooms. Cones of cellophane envelop a vivid display of colour. All types of flowers, perfectly presented, seem to shout my name from their white enamel buckets.

'What amazing roses. I'll have two bunches of the dark red, please,' I say on impulse, then hold them to my face and inhale. Their rich, overwhelming scent swirls about, playing with my senses, and I know they'll please Uncle.

I let myself into the flat, call, 'Good morning! Tea in five minutes!' then hide the roses behind his armchair. I go straight into the kitchen and pop the kettle on before even taking my coat off. My uncle comes into the big room, mutters, 'Morning,' and settles in his chair. 'I'm going to miss my breakfast cuppa, Olivia. Are you ready to go?'

'I am and I've brought you something so that you don't forget me while I'm away.' I reach behind his chair and place the roses in his lap. 'Ta-da!' I cry dramatically and grin.

My uncle gasps, lifts them to his face and closes his eyes. He inhales their perfume, long and slow, as if they are the finest red wine.

'Damascus roses. Dear Rosa,' he whispers. His chin quivers as he looks up. In an emotional moment, tears spring to his eyes and he fumbles for his handkerchief.

'Oh, Uncle,' I whisper. 'I didn't mean to upset you. Shall I take them away?' I'm confused and regret having saddened him. But why should a grown man cry over a bunch of flowers? I turn away to make his tea while he recomposes.

He sniffs and dries his eyes. 'No problem, it's me, a bit topsy-turvy after the hospital. I'll be all right, I promise. What a lovely gesture, Olivia, thank you.'

'No, really, I can take them away. I'm sorry.' I wonder if he wants to talk about it.

'It's not you, it's darling Rosa, my dearest niece. She was a little older than me, but much smaller and very delicate-looking.' He's silent for a moment; I guess recalling the past. 'Such a beautiful girl, not just in appearance, but her generous personality too. I admired her tremendously. All she wanted was to make people forget their troubles. This was a great gift and one that many Castellorizons needed as times got harder. You see, it was a time of war, of bombings, of starvation and loss. So, she danced for the people of Castellorizo. Little Rosa shared her great talent with all those she loved.

'Her favourite saying was, *God gave me these feet to dance away other people's sadness*, and she really believed it.' He closes his eyes and a tear slides out. 'I loved her dearly, but the tragedy! A trick of fate so cruel, I still can't talk about it. The flowers brought it all back, what happened to poor Rosa.'

My heart aches, he seems to carry such a burden. I want to comfort him, but I'm not sure what to say and fear upsetting him further. I put his tea and a couple of shortbreads on the side table next to his chair.

'Rosa is such a beautiful name, but it doesn't seem very Greek, Uncle.'

He smiles and my heart lifts.

'Ah, her name.' He lifts the roses from his lap and inhales their scent again. 'Best put these in water, if you don't mind.' He hands me the flowers. 'Rosa's name was an inspired choice. Mamá, María and Sofía were making precious oil from the Damascus rose, a very heavily scented bloom with large, dark-red velvet petals. This was the most expensive and valuable oil we made because there's very little oil in roses. The petals have to be gathered before sunrise, shipped to Castellorizo and distilled the same day.'

'Where do they come from?'

'The Damascus rose comes from across the water, in Turkey. Even today, most roses grown for perfume come from there. Many hundreds of acres of them, a magnificent sight. Anyway, in our distillery there's an open cement tank in the floor where the ingredients were collected and kept cool. When María was pregnant, they say she slipped and fell into this tank when it was full of rose petals. After that, it was as if she had an addiction to the smell and taste of roses.'

'The smell I understand . . . but the taste?'

'Ah, *loukoumi*, Turkish delight – made from rose water and gelatine – tastes of roses. She couldn't get enough of it. So, when the baby girl was born, they named her Rosa.'

'What a lovely story, Uncle. Why does it make you sad?'

He shakes his head, then his face crumples. 'Will it ever leave me, Olivia? The events of 1945. Poor Rosa. If only I could forget what happened, but I see it so clearly. I was standing right next to her. It was terrible and me just a boy. I idolised her, you see. I can't find the words to describe . . . I'll try to tell you the story when you return from Castellorizo.'

'No pressure, Uncle. Anyway, I'm taking my tablet so you can speak to your Castellorizo friends, via video, before I return. I think you'd enjoy that.'

*   *   *

My flight to Athens is over an hour late, so my plans to take a tour bus around the city are scuppered. Waiting for my flight to Rhodes, I wander around the airport departure lounge, gazing at handbags I can't afford and sampling perfumes in the duty-free shops. Some famous scents have been around since before the Second World War and I wonder if any of them once contained precious oil from Castellorizo. I still feel a little sad that my uncle's memories of Rosa upset him so much and I wonder what sort of tragedy could continue to break a man's heart after more than seventy-five years.

I love airports, but worry for Uncle undermines my enjoyment. *Olivia, you're a very shallow and superficial girl!* I tell myself while dabbing another scent sample onto the inside of my wrist. I'm going to smell like a tart's handbag by the time I get on the plane. You have to make the most of things while you can. My uncle's such a nice man, I wonder why he never married, but then again perhaps he did. I know so little about him.

Annoyed that I have allowed myself to be bullied into going alone, I punch his number into my phone . . . three rings, four rings . . . five rings. The echoing acoustics and bleachy smell of my surroundings add to my sudden gloom. I sigh and hang up, then realise I've absentmindedly stopped before a couple of flight monitors.

Destinations, gates and times scroll down. RHODES catches my attention but before I have chance to read the information line, the monitor changes to the Greek alphabet. Not an R to be seen and I've lost my place.

'Bugger!' a man's voice beside me exclaims.

'Double bugger!' I reply without looking at whoever it is. 'Why can't they have the English on one monitor and Greek on the other?'

'Hang on, mate, it's back,' he says. I catch an Australian accent.

'Damn – an hour's delay, again,' I mutter to myself.

'Just what I need!' he moans. 'Fly halfway around the world, all perfect timing, only to be felled at the last hurdle. I should have listened to the pilot. *Ladies and gentlemen, welcome to Greece. Keep your seatbelts fastened until the sign goes off and put your watches back fifty years.*'

I laugh and glance sideways. He is already looking at me, awaiting my attention. The faintest alarm bell is triggered by the twinkle in his friendly eyes. I smile politely at a younger version of Nick Dundee in jeans and T-shirt. He also wears the sallow tan that comes with tiredness. My flight's the only red on the screen, so I guess he's flying to Rhodes too. 'Hard luck,' I say.

'Fancy a beer?' he asks, nodding sideways.

Suddenly I'm thinking of Andrew. Is this how he did it? Bold as you like. I wonder if the tall Aussie has an unsuspecting wife at home. 'Actually, I'm just going to the bookshop, then I'll grab a coffee. But thanks anyway.'

'Here, take this. Wilbur Smith's last novel. Really good. Read it on the way over.'

I glance at the tome. 'Come far then?'

'Oz.'

I didn't roll my eyes, did I? Damn!

'I'm Rob. Pleased t'-meet-cha.' He makes an exaggerated handshake gesture, elbow out, stiff-fingered hand slicing towards my breastbone. I don't know why but it makes me laugh, then my guard's up again. Am I just another conquest? One thing's for sure, my knickers will *never* end up in his pocket!

'Olivia,' I say, feeling empowered now. We shake. His hand, warm and firm, grips mine comfortably.

By the time I return with my coffee, Rob is asleep, arms folded, chin on chest and knees pointing in opposite directions as if they'd had a row. I take the opportunity to scrutinise him. Sun-bronzed skin, maybe six-two, athletic, muscular. I guess his floppy, sandy hair would be brown in the UK. No sign of a wedding ring but why am I looking?

I call Uncle again and this time he picks up.

'Sorry, dear girl, I was answering the door. Just about to call you back. My lunch arrived. Shepherd's pie and jam roly-poly. Jolly good too. They brought me my carer yesterday, Amy; one hour in the morning and one in the evening.'

'You sound much better. Promise me you won't overdo things, Uncle.'

'I feel good, Olivia. Also, I've started a new painting and this one's especially for you. Look, if you need any information, or I can be any help while you're on the island, just give me a ring. I'd love to hear what you're up to.'

'I will, thanks. I'll call you every day, if that's all right, just to put my own mind at rest. I'm in Athens airport right now so I'll phone you from Rhodes, tomorrow, OK?'

'That will be lovely. *Kaló taxídi.* Good journey,' he says with feeling.

The flight to Rhodes is called. I nudge Rob's shoulder to wake him then quickly sidestep the queue, glad I've booked priority boarding. I don't see Rob on the plane, or in the Arrivals hall.

* * *

On a hotel sunbed at the side of the pool, I close my eyes against a sky as blue as a Santorini church dome. Apart from an occasional swim in the pool's crystal water, I will remain on this plush, lemon-coloured beach towel until it's time for a pre-lunch prosecco served by handsome young Markos. I'm primped and pampered and should be in heaven but the truth is I'm struggling with worry about Uncle. Also, why can't I enjoy a single moment without wishing Andrew could see me now? I don't want to think about him, yet it's as if he's still deep in my heart and I can't exorcise him.

I'm also trying to figure out why my mother and grandmother, both of whom I loved, would never talk about the island of their birth? It's never bothered me before, but Uncle has sparked my curiosity. What will I discover when I get to Castellorizo? Were my family expelled for some terrible misdemeanour? Did Uncle *have* to leave with Sofía, or was he being brotherly?

So many questions.

I am having a wonderful time, so long as I don't think. Was it my fault Andrew was attracted to other women? Of course not! I try to lose myself in a book, but it doesn't work. My eyes drift along the lines of print, but my mind is with Uncle. It was a huge mistake to come without him. I reach for my phone again.

'Olivia, relax! I'm on the mend, really, everyone's taking excellent care of me. It's important that you enjoy your holiday. I don't want to be worrying about you worrying about me worrying about you. All right?'

'Sorry, Uncle. I *am* thrilled to be taking this holiday, honestly and I know you'll take care of yourself.'

Still, my thoughts keep returning to my uncle's delicate heart, my ex-husband and my deceased mother. I should be concentrating on my new cookery book.

The sun seeps through my skin, warming me to the bone. I feel that same sun bathe me in glorious elegance. Its sparkling light shines down on my body and illuminates my very spirit. I lift my shades and smile at Marko as he delivers my prosecco.

Too much pressure lately has made me stressed and depressed, but I will learn to love myself once more. I sip my sparkling drink then close my eyes for another ten minutes. I remember poor Uncle and feel sad. There is no escape from my concern. Perhaps on the island of Castellorizo I will find out what happened to Granny Sofía's family.

*   *   *

After three days of relaxing at the poolside of my five-star, drinking exotic cocktails and using the gym each morning before breakfast, I rise from my sunbed, pack and check out of my beautiful hotel. The Wednesday ferry to Castellorizo takes four hours. I could fly. There are planes from Rhodes several times a week. However, Uncle insisted that I sail from Rhodes when I travel to Castellorizo for the first time.

'This will be an experience you'll never forget, Olivia,' he promised.

'I wish you were coming with me.'

'I will, next time.' He closed his eyes and smiled, seeing the scene in his mind's eye. 'The commercial harbour's right next to the castellated city of Rhodes Old Town. It was built by the Knights of Saint John, you know. When the ship leaves, it will pass the lighthouse of Saint Nikolaos and you'll catch a glimpse of Mandraki harbour where they say the great Colossus of Rhodes once straddled the entrance.'

'Will I see any remains of the statue?' I asked.

'No, they blame an earthquake. Poor Helios lay there for hundreds of years. A famous sight, apparently.'

I imagined his students spellbound and found myself smiling as he continued.

'Later, when Arabs ruled the island, they sold the fallen Colossus to a Jewish merchant. They say, the Jew needed 900 camels to move it.'

'It's difficult to imagine anything that big. Maybe the Statue of Liberty?'

He nodded. 'Yes, perhaps. Now, Rhodes harbour is marked by two stone columns topped by two bronze deer, a doe and a hind. Worth sightseeing around there. The cathedral, the bishop's palace, the charming old Muslim cemetery, the fish market, the lighthouse and of course, Rhodes Old Town. You must see them all.'

'Next time, you're definitely coming with me.'

'It was an ambitious plan, but I need to be stronger first. I knew I have a dicky ticker, I should have told you. Damaged it when I was a boy. The fire, drowning, the submarine, seeing my niece and my sister . . . Oh, God! It's still impossible to . . . After all these year. Will it ever go away?' He rubbed his hand across his eyes, then sighed as the exhausting memory drained him.

I looked away, conscious of his battle, yet helpless. There are things he wanted to say, events too terrifying or dramatic to pass his trembling lips. His eyes stared into the past. The eyes of a screamer – of nightmares – of horrors conquered for the moment but bound to return.

After a long, shaky breath, the Uncle I know returned. 'But I don't want to think about all that now,' he continued. 'My past was a bit of a nightmare. I don't know how we all survived. But then again, we didn't, did we?' He crossed himself, one of the few Greek mannerisms he's retained.

'It sounds as though you have a huge story to tell me, Uncle.' I don't think he heard me.

'Poor Rosa ... Poor, poor Rosa. Life was so unfair to her. And the soldier ... That soldier changed everyone's lives. I wonder if you can find Granny Sofía's history book. It might be in the attic, or it could still be in the Castellorizo house. A first-hand account of modern history. It would be marvellous to see it again, even though she wrote it all in Greek.'

'You must have some incredible tales stored up here.' I tapped the side of my head. 'Why don't you tell me one, each time we meet? I'd love to hear them.' He smiled, clearly thinking about it, so I continued. 'You mentioned a soldier. What was that all about?'

'Ah, the soldier. If not for him, where would we be now? Anyway, I digress. Before the ship turns into Castellorizo's harbour, go back up to the top deck, port side and you'll see the islet of Ro flying under a Greek flag.'

'Port?'

'Left. Remember: port has four letters, left has four letters. Now you'll never forget.' We grinned at each other and I imagined the pleasure he gave his students. 'I promise you an unforgettable arrival, Olivia. Picture-postcard pretty.' He spoke quickly, as if he isn't sure there's time to say all he needs. 'Remember me to the old people and show them pictures of me and your grandparents and parents, of course. Make friends with the mayor, whoever he is now. Give him my regards. Tell him I'll visit soon and inform him that your mother's name was Tsambika Konstantinidis, daughter of Sofía. Ask him about the house ...'

'House?'

'Find a lawyer. You have a fine house and a distillery in Castellorizo – I planned to show you myself – surprise you. One of the reasons I wanted to go with you.' His eyes closed. 'Too tired now.'

CHAPTER 10
SOFIA

Castellorizo, Greece, 1941

THE KONSTANTINIDIS MEN WERE EATING their food outside while discussing Greek politics.

'Damn Churchill and his blockade. He's supposed to be on our side!' Kuríllos yelled, throwing a chunk of bread into his chicken-egg-lemon soup, which was mostly boiled rice and wild herbs. The War had finally reached Castellorizo although only two things changed. A terrible shortage of food and a lot more Italian soldiers controlling the island. 'His goal of starving the Germans and Italians out of the country pays no regard to Greek civilians. They say 300,000 Greeks have died of hunger around Athens and the larger islands. There won't be any Greeks left the way he's going on! What are *we* supposed to do?'

'We should move over to Turkey. Castellorizo has no arable land and no natural water supply,' Babá said.

Kuríllos scratched his head, stared at Babá, then yelled for Sofía. 'Sofía! I want you to write a letter to Churchill. Get your pen and paper and I'll dictate.'

'You can't just write to the prime minister of England, Uncle,' Sofía said.

'He's prime minister of Great Britain,' Babá corrected her. 'I hope you know how he should be addressed.'

Mamá said, 'Write to Mataxa, or the King of England, if you write to anyone – then you might expect some sense.' Both men stared at her, both wondering what she knew about politics. 'I'm taking Zafiro and the girls down to Mandraki to wash them in the sea while the midwife's here with María,' Mamá said. 'Sofía, keep an eye on little Fevzi, Panayiotis, and young George while I'm gone. They're sleeping.'

'Yes, Mamá.'

'I'll be back to cook in half an hour. Bring the washing in if it's dry and mind you fold it as you do. Also, light the fire under number one kiln for the next batch of oil.' She glared at her husband and his brother. 'One last thing, Sofía, don't let the men leave the patio before I get back . . . do you hear me, you two?'

Babá and Kuríllos nodded. Sofía said, 'Yes, Mamá,' as she watched the band of children with towels under their arms head for the sea. She would stay with the men and listen to their discussion about the war for as long as possible.

'It's us – those who depend on food that's shipped in from Rhodes – that suffer the most,' Babá said. 'Everyone's turning to Turkey for their essentials, but demand's driven prices through the sky. Nobody can afford even a loaf of bread.'

'Where's Mustafa? We should send him a telegram and ask him to bring some sacks of flour and yeast.'

'We're all right for food at the moment. I checked the storeroom. We're only halfway through the sacks of lentils, chickpeas, dried beans and rice and we've still got two gallons of oil Mustafa brought last time. Besides, he sent a telegram from Rhodes, he'll be here today. Anyway, he knows what we need. That's his job and his father taught him well.'

'More families are packing up,' Kuríllos said nodding at a family waiting at the port. 'Look – the Hatzidakis family are leaving for Port Said, hoping to get a ship to Australia next week. Who can blame them? Ah, look, speak of the devil, here comes Mustafa sailing into port.'

A loud groan came from indoors. María was about to birth another baby. Her last child was another glorious boy, Panayiotis. On that occasion, a joyous Babá and Uncle Kuríllos got so drunk that eight men had to carry them home. Mamá made them sleep where they were dropped, outside. She stuffed a pillow under each head, then gave them both a fierce kick in the thigh before locking the door.

'I swear if I had honey to spare, I'd drizzle it over their sweaty faces, for the ants,' she muttered, narrowing her eyes as she imagined black insects crawling into her husband's ears and nose.

'Do you think I'll ever get married and have children of my own, Babá?'

'Of course you will, Sofía. It's not your fault eight of María's children are girls – and nobody wants to marry into a family that's prone to birthing useless females,' he said.

Yet Sofía remained single despite Babá's generous dowry. Her grand traditional costume, worn by the bride on her wedding day, lay on top of her dowry chest full of carefully crocheted linen.

Uncle Kuríllos added, 'You've just been a bit unlucky, after the earthquake that accompanied your birth, then your sister producing a glut of girls. Then, when you managed to knock Pavlos unconscious – I was proud of you, what a left hook – but, it didn't help your chances of a betrothal.'

This incident happened when Pavlos, emboldened by his gleeful friends, crept up behind Sofía as she pegged washing out one blustery day. He tried to put his hand on her waist. Nobody, including Sofía, expected the force in her fist when she swung around. Unfortunately, the punch rendered Pavlos unconscious for all of thirty seconds. Sofía was certain she had killed him and broken her knuckles in the process. His friends scattered as she screamed hysterically.

Later, she took comfort when many village women patted or squeezed her shoulder in a display of female camaraderie. Hardly a word was said, just a nod, a wink, or a smile occasionally accompanied by a languorous utterance of, 'Ah, Sofía, if only I had . . .'

* * *

Sofía sweltered on a stone banquette, between Babá and Kuríllos, outside the front door. 'I can't believe October's over already, Uncle, it's still too hot. What will happen now we're at war with half the world?'

'Same as last time,' Kuríllos replied. They spoke quietly in Greek, although this was still against the law according to the Italians. 'We were short of food in the Great War and we're short of food now, but forewarned is forearmed. We're sacked up with rice and dried beans.'

'Why have the Italians sided with Hitler?' Sofía asked. 'Anastasia said she heard the Italians had invaded Greece from the Albanian border without informing der Führer. She says there'll be terrible trouble.'

Uncle Kuríllos scratched his head. 'How does she know these things, Sofía?'

'She's a teacher, she knows everything.'

Babá shook his head. 'She might be a spy for the Italians!'

'Could be, she's beautiful enough to be a spy,' Kuríllos agreed, smiling softly. 'With legs that long, I'd want to be on her side any

76

time.' Babá grinned and Sofía tutted, then Kuríllos continued, 'perhaps we should interrogate her. What do you say, brother?' He winked at Babá.

'Stop it, both of you!' Sofía said crossly. 'She's not a spy and that's the end of it!'

Babá continued, 'We're the furthest island from Athens and we have no assets. Who's going to waste their bombs on us? We're safe.'

'They say we've the only safe harbour between Rhodes and Cyprus. What will happen when the Allies and the Axis fight over our port?' Kuríllos asked.

'Anastasia says the other worry is Turkey,' Sofía said. 'Turkey might be neutral now, but whose side will she be drawn to? Anyway, Germany and Italy were supposed to be on the same side, the Axis – united in fighting us, the Allies?' She was proud of her grasp on the political situation. 'Until now, the Allies were mainly the British and French . . . but not even the French now, because they've already surrendered to Hitler, haven't they?'

The two men stared at each other, neither of them ready to admit they didn't know what Sofía was talking about.

'You can say what you like, no war in Europe's going to affect us on this distant outpost,' Uncle Kuríllos said. 'I'm quite sure we're safe.'

Babá disagreed. 'We're so short of food, some are starving but too proud to say. Also, if Turkey decides to join in, we'll be slaves in our own land.'

'Anastasia said something similar, Babá,' said Sofía.

Her father continued, 'Whichever side Turkey chooses will rule us. In the Great War, she chose the Germans, but Germany lost, so this time she'll choose the Allied Forces if she has any

sense. Mind you, where do we stand when our Allies are determined to starve us all to death?'

* * *

A newborn's cry drifted through the open door. Sofía peered
under the olive tree at the other end of the courtyard, where the
two deaf grandmothers were crocheting. She stood, folded her
arms and made a rocking motion. The two old women turned
to stare at each other, so they could lipread.

'Looks like she's given birth, then,' Mikró Yiayá said.

'Wonder what she's had?'

'Probably a baby.' Mikró Yiayá shrugged. 'What were you
hoping for?'

Megáli Yiayá giggled. 'A donkey would be useful,' she shouted.

Mikró Yiayá pouted as she recalled, then nodded. 'I'll bet it
felt like a donkey.'

They sat like a pair of crusty bookends with their backs
against the ancient olive tree. In the shady nook, dressed in col-
ourless clothes, they seemed carved out of bark and could easily
be overlooked.

'If that María has had another girl, I'm going to crochet her
legs together,' Megáli Yiayá yelled, jowls a-quiver. With a meaty
fist, she thrust her crochet hook into the next loop of thread.

Mikró Yiayá cupped a thin hand around her ear and tilted it
towards the lady. She squinted into the distance while decipher-
ing what at first came to her as mumbled monotone. When the
light went on, she screeched back. 'If that María has another
girl, I'm going to castrate that Mustafa and make an *amelétita*
fricassée.' She stretched her scrawny neck, swiping her thumbnail through the air in a threatening manner at knee height.

'A free what?' Megáli Yiayá shouted back.

'A fricassée, you deaf old cow!' Mikró Yiayá squawked a little louder, her tinny voice trembling with the effort.

'Ah, a fricassée?' Megáli Yiayá grasped her roll of crocheting and made a slightly obscene gesture. 'Well, according to gossip, you'll be able to feed the whole town. Hung like a ram, they say.' she blasted back.

Mikró Yiayá narrowed her eyes and smiled slyly. 'Better buy a bigger pan then,' she squeaked, her bony shoulders jigging up and down.

* * *

The two men had gone down to the *kafenio* when the doctor arrived and then Mustafa the Turk strode onto the patio and straight in to see his wife. A heated discussion went on inside. Sofía glared at the proud father and exasperated doctor as they came back out. They talked about María as if Sofía wasn't there.

'If she has another child, it will kill her!' Doctor Iohannis couldn't contain his anger and frustration.

The big Turk, deaf to the doctor's reprimands, grinned proudly with the news that he had another son.

The doctor tried again. 'Mustafa, listen, a child a year would take too much out of any woman. In the name of God, can't you see it? Her body is old before its time. She was married too young and she's had too many babies. What will you do with all these children when she leaves you for a better place?'

'María will never leave me, she's blind to the *kamáki* of other men. Look at her, strong as an ox and just as beautiful.'

'She's neither,' Doctor Iohannis said. 'She was very beautiful. Now, she's the exhausted mother of all these children.' He lifted

79

his hand and indicated the line of freshly washed girls, headed by their oldest brother, tramping onto the patio. The doctor sighed and continued to scold Mustafa. 'If you don't mark my words, María will depart on a journey to heaven before the year is out! Keep it in your pants for six months while your wife gets her strength back, Mustafa. Do you understand?'

The big Turk squared his shoulders. 'Don't worry, Doctor, I have a plan. Each time a baby is born it's given to the next oldest daughter. This one will go to the nine-year-old, Rosa. Pretty little thing. Going to be a ballet dancer when she grows up.' He smiled adoringly as Mamá herded the last of his freshly bathed children through the gate.

The youngsters threw themselves at their father, prancing around him, hugging his legs, uproarious in their welcome. He went to the edge of the patio, placed two fingers in his mouth and produced a whistle that made everyone, apart from the grandmothers, clasp their hands over their ears.

'My men will bring presents for all those who have been good for their mother and Aunty Sofía. Who's been good?' All hands went up. 'Go and sit on the wall and wait quietly,' he ordered. 'Ayeleen, see if Aunty Sofía needs help with anything in there.' He nodded towards the house.

Sofía smiled; it was true that Mustafa made a wonderful father.

'Rosa,' Mustafa called remembering the book on ballet that he brought for the girl on his last trip. 'Show us what you've learned while I've been away.' The younger girls sat around their sister, clapping as she bowed. Rosa tucked her skirt into the legs of her knickers, stretched her neck, and moved her arms as elegantly as the wings of a flying swan. She went through her positions and then, much to the delight of her siblings, she twirled and pranced about the patio.

Mustafa rested his big fists on his hips and grinned, gleefully. 'Bravo! Bravo!' he called out. The midwife approached and thrust a bundle into his arms.

'You can hold him for a minute, while I see to his mother,' she said. 'Another boy for you.'

'This is a miracle, is it not?' Mustafa whispered. Clearly emotional as he gazed down at the swaddled baby. 'At first I thought Allah had cursed me for marrying an infidel, one girl after another.' He turned to the doctor while he stroked his son's cheek then glanced at Rosa leaping and twirling before her siblings. 'But now I understand, this is Allah's great plan. Have you ever seen so much love and joy in one family, Doctor?'

Doctor Iohannis shook his head. 'I give up! For delivering a strong healthy baby, Mustafa, you owe me a sack of dried beans. No, wait a minute, two sacks. You didn't pay me for the last birth.'

Mustafa, a head taller than any Greek on the island, was a handsome but formidable figure. His wide, good-humoured smile spread above a thick black beard that reached his broad chest. Two gold teeth and one gold earring proclaimed the man's wealth. All the women of Castellorizo and beyond admired his dark long-lashed eyes and narrow hips, but he had adored nobody but María from the first moment he saw her.

Sofía greeted the doctor hurriedly, pausing only to glance at the house and ask, '*Ola kala?*' All's good?

'Yes, Sofía, all's good,' Doctor Iohannis assured the girl. 'But your sister's very tired. She needs to rest.'

CHAPTER 11
OLIVIA

Castellorizo, Greece, present day

I STEP OFF THE FERRY and quickly move away from the clatter and diesel fumes. At last, I've arrived at the birthplace of my mother, grandmother and uncle.

My first impression of Castellorizo is that it is dazzlingly beautiful, so perfect that I can't imagine why anyone would leave. I hurry towards the curve of the bay where the majestic bastion of Christianity, Saint George of the Well, stands like a huge white cake; a triumphant thumbed-nose at the Turkish coastline in the distance. I wonder if a magnificent mosque stares back with challenging minarets and sturdy domes, displaying even greater splendour in a duel of religious architectural supremacy. According to the travel company, next to this splendid church, I will find my very reasonable accommodation with a balcony overlooking the beautiful harbour. Feeling rather pleased with myself, I drag my case through the tide of people hurrying towards the ferry.

My need for coffee hits home so I order one at Eleni's Place, a waterside taverna. The royal-blue chairs and turquoise cushions, perfectly match the unbelievable colours of sea and sky. After a frantic five minutes of embarking passengers and disembarking packages and pickups, the ferry hoists its tailgate. The quayside clatter subsides and the promenade empties. Agitated water swirls and foams in a maelstrom as powerful propellers turn the ferry in preparation for departure. Café tables fill. People sit and dreamily stare across the water.

My chair, dangerously close to the unguarded edge, gives me an uninterrupted view of the bay. Beyond the harbour mouth, I see a scatter of charming islets. Across the water, the Turkish mountains are dotted with white houses belonging to the small town of Kaş. I hope to take a day trip. The idea of two very different cuisines so close together excites me.

Mesmerised by the view, a sudden snorting comes from near my feet. I am shocked to see an enormous turtle paddle its flippers right next to the quayside. I stare disbelievingly as this magnificent creature sticks her haughty head out of the water and blinks round ET eyes at me . . . just like that!

I snatch my phone and take a short video of her paddling. For a crazy moment I almost expect the turtle to say, 'Welcome to Castellorizo, Olivia.'

The town seems surreal, like a Spielberg film set with life-size dolls' houses. An impossibly clear sea shimmers under a ridiculously blue sky. Chunky wooden boats, straight out of Uncle's paintings, have gloss paintwork in clashing primary colours. They pose on their acrylic reflections, along the harbour's edge.

I understand why Uncle insisted there was no point in telling me anything until I'd seen this place for myself. How could he describe the saturated colours of Castellorizo without sounding implausible?

Shaking my head, I ask the woman who comes with my coffee, 'Is there a tourist information place nearby?'

'What you want? I will help you,' she says with a practised smile.

'I need to find my grandmother's house. My family come from here, but they left after the war.'

'You come from Australia?'

'No, from England.'

Her smile falters and despite the riotous clash of colours and fabrics she wears, she seems to dull a little. My uncle's words come back: *things happened*.

'Ah, you come back here in one hour, yes?' A slight Australian accent seems strange coming from this smart, upright woman, although her strong features and dark hair pulled into a tight chignon are undoubtedly Greek.

* * *

I finish my drink, then drop my suitcase off at my harbourside room. Back at the café table a little later, I find the mayor waiting. After introductions, he offers to take me to the house and old distillery of my family.

The streets are lined with houses of peach, lemon and dusky pink, tall and elegant with ornate plaster finishings and shutters of wine red, blue or ochre. Not a bit like the white, sugar-cube homes of the Cyclades Islands. These two- and three-storey dwellings shimmer with colour. The geometric shapes under terracotta-pitched roofs have wide balconies that contrast with a riot of bougainvillea. The show-stopping vermillion vine climbs and intertwines from street to street like a single deep-pink satin ribbon unravelled around buildings and binding the town together. In colours that clash outrageously, clay pots burst with flamboyant lilies and geraniums.

Castellorizo's only town, Megisti, clusters around the deep, U-shaped anchorage. Café tables crowd the pavement, centimetres from the water's edge. Brightly painted metal ladders, like an upended J, make light of entering the crystal harbour water for a swim. I lift my phone and take photographs for Uncle.

Feeling slightly drunk on the island's exquisiteness, I call to my guide leading the way and try to make conversation. 'How come no one's ever heard of Castel . . . Castel . . .'

'Eh, what you say?' the old man calls back over his shoulder. 'Ah, Castellorizo. Cas-tel-lor-ree-zo! Is easy.' Under a slick of hair that is too black to match his age, I catch his frown and an impatient tone in his voice, but it's soon gone. 'We is nearly here at your *spíti* . . . your house, lady.'

'I can't believe this place, I feel like Alice in Wonderland!' I remind myself to show respect. Not all cultures understand my own country's ways and some might misinterpret the British sense of humour as mocking. Giddy with the strange euphoria that fizzes in my head, I still find it hard to believe I'm not dreaming.

The mayor turns towards me. 'Why you laugh, lady?'

'I can't believe it's real. It's all so amazing!' I raise an open hand and gesture across the landscape. 'Absolutely spectacular!' Something about the mayor unsettles me.

'But of course! Castellorizo is the most beautiful of all the islands.'

We stop outside a dilapidated house with crumbling walls and peeling shutters. A property abandoned for many years. Three storeys of stone covered by stucco, much of which has fallen away and lies in a drift against the front wall. A neoclassical Venetian-style building, like all the others I've seen so far. The balcony has gone, but support rafters protrude from the front like four fingers of an upturned hand. A few smashed terracotta roof tiles lie around my feet.

I would never have found the house on my own. A row of wide pine trunks sawn off at knee height are half hidden by clumps of common hawkweed and gripped by the searching stems of ivy. The yellow, dandelion-type flowers nod their heads as if talking about me, the stranger in their midst.

I can imagine their gossip: *'This woman doesn't belong.'* *'Legally, she owns the property.'* *'But after what happened . . .'* *'No, everyone will have forgotten that time by now.'* *'Not everyone. Not here.'* *'And the Castellorizons never forgive.'*

'Madam!' the mayor interrupts my silly daydream. 'You want me to open this door for you?' There is something sly about his eyes.

I nod. 'Yes, please.' The heavy wooden door has rotted along the bottom. Once a vivid blue, the paint has faded to a charming chalky hue. A hand-carved architrave surrounds four rectangular panels, the top two of which were once filled with glass. One has been replaced by a sun-bleached plank of ply with stencilled lemons, and a rusting, ornate, cast-iron grille is all that remains of the other.

I try to imagine some of the people who have passed through that doorway and how safe they must have felt behind such a solid portal.

The mayor tilts his chin towards the lobbed pines. 'The locals, they cut the trees for their fires. Many people still cook with the wood oven.'

'Why would anyone build a house behind trees when they blocked this beautiful view?'

'Ah, the house, it needed much shadow. They make the perfume here a long time before. Also because it is hidden, the house was saved from the *bombes*.'

'Oh, yes – the perfume – I'd forgotten. Granny Sofía had mentioned it.' But what was this about bombs?

'Your grandmother was Kyría Sofía, Mrs Sofía, yes?'

'Yes, she was.' I imagine Granny Sofía gazing between the trees towards the town below.

'This *spíti* ... this house, it belongs to Kyría María ... Mrs María. You find the factory belongs to the younger sister, Kyría Sofía, at the backside.'

I hang on to a straight face – after all, his English is far better than my Greek.

'We go to see now,' the mayor says. 'Here they make the famous oil for perfume, long ago.' He sighs, glances at his watch then at me. Then he smiles his big, open, Greek smile. 'They build the house from the rocks of houses that fell in the earthquake in ...' He says something in Greek that I can't make sense of.

'Sorry, I don't understand.'

He reaches into his pocket for a penknife, then pulls the hefty blade out.

I step back, suddenly wanting to leave.

'Ah, I no speak the good English.' He scratches *1926* into the stone doorframe before he slips the knife into his pocket. With a short grunt, he untwists a length of wire threaded through the bolt and hasp.

'You mean this wire is all that's kept the door shut for over seventy years?'

'Yes, is true. You are lucky. The British and the Italians steal everything from the houses ... everything, you understand?' He makes a clawing motion with his fingers. 'And the big fire and the German Stuka bombs and the British bombs, too – they fall all around and destroy everything that was built after the big earthquake. But they all miss the *spíti* of your family because it hide behind the trees.'

'The British? That can't be right.' What an alarming thought. 'You're not saying the British robbed the local people and bombed the island?'

He lifts his chin and peers down his nose. 'They gathered all Castellorizons – even babies, old grandmothers – and forced them onto the big ship. They say, *You go to Kaş for a few days.*' He points over the harbour to the Turkish mainland. '*To be safe from bombs*, they say.' His anger is apparent. 'The Castellorizons and Turks were great friends, so the Greeks feel safer with the Turks, who were not on any side, than suffering the German dive bombers, the Stukas. The English soldiers say to hurry, no lock the house, leave, quickly now! Straight away! They tell us we soon come back, no worries. Is lies to all our people.' He lifts his chin higher and narrows his eyes. 'The English warship – with all Castellorizo's families, except not our strong boys, they is far away in the Greek army – set sail and *then* the people are told they go to Cyprus. Cyprus! What they do, lady? Is too late. They can no get off, can no leave the navy ship. The English *capitanos*, he no care about the grandmothers' cries! You understand?'

I am finding all this hard to believe and promise myself to ask Uncle when I get home. 'Can I just ask, how old were you when all this happened?'

He squints at me, hesitates, then says angrily, 'I was three years old, but I remember everything very clearly!'

It is impossible to believe that my own countrymen would trick the island's entire population into leaving and then rob their houses . . . surely not?

'Are you sure the British soldiers did that?' I ask again. 'You know the penalty for looting is execution in the British army?'

'Yes, they did it, madam. I know, I was here.' He hesitates then, realising he has made a mistake. 'But when they steal all the treasure from the Castellorizo houses, they miss this place, the family house of you, they no steal the things in here. Nobody dares even to go inside because if the big Turk, Mustafa, or one of his sons find out, then they cut the throat, ear to ear. Everyone knows this for sure.'

The mayor runs his fingertips across his neck in one swift action to ensure there is no misunderstanding. He pushes the old door until it shifts decades' worth of grit. Golden sunlight floods the room.

I can't believe what lies before me. 'Oh, my goodness, look at this place . . .' I whisper, reluctant to disturb silver cobwebs that round the corners, like old ghosts that peer back at me from the distant gloom. My thoughts go to Uncle. When did he last see the place – when he was a small boy, or was he here after the war? I peer at the floor.

'Is there a cellar, do you think?' I ask the mayor, imagining the floor collapsing as I step inside. 'I mean, do you think it's safe to walk on?'

'Of course it's safe,' he cries, as if I have insulted him. 'Go in, go in!'

I'm just about to step inside, when a man's voice rings out behind me. 'Stop!'

I turn to see a tall man wearing navy bib-and-brace overalls over a white vest. He has a huge beard, a loaded toolbelt slung around his narrow hips and a concerned look on what I can see of his face.

'Don't go in, it's not safe!' he shouts as he approaches. He turns to the mayor and a big argument takes place with raised voices and lots of arm waving. The stranger turns his attention back to me. 'You speak English?' I nod. 'Is not safe in there,' he repeats. 'The beams have rot, there's a big hole in the roof. Please, talk to the builder first.'

'Thank you. I appreciate your help. I'm Olivia, the grand-daughter of Sofía Konstantinidis.'

He reaches to shake my hand. 'I am Gregoris, the local electrician. Pleased to meet you.'

I wonder if Gregoris is Greek for gorgeous, because from what I can see, he is. The man has an open, honest face above his enormous beard and, oh goodness, the most amazing, deep brown eyes. Tall for a Greek, with the arms of a weightlifter, a broad chest, flat stomach and narrow hips, it's difficult not to stare.

'According to the mayor, the house hasn't seen another human cross the threshold for seventy years,' I say. 'So how do you know about the hole in the roof?'

'You can see it if you look down from the cliff path'

'Right. I'm just going to call my uncle. He owns the property.'

I speed dial Uncle. He picks up on the third ring.

'It's me, Olivia,' I say. 'How are you? Where are you? Ah, at home . . . social services looking after you? That's good to hear. I'm here at your house. I'm with the mayor.' I look into the mayor's face. 'I'm talking to my uncle, Yeorgos Konstantinidis,' I say.

The mayor's eyes widen and he blinks rapidly. 'Yeorgos Konstantinidis is alive?' He stares, disbelievingly.

CHAPTER 12
SOFIA

Castellorizo, Greece, 1941

Sofía took the newborn from Mustafa, then crossed herself and the baby as she entered the house. She screwed her sensitive nose at the cloying odour of childbirth, laid the infant next to her sister and then hurried to fling open the windows. Gathering the rubber sheet and soiled bedding discarded next to the bed, she dropped them into the dolly-tub outside. Back in the room, she took a natural sponge from a pail of cold water and wiped her sister's face.

'How do you feel, María?' You must be exhausted by *bravo* for giving us another boy!'

'I'm weary, Sofía. But he's beautiful, isn't he?' She opened one eye and a hint of mischief passed between the sisters before she closed it again, leaving nothing but a fading smile.

'Then sleep,' Sofía said. 'I'll see to the children.' She lifted the newborn from her sister's breast and held it against her own chest. 'Do we have a name?' she asked, laying the infant in the baby hammock that hung from the canopy above María.

'He's Christos,' María murmured.

'Christos! I'm surprised Mustafa allowed that.'

'He doesn't know.' Her smile widened. 'He thinks the baby's name's Emre, after the great Turkish poet. The Papas is coming to bless the little one at six o'clock. If you can make sure Mustafa's occupied elsewhere for an hour, I'd appreciate it.'

''Course I will. Don't worry about a thing. Four boys in as many years: Christos, Panayiotis, Fevzi and Zafiro, well done you!'

Still smiling about the conspiracy, Sofía stepped outside and raked the tiny leathery leaves from a stalk of myrtle. She crushed the greenery in her palms then returned to scatter the leaves over the bed. 'There, that should help you sleep,' she whispered as the sweet liquorice scent drifted over her fatigued sister.

Outside, she challenged Mustafa. 'What food do you plan to give the children?' Her heart thudded, yet she felt indignant, knowing he would not have thought about anyone's sustenance.

He shrugged. 'I've just arrived back, how can I know? Mamá told me she's made fish stew in the pot and there's bread and oil.' He grinned, clearly pleased with himself. 'Aren't you going to congratulate me? You have another fine nephew and I'm a very happy father.'

'No, I am not going to congratulate you! The doctor's right, my sister's half dead from childbearing and my mother and I give up our lives to take care of you and yours. You do nothing to help!'

'The cockerel doesn't care for the chicks, Sofía. I earn plenty of money for this family, I work for six months without one day off. You only see me relax for a few days, but this is not how I spend my time away from here. There are pirates out there—' he nodded towards the sea, 'and storms that could sink my ship and drown my men. Also, I miss my beautiful and loving wife every day. I do my best in the things at which I am expert and I leave the rest to you. You know what a family needs to eat and drink and what clothes need buying. All I can do is hand over money. You don't see me wasting it in the bars or gambling houses, do you? What more you expect me to do, little one?'

Her shoulders dropped and the tension left her voice. 'Do you think *we* ever get a day off, Mustafa? It would be amazing if you could help in the upkeep of your family. Can't you at least organise their food for a few days.'

Mustafa's green eyes flashed as he delved into his baggy breeches and pulled out a fat roll of Italian lira. He shoved it into her hand, keeping hold of her wrist. For a moment, she sensed the great strength of him and fear gripped her stomach.

'Here, Sofía, you do it.' He looked her up and down. 'You look tired, get something nice for yourself, while you're about it. You're growing into a beauty. Make yourself look pretty.'

Angry that he demonstrated his power over her, she protested. 'Mustafa! Let go of me, or I'll tell María!' she hissed.

'It's time to betroth you,' he said in a kindly way. 'I was only a year or two older than you when I first met your sister.'

Feeling bullied, she snarled, 'I'm not getting married!' Her heart thudded. It wasn't her norm to answer people back. 'I'm not ending up like my sister with too many babies. It's horrible, you treat her like a slave!'

Mustafa laughed. 'Of course I do, she's my wife,' he joked, glancing around the forecourt crowded with his children. 'Ayeleen!' he called. 'Give your aunty a hand while your mother rests. I'm going to eat and sleep on the ship while I'm here, this time.'

Ayeleen sometimes worked in the perfumery behind the house while her two younger sisters, Rosa and Popi, took care of the toddlers. With only a few years between Sofía and her niece, they were the best of friends.

Ayeleen shifted the weight of the twelve-month-old toddler on her back and looked up from the sheep she was milking. 'Yes, Father.'

The late-afternoon sun caught her beautiful face; her full lips and large, heavily lashed eyes were so like her father's. There wasn't a young man on earth that wouldn't want Ayeleen for his wife in a few years. She was beautiful, hard-working and possessed the wide, child-bearing hips that promised a fertile womb. Mustafa was protective of every youth that laid eyes on his girls. He loved and guarded his children and wouldn't allow any boy near his precious daughters.

*　*　*

Reluctant to go the long way around to enter the distillery from the outside, Sofía ducked behind the half-woven carpet that hung from the beam-loom at the back of the room, then passed through the hidden door. In the hot, damp workshop, she checked the latest batch of oils, extracting by steam distillation. Three copper stills filled the centre of the workshop. A mattress lay at one end to accommodate those who had to work through the night when Mustafa telegrammed with too many orders. A mound of myrtle leaves, gathered fresh to distil that day, filled the square pit in the floor, another bank was heaped against the wall. Myrtle oil had so many uses it was their best and most profitable product.

At this time of austerity, the Konstantinidis family often placed a poster in the port informing the locals they would buy myrtle on a particular day. Local women went over to Turkey in their husbands' small boats and gathered sacks of leaves from the wild shrubs. Babá bought this vegetation from them for a few welcome Italian lira.

The air swirled around Sofía, lulling her with its drowsy intoxicating aroma. Her eyelids drooped as she slipped the block and tackle hooks under the heavy copper top of the still and hauled. Perfumed steam dampened the air and her skin. Once she had lifted the kettle lid, she wound the rope around a cleat on the wall. She wheeled the wooden barrow to the holding tank of myrtle leaves, singing a sweet refrain as she shovelled the spear-shaped, leathery leaves into the barrow. Lost in thoughts of the new baby, she jumped in fright when the myrtle mound exploded and a soldier leapt up from the pile, throwing leaves into the air like a volcano.

He lunged towards her, yelling foreign words she couldn't grasp.

Instantly terrified, she slammed the shovel down on his head with all her strength. Blood gush from his scalp, his startled eyes widened, then rolled back in his head as his knees buckled.

Sofia screamed, her heart thudding. 'Holy Virgin, I've killed him!' She threw the shovel down as sweat beaded on her face. An irreversible situation that would condemn her to hell in the hereafter. 'God forgive me! What shall I do?' Clasping a hand over her mouth, she backed away. He lay deathly still on the pile of leaves. His terrible wound stopped spurting almost as quickly as it had started. Crimson blood covered the side of his face and one shoulder of his uniform.

In her shock, she had thrown herself against the distillery's stone wall. She ventured forward. The man, she now realised by his uniform, was British. They would shoot her! What should she do with the body of a dead soldier? She glanced at the steaming still and trembled so much her legs almost folded.

'Dear God, what shall I do? My sister's just had another baby and her husband may leave – never to return – if he knows he's married into the family of a murderer. A murderer! Me! My mother will die of shame. Besides all this, my father and uncle might do something stupid, or irreversible, like bury the body, or drop it out at sea, I know them that well. Please, Dear God, tell me what to do.'

Her prayer was answered immediately. She must tell her hero, the teacher. Anastasia would answer all her questions. Sofía's panic returned and before she had even thought the idea through, she found herself racing out of the rear door and down the back streets. Within minutes, she was running around the sandy bay of Mandraki.

* * *

The teacher lived in a neat cottage near the shore. Sofía pounded on the blue door, then fell, sobbing and breathless.

'What on earth is the matter?' the teacher asked lifting her to her feet. 'Sofía, isn't it?'

'Miss! Oh, miss! I've killed a soldier in the distillery!' She threw her arms around the teacher and collapsed in tears. 'What shall I do . . . oh, what shall I do? They'll shoot me!'

'Let's calm down. Take a sip of my coffee.' She stirred more sugar into it. 'They won't shoot you, you're too young, so stop fretting about that. You're over-excited, perhaps in shock.' She put the little coffee cup into Sofía's hands, but they were shaking so much she spilled half of it. 'Now, sit down, take a deep breath and tell me what happened.'

Sofía took a sip of the bittersweet drink. It was the first time she had drunk coffee. 'I was about to shovel myrtle leaves into the barrow. This soldier just leapt up out of the pit. I didn't mean to do it, honestly, but he gave me such a fright. I was holding of the spade, so I just whacked him. He went down, miss, blood gushing from his head. I'm sure he's dead. Completely dead!

Oh, what will I do? María's just had the baby and no one's in any state to deal with such a catastrophe.'

'There's only one thing we can do, Sofía. Come on, let's go and take a look.'

'I'm truly sorry. I didn't mean it! Will they put me in prison?'

'One thing at a time. Let's see the soldier first. Perhaps he's just unconscious, who knows?'

They hurried around the bay, through the back streets again and in through the back door of the distillery.

'What?' Sofía stared at the leaves.

Anastasia also stared around. 'Where's the soldier, Sofía?' she said with a tinge of irritation.

'He was there, right there on the myrtle leaves.' She pointed at the heap, unable to see any sign of blood. 'He was, honestly. Perhaps he slid back under the pile.' Her heart was still thumping with terror and she stepped back with the thought that the whole incident might happen over again. 'He must still be under there.'

Anastasia dragged her eyes away from the leaves and stared at Sofía for a moment. 'You are quite sure you didn't imagine the whole thing?'

'I'm quite sure.' Sofía picked up the shovel. 'Look at all the blood on the end. Oh, miss, I've killed him, haven't I? His dead body must have slipped back under the leaves!'

'Stay calm. Can we lock the door from the outside?' Sofía nodded. 'Where does the other door lead to?'

'It goes into the house, but we keep it locked to stop the little ones coming in here. It's too dangerous when the stills are running. Usually, we only use that door when it's raining.' She went over, turned the key and then slipped it into her pocket.

'Then I think we must go and tell your father what's happened. We don't know what we're dealing with and the soldier will probably have a gun.'

*　*　*

They backed out of the distillery, neither of them taking their eyes off the mound of leaves. Once outside, they locked the door and hurried around the building straight into the house where Mamá and María were sitting on the bed, feeding the babies. Rosa was holding onto the windowsill, practising her ballet moves. Babá and Uncle were stacking wood next to the fire. At first glance of the teacher, both men stood tall and sucked in their bellies. Sofía was relieved to see that Mustafa had left for his ship.

'Miss Anastasia, welcome, please take a seat.' Babá spoke Italian, as was the law. He pulled out his chair and dusted the cushion, his eyes flicking nervously to his wife, then his brother.

The teacher went over to Rosa who was still practising her ballet, holding onto the windowsill. 'Very good, you're coming on nicely, Rosa.' She used one finger to lift her chin, then eased her shoulders back and gently turned her extended arm into the correct position. 'Good,' she said to the child. 'Keep practising.' Anastasia faced the men and spoke in Greek. 'Forgive me, but which one of you is Sofía's father?' She sat and folded her delicate white hands in her lap. 'I don't recall either of you coming to the school to see her fine work or discuss her future.'

The men blustered. Mamá smiled broadly. 'That's because he's never shown interest in his daughter's future, Miss Anastasia,' she said. 'Although I believe Sofía has the capacity to embrace a fine career.'

Sofía cringed and felt her cheeks burn as her mother tried to impress the teacher by using fancy words.

Anastasia tilted her head to one side and smiled understandingly. 'No doubt, Mrs Konstantinidis, but that's not why I'm here. Sofía's father?'

Mamá returned to straight talk. 'The fat one.'

The teacher turned to Babá. 'Allow me to come straight to the point. Your daughter believes she has killed a British soldier. Do you know anything about it, Mr Konstantinidis?'

CHAPTER 13
OLIVIA

Castellorizo, Greece, present day

From the doorway of the old building, I peer into the living room and try to imagine life as it was for my ancestors. Unease grows in the pit of my belly and I feel exposed and vulnerable in this lonely spot on the outside of town with only the mayor and the electrician for company.

'Yes,' I say to the mayor. 'My great-uncle, Yeorgos Konstantinidis, is very much alive. Would you like to speak to him?'

I call George's number then thrust my phone at the mayor. A rapid conversation, with much hand waving by the mayor and raised voices, sounds to me like an enormous argument. Finally, the mayor returns the phone.

'*Bravo!* Yeorgo . . . George, he was my big friend, we were like brothers. Ah, Yeorgo, ah, man.' The mayor shakes his head. 'It was like he came from my mother's own womb!' he cries, which I think is a little overdramatic.

I put the phone back to my ear and listen. 'Olivia, are you there?'

'Yes.'

'Don't trust this man. Skyfalos was like his father: the biggest liar in Greece and a *mafioza* cheat. He would sell his own mother. He was the biggest snake in the country and a coward too. A nasty piece of work. Married a foreigner because no Greek family would let him near their own daughter. I know this from my friend Constantino. Also, he hates foreigners, especially those who are more intelligent than him, which must be everyone that arrives on the island. This makes him dangerous.'

'Thank you, Uncle. Tell me, do you think the floor of the house is solid and safe for me to walk on, or is there a cellar? There is an electrician by the name of Gregoris here, who says it's not safe.'

'Ask Gregoris his grandfather's name.' I do, then reply to my uncle whose response is joyful. 'Bravo, Olivia. He says his grandfather's name is Demetriou. My dear girl, he was one of my best friends! He had my boat, the one in my paintings. Ask him how his grandfather is.'

'Why don't *you* ask him?' I pass the phone to Gregoris who peers right into my eyes.

After a clearly joyful exchange in Greek, he hands it back to me and says, 'My grandfather will be happy to know his good friend, Yeorgo, is still alive and plans to return.' He gazes into my eyes again, sending a shiver down my spine.

Careful, Olivia! You're on the rebound, remember!

I return my attention to the phone. 'There's a cellar, Olivia. The electrician believes the floor is unsafe. Don't risk it,' my uncle says.

'What about the distillery?'

'Ah, that floor's solid. It had to be because of the weight of the copper kettles. There were three. I hope they're *still* in there, pardon the pun. You can go in through the outside door at the back if it's clear. Good luck! Call me tomorrow.' I can hear the tiredness in his voice.

'Get some rest, Uncle. If you think of anything important, just write it down and keep it by the side of the phone. Bye now.'

After the call ends, the mayor bids me goodbye with the excuse of work waiting and hurries back towards the port.

Gregoris says, 'Really, this place is too dangerous. My cousin's a builder, he'll fit some supports under the floor, but until then, best stay outside.'

'I'm not going any further. I just want to see what's here. I'm so excited.' The floor groans in protest and I feel it tremble. Horrified, I leap back in fright, straight into his arms.

He laughs. 'No need to throw yourself at me, Miss Olivia!'

'No, the floor . . . it gave me a fright,' I stammer. 'I thought I was going to crash through it. I'm longing to explore inside.'

He laughs again as if he understands my excitement. 'Let me help.' He unclips a torch from his toolbelt and passes it to me. His eyes narrow ever so slightly as our hands touch. I can't explain why I feel slightly triumphant.

The torchlight dances around the room. I'm impressed by an exposed stone fireplace to my left. It takes up a third of the wall. Pots and pans hang against crumbling stucco either side of the chimney. A black cauldron stands in the fireplace over an empty grate. I remind myself that María had sixteen children, so cooking must have taken up the greatest part of her day. To my right, the width of the room is filled by a sleeping platform and a staircase. Momentarily forgetting the fragility of the floor, I step towards it excitedly.

'No!' Gregoris shouts.

The whole bed seems to move. 'Crap! Someone's in there!' I leap back.

'No, it's mice. The place is infested,' Gregoris says as I bump into him again.

The vermin scatter like one vast grey scurrying blanket that seems to slip off the bed. I shrink with horror and step out of the doorway. A shelf has collapsed at the back of the bed, dropping piles of folded linen into a dust-covered heap, which I mistook for a sleeping person. Leaning forward, I stare around, convinced something is about to leap on me from the beams. The corners of the room are concealed by decades of undisturbed cobwebs that waft to and fro with the draught from the open door. It's as if the house itself is alive . . . breathing. The steps to the sleeping platform have crumbled. A huge centipede, at least ten centimetres long, scurries across the floor. Every kind of infestation has set up home and now my skin crawls with revulsion.

A confusion of planks and beams at the back of the room tells me something has collapsed, but it doesn't appear to be the upper floor. Also, there is a door hanging off its hinges. Where will it lead . . .?

* * *

Turning back into the dazzling sunlight, I say, 'Can we have a look at the distillery, Gregoris?'

'Yes, Miss Olivia,' he replies, glancing at his watch.

'Please, must call me Olivia.'

'Then you call me Greg, OK.'

I nod. 'Look, don't let me keep you, but, if you have time later, I'd like to talk about connecting the house to the mains, or better still, to solar. You'll find me at the harbour in the evenings, at Eleni's Place.'

'Sure, sorry, but I do have to go soon.' He smiles, his eyes crinkling and perhaps a question on his lips. 'Keep the torch for now. Is there anything else I can help you with?'

'You're very kind, thank you. I'd just like to see if it's possible to get into the distillery from the back.'

He nods and I follow him around the outside of the building, but we find the perfumery inaccessible, unless we break a window that is. Part of the cliff behind the back wall has slipped and a mound of scree comes halfway up the back wall. It's a job for a mechanical digger. I place my hand against an exposed quoin. The stone is warm, full of the day's sun, yet around the corner, the wall is cold and dark as a tombstone. A shiver runs through me. I imagine my superstitious mother, shoulders up, rubbing her arms as she says: *Brrr, someone just walked over my grave.*

'It's such a special place,' I say to Greg. 'My Uncle George was born inside this house.'

'Yeorgos Konstantinidis, yes, I know. He left his fishing boat with my grandfather,' Greg says. 'Is he coming back?'

'I hope so, but he's poorly right now.'

'Poorly, you mean he is poor, he has no money? What happened? They say he was very rich when he left here . . . ten times more money than anyone else on the island.'

I laugh, but Greg's words strike me as odd, *very rich when he left the island* – why was that? 'No, it's his health, his heart,' I reply. 'But he'll soon be able to fly.'

We close up the building and walk back down to the port.

'Thank you for your help today. I suspect you saved me from a nasty accident. If that floor had collapsed, God knows . . .'

'No problem. Glad to help.' He gives me another disarming smile, then leaves for the customs building where he tells me he is installing sockets.

*　　*　　*

I stroll around the harbour until I reach Eleni's.

'Hey, Livia!' I spin around. Only Andrew calls me Livia and suddenly I realise I haven't thought about him for two whole days. I stare about, searching for the guy I once adored, but of course he isn't here.

'How's it going, mate?' the voice continues. Recognising the Australian, I'm filled with relief, regret – and an irritating amount of disappointment.

'Hi, sorry, you startled me.'

'No drama, I have that effect on women,' he says through a wide grin. I must look puzzled because his next words get me out of a predicament. 'Rob, remember?'

'Ah, yes. Sorry again. A lot's happened since we last met.'

'All good, I hope?'

I nod. 'Pretty much. I didn't see you on the ferry, when did you get here?'

'Just arrived this arvo. Flew in from Rhodes. Can I get you that beer now?'

I really want to sit alone and think for a while. 'Can we share one? A quick half before siesta will be lovely.'

'You siesta? I didn't think people did any more. My sleep map's so disorientated I just go with the flow. I'm in Greece for two months, so I kind-a hope to see a few other islands.' We sit at the first table we come to, at the water's edge and order a large Amstel and two glasses. 'It's pretty here, don't you think?' Rob continued.

'It's amazing,' I agree. 'Have you seen the turtles yet?'

'Turtles? No way, man! That's so cool – no crocs, I hope.'

I laugh. 'Definitely no crocs. You're a bit off the beaten track for a tourist, aren't you?'

'True, but my grandparents are from this island and they made me promise to visit. Still, it seems half of Sydney have their roots here. They say most of the locals left after the last war and settled in Oz.'

'My grandparents, too, but they settled in England, on the south coast. Have you heard of Brighton?'

He shakes his head, then takes a great sip of beer while I wonder if we'll end up becoming more than friends. Probably not, definitely not, but it's a sort-of-nice idea. The truth is, I still feel as though my heart belongs to Andrew . . . damn, that's the second time I've thought about him in five minutes! What's going on? Then clarity turns its spotlight on and I realise my problem . . . I still feel I *belong* to Andrew and Andrew always felt he *owned* me.

'Ace!' Rob says, lowering his glass. 'I needed that. Anywhere you'd recommend for lunch?' He looks up, straight into my eyes, catching me off guard and for some reason, makes my heart jump.

'No, I've not tried anywhere yet. Why not check Tripadvisor?'

I learn that Rob is an architect and part-time professional footballer. He likes to talk, especially about Aussie Rules.

In the end I can hardly suppress a yawn. 'Sorry, Rob, I had such an early start and a hectic morning, I need to sleep.'

'Sure, no worries. Shall I walk you to your room?'

I want him to go away. 'Thanks, but no need. I'm right here by the church.'

* * *

I resurface two hours later. What bliss! After opening the windows onto the balcony I stretch out on the bed to think. This is the greatest opportunity of my life. I have to find the lawyer and organise my property deeds. I shower, dress in white linen capri pants, a stylish black slash-necked top and low-heeled sandals. My scarlet nail polish is good to go, so I simply twist my dark, shoulder-length hair up and take a little extra care over my make-up.

After walking around the harbour, I look in at the gift shop and buy a fridge magnet. Eventually, I find myself back at the same café table. The sun is low in the sky and bathes everything in warm orange light. A warbler – perhaps a nightingale – sings its heart out somewhere nearby, notes undulating in a magical melody. Waiters light candles on their waterside tables and peer around, searching for prospective diners. Taverna music, turned down low, adds to the ambience of this most idyllic setting. I decide it is time to try speaking Greek to the woman who approaches my table.

'*Kalispéra*,' I say boldly.

Her face lights with a beaming smile. She echoes my greeting and follows it with a rattle of Greek that leaves me bewildered. 'Sorry,' I say. 'I've only learned to say *good evening*.'

'Ah, no problem! I help you. What you want to drink? You want to eat? I bring menu, yes? I am Eleni. You tell me what you want.'

'I need a solicitor, I think.'

CHAPTER 14
SOFIA

Castellorizo, Greece 1941

SOFÍA'S PALE FACE CRUMPLED AS she ran to her mother. Mamá put the baby down and embraced her daughter. 'Don't cry. It will be all right, Sofía. We'll stand by you, whatever happens,' she said.

Babá stared at the teacher, then at Sofía. He shook his head. 'I know nothing about any soldier.'

'Well, the body seems to have disappeared. I'm here to support your daughter as she asked me for help. It appears that as the soldier leapt out of the myrtle leaves, she instinctively hit him over the head with the shovel. Sofía believes she split his skull open, thereby killing him. However, the body has disappeared. Did any of you know there were British soldiers on the island?'

They all shook their heads.

'Then – just in case the young soldier is part of a liberating force – I suggest we don't mention this to anyone. I can only presume the soldier's recovered, or has been taken care of by his own forces. We must agree to say nothing and carry on as normal because some, including the mayor, are very close with the Italians and, therefore, our enemies.'

Everyone nodded.

'Good. The two men should check the soldier hasn't slipped to the bottom of the myrtle leaves.' They nodded but didn't move. 'I mean *now*, before I leave and please let me know if there are any further developments. Also, I suggest you continue to keep both distillery doors locked.' She passed Babá the outside door key.

The men returned and, to the relief of the women, said there was no sign of the soldier.

Sofía pulled out of her mother's embrace. 'Miss Anastasia, thank you. How can we repay your kindness?'

All eyes were on the teacher. 'There is something you can do, Sofía, if your parents allow it. Come and help me in the school on Monday mornings.' She went over to Rosa and said, 'Keep your back straight, child. Very good, now, from the beginning . . .'

Sofía found her voice. 'Oh, may I help in the school, Mamá, Babá, please?'

Her mother didn't waste a heartbeat. 'Of course you can, child. It's what you've always wanted to do.'

*　*　*

Later, Sofía, Mamá and María gave the children their last drink of the day – warm milk – then got them ready for bed. Luckily, Sofía's little brother, George, behaved himself for once, drinking his milk and going up the stairs without his usual commotion.

Sofía lay in bed that night and worried her way through all that had happened. Had she killed the soldier or had someone rescued him? Would she learn to teach, as she had always wanted? Who would make the precious oil, look after the little ones, forage for food or mend the clothes if she didn't?

She had become obsessed with writing the history of Castellorizo in Greek, which everyone thought a great joke. After all, who would be interested and who would be able to read the forbidden language anyway? Sofía only cared what the teacher would think. She planned to take her history book into the school on Monday.

* * *

At sunrise on the morning after the soldier incident, there was a great commotion as British commandos appeared, hammering on doors, demanding that people stay indoors. Sofía feared they were looking for her soldier. Later that day, as February's early dusk descended and the island fell under darkness, Uncle Kuríllos came crashing into the house. The entire family had remained inside all day for fear of over-enthusiastic soldiers and their rifles.

Mikró Yiayá and Megáli Yiayá sat elbow-to-elbow on Sofía's dowry chest, crocheting Ayeleen's dowry linen. The older girls helped to bed María's younger children while Mamá prepared food for the adults.

Uncle Kuríllos appeared so excited, Sofía expected his bad eye to fly open and reveal he'd grown a new one. He sat close to Babá in the big hearth. Driftwood and pinecones smoked and spat under a simmering cauldron of marrowbone and wild carrot stew with pitta breads made from cooked cactus pads, for the adults' meal.

'Have you heard the news?' Uncle asked dramatically.

Mamá frowned at the older girls, telling them to keep quiet. They all turned their heads so that one ear tilted towards the men, the way that a wild lily follows the sun. They continued to wash the younger children's hands, faces and then got them into their nightgowns.

Babá jerked his chin upward in a *go on* gesture.

Uncle Kuríllos glanced melodramatically over each shoulder then hunched forward, hinting of conspiracy, before speaking to his brother. 'The British commandos are trying to take Castellorizo from the Italians!'

Babá rolled his eyes. 'We guessed that, sport. It started last night. Where've you been? What's happening now, have you heard the latest?' He poured his brother a tot of *tsipouro*.

'Simonos was fishing out near Punta Nifti, at sunset, yesterday,' Kuríllos said, unbuttoning his leather waistcoat. 'He was packing up because it gets so dark out on that point, but he got his hooks caught in the rocks. While he was down in the crevices trying to rescue his fishing gear, he heard noises – British voices – so he hid and watched.' Kuríllos banged the bottom of his glass on the wooden arm of the chair and cried, 'Yammas!' then took a sip of the fiery liquid and a drag on his cheroot.

'*Ela, maláka*, get on with it!' Babá said impatiently.

'All right, keep calm. Simonos realised there were several whaleboats just offshore, approaching the island. Thinking it was best not to move until they'd gone, he hunkered down in the gully. One boatful of commandos, fifty soldiers he guessed, eventually made land and disembarked. More arrived, but then it became completely dark. He couldn't see the warship; it was either too far out, or had pulled away already. There were other whaleboats, but he doesn't know where they went because there was no moon just yet.' He held his glass out and Babá filled it again. 'It seems the British could have been quieter. Those fools from the Italian garrison on the old fort heard them and sent the young sailors, Bosco and Trojan, to investigate.' Kuríllos snorted. 'A big mistake. The Italian boys hurried across Mandraki Bay, past the cemetery and then ran straight into the path of commandos who were marching towards the port.' He took another sip of his drink.

111

The girls had tucked the little ones into the big bed and now moved closer to sit on the rug, around Babá and Uncle Kuríllos's feet.

'Will you stay and eat with us?' Mamá asked while stirring the soup.

Uncle Kuríllos nodded, then resumed the story. 'So, a gunfight kicked off and Trojan fell immediately, ending his life as target practice for the British. Bosco caught a bullet in his foot but still managed to escape to the cottages on the far side of Mandraki, losing his gun on the way. You know where the teacher lives?'

Kuríllos bobbed his eyebrows and Babá nodded, leaning his elbows on his knees and prayer-locking his fingers. 'Who doesn't?'

Mamá sat straighter and stared at Babá suspiciously. María, whose numerous children were almost all asleep now, sat on the edge of the bed. She lifted her newborn off the breast and handed him to Sofía to wind.

'Go on then,' Babá said impatiently, filling his brother's glass again. 'What happened next?'

Kuríllos nodded. 'Anastasia heard the sailor crying for help and ran out of the house, just as the commandos came into view.'

Sofía's hand flew across her mouth. 'No! They didn't harm the teacher?'

Kuríllos stuck his chin out and raised his eyebrows. 'Tut! Wait.' His older nieces and nephews gazed at their uncle with a mixture of dread and wonderment. 'The British surrounded the wounded Italian boy and Anastasia who was in her nightdress.' He threw Babá a smile. 'One of the British commandos pulled his gun and aimed at the Italian's temple, ready to finish him.

112

Coup de grâce, they call it. The poor boy pissed his pants. That's when the teacher stepped between them.'

Mamá was almost in tears. 'Please, don't tell me they shot Anastasia. I promise I'll never say anything bad about her ever again. It's not her fault she's beautiful, or that her mother was Italian, or that weak men can't take their eyes off her behind. It's not as if she encourages their attention.' She glared accusingly at Babá who seemed fascinated by the cauldron of soup.

Uncle Kuríllos shook his head. 'Anastasia saved him from certain execution at that moment. She held her hands out like El Greco's *Christ Crucified* and challenged the British soldiers. *Shoot me instead, he's wounded!'*

'What a brave woman!' María half whispered. Sofía nodded emphatically.

Kuríllos relit his cheroot, exhaled a cloud of smoke towards the beamed ceiling, then continued. 'Anastasia told the British commandos, *I'm saving you from certain death, do you understand? If you execute this wounded, unarmed sailor you'll be guilty of a war crime. If you kill me, a defenceless, non-aggressive, female civilian, you'll be guilty of murder. Both carry the death penalty.*

'The British commandos were shocked – they had never come across such a courageous woman before. They stood, open-mouthed, while the teacher continued. *May I remind you; we are on the same side and you're supposed to be defending the people of Castellorizo. It's your choice.* She stood there, facing the commando's pistol, proud and brave as Joan of Arc! Can you believe it?'

Kuríllos glanced around his enraptured audience, sipped his *tsipouro*, then carried on. 'The British commando was shocked by the Greek woman's gesture. He pulled back from the execution and took the young Italian prisoner instead.'

'*Bravo! Bravo!*' the girls cried, with Sofía adding, 'Mamá, *I'm* going to be a teacher and *nobody*'s going to stop me!'

'That's not all,' Kuríllos said. 'Because it was not known precisely where the Italians were, nor did they know the coastline around Punta Nifti, there was another catastrophe.'

'What, not more *malakías*?' Babá swore.

'Shush! Remember the children!' Mamá cried, objecting to Babá's bad language.

Kuríllos said, 'Apparently, there were ten whalers, like giant rowboats, to transport the attacking British from the warship to the island. But in the thickest darkness, the commandos rowed so close together they all bumped into each other making a terrific racket. So, they spread out, scattered and lost each other in the dark. The majority passed the landing point at Punta Nifti and rowed to the other side of the harbour mouth. The leading rowboat proceeded, while the others thought they were following in blind faith, but perhaps they were following each other in a big circle. The lead boats gradually recognised dark silhouettes of buildings on both sides of the port. One of the seamen whispered, *Where the hell are we? They said Punta Nifti is completely uninhabited!* Then, they heard Italian voices above and all looked up, remembering the old castle on the map. At this point, they discovered the lead boat was rowing at a slower pace and several of the following boats bumped into it. After making so much noise and being unsure of where they were, the lead boat commanded that they row, full speed, back to their cruiser, HMS *Decoy*.' Kuríllos lit a fresh cheroot while his audience digested this information.

Sofía scribbled like crazy into her history book, then stuck her finger in the air. 'Excuse me, Uncle, where did you get all this information?'

'I have my ways, Sofía. Namely, a packet of cigarettes to Simonos and another packet along with several glasses of *tsipouro* to my new friend, a soldier who shall remain nameless.'

'Mamá, let's have more *tsipouro*,' Babá said.

One of the younger children whimpered in their sleep. Instantly, everyone remembered the kerfuffle of slobbering, snot-nosed, teething toddlers. They all turned to stare silently at the big bed, wishing the babies a peaceful night.

'Give me the limbs of an octopus,' Mamá said quietly while she put a baby over her shoulder and filled the men's glasses.

Kuríllos continued, 'Well, when the last boat turned back, it lost sight of the others. As the moon came up, the skipper realised they were approaching the original destination of Punta Nifti. Then, coming ashore on the point, they came across the two Italians and you know the rest.'

Babá frowned at Mamá. 'Let's have some food, all this is making me hungry.' He returned his attention to Kuríllos. 'Then what? We know nothing.'

'After a fierce defence, the Italians surrendered. The British commandos seized the Italians' weapons, ammunition and gasoline. They hoisted the British flag above the government building by the port. When the Italian postal boat arrived from Rhodes, the British captured it and confiscated all the mail too.'

Babá stared at his brother. 'I can't believe you got all this information out of them.'

'Not me, Simonos is acting as a translator, as I said. They told him he'd be shot if he passed on any information. Anyway, the British have returned and occupied the port, the customs building, the radio station and the town hall. This morning, I went to the town hall and declared myself a local merchant. I asked if there was anything they needed.'

'You! A merchant? You're a black-market racketeer!' Babá roared.

'Perhaps, but they don't know that and the mayor had more sense than to say anything. Anyway, they told me they've got no food until a ship arrives from Cyprus in three days' time.'

He turned and watched Rosa as she practised her ballet exercises in the centre of the room. Everyone followed his eyes, knowing without question that the girl would be a great dancer one day. They imagined themselves applauding from the front row of a grand theatre in Paris, London, or even New York. They would throw red carnations onto the stage and call, 'Bravo! Bravo, Rosa!' proud of their sister. No one had ever been in a theatre or seen a ballet, but that did nothing to dampen their enthusiasm.

'Great and us starving as it is,' Babá said breaking everyone's dreams. 'What fools, to bring a boat full of soldiers and not enough food for every eventuality!'

'Trust me, I have a plan. I'm rowing over to Kaş tonight, to get two sheep from the doctor's flock. The army will pay double, which means we'll get one sheep for free and I'll sell half of the free one to the mayor at double price, so we'll end up with half a free sheep for ourselves and the money for half a sheep on the black market, which is the same price as a full sheep.'

Rosa did a pirouette, then made a low and graceful bow. Everyone applauded.

Babá called, 'Bravo, Princess!' then frowned, staring at the floor as he tried to work out the logistics of his brother's plan. 'They should have brought more food in the first place, idiots!'

Sofía sat on the low stool at one end of the loom and knotted a row of carpet tufts. She had become the island's expert and was sometimes paid to help finish a carpet if a wedding was brought forward. She had designed the pattern of her own carpet, where many small pictures told of the most important things in the life of her family. In the centre was the tree of life and the earthquake that marked the day she was born. A blue and white amulet, the lucky eye, would stare out of the four corners to ward off evil spirits. The rest of the carpet would show the major events in their lives as they happened.

Kuríllos shrugged. 'The British had plenty of food when they left Crete, but they came the long way around the island to Castellorizo, sailing almost 200 miles further! Consequently, they ran out of fuel. So, they had to steer as they drifted, which added an extra two days. By the time they landed, their five days of supplies were gone.'

'Oh, for God's sake!' Babá cried. 'And these are the people who are going to save us from the Germans and Italians? Give me strength.'

'It's not such a disaster,' Kuríllos said. 'It turns out that six Italians fell in combat, seven were injured and thirty-five were taken prisoner by the British.'

Babá stared at his brother. 'Have you any ammunition left? We should clean the rifles.'

Mamá's eyes widened. 'Don't think you're keeping loaded guns in this house with all these children!' she yelled, startling the baby who started crying.

CHAPTER 15
OLIVIA

Castellorizo, Greece, present day

AFTER SOME BANTER WITH ELENI, I phone Uncle George. It's such a relief to hear he's feeling stronger. He speaks to Eleni, then to me. 'I don't know Eleni, but her family were the decent sort. Her grandmother was the friend of Sofia's that I wanted you to give the table runner to and her father is another of my very good friends. She'll send you a notary to sort out the title deed. I wish I was with you.'

'So do I, Uncle.' I take a breath, unsure and a little nervous about how he will react to my next statement. 'When I return, I've decided to move in with you for a couple of weeks, to look after you. How do you feel about that, Uncle?' The line goes quiet. 'Uncle?'

'That would be wonderful, dear girl.' There's a heartbreaking silence again and I sense he is struggling with his emotions. 'Thank you,' he says quietly. 'That's the kindest thing.'

'Good. I'll call tomorrow morning, OK?'

'Any time. It's so lovely to hear you.' Suddenly, I realise he's desperately lonely.

Eleni recommends the fresh sardines baked on grapevine leaves and drizzled with fruity olive oil and lemon juice, flavoursome local bread sprinkled with toasted sesame seeds and a Greek salad that trumpets colour and flavour as if they're royalty. She serves the food with a carafe of crisp white wine so cold it takes my breath away, then she lights a small candle on my table.

This is heaven. I pull out my notebook, analyse each mouthful and jot down my first thoughts. Smoky, salty, fruity and so on.

At the edge of the sea, where turtles occasionally stick their heads out of the water, I'm mesmerised by the beauty of my surroundings.

'All is OK?' Eleni asks.

'Perfect, Eleni, thank you. Did you cook this wonderful fish?' I prod a sardine with my fork.

'No, my husband, he catch and cook all the fishes here on the menu. You like, good; I tell him.'

'It's delicious! Can he give me some cookery lessons?' I laugh at my own light-hearted joke, but Eleni takes me seriously and minutes later her husband, Dino, is at my table telling me how to prepare the sardines while I frantically scribble the information into my notebook.

'Thank you,' I say and shake his hand, which seems to please him a lot. His round face beams in its frame of thick, curly dark hair. He returns to the kitchen then reappears with another carafe and glass and, uninvited, sits at my table.

The next five minutes are an inescapable interrogation. Where did I live, who were my parents, did I own my house in England, was I married, how did I earn a living and why was I in Castellorizo? The questions go on.

'So, you're from the Konstantinidis family?' he asks. 'My good friend, Yeorgo . . . George Konstantinidis! I have his boat, *Sofía-María*. He went to school with my father, Demetriou, who looked after his boat for many years after he left, but now he's not so strong, he stays in his bed most of the time. I was in the boat of Yeorgos when I catch your *sardelles*, this morning!'

My spirit soars. This is just what I need.

In the beautiful, ambient light of early evening, I want to share this moment with Uncle George. 'Will you tell my uncle, please? He's not too well, his heart – you know? This will cheer him up so much,' I plead while video calling my uncle.

He answers almost immediately. 'You forgot something?' he says smiling into the camera.

'Uncle, I have somebody here to speak to you. I've just had a wonderful meal of sardines that were caught from your very own boat, *Sofía-María*, by Dino the son of your friend Demetriou!'

I hold the phone up for Dino who shouts so loud at my small screen that he captures the attention of everyone in the vicinity. People gather around the fisherman-chef, boisterously calling greetings and waving at the screen. The moment uplifts me and as I turn to stare over the water, a turtle sticks its majestic head up as if to join in the fun. I know dear Uncle will feel better because of the call. Concerned for my battery, I withdraw the phone and tell my audience I'll be back online with my uncle tomorrow.

'Thank you, dear girl,' he says huskily. 'What a wonderful experience to see my friends again after ... how long has it been, half a century?'

'I promise to call again tomorrow, Uncle. Take care now.'

Eleni clears the table. 'You want to wait a little before the main course? My husband, he make the best moussaka in all of Greece. Is very fresh, he make it today. You will like very much.'

Oops, I'd forgotten the sardines were only a starter – and I've eaten half of the bread basket too. 'Wonderful, Eleni; but if you don't mind, I'll wait a while.'

'No problem.' Eleni peers along the promenade and smiles. I follow her eyes.

A tall, broad-shouldered man approaches, his short dark hair is impeccably groomed. Arrestingly handsome, he has a strong nose, smooth golden skin and a boldly defined jaw. His eyes are on me and it's only when I glance into them, I realise I'm looking at the electrician. Heat rushes into my cheeks. He has shaved off his enormous beard and paid a visit to the barber. Gregoris looks so different without all that hair, but his eyes are the same captivating, warm brown and they soften with a twinkle of mischief. His lips curl slightly, acknowledging my reaction to his changed appearance with undisguised pleasure.

Do I play it cool, or make it honest? I turn back to my food notes, hoping that my throbbing heart and rosy cheeks don't draw unwanted attention. Yes, I am attracted to him . . . really. Like weak knees – really.

'Ah, Gregoris, have you eaten?' Eleni calls.

I try not to look at him again, but the desire to do so is overwhelming and I can't resist glancing over the top of my recipe page. Instantly I withdraw my attention, as if the sight of him scalds me. He looks so much younger and sophisticated without all the wild hair, as if his village roughness had also been cut and styled. I thought him attractive before, but now he is devastatingly so. I run my hand around my neck to try and dissipate the heat of my blushes.

He smiles my way as he kisses Eleni's cheek. 'No, Mamá, I'm too busy now, but I'll be back later.'

Mamá? I'd forgotten Eleni is his mother.

Then I wonder why they're both speaking in English. I can't think of a single sensible thing to say, so I turn to my phone and concentrate on putting it away. In the end, I string a sentence together. 'Hi, Gregoris—'

'The English call me Greg, remember?' His dazzling smile throws me off balance again.

'I don't suppose you can give me an estimate for wiring the house?'

'Yes, of course. You did ask me.'

'Did I?' Heat floods my cheeks again, I'm in bits, he must think I'm stupid. 'Ah, so much going on, I forget where I'm up to.' He peers into my eyes, I go weak at the knees and have to look away.

'I have another job, but I'll be back soon. I'll call over soon, OK?'

I nod once, but as he turns and walks away I follow him with my eyes. Then, I feel the town is watching me.

* * *

As the day draws to an end, I have more questions than answers about the property, but I hope the notary will clarify the situation. The cookery book is another story; I have to make a definite plan or shove it on the back-burner until I've sorted out the house.

Staring across the bay, a kind of magnetism that I can't explain draws my attention over the water. I notice that everyone else, whether tourist or local, appears spellbound by the sunset too. I don't notice Rob until he drags a chair from under my table and plonks himself down. He also gazes across the harbour where lights twinkle from half-empty tavernas and a few tourists stroll along the promenade.

'Hi there, Livia, how's it goin'?'

So much for my quiet evening. 'Hi, Rob, everything's fine, thanks. Had a great day, in fact.'

'Wish I could say the same. Can I offer you a glass of wine?'

There is no escape. 'Very kind, but you must have some of mine because I can't drink all this while I'm working.' I indicate the carafe, then my cookery notes on the table. I speak softly, hoping he'll catch the mood of peace and serenity that seems to touch everyone else and stay silent for a while.

'Everything's gone tits up,' he says brusquely. 'Gran'ma had a house here, so I've come thousands of miles to claim it, but the lawyer's pretending it's a myth. Crooks. I wonder which building . . .' He gazes around the port.

Alarm bells ring! Best not arouse Rob's suspicions that I'm also laying claim to a property or he won't give me a minute's peace.

Eleni comes to the table and I order the moussaka.

'Mind if I join you?' Rob asks. He's already at my table, so what can I do? 'The meal's on me, by the way,' he continues.

'Really, Rob, you don't have to . . .' I sigh. 'I won't be very good company. I'm here to work, you see, so I need a certain amount of time alone.'

'Work?' he exclaims.

'I'm writing a cookery book, so I need silence to concentrate on the food and its flavours and make notes while I'm eating.' I might have decided to take a rest from the cookery book idea, but it's still a good reason to demand a little peace.

'There's a bummer, me messing up your plans, sorry. No worries, I'll sit somewhere else.'

Now I feel awful. Would it hurt to give him a couple of hours of my time? 'It's fine, really. It'll be nice to relax this evening, then start in earnest tomorrow.' Will he get the message?

'If you're sure?' He lifts his arm to get Eleni's attention and then says, 'The same for me, OK? Moussaka and a glass, please.'

I decide to keep him busy with questions, so he doesn't have a chance to interrogate me. 'Now, tell me exactly what happened to spoil your day, Rob.' It can't possibly be the same house . . . can it? That would be really weird. Nevertheless, I might learn something from his experience that will help me in my own quest.

'Every time I ask a question, they do this . . .' He shows his palms to the sky at the same time as lifting and dropping his shoulders. 'And they say, *What I do, sir?* like I'm asking the impossible.'

'And are you?'

'Asking the impossible? No, just enquiring where's the old house of María Konstantinidis.'

Crap! This will not end well. Uncle has informed me that most Greek women keep their family name after marriage; also, property usually transfers through the females, for tax reasons. I hope to know more tomorrow, after speaking to a notary or a lawyer. Why can't this be straightforward? I'm really not good at subterfuge.

'Just be grateful you're writing a cookery book, and not chasing after a property yourself, Livia,' he says loudly as the food arrives.

My creamy moussaka is to die for, packed with flavour and texture, but after Rob's statement, it's hard to concentrate. I glance at my notebook.

'Don't let me stop you,' Rob continues. 'Make notes if you want.' He shovels food into his mouth.

I can't resist jotting down a few first impressions while trying to detect which herbs and spices were used. Cinnamon, oregano and a hint of nutmeg just discernible beneath the smoky taste of charred aubergines. The tender minced lamb lies under a blanket of the lightest, creamiest béchamel sauce I've ever tasted. Heavenly!

Rob continues to bemoan his property situation, then I notice the mayor strolling our way. A spark of panic fires off. 'Excuse me,' I say to Rob, 'ladies' room.' I dash into the taverna. The last thing I want is the mayor talking to me about Sofía's house in front of the Australian.

'Everything OK?' Eleni asks.

'I want to compliment the chef. Did I tell you I write cookery books? Later, I'd like to talk to you both about the special flavours of Castellorizo.'

She beams, clearly thrilled. We chat about food, then I return to the table. 'Sorry, Rob, I was just asking the chef about the moussaka. What did you think of it?'

He shrugged. 'Yeah, OK, I suppose. So, you're here to write your cookery book?'

'Amongst other things, yes. Are you interested in food – cooking, baking?'

'Me, not at all. I make a sarnie, order in, or grab something at the boozer.'

'No wife, partner, girlfriend?'

He blanks, stares into the distance for a moment then takes a breath. 'No, I tried that, even bought a dishwasher so she didn't have to wash up after cooking, but it didn't work out.'

I nearly choke on my wine. 'You're all heart, Rob.' Then I catch his grin. 'You're kidding, right?'

'Of course – what do you take me for?' he says good-humouredly.

'Sorry, I've a lot on my mind.'

'Come on, Livia, lighten up. You're taking a night off, remember?'

He seems such a nice guy – and here was I riddled with guilt, still being devious. Shall I tell him? I fear he might railroad me out of my fair inheritance. I wish I could talk to Uncle. I pull the scrunchie from my hair and shake it out. 'There, how's that?'

His grin widens. 'Great! Now, I can take you clubbing until the sun comes up.' Eleni arrives for our plates. 'Excuse me,' Rob says. 'Is there somewhere we can go dancing . . . a nightclub or something?'

Eleni blinks at him, then me, then pulls her chin in. I roll my eyes upward, hoping she'll understand.

'I believe Mykonos is good, the travel agent will book you a flight if you hurry over there.' She jerks her chin towards the square, then spins around and walks away.

'She doesn't approve of me,' Rob mutters.

'I don't think it's a clubbing type of island,' I say. 'Besides, aren't we a bit long in the tooth for nightclubs?'

He develops a slightly panicked expression. 'Speak for yourself! What are we going to do, trapped here for a week?' His alarmed stare darts about the harbour. 'Mind you, it seems we've stumbled on a great business opportunity. Just imagine . . . Are there any large, vacant buildings, do you know? A warehouse or something like that, with road access?' He's twitching, excited now. 'Just imagine, the most exclusive clubbing paradise . . . *ever*!'

'Ha, I've only seen three cars, an airport bus, and a taxi since I arrived. This isn't Australia, you know.' I can't believe he is so insensitive to the charm of his surroundings. 'Look, there's a bit of a beach in the next bay and there's the Lighthouse Café Bar next to the mosque, across the harbour. What more do you want? This is not – and never will be – a nightclub island.'

Before he can answer, a voice comes from behind me. 'Ah, madam! Did you find the lawyer? You must make the property papers as soon as possible. Here, I bring you the notary.'

I look over my shoulder and see the mayor again. Damn! Rob's jaw drops. The mayor continues around the harbour, but the notary, a woman of fortyish, pulls a chair out and, uninvited, sits next to me then notices my company.

Turning to Rob, she says, 'Oh, hello again, I didn't realise you were together in this.'

We both shake our heads and say, 'We're not!'

She frowns and looks from me to Rob and back again. 'I see. I'm a little confused as Mr Robert came to see me about a property earlier today. Eleni is a very good friend of my family.' She nods towards the kitchen. 'In fact, she is my godmother, so when she asked if I can help you, Miss Olivia, I agreed.'

'Speak of the devil,' Rob says as Eleni scurries towards us.

'Thank you, but I don't want to interrupt your evening,' I murmur, very aware of Rob hanging on to my every word. 'Perhaps it's better if I come to your office in the morning.'

She smiles. 'This is also a good plan. I will need your passport, and if you can make a list of these things for me, it will save time. Your tax number, father's name, mother's name, mother's maiden name, any siblings of your father, your mother, or you. Also, all those things relating to your grandparents on both sides. From the generation before you, I want their tax numbers, wedding certificates, dowry contracts, death duty tax certificates, any legal documents with their names on such as utility bills from here or elsewhere. In fact, anything at all relating to anyone from your family. Also, any proof that you have legal entitlement to the property, any photographs that bear a date stamp and statements from any witnesses to the weddings or betrothal contracts, or baptismal certificates. I also need proof of residency in Greece for all those people and witnesses that will verify your statements under oath. Then, I will need everything translated by a government registered translator, so that I have all the information both in English

127

and Greek and stamped by the records office. Do you have any questions?'

To my relief, Rob laughs. 'This will be interesting,' he says. 'I'll watch how you get on before I attempt my own legalities.' He sits there grinning.

The notary continues. 'Of course, if Mr Konstantinidis could come over, everything would be much simpler, as other locals will vouch for his credibility by signing a statement for the court. Is there any possibility of Mr Konstantinidis coming to Castellorizo or Rhodes, or better still, give me his phone number and I'll talk to him myself.' She slides a small notebook and a pen towards me.

My eyes flick to Rob's face. The grin has gone – replaced by a murderous expression.

'Konstantinidis!' he gulps. 'Did you say, Konstantinidis?' he growls between his teeth as I write.

The notary places a business card next to my plate. 'Here's my phone number. I'll prepare a list of procedures for you. Come to my rooms here at ten tomorrow and we'll get through as much as we can. When you're ready, make an appointment with me in Rhodes, where we'll settle any disputes over the property in court. I look forward to your visit.'

She reaches out a slim, perfectly manicured hand, we shake and, without a glance at Rob, she gets up and leaves.

'Konstantinidis!' Rob mutters vehemently. 'We're related! Probably both trying to claim the same house! Hell, you've kept that quiet.'

* * *

That evening, Uncle ended the call from a notary in Castellorizo and smiled to himself. Clearly, Olivia had the legalities well in hand. The notary had wanted the names of his sisters and their husbands. He recalled María's husband – Mustafa, the big Turk – whom he had known all his life. Then he remembered Sofía's husband, Jamie, the British soldier. He closed his eyes and drifted back through the years to his first meeting with that same soldier, perhaps his earliest childhood memory.

George must have been about four years old and no longer regarded as a baby. Mamá and María were feeding the infants, as they did from morning until night. The two men, Babá and Uncle Kuríllos, relaxed before the fire, drinking raki, as both grandmothers sat on the chest with their handiwork.

He can see the scene so clearly and even smell the chicken soup in the cauldron.

CHAPTER 16
GEORGE

Castellorizo, Greece, 1941

SOFIA GAVE YOUNG GEORGE a cup of warm milk. 'You drink that up like a good boy, then off to bed.'

He didn't want to go to bed, to be up there all alone, waiting for the *Bamboulas* – the Bogeyman – to find him. Nobody would listen, they all said, 'Don't be silly, of course there isn't a *Bamboulas,*' but he knew there was. Sometimes he hid under the bed, but it was too dusty there. Other times he pulled the sheet over his head, but it got so hot that the horrid monster would surely hear his breathing and hear his thumping heart. This indescribable fear filled the boy with panic as soon as he was alone in the bed, so each night, he lay awake, staring into the dark, terrified!

While the grown-ups in the big room were having a big discussion, little George ducked into his special hiding place, behind the carpet loom. Imagine his surprise, then, to see a man sprawled along the narrow space. The stranger had the biggest bump on his head. They stared at each other, then the man put his finger across his lips, telling him to be quiet. He didn't look well, but he was going to have a magnificent scab on his head, which would be the envy of every boy on the island. Still, George knew it must hurt even more than his own knees when he fell off the wall. He offered the man his milk and to his surprise, he took it and drank it all down. With great relief, George noticed the man was a soldier. No Bogeyman would come near if there was a soldier in the house, everyone knew that. On a mission to keep the soldier behind the carpet, George put his own finger across his lips, at which he saw the glimmer of a smile come from the soldier. He took his cup back, stepped out and asked Mamá for more milk.

'Oh, you good boy! Here you are,' she said. 'Once you've drunk it, straight up to bed with you, Georgikie.'

This, George's first exercise in subterfuge, went well. He pretended to sip the milk, peering from under his long lashes. When unobserved, he slipped behind the carpet again and gave the soldier his drink. To his delight, the soldier saluted him. He would sleep easy with a real soldier in the house. Tired now, he was eager for bed. Leaving the drink with his warrior friend, he slipped back into the room and climbed the stairs.

* * *

Sudden hammering on the front door made everyone jump. Two of the little ones woke with a fright and started bawling at the top of their lungs. The hammering started again.

'Kuríllos!' an angry voice shouted.

Uncle Kuríllos leapt from his fireside seat and dived behind the carpet. Babá got up, opened the door and saw Simonos and two British soldiers with faces like thunder.

'Yes, what do you want?' he asked the soldiers.

Simonos replied, 'They want to know where Kuríllos is. They've paid him for a sheep and he left with the money but didn't come back with the sheep.'

'He's not here. If you ask me, he's probably halfway between here and Turkey sharing a small boat with a couple of sheep right now. Be patient.'

'We're going to search the house!' the soldier bellowed and Simonos translated.

'Are you mad?' Babá shouted at them. 'There are too many people in this house, most of them women and children, each with the cry of a thousand cats!'

The two grandmothers, seated on the dowry chest, started screeching at the soldiers, beating their breasts and shaking their fists. Fevzi and Zafiro also started to holler and several of the youngsters scrambled out of bed and hugged Babá's and Mamá's knees. The noise was so great, the soldiers had to step away from the door to have a conversation. Eventually, they spoke to Simonos and he translated.

'Tell Kuríllos to return with the sheep as soon as possible. Do you have any food for our soldiers?'

'Yes, of course,' Babá said. 'Please, enjoy these with our compliments. It's a local delicacy.' He lifted the cactus pads out of the hearth. 'Very nutritious!' he said with gusto, giving Simonos a warning glance as he handed them over.

The soldiers and the fisherman turned and left. Babá stood for a moment, watching the three lead their long shadows down to the harbour. He closed the door and dropped the bar over the receivers on the inside.

The grandmothers got back to their crocheting and Mamá, María and Sofía settled all the children back to sleep.

Babá called, 'You can come out now, you whore of the devil!'

Sofía grinned at María.

Kuríllos stuck his head out from behind the carpet. 'Have they gone?' Babá nodded. 'Then look what I found,' Kuríllos said, stepping out sideways from between the carpet and the back wall. He had the soldier's arm up his back and his other hand over the commando's mouth. Sofía yelped when she saw the caked blood all over the boy's head and the right shoulder of his uniform.

Babá got to his feet. 'Is he armed?'

'I'm not armed,' the boy said in Greek, pulling back from Kuríllos's hand and reaching for his shoulder. 'You're hurting me!'

'You speak Greek?' Kuríllos asked.

'My mother's Greek. I'm on your side. Please, I need some water.'

'How old are you?' Babá asked.

'Eighteen. Water, please?'

'Babá, give the boy some water!' Mamá ordered. At that moment the boy stumbled forward and collapsed. 'The poor child, now look what you've done! Bring him over to the bed and let me have a look at that wound on his head. He's so pale, seems to have lost a lot of blood. He must have been there since yesterday evening!'

Sophia gulped. 'I did that. This is my fault. Tell me he's not dead?'

'Bring him a cup of water,' Mamá repeated. 'And fetch me a dish of brine and a sponge so I can clean this wound up.' Sofía stared. 'This week!' Mamá cried.

Soon the soldier's eyes opened and he stared about, clearly confused. 'Where am I?' he asked in English.

'Speak Greek,' Mamá said. Zafiro started yelling again. Mamá huffed and passed the water and sponge to Sofía. 'Here, clean that blood off him so we can see how deep the wound is and get him to drink some water before he passes out again.' She picked Zafiro up and rocked him back to sleep.

* * *

133

The next morning – refreshed after twelve straight hours of sleep – George hurried down and slipped behind the carpet loom. The gap was empty, only his cup on the floor confirmed it had not been a dream. It had to be magic! Perhaps the soldier had actually come out of the carpet to save him from the Bogeyman. He stepped around to the front of the vertical loom and peered at all the figures, the trees, animals and people woven into the family story.

'Georgikie, what are you doing?' Sofía asked.

'Where's the soldier?' he said. 'The one that comes out of the carpet and frightens the Bogeyman away.'

Sofía stared at him for a moment, then pulled him to her. She hugged him and kissed his sleep-warmed cheeks. 'Ah, that soldier,' she said humouring him. 'He's still there in the skeins of thread, but today he is going to start making an appearance in the carpet. All right, little man?'

George was quite happy with this explanation. So long as the soldier was somewhere in the house, he would be safe. He peered at the skeins of wool in the basket at the side of the carpet. There, he saw the brown of the soldier's uniform, the pink of his pale face and the red that would tell of the blood that covered half of his short hair and some of his shoulder. He stood tall and saluted the basket.

* * *

Sofía watched the children out on the patio while María and Mamá checked on the stills in the distillery.

She thought about the soldier and all that had happened the previous evening. Once the stranger was cleaned and watered and all the youngsters were settled, the house became quiet.

'I must report to my station,' he said.

'What's your name, boy?' Kuríllos asked. 'And how did you manage to get yourself knocked out by a useless girl?'

'Jamie Peters, sir. I was exhausted, walking and climbing through the night. Hiding from the Italians. I must have fallen asleep in the building behind here. The ship dropped us off, you see, but I've lost track of how long ago. Me and another soldier rowed ashore at the other end of the island, on a reconnoitre. We were supposed to map the land then meet the troops at somewhere called Punta Nifti, but we became separated ... lost; no roads and pitch black. Not what we expected. What's happened, do you know? Was it a success? Do the allies rule the island now?'

'Bedlam, chaos, that's what happened,' Babá said. 'There's about 200 of your lot here now, but they've no food or water and they're only just managing to hold on. You better eat with us before you go down there to report in, Jamie Peters.'

The cauldron of marrowbone soup had more lemon and rice in it. Mamá ladled a bowlful and placed it on the table. 'There, get yourself on the outside of that and you'll feel better.'

When the soldier had eaten, Mamá passed Sofía a basket. 'Show the soldier where the headquarters are and collect some fresh cactus pads from behind the chapel while you're out. And don't speak to any boys!' She turned to the soldier. 'Can I trust you with my daughter, young man?'

'Of course. I'll be the ultimate gentleman.'

'You'd better be, or I'll break both your legs before I kill you myself!' Babá threatened.

Sofía, shocked to be let out, alone, with a man, stared at her mother for a moment and caught a look she didn't quite understand.

Once outside, she led the soldier around the outskirts of town. There was so much she wanted to talk about, to ask about the war, yet words eluded her until eventually she blurted, 'I'm sorry I hit you! It's just that you gave me such a fright. The hours since have been like a terrible nightmare.' Once she had managed to get the words out, Sofía was so emotional she just wanted to cry. Severely disappointed with herself, she glanced up to meet his eyes, hoping he would understand the horror of that moment when she had thought the worst. 'You can't imagine how awful it is to think you might have killed somebody.' Trying to swallow her distress, she stared at the ground.

He placed his hand under her chin and lifted her face until she met his eyes again. 'I'm a soldier. I think about those I may have killed every day.'

'Of course, you do,' she whispered. 'Silly me. That must be difficult.'

'Don't worry about it, I forgive you, it's forgotten already.'

So many new emotions rushed into Sofía's head, she gulped, struggling to speak. He took his hand away and they continued to walk. 'How come you were behind the carpet loom?' she asked.

'I was just leaving when I saw you and another woman coming towards me. I didn't know which side you were on, so I ducked back inside and went to leave by the other door, but it led into the house. I've never seen so many children in all my life and they were making a terrific noise. Anyway, I decided to hide behind the carpet but I guess I passed out again. You know the rest.'

'Wait, I have to collect some cactus pads. We've got no bread.' She thrust the oversized wicker trug at him then pulled a pruning saw and a piece of oilcloth out of it.

After all the rain of previous weeks, the pads were fat, bright green and long as her forearm. She threw the cloth over one particularly healthy-looking pad and hung on to it as she sawed through the joint. A sudden blast of machine gun fire made her jump as the cactus pad broke away. She lost her grip; such was its weight. The soldier dropped the basket and grabbed the pad just below the cloth with both hands.

'Gosh, it's much heavier that it looks, miss.' He placed it into the basket.

Sofía rolled her eyes. 'Now you've got spines in your hands!' She took hold of them and peered closely. They were strong hands with out the scars of a labourer. A little tremor of unexpected pleasure quivered through her. So this was what it was like to hold a man's hand. Sweet sensations made her cheeks tingle. She looked up into his eyes again. His face was gaunt and pale and dried blood marked the wound on his head. She put her fingertips to the injury.

'I'm really sorry,' she said. 'How can I make amends?'

His eyes sparkled, then, as a mischievous smile appeared. 'Well . . .'

She blushed again and returned her attention to his hands. 'It's not the small spines, they can be removed, it's the golden tufts that the spines grow out of that will drive you mad in an hour's time.' She looked up, right into his eyes again. Suddenly awkward, her face was surely burning now. Another machine gun fired nearer the port, making her drop his hands.

He studied his palms. 'Really, don't worry, it's just a few prickles. I didn't realise how heavy they were. Here . . .' He took the saw and cut down another three, stacking them in her basket. 'Can you manage them, they're quite a weight?'

'Yes, don't worry, but your hands . . . you must run hot candlewax on them, then peel it off when it's set. It'll pull the fine spines out.' She glanced around, apprehensive.

'Don't worry, miss. Look, you'd better get off the street, it sounds like there're skirmishes going on. It's too dangerous.' He plucked a hibiscus from a shrub growing against the church and quickly tucked it behind her ear. 'I have to report in. Perhaps I'll see you tomorrow? What's your name?'

Sofía lifted her hand to the blossom, her eyes wide with surprise. What did he say? Would he see her tomorrow? How could she know? She shrugged. 'I'm Sofía. Will you get into trouble? You can kiss me if you want. I've never kissed a boy before.'

'I don't want your father coming after me with a gun.' He grinned, eyes sparkling again as he slipped his hand around her waist, pulling her to him.

'He'll never know, unless you tell him.'

Jamie dropped his head to one side, then the other, studying her face as if he were an artist.

Sofía was afraid; perhaps she wasn't beautiful enough. She stood on tiptoe, closed her eyes and tilted her face to meet his. His breath caressed her eyelids and cheeks as he moved closer, then his arms pulled her more firmly against him. Their bodies were hard against each other, his mouth over hers. He made a soft moan, rather like a cat purring, the thrilling sound made her toes curl and her body melt against his. Wonderful feelings exploded inside her for a few glorious seconds. Once he had broken away, she kept her eyes closed for a moment and smiled as the happy occasion settled in her memory. He smelled of myrtle, musk and warm chicken soup. The scents would be associated with her first kiss for the rest of her life.

'I must go,' he whispered, then made a casual salute before he turned towards the port.

'Goodbye, Jamie Peters,' she whispered, hoping he would not get into trouble. As she stood watching him, he turned and waved just before disappearing around a corner.

'Goodbye, beautiful Sofía!'

Oh!

An ear-bursting explosion went off. Her heart leapt, she whimpered, grabbed the heavy basket and hurried towards home. Despite the danger, she could not drag her thoughts away from the soldier and found herself bubbling with joy. Her heart beat a little faster and she had a strong feeling that she stood on the verge of adventure.

She threw herself into the house and dropped the cumbersome basket. Mamá and Babá stared at her.

'Why is your face so red and why is there a flower behind your ear? He didn't touch you, did he?' Babá demanded.

'Babá! What a terrible thing to say!' Sofía cried, terribly afraid there was some secret way her parents could tell. 'The basket's heavy and there are guns going off everywhere. I ran for my life.'

Babá frowned at her. 'If he touched you I'll cut his bits off and stuff them down his throat before I kill him. Are you sure, Sofía?'

'Of course I'm sure.' She sighed dramatically and used the oilcloth to lift the cactus pads onto the grill under the cauldron. The tufts of spines burned off in a flurry of sparks, as if celebrating her personal excitement, then the pads roasted to a delicious, nutritious pulp.

* * *

The next day started like any other, except that Sofía was terribly tired and completely in love. It seemed she had tossed and turned all night, dreaming of Jamie Peters and her first kiss.

A British officer came knocking on the door wanting to know if they had a Greek flag. Nobody would admit they had, so a British soldier hurriedly hoisted his union flag over the Customs House. Word spread quickly and in a magical moment – for the first time in anyone's memory – Greek men and women came out of their houses, stood proudly together and sang their national anthem. The 'Hymn to Liberty' rang out over the town – over the whole island – without fear of punishment. The all-important lines were chanted with vigour and the utmost reverence. Most importantly, they sang the beautifully poetic words in their own Greek language, which brought heartfelt tears to the eyes of every local man and woman on Castellorizo.

I shall always recognise you (Liberty)
By the fearsome sword you hold,
As the Earth with searching vision
You survey with spirit bold.
From the Greeks of old whose dying
Brought to life a spirit free,
Now with ancient valour rising,
Let's hail you, our Liberty!

Men, so moved they could not speak, wrapped their arms around their wives and pulled them to their chests. Women squeezed the hands of their children and thanked God they were free at last.

* * *

Sofía's heart burst with pride at every Greek word she wrote in her history book, the moment she got home:

> *Being freed from oppression and Mussolini's fascism by the British is the greatest event to date in my lifetime.*
>
> *I want to swim over to the little island of Ro where the old woman, Despina Achladiotou, defies Italians, Germans and Turks by raising the Greek flag every day at sunrise.*
>
> *She is the bravest person I know, apart from Anastasia, and also a certain soldier who dared to forgive you-know-who, the person who almost killed him.*

* * *

For five days the British occupied the jubilant island. Sofía and her cousins scurried about on their daily chores, linking arms, giggling and batting their eyelashes at the young soldiers. Each evening, under the pretext of studying with Anastasia, Sofía slipped out of the house and hurried to her secret meeting behind the chapel where Jamie Peters waited. His eyes burned as she fell into his arms and turned her face up to receive his kisses. The sensible part of her was silenced by desire, which grew with each meeting. They made love in the old-fashioned sense of the word, exchanging whispered promises of love as eternal as the moon and stars. However, each evening their passion gained strength and soon they were in danger of breaking their own rules of celibacy.

With her back against the cold chapel wall and his warm uniform pressed against her, Jamie needed no invitation. He slid his hand under her scarf and into her hair, then pressed his lips against hers. She closed her eyes and let him kiss her deeply. His skin smelled of soap and his mouth was warm and passionate and tasted of spearmint. For a long time she existed in the moment, only aware of the waves of pleasure running through her body, then she kissed him until they both trembled with desire.

CHAPTER 17
OLIVIA

Castellorizo, Greece, present day

I REFUSE TO LET ROB rile me now the notary has left us. Eleni serves what looks like chocolate cake and ice cream to the next table. She turns to me, ignoring Rob and asks, 'Everything all right? Can I bring the dessert menu?'

'No need, Eleni, I'll have some of that, please.' I nod at my neighbour's pudding.

She stoops and comes in close. 'Is the best! Dino, he make the Greek way with black-cherry spoon-sweet and the darkest chocolate. Very delicious.'

'Perfect. I need something sweet.'

She glances at Rob and nods. 'I understand, I bring the big slice.'

Rob glares at me across the table. 'You know where the house is, don't you?' He speaks quietly but with a vicious tone. Each word gathers more anger until he is shouting. 'What are you planning to do, have it put in your name, then move in when I return to Oz?' His fist hits the table with such force the bread basket skips.

'Hey, no, calm down! How dare you yell at me like that. Look at this place. There are dozens of old ruins.' My heart hammers like mad as I leap to my feet. Something I learned from Andrew; if you want to stand your ground in a row, do it on your feet, then leave. 'We don't even know if we're talking about the same property, or even if we're from the same family, so don't you dare speak to me in such an aggressive manner! In fact, you owe me an apology and I'll be back for it in a moment.' I go inside, to the ladies', passing Eleni on the way.

'OK?' she says looking alarmed. 'We could hear him in here.'

'Sorry, Eleni. He thinks I've come to steal his house.' I place a hand on my chest and gulp, feeling a little shaky as the adrenalin dissipates. 'Oh dear, I'm afraid he's upset me.' I dash into the ladies' and give myself a talking to.

You've got two choices, Olivia: let his bullying overwhelm you, as you did with Andrew; or rise above it.

I give myself a hug, sniff hard and tell myself not to be a wimp. He has no right to speak to me like that! Dino comes out of the kitchen with a tot of *tsipouro*.

'Straight down,' he orders with a little uptilt of his head. 'Then I throw him in the sea, OK?'

As the fiery liquid hits my throat, I splutter, then laugh. 'No, it's fine, thank you.' After I square my shoulders and stretch my neck, I march confidently back to my chair.

Determined not to look at him, I stare away reminding myself *he* had been incredibly rude. Eleni arrives with the cake and ice cream. Perfect timing. There has never been a moment when I needed a sugar hit more.

I close my eyes and savour the distinctly different tastes, that first rich mouthful of dark-chocolate sponge filling my mouth, the sharp flavour and slinky tartness of bitter-cherry preserve rolling over my tongue, then the cold clean vanilla ice cream melting into the back of my throat. As I concentrate on writing the description into my notebook, I sense everyone is looking our way. I take a breath and look up. A couple of sympathetic glances come from the women on the next table.

The silence builds up between us. Despite my quaking insides, I'm determined to ignore him until he apologises. I don't have to wait long.

'Listen, I'm sorry,' he mutters.

'Excuse me, I didn't quite catch that. Could you speak up?' I say it loud enough for the neighbouring tables to hear.

He glances around, slightly shamefaced. 'I said, I'm sorry. I overreacted.'

'Yes, you did. I didn't invite your attention and I did tell you I was here to work but you insisted on joining me.'

'I thought we were friends.'

'Friends? I don't even know you!' I catch his hurt look and regret being so hard. 'Look, Rob, perhaps I owe you an explanation. Last month I received my decree absolute after seven years of marriage, my mother's just died and I'm here to scatter her ashes and my darling uncle who was supposed to come with me had a heart attack last week. *On top of that*, I've been made redundant from a job that I loved. Do you understand? I'm not about to throw myself into a relationship, or even a friendship. What I need is space, time for myself, and you are overcrowding me.' My emotions bubble dangerously close to the surface. 'Thank you for the meal but I want to be alone, so, goodnight!'

I stand and walk away without giving him a chance to reply.

* * *

In the privacy of my room, I am overwhelmed by everything and the tears I've been fighting for so long break free. I can't even say why I am crying, then a knock sounds on the door. I wipe my eyes and open up.

'You left your sunglasses.' He thrusts them towards me. 'I thought you might need them if you're out early tomorrow.'

'Thanks.'

'Look, I'm really sorry, Livia.'

'It's forgotten.'

'Can I come in?'

'No, you cannot! Goodnight.' I close and lock the door.

* * *

The next morning, I lie in bed and think everything through. What a disastrous start to my time in Castellorizo. I wonder how Uncle is and decide to call him after breakfast. 'Never do anything on an empty stomach,' Mum had often said.

I shower, dress, then dash to the bakery and buy two fancy cakes in a little box. Next, I hurry to Eleni's taverna and present her with the luxurious tarts.

'What is this?' she says.

'Just to say I'm sorry if I embarrassed you last night; and to thank you for your kindness.'

'Virgin Mary! You do not have to do such things.' She turns towards the kitchen. 'Dino!' The chef hurries out and Eleni greets him with what sounds like a tirade of scolding. Dino plucks my hand to his mouth, kisses it and makes a little bow.

'I just wanted to say thank you,' I explain.

'No worries, be happy,' he says, beaming. 'I make you eggs, yes?'

Five minutes later, Eleni presents me with two eggs in a small, cast-iron skillet. Their yolks are the colour and size of tangerines, sprinkled with freshly ground black pepper and chopped, fresh parsley. She slides them onto thick slices of newly baked, nutty, wholewheat bread. What a simple yet delicious breakfast. Now, I am set for a productive day.

But before long, I'm staring out over the sea, my mind in a dream-like state. A ring of bright water catches the sunlight and ripples outward as a turtle sticks his brown and cream jigsaw-patterned head out of the sea.

'Good morning, Mr Turtle,' I mutter, then quickly glance around, feeling silly. Eleni comes and sits at my table.

'Everything OK?' she asks, softly, patting the back of my hand.

I nod. 'I should see the notary, have the deeds put in my name, but I can't seem to move myself.'

Eleni smiled. 'I see you have plenty of stress, Olivia, you need to relax, *koritsie mou*. Relax, my girl. I bring you some mountain tea now, is good for the body. Be calm. Look at the turtle; he live for a hundred years because he is always calm.' A sparrow lands near my feet, pecking at a few spilt crumbs. Eleni continues. 'Look at that little bird, he live one year, two at most, because he never relax. He is up and down, flitting from here to there, always fighting with other birds. Be a turtle, Olivia, slow down, take time to enjoy, live for a hundred years.'

Her voice is so tranquil, it seems to drench me in harmony and I feel the tension leave.

'Hi, Livia, there you are!' Rob's voice. 'Mind if I join you? I've got some news.' He plonks himself in a chair before I can answer, sticks his elbows on the table and leans towards me.

Eleni and I exchange a glance. 'Remember the turtle,' she says, then turns to Rob. 'Can I get you something . . . breakfast? Fried eggs? A flight to Mykonos?'

'Mykonos?' Rob blinks at her. 'Not just now, thanks. Coffee, Americano if you have it.' He turns back to me.

'Look, Rob, I'm going to visit the notary today and see if there's a problem with your family and my house. I don't want to fight with you and it's foolish to second-guess the legal situation, so let's leave it until we know what's what, shall we?'

'No need, I already found out. You left her card on the table last night, so I went to see her.'

From where does he get this intense power to rile me? 'And?'

'It seems the property belonged to three siblings, María, Sofía and George. María is my great-grandmother, Sofía is your grandmother and then there is George, who seems to have disappeared, probably dead by now like his sisters, which means the property is divided equally between us – me and you.'

My angst swirls. How can he dismiss darling Uncle as, *probably dead by now*? Heartless bastard.

'Wait a minute, Rob. María had sixteen children, one of whom I presume was your grandmother or -father. So, her third would be divided by sixteen and one of those sixteenths would have gone to your grandparent, unless a will was made that skipped a generation for tax reasons and bequeathed what amounts to one forty-eighth of the property to be divided between your parent and any siblings they may have. Even if they only had one, that means a ninety-sixth of the property heading your way . . . Unless you have any siblings.'

His jaw drops. 'No, no, no. That can't be right.'

'Well, maths isn't my strong point, but I'm sure the notary will come up with the right figures. I presume you know that death duties are incurred by the next of kin, by all those who inherit and a penalty, which is double, if person's taxes weren't up-to-date before they died? As I said, I'm sure the notary will tell us the facts when I give her the house documents from my great-uncle.'

'María's brother? You mean, he's still alive – you know him?'

'He lives in my house.' His jaw drops. 'You're disappointed, but I can't change the facts. Look, I'm not trying to cheat you. Whatever your share of the property's worth, I'll buy it from you at the going rate.'

He runs a hand down his face. 'That's a bummer. What will I tell my mother? She's desperate to come back here. There's no hope, you see. Cancer, she's got six months they say.'

Rob's mother is dying? God, what sort of person am I to judge him the way I have? Poor guy, no wonder he's desperate to get the house. 'I'm sorry, that's awful.'

He stares at the water. 'It's always been her dream to return. Her parents brought her here when she was a little girl and it made a huge impression on her. In Oz, they pass Castellorizo stories down from generation to generation. There's even a website where people share their memories. As you point out, we're a massive family and many of the old ones have this same dream. They gather every Easter and discuss plans to return.' He folds his arms across his chest and hangs his head. 'To tell you the truth, they clubbed together to send me here. What am I going to tell them, Livia? That I failed, wasted their money? Mum will be broken-hearted. This dream was the only thing that got her through chemo, you know. *Leave it to our Robert*, she told them. *He'll sort it, no worries.* Now I will have to admit, I failed them all.'

We sit in silence, glum with our thoughts. 'We need to think this through.' I turn towards the kitchen and see Dino and his wife relaxing at a back table. Eleni hurries over. 'Can we have two coffees, please?'

We peer across the water, contemplating the situation. After a few minutes, he says, 'Livia . . .'

I put my hand up. 'Shush, let's just think.'

Eleni brings the coffee and two slices of confectionery. 'This is *galaktoboureko*, egg custard in crispy filo pastry. Enjoy.'

'My mother made the best *galaktoboureko* in the world,' I say. Remembering how I loved her baking, I stare at the pie, my chest filling with sadness.

'You're completely mad,' Rob says, the corner of his mouth twitching with an attempted smile as he picks up a fork.

'You might be right, but I think we should go to the notary together, do you agree?'

Without hesitation, he nods.

CHAPTER 18
SOFIA

Castellorizo, Greece, 1941

AT DAYBREAK EVERY MORNING, ROWBOATS headed for the small islets where men scoured the sandy beaches for turtle tracks. One nest would provide omelettes for two dozen starving families. The population of cats, dogs, tortoises, hedgehogs and falcons had decreased dramatically as the meat in pies and stews took on a slightly unusual texture and flavour. Later, the Castellorizons only ate meat on a Sunday. Before the year was out, this deteriorated to the first Sunday of the month. When meat was available, nobody asked where it came from. They wasted nothing. Bones were boiled for soup and offal became brawn or sausage. The island's horses and donkeys disappeared and fresh meat was hung from rafters to dry. Every unnecessary animal helped to save the lives of hungry children.

Even so, there remained a huge discrepancy between supply and demand. Children had swollen eyes and bloated bellies. The proud Castellorizo people struggled on without help. Every item of value they owned was taken over to Turkey and traded for essential supplies such as flour, cheese and dried beans. Grandmothers pulled the rings from their fingers and dug the gold from their teeth. One by one, the silver brooches were removed from women's traditional costumes. Old men sold their prized amber, or carved ivory worry beads, until eventually they also found themselves without the money for food.

Reduced to skin and bone, everyone became more resourceful in ways to feed their children. The economic hardship was unrelenting and the island's population continued to decline. Emigration to Australia gathered momentum. Men went first, setting up home, then sending tickets for the rest of the family.

'Why do they all go to Australia?' Sofía asked Anastasia one morning after class.

'Good question, Sofía,' she replied indicating a world map next to the blackboard. 'This pinprick is us, there's Great Britain and here's France.' She paused while Sofía took it in. 'During the Napoleonic wars, Castellorizo had an armada armed with cannons. Local captains tried to dodge Britain's sea blockade of the south of France and supply food and other essentials to Britain's adversaries. Whenever the Royal Navy caught the culprits, they shipped them off to their Australian prison colony. After their release, those prisoners saw Australia as a land of opportunity and sent for their families who were struggling on our tiny island.'

'So that's how the colony of Castellorizons started in Australia?'

'Yes indeed.'

* * *

Two days later, Sofía was collecting more cactus pads behind the church when a 'Pst!' interrupted her daydreaming. Her heart leapt, she knew it was him. A pair of hands slid over her eyes and, for a thrilling moment, she felt his breath on her neck and his body pressed lightly against her back. 'Guess who?' he whispered.

'Jamie Peters, you'll get me into trouble. Take your hands off me and step back, right this moment!' She said the right words though her body ached for him.

Canford Heath Library

For renewals and enquiries
please call
01202 127127

Borrowed Items 03/09/2022 11:20
XXXXXX7960

Item Title	Due Date
* The summer of secrets	24/09/2022
* The escape artist	24/09/2022
! The perfect gift	24/09/2022
* Turning point	24/09/2022

* Indicates items borrowed today
! Indicates items with problems
Fees charges are changing 5 July see
poster in library
Thank you for visiting BCP Libraries
www.bcpcouncil.gov.uk
Twitter @BCPlibraries

'Only if you promise me another kiss.' He nuzzled her ear while his voice sent a thrill down her spine. 'I've brought you chocolate.'

'Chocolate! How dare you think you can buy my kisses with chocolate.' She leant back, intensifying the pressure between them. Her toes curled and her eyes closed as every nerve seemed to dance, then clench with delight. 'Oh!' she gasped. 'I really should slap you. You're too bold, Jamie Peters ... How much chocolate?'

He laughed and swung her around. As her heart soared, his lips were on hers and she tasted chocolate in his kiss.

* * *

All night, Sofía tossed and turned. Jamie's kisses and the wound on his head repeatedly returned to her thoughts. She feared whispering his name, declaring her feelings and everyone knowing they had kissed. Babá would beat her and Mamá would cry.

She longed to lie in Jamie's arms, taste his sweet kisses again, feel his breath on her skin as he promised her the earth and his undying love. At dawn, she got up and brushed her hair until it shone. She would tie her scarf a little looser next time she ventured out for cactus pads. If he saw her, perhaps she could shake it loose and display her captivating tresses.

* * *

Over the next days, they met often and whispered endearments, oaths of undying love and promises of restrained ardour until they joined in wedlock.

'I love you and I want to make love with you, Sofía. I am holding back only because I respect you so much,' he whispered. 'I have never felt this way before. Do you really love me, Sofía?'

'Oh yes I do! But this is madness. We have only known each other for a week and I . . . I want to give myself to you and no other, Jamie Peters.' Desperate to keep this man that she was falling in love with, she took his hand and pressed it against her breast. 'Can you feel how my heart beats for you? I am on fire, I want you so badly.' In the inescapable grip of passion for her Jamie, she could not hold back now. His mouth was on hers, so hard she felt her lips bruising. Their hands were tugging at each other's clothes. Neither of them had experienced such intense longing before.

Suddenly, they froze, aware of marching feet coming closer. They broke apart, tucking in garments, smoothing hair and trying to calm their racing hearts.

'Damn, it's the night patrol!' Jamie whispered urgently. 'I must go, Sofía.' He picked up her scarf from the floor and placed it around her shoulders. 'Will you be all right? Wait until they're further down the street, then hurry home. I'll see you here, tomorrow evening, OK?' She nodded. 'I really do love you, Sofía. One day, I *will* ask to marry you. Promise me there'll be no other.'

She could hear a slight tremor in his voice and knew they were both still quivering with passion. 'I swear on my life, there will never be anyone but you, Jamie Peters.'

*   *   *

Sofía approached the house, knotting her headscarf and smoothing her skirt. Uncle Kuríllos appeared with half a sheep slung over his shoulders.

'Are you all right?' he asked, giving her a knowing look.

She nodded, suddenly afraid that the evening might turn bad.

'Then you'd best go straight to bed when we get inside,' he said with a smile. 'I'll cause a distraction.' He tapped the spot beside her mouth. 'A little olive oil will help with the beard-burn.' His one eye sparkled and she loved him for his understanding. 'Just promise me you'll not go past that point of no return, before you're married.'

She shook her head, more grateful than she could say for his understanding. 'I swear, Uncle.'

*   *   *

For several days, everyone enjoyed the unmistakable taste of mutton, though Sofía had lost her appetite. She hungered only for the arms of her soldier.

The British were very different from the Italians. Hundreds of commandos overran the island. The pink-skinned, blue-eyed soldiers with their smart uniforms and their heads almost shaved seemed so alike, distinguishing one from the other was difficult for the young girls. Fathers watched their daughters for any sign of happiness, a sure giveaway that they were flirting. Mothers swung the back of their hand towards blushing cheeks at any hint of coquettish behaviour. Yet the girls stood taller and swung their hips with a little more vigour when far from parental observation.

*   *   *

The next evening, Mamá, María and Sofía had just finished putting the children to bed when terrifying explosions rattled the windows, waking the youngsters again.

Amidst the ensuing hullabaloo, Uncle Kuríllos burst into the house. 'Where's Sofía?'

'I'm here,' she said, rocking a baby with a bottle in its mouth.

'Thank God! Don't go out now. The *maláka poutána* Italians are back!' he cried. 'Two of Mussolini's torpedo boats just sailed into the harbour. They've massive searchlights and guns and they're trying to blow all the important buildings to kingdom come! Virgin Mary, there'll be ructions tonight, you can count on it.'

Babá rolled his eyes. 'How did that happen?'

'The Italian forces regrouped and retaliated. Some say they've already overcome the British and recaptured the island. Two British commandos lay dead in the street for everyone to see!'

'Oh, Blessed Mother!' Sofía cried. 'What if it's Jamie?' Before anyone could stop her, she dumped the baby onto the bed, leapt up and lunged through the doorway.

Mamá cried, 'Stop right now, Sofía, or I'll kill you myself!'

'I'll bring her back,' Kuríllos called, racing after Sofía's shadow. Halfway down the steep path towards the harbour, he pulled her to a halt.

'Are you mad? You'll be shot!' he whispered, his fierce grip bruising her arm.

'I have to see, Uncle, make sure it's not my Jamie that was k-killed,' she stammered. 'You see, I love him. He wants to marry me and in truth, I will marry no other.'

At that moment, the Customs House exploded and debris hailed around them. He threw her into an arched doorway and protected her with his own body as rubble fell about them. 'We'll both be killed. Let's get home!'

'No, Uncle, I have to know! Don't you understand? I love him.' At that moment, three commandos came hurtling around the corner and raced past them. 'Jamie!' Sofía called out, not sure if he was one of them. They pulled up sharp.

Jamie stepped out of the gloom. 'Sofía? Sofía, go home. It's too dangerous. The Italians are attacking from the harbour.'

'What's happening?' Kuríllos asked.

'We don't stand a chance, sir. Three commandos killed, seven wounded. Another two Italian vessels have just arrived in the port. Most of the island is surrounded.' His two companions pressed themselves against a small house and peered around the corners towards the port as Jamie continued. 'We have no food, no water, only a few weapons and hardly any ammunition.'

At that moment a heavy plane droned over the island so low Kuríllos ducked and they all felt the air vibrate over them. Jamie put his arms around Sofía and they both dived into the doorway. 'Orders are to regroup at Punta Nifti, but we're not sure of the way. Go home, you'll both be shot – or blown to smithereens when that bomber drops its load!'

As if to confirm his statement, a loud explosion came from the port's direction.

Sofía grabbed his arm. 'It's you who'll be shot if you go down there. Come up the back streets, follow us to the other side of Mandraki, *now*!' She turned to her uncle and begged, 'We have to help them. At least take them as far as the teacher's house.'

'You're so stubborn,' he muttered. 'But we're not going near the beach. That's what they'll expect.' He turned to the men. 'Don't make any noise and stay close together – it's pitch dark out there. Follow me, soldiers.'

A blast of machine-gun fire went off somewhere nearby. Kuríllos spun around and hurried inland, up to the magnificent but unfinished church of Saint George Santrape, then around the back the building. They plunged onward, through an olive grove and down the other side, travelling inland from Mandraki harbour. Breathless, they rushed under cover of a copse of pine trees, then the black mountain cliffs. Heading for Punta Nifti, Kuríllos led, followed by two soldiers, then Sofía holding Jamie's hand. In another small woodland area, Kuríllos stopped them.

'On the other side of these trees is Punta Nifti. We're going to leave you here.'

Jamie swooped Sofía up. 'I'll come back for you, after the war. Wait for me!' he whispered urgently, before planting a fierce kiss on her mouth.

'Enough! Come on!' Kuríllos hissed. At that moment, a rush of dark shapes hurtled out from the trees. Soldiers, with guns raised, rushed upon them.

'Hold your fire! They're ours,' someone said.

Weapons were lowered. Sofía, sick with fright, trembled like a kicked dog. Jamie pulled her against his chest and wrapped his arms around her. 'Don't be afraid now, they'll protect us.'

In the darkness, she guessed there were over fifty soldiers and – feeling unsure of their safety – Sofía sobbed. 'Tell them not to shoot us.'

'Permission to speak, sir?' Jamie said quietly, standing to attention.

'Go on, soldier.'

'These two locals, they helped us get out of town, sir. They're on our side and this one is to be my wife when the war is over.'

Sofía gasped.

'Right, good show.' He turned to Kuríllos. 'Is this Avlonia?' he asked, pointing at the cliff to his left. Kuríllos understood and nodded. 'Then perhaps you can tell us how to get to the top of the cliff.'

Jamie translated quietly to Kuríllos, then turned to his commanding officer. 'They'll lead us to a goat track that goes all the way up, sir.'

'Come on, chaps. We've no time to lose,' the captain ordered. 'You, Kuríllos, take the lead. Corporal Peters, bring up the rear and take care of the young lady.'

They scurried upward as the moon rose and lit their way. Jamie tugged Sofía by the hand. Perspiring and breathless, they reached the summit then dropped into the scrub so their silhouettes were not visible from below against the moonlit sky. A sudden break in the bombardment made Sofía wonder if it was over.

Once everyone stopped panting, the silence was intense. Sofía's sensitive nose picked up the scent of sweat and fear, which dissipated, replaced by the perfume of night scented wild flowers. The only sounds were faint rustlings of nocturnal animals. An owl hooted. Sofía's eyes bored into the dark. A dog barked down in the town. Everyone listened for footsteps. The captain lay on his belly and, using a hefty pair of binoculars, peered out to sea.

'Can I suggest something?' Kuríllos whispered to Jamie who translated for their leader. The captain nodded and Kuríllos continued. 'As soon as you stand, your silhouette will be seen from the town. A narrow path along the precipice leads to a small beach about 200 metres from Punta Nifti. There's an overhang about thirty metres up. High enough for a good view out to sea, but invisible from the point – where the Italians will be expecting you. We can lead you there, it's much safer.'

'Champion! Go right ahead, my good fellow,' the captain said. 'I believe the Royal Navy are on their way.'

Within an hour, the dark silhouette of a frigate slid over the horizon and approached on a silvery sea. Once the commandos were sure of its allegiance, they made themselves seen by lighting matches and signalling with a torch. In a tense half hour, boats with muffled oars rowed to shore and the commandos embarked.

The commanding officer turned to Kuríllos and shook his hand. 'On behalf of King George VI and the British Empire, I thank you for your assistance.' Then, to Sofía's jubilation, he repeated himself while shaking her hand.

'I'll come back!' Jamie whispered urgently. 'I'll return to marry you, Sofía. Trust me. I'll write every week and await your reply.'

* * *

Uncle Kuríllos and Sofía hurried home. 'We'll be in trouble, Uncle ... but we have the thanks of King George, can you believe it?' They both grinned.

Mamá, demented with worry, swiped at them both from the moment they entered the house. 'How dare you come back here at one o'clock in the morning and me completely out of my mind with worry, you *stupid*, stupid people! You could have been killed! I want to murder you both myself.' One of the children woke and started crying. 'What sort of crazy fools are you?' she yelled. 'How would we manage with all these babies if you never came back? You're so selfish, the both of you. No thought for anyone but yourselves!' She ranted on and on. Both Sofía and Kuríllos realised the poor woman was hysterical with worry.

Sofía put her arms around her mother's neck and kissed her cheek. 'Sorry, I was only thinking of Jamie.'

Kuríllos made the mistake of giving Mamá a condescending pat on the head. 'Calm down, woman. Everything's all right, she was with me. Nothing to worry about.'

Mamá's rage peaked. A fierce jerk of her sharp elbow whammed into his belly, just below his ribs. Kuríllos wheezed and doubled over.

'I'll give you, *calm down!* I've warned you before, you ever do that again and I'll kill you myself!' Mamá shrieked.

The Baby hollered and María tried to calm him, but matters just got worse. Babá, asleep in the chair when the pandemonium broke, woke with a start and shouted at everyone to, '*Be quiet!*' which woke the remaining children.

Sofía, exhausted, found the noise unbearable. She slipped upstairs to bed and once in her nightgown, blew out her candle. The muffled bedlam that rose from the ground floor subsided. She opened the wooden shutter and peered out into the star-spangled night. The moon was on the wane and at last the town had fallen into silence. Her heart pounded with the fullness of her love for Jamie. She imagined his lips on hers again and his hands on her body. She guessed everyone had been woken by the hullabaloo of her family, but she didn't care. Somewhere out there, on the dark sea, was the man who had stolen her heart.

* * *

By morning, the island had returned to normal. Rumours flew about concerning the British. Some said one commando tried to swim across the strait to Turkey. Although only a mile, the fierce current had pulled at him until, in the morning, his body washed up near Punta Nifti. The Italian police came around the houses and arrested thirty Greeks accused of conspiring with the British. They were deported to an Italian prison in Brindisi to stand trial. Babá and Uncle Kuríllos dived behind the carpet and into the distillery whenever one of the children hurried inside and said, 'Soldiers!'

In the empty classroom after lessons, the teacher encouraged Sofía to continue with the journal and, because she wrote it in Greek, the forbidden language, Anastasia insisted they keep the book hidden in the school.

'Fourteen Italian soldiers died in the conflict, Sofía.' Anastasia, the only woman on the island who refused to cover her hair, raked the long tresses back and held them away from her beautiful face with a comb. 'Fifty-two injuries and twelve Italians taken prisoner by the British, so, a good result for us Greeks.'

'But, Miss Anastasia, you're half Italian. Aren't you sad for your fellow countrymen?' Sofía asked.

She shook her head, got to her feet and paced the classroom. 'No, I'm not sad, Sofía. My father was Italian, but too many times he got stinking drunk and beat my mother.' She was silent for a moment, staring into the past, her face indescribably sad. 'My sister would have been the same age as you, Sofía, if he hadn't kicked my mother in the belly in a jealous rage when my sweet and gentle Mammon was seven months pregnant. He left me to take care of her, to gather the shallow breathing infant that was born too soon and died after a few minutes of life. For many years I blamed myself for her death.' A tear rolled down her pale cheek. 'I'll never forgive him. I buried my baby sister under an ancient olive tree and carved her name and the date of her birth through the gnarled bark, *Zoe* . . . Life . . .' She smudged the tears from under her eyes and sniffed. 'Perhaps, one day, we'll go there together, what do you think? Lay some flowers and say a prayer in the olive grove.'

Saddened for Anastasia, Sofía struggled for the right words. 'You must have been very lonely as a child, being the only one. I can't imagine.'

'A little, that's why I became a teacher.'

That night, Sofía wondered if that was the reason the teacher never married. She couldn't imagine what it would be like if the man you loved became violent. Her Jamie would *never* do such a thing.

CHAPTER 19
OLIVIA

Castellorizo, Greece, present day

'TELL ME ABOUT YOUR FAMILY, Rob,' I say as we sit at the harbourside. I notice his face is pasty with a sheen of sweat on his brow. 'Are you all right – you look tired?'

'I didn't sleep too well. Look, Livia, you can have the house without a fight, so long as I can bring Mum over and stay now and again.'

I want to hug him, poor thing, letting all those people down. 'My uncle says María had sixteen children. How many people are in your family in Australia today?'

'I don't know . . . hundreds. Why?'

'Because I believe they're all entitled to a share of María's third of the house, but they're also all bound to pay the taxes, death duties and accountant's fees. Sofía left her third directly to me in her will and my great-uncle tells me he's done the same.'

Rob drags his eyes away from the water and stares into my face.

'You mean if María didn't make a will the property would be divided between us all? I can't just come over and claim it?'

'That's right, I think. As far as I know, if María didn't make a will half of her third goes to the government and the other half is divided again. One quarter to her husband and the other quarter is split equally between her children. If her husband died before her, without leaving a will, then the same applies to his share. It's a minefield of legalities. Let's make a list of questions we want to ask the notary.'

*   *   *

Stunned is the only way I can describe my feelings as Rob and I step out of the notary's rooms onto the sun-warmed pavement.

'How can we pay the death duties of all our ancestors?' Rob cries. 'I mean, if they didn't legally own the property, then surely they don't legally owe taxes on it? Jeez, what a bummer! I've never heard such a complicated set-up in all my life. What am I going to tell the folks? My sister, Tilda, texted me this morning to say Mum's really picked up with my news. She's talking about getting a flight. I said it's best to wait until we've sorted things out and anyway, the house isn't habitable. She made me promise to send photos.'

'How tragic. Let's sit at Eleni's while we think.' We walk towards the taverna. 'What if we find a lawyer and ask him to explain our options? There must be a way around this.'

'You could show me the house, so at least I know what we're fighting for.'

'What? You haven't seen it yet?'

'It seems you have the island on your side. Nobody will tell me which house it is. I'm hoping it's one of these near the water.'

'Ah, sorry, you're in for a disappointment. See the cliff with the white steps going up at the back of the town?' He nods. 'It's at the base, to the left of the steps, practically the furthest house from the sea. Great view though.'

'Can we take a look while it's still light?'

Eleni approaches as we draw near her tables.

165

'Say, *kalispera,* Eleni. It means, good evening,' I say to Rob. He frowns at me so I sound it out for him. 'Ka-lee-spare-ra.' He repeats it to Eleni, who in return squints at him suspiciously, then throws me a questioning glance. 'We'll be back to eat in an hour, Eleni.'

'He no go to Mykonos?'

I laugh. 'No, he likes it here. I think your cake captivated him. We're just going up to look at the house, then we'll be back.'

* * *

We hurry along twisting narrow paths between houses, steadily climbing towards the back of the town. Scarlet hibiscus nod their heads as we pass. Bright buttery-yellow forsythia seems to light our way, leading us into tunnels of green that drip with vermillion bougainvillea and mauve-blue plumbago.

The heat of the day has passed. People emerge from their houses and sit on stone steps or rickety chairs outside their doors and call, '*Yiasas!* Come for coffee!' tilting back and grinning in welcome. Little groups of women gather under trees with their crochet or needlework and children run riot, unsupervised, yet safe and happy.

'This island is such a special place. Do you know, I haven't seen anyone distracted by their phone, not once, since I've arrived.'

'Probably a shite signal.'

'You're so cynical. The signal's fine.' Suddenly, I remember Uncle and remind myself to call him when we get back to Eleni's. We continue up past the church. The buildings thin out; some are little more than rubble. Cement mixers, bags of sand and piles of scaffolding indicate that other dwellings are in the process of restoration. Moments later, we find ourselves on the patio in front of the house.

I stand for a moment, taking in the strong stone building, feeling like a princess on the drawbridge of a fairy-tale castle. I thrust my hands into the pockets of my white linen shorts and bump my heels together twice. 'There's no place like home.'

'What?' Rob says.

'Dorothy, *The Wonderful Wizard of Oz* . . .'

He squints sideways, clearly thinking I'm nuts. 'This is what all the fuss is about?'

'It is,' I say. 'Isn't it wonderful?'

He shakes his head. 'What a disappointment. Can we look inside?'

'No, the floor's not safe.'

He rolls his eyes and mutters, 'Just my luck. A dump that needs flattening.' He moves to the side of the building. 'Not even a good spot for a guesthouse. Look up at that cliff. One good quake and my luxury hotel might be flattened. Just imagine the insurance!'

I can't believe my ears. A hotel!

'Clearly, the place is a liability. Best thing would be to get rid ASAP.'

My forehead prickles with sweat. I huff. 'Let's see if we can get in from the other side. I'll just take a look.'

At the gable end, a tree growing too close to the wall has been pollarded. Now, a tangle of leggy green branches make an impenetrable wall against the side of the building. We scoot around them. My heart beats faster. I'm longing to look inside but find myself thwarted again. A mound of fallen earth blocks this side too. There is no way in unless we break one of the half-covered windows and its shutter, which I was loathe to do on my first visit. I've never seen an industrial still, never mind one a hundred years old, but all my excitement bottoms out.

Rob picks up a hefty rock. 'Wait! What are you going to do?' I ask.

'I'm going to smash that back shutter and window in, that's what.'

'You can't do that, it's not our building. Let's think for a minute.' I sense there's a huge story behind this place. I feel its magic and wish Uncle was with us. A sudden sensation of foreboding surges up inside me. My instincts are trying to tell me something. 'Wait!' I cry again.

He swings around and lowers the rock. 'Why? I want to see inside.'

'Look, we may own some fraction of this place, but the truth is, my great-uncle legally owns most of it. I must video call him first. You can introduce yourself.'

'We can call him later. Anyway, there's probably no signal.'

I glance at my phone. 'The signal's fine. This building is the stuff of his dreams. He's the only living person, as far as I know, who was actually born here. Don't you understand, Rob? Like your mother, he longs to come back. Do you know what happened to make everyone leave the island?'

Rob pulls his chin in. 'They just left, that's all. Emigrated for a better life.'

'So why are they all desperate to return and reclaim their little patch of home? I'm sure something happened – something so awful that nobody will talk about it – even though time has passed and wounds have healed. It seems to me there's still a lot of pain under the surface.'

His brow furrows. 'I haven't a clue. All right, call the old man if you must.'

'Hey! What's going on?' a man's voice calls.

I turn and see Greg heading our way. His long strides and loose-limbed walk are graceful for such a big man. A role of white electric cable sits on his shoulder. His face breaks into a wide smile.

'Hi, Miss Olivia, my mother sent me. She said you might need help.' He drops the cable, turns to Rob and sticks out his hand. '*Yiasas*. I'm Gregoris the local electrician.'

'Your mother's too kind,' I say then indicate Rob. 'This is Rob, a relative from Australia.'

The two men shake hands. 'Welcome!' Greg says.

Rob frowns and mutters, 'G'day, mate.'

'You coming to live here too, Rob?' Greg asks. 'If you need an electrician, just call me, OK.' Without waiting for an answer, he turns to me. 'I've worked out several prices for you, in case you need to do this in stages. It will take time to explain everything so I suggest we eat together this evening and discuss the situation.'

'That sounds wonderful.'

Rob sticks his hands in his pocket and clears his throat, waiting for his invitation.

Greg turns to the Australian. 'It was nice to meet you.' Then walks away.

'What now?' Rob asks, frowning.

'I'm video-calling my uncle to show him the house.' After a minute, the call times out and it's my turn to frown.

Where is Uncle?

CHAPTER 20
SOFIA

Castellorizo, Greece, 1943

EVERY SATURDAY, SOFÍA RECEIVED A letter from Jamie and every Sunday, she replied. She longed for him to put flesh on her fantasies and dreamed of the moment she would fall into his arms again. Although she hardly saw him over the following two years, she learned everything about him, as he did her. Their love grew with each letter and she felt rich, embellished and adored. Days, weeks and months vaguely leaked away, pierced only by the surge of anticipation that came with Saturday's tootle of the mail boat as it sailed into harbour.

Sofía taught at the school every Monday, but this soon turned into three days a week and earned her a small wage, most of which she saved towards the time when she and Jamie would have their own home.

Six months into her next pregnancy, María lost her baby, a boy, and nearly died herself. This gave Mustafa the jolt he needed and, to everyone's relief, it was several months before María got pregnant again.

The distillery's fame put everyone under pressure. Despite the acceleration of war, lack of food and shortage of money, the perfumiers of Paris demanded even more of the precious oils. Everyone worked to increase the factory's output, even María's children helped gather blossoms as soon as they were able. That summer was particularly good for local flowers; consequently, everyone's hands, hair and clothes smelled of jasmine, honey-suckle, or myrtle for most of the season.

Life changed little over the following eighteen months, every day challenged them to put food in bellies. However dire were the unfortunate circumstances and isolation of the island under Italian rule, it only served to draw the people closer together.

Mustafa returned home three times that year bringing gifts for everyone. His kindness and generosity saved lives when twenty sacks of rice and lentils were shared between the people.

The Konstantinidis family struggled along with the rest; money could not buy food that wasn't there. Sofía's load was lightened by dreams of Jamie and the day they would be together. In his letters, he promised her that when the war was over, he would marry her.

*　　*　　*

As the year progressed, food became a bigger issue. Even the hens were starving. Through July, a few turtles nested on the tiny islet of Saint John. Each nest put some protein into the bellies of fifty hungry children, with two small eggs each. Sawdust bulked out wholemeal flour which in turn made coarse brown bread. Carefully roasted acorns – collected from under the holm oak trees of Kaş – produced a form of coffee. Housewives infused herbal tea from anything edible, including chopped olive leaves. Highly prized wild rocket, purslane and stinging nettles added welcome colour and nutrition to a daily meal of boiled rice or the roots of anything that wasn't poisonous. Everyone gathered sea urchins on the eve of a full moon, when the females' ripe, pink eggs were most abundant.

*　　*　　*

One restless hot July night, when windows and doors hung open, the Castellorizons lay restless in their beds, hardly able to sleep for hunger. A blast of gunfire rang out. Fear exploded in everyone's heart. An invasion, they thought. Those who were prepared, gathered startled children and hurried to their cellar. Others peered out to see if the danger came from air or sea, soon realising neither direction posed a threat. Another volley of gunfire came from the castle's summit – the Italian lookout post. As the discharge faded, the confused locals heard cheering and laughter. Shutters were hurriedly bolted to avoid the danger of flying glass injuring the children. But what were the crazy Italians up to now?

The first thought that came to everyone's mind was that the war had ended. Peace at last!

'I'll find out what's happening,' Kuríllos said, returning shortly with news. 'God save us from drunk Italians! King Victor Emmanuel's banged Mussolini in prison and changed the government. Nobody knows whose side Italy's on now but there's talk the war's almost over.'

'Let's thank God we're not being invaded and get some sleep!' Mamá said.

* * *

On a glorious September morning, swallows dipped and dived over the sparkling harbour water, catching insects to fatten themselves in readiness for their long migration to Africa. Leaves on the apricot trees turned amber then startling yellow, like beautiful candle flames flickering in the breeze. The white, waxy flowers of frangipani trees fell to the ground, still exuding the sweetest perfume with their dying breaths.

Women softened dried rusk with hot water, then drizzled a little precious honey over the top to feed their hungry children. Everyone prayed the war would end soon and food supplies to the island would resume.

Sofía rejoiced in the beautiful day and all they had to be thankful for. She wondered if King Emmanuel and the people of Italy knew that Castellorizons were suffering so badly. She had kept pictures from the newspapers all through the war so far, pasting them into a scrapbook. Thousands had died of starvation on the streets of Athens where mobs raided bins, searching for scraps to feed their children. Other photos showed wagons piled with corpses gathered from the streets each morning. She remembered the accompanying words with a shiver:

Hunger has become a national epidemic. 300,000 Greek people dead of starvation, most of them on our city streets. This devastation is the result of the brutal British blockade that started on 27 April 1941, when Germany occupied our capital city. The Axis took everything, including sheep and cattle, from our countryside, and the Allies continue to stop food supplies from coming into Greece until the Germans leave.

That blockade was over, but she wondered if the British people knew they had caused such a tragedy. Despite their struggle for food, surely it would never come to that on Castellorizo, even though the recent few days had been dire. She put the past out of her mind and hurried towards the harbour and the mail boat, eager for Jamie's letter. To her jubilation, she spied Mustafa's magnificent three-masted schooner, the merchant sailing vessel *Barak*, furling its square topsails as it approached the harbour.

The buccaneer returned from exotic places with a hold full of staples and treasure. Sofía's heart leapt with happiness for her sister.

María missed her husband terribly. 'Mustafa's back!' she yelled at the top of her voice.

The miserable Castellorizons, pale and stick-thin with dark rings around their eyes, had nothing left to sell or swap for overpriced food. They looked up, daring to smile. The big Turk always brought some treats, along with the cinnamon, cloves, sandalwood and patchouli for the distillery. Perhaps from Fodele, the village of the artist El Greco in Crete, there would be a sack of its famous juicy citrus fruit. Potatoes – the best in Greece – came from high on Crete's Lassithi Plateau. A new food came from Crete's south coast: bananas. In a matter of days, the hard green fruit turned into fat yellow fingers of sweet and delicious nutrition. Would Mustafa bring a barrel of the high-quality olives from Kalamata which were so fat and black that strangers mistook them for damsons? Or the best pistachios in the world, from the island of Aegina? Perhaps there were bottles of mastic liquor, made from the trees that cry golden teardrops of prized resin on the island of Chios.

Everyone rushed to the quayside, cheering and waving to welcome the Turk. Others shouted, 'Congratulations! You have another son!'

Mustafa had heard about his latest child from a merchant in Rhodes and was determined the whole island of Castellorizo would rejoice with him. The handsome buccaneer with the wide smile, generous heart and flamboyant clothes dragged a sack, bulging with oranges, down the gangplank and then tipped it over for the starving children. He roared with laughter, irrepressibly joyous to hear their squeals of delight as they scrambled around the quayside after rolling fruit. He brought gifts for the whole town, sacks of dried pasta, one of which he sent to the Italian garrison to keep them sweet, bags of lentils and dried beans, delicious nougat with chunks of almonds. A few squares of Turkish delight, delicately perfumed and coloured by red rose petals for the old toothless matriarchs. There were balls of white silk thread for the younger women and swatches of prized fabric for those with a sewing machine like Mamá. Richly embroidered black scarves delighted the two grandmothers who sat under the tree and shared a small mirror. They peered at each other, grinning like a pair of happy gargoyles. All these gifts Mustafa gave away in celebration of his newborn son and his enormous act of generosity greatly lifted the spirit of the Castellorizo people.

For María, Mustafa brought a red lipstick and diamanté combs for her hair; and for Sofía, a music box with a ballet dancer that twirled around when she opened the lid. A fancy gold key kept the contents away from prying eyes. Against all rules, Sofía wrapped her arms around his neck and kissed his cheeks, then ran up to the room she shared with her parents. She took all Jamie's letters from under the straw mattress and locked them safely away, to be guarded by the pirouetting ballerina.

Rosa, who practised her ballet every day, stared at it in wonder.

'Can you keep a secret, Aunty Sofía?' Sofía nodded. Rosa stared at the twirling ballet dancer for a moment, seeming unsure of herself. 'This is my biggest dream. When I grow up and I have learned to dance properly, I hope to travel to Athens and perform on the great Herodian stage at the Acropolis,' she confided. 'I've seen pictures. Do you think it's possible?'

'They say if you practise hard enough, anything is possible.'

Rosa's eyes widened. 'I will . . . oh, do you honestly think so?' She clasped her delicate hands between her knees, raised her shoulders and closed her eyes. 'Can you imagine, thousands of people sitting on those marble steps watching me dance? Do you really think it might happen one day – I could become a beautiful dancer? A real prima ballerina?'

'Come here and give me a hug,' Sofía said. 'Who knows what's in the future? But one thing is for sure, you are already a beautiful dancer. Your dancing gives people a lot of pleasure. When they watch you, they forget their troubles, their hunger, their worry. That is a marvellous gift, truly astonishing.'

* * *

Early that evening, once the children were asleep, Mustafa called a meeting.

'Sofía, María, come to the table to talk with us, I have some news. The reason I was longer than expected on this trip was because the French held me up in Paris. Your precious oil, formula twenty-five, is the inspiration for their latest perfume, which they are marketing as *Vingt Cinq*. Despite the war, it's the most successful perfume ever produced. In fact, we can't distil enough oil for them so they're offering to buy the recipe.'

'No way!' María said.

'How much?' Babá asked.

'Let's not be hasty,' Mamá added matter-of-factly.

'What're they offering?' Kuríllos asked.

'Whatever they offer, we should demand more,' Sofía insisted.

All eyes fell on Mustafa. He drew in a slow breath. 'Five million Italian lire.'

Mamá jumped to her feet and ran to the door. 'I'm going to be sick!' she muttered before slapping a hand over her mouth.

María shook her head disbelievingly. 'Five million Italian lire? I can't even imagine that much money.'

The figure was too big for Sofía to deal with. They stared at Mustafa.

'Look, I've got a lot going on,' Mustafa said. 'I must return to Rhodes tonight to meet another merchant. Please think about this and we'll discuss it later, all right?'

'Good plan,' Kuríllos said, grinning when the tootle of the mail boat drifted through the open door. 'Sofía, don't you usually meet the post?'

She nodded frantically. 'Anyone need anything from the port?' she said, hurrying towards the door.

* * *

The tissue-thin blue airmail letter said Jamie – her wonderful Jamie – was on his way back to Castellorizo! Sofía raced back up to the house where the three men enjoyed a *carafaki* of *tsipouro* on the patio and the women and older children worked in the distillery.

'Babá, Jamie's coming back!' she cried, waving the letter.

'Forget such dreams, Sofía. He's a British soldier. Now the Italians are on our side, there's no need for the British to come here.' Clearly happy that Mustafa was home, he grinned at the big Turk.

Mustafa's eyes twinkled mischievously. 'Ah, little one, you are in love with this British soldier, I think, yes?' Sofía blushed. 'Listen, something urgent has come up. You must brush your beautiful hair, then run down to the port and give this note to my skipper, OK.'

177

Sofía's smile fell. She wanted to be alone and read Jamie's letter over again, as she always did. Unable to imagine what could be so urgent, she hurriedly brushed her hair, then raced out of the house, hearing the men's laughter behind her. Down the hill she hurried, along the quayside to the gangplank where she handed Mustafa's note to the schooner master.

'I'm not happy about this!' The skipper's round face darkened with a frown. 'It's bad luck to have a woman on board. Follow me to the captain's quarters. He's given me orders to shut you in.'

He unlocked the door, Sofía stepped into the darkness and the door swiftly shut behind her. She heard the turn of the key. The room was perfectly still. Her tingling anticipation changed to fear. Was this a trick? Had Mustafa sold her to some distant oriental merchant for his harem? She had heard gossip of such things, and now she had reached the awful age of seventeen without a betrothal. Another year and she would be shamefully labelled a spinster like her hero, Anastasia.

'Is anyone here?' she whispered. Almost immediately a match flared, an oil lamp glowed and in its light stood her beloved soldier. 'Oh, Jamie!' She rushed into his embrace and at last, felt his lips against hers. She had dreamed of this moment for so long, her emotions exploded and tears sprung forth.

Jamie stroked her hair. 'Don't cry my darling, Sofía. I'm only here for one day, you mustn't waste it on tears. Will you marry me? Say yes and I'll speak to your father before I go back.'

Her emotions were so intense she could only whisper. 'Go back? I've waited so long.'

'I'm stationed in Rhodes; I can't say more than that. I couldn't bear to be so close and not see you. When I heard Mustafa was in port, I went to see him. He couldn't bring me because the port authorities search his ship thoroughly. He suggested I came on the mail boat, then slipped onto the *Barak* once I got into port. He's taking me back at midnight.' He took both her hands. 'Tell me you'll marry me, Sofía. Make my dreams come true. There'll never be anyone else for me. I want you to be the mother of my children. The love I have for you gives me responsibilities, but not rights. I have no right to your heart, but I'm asking you to give it to me. You have mine. There will never be anyone else for me, Sofía. Tell me what would make you most happy and I'll do everything in my power to give it to you. When you hurt, I hurt too; but when you're happy, there is nothing more in life that I want. Marry me, Sofía, marry me!'

It seemed she had lost her voice. Like trying to speak in a dream, the words would not come, until she nodded furiously and cried, 'Nothing would make me happier. Yes, Jamie Peters, I'll marry you.'

'Then go and tell your father to bring the priest.'

She stared at him. The ornate captain's cabin and the sounds of the harbour all faded to nothing. 'What, now, right at this moment?'

'Yes, we'll be married in the eyes of God, today. As soon as this war is over, we shall have an official wedding, more grand than this island has ever seen.'

'Just one thing, Jamie. Promise me we'll have no more than four children, regardless of whether they're girls or boys.'

He grinned wildly. 'I swear! Thinking about having our own children brings me great joy. Now go, my lovely bride, we don't have much time.'

Sofía pushed herself out of his arms, her heart thudding joyfully. She hammered on the highly polished cabin door to be set free, then rushed up to the house and burst inside. To her surprise, she found Mamá, Babá and Uncle Kuríllos in their best clothes, also Mustafa wore his black-tasselled fez and flamboyant *vrákes* – breeches.

'Ayeleen, run and get the priest,' Babá ordered. 'Tell him there's about to be a wedding.'

Mamá turned to Sofía. 'Bathe and dress, María's waiting for you upstairs, then we'll go to the ship.'

They all knew!

* * *

She hurried upstairs to the water pump on the landing where they gave her privacy to wash. The women helped dress her in the traditional wedding clothes set out on the bed. Since María's marriage to Mustafa, the richly embellished costume and special jewellery had lain in the olive-wood chest awaiting this day. Mamá and María sang the time-honoured wedding melody while they eased her into the cumbersome Castellorizo finery. Finally, she slid into the heavy, gold embroidered coat which was lined and trimmed with the finest mink. The wine-coloured brocade garment weighed as much as she did. As Sofía started downstairs, her sister slipped a special bottle of precious oil into her pocket.

'Here, use a little of this, just before he takes you for his wife,' María whispered hurriedly. 'It will dull the sting and make things easier.' She kissed her sister's cheeks. 'Don't let him near you in the middle of your month, or you'll end up like me, with too many children. *Na zisete,* long life, Sofía! Be happy, little sister.'

Out on the patio, sitting under the olive tree, the two grandmothers dropped their crocheting and flashed pale pink gums in a wide smile. They clapped as Sofía passed them in her finery and called the traditional salute, '*E óra e kalé.*' The time is good.

Sofía's unstoppable smile dazzled everyone. At last, the girl and her handsome English soldier would be united. Yet suddenly, she experienced a great aching hollow and – wanting her mother's arms – she felt her tears rise.

'I love you, Mamá,' she whispered. 'I hope I make as good a mother as you have been.'

Now her mother was crying and María huffed at them both. 'Come on, dry your tears, we don't have time for this. The boy has to leave at midnight!'

Sofía was already dreading Jamie's departure. 'I know, but why, María? He didn't explain.'

'Something's happening, there's no leave for soldiers this month,' María said. 'He'll apply for leave and return as soon as possible. Right now, they'll only give special dispensation to single men in the case of a parent's death. Come on, let's hurry back to the ship.' She glanced around the house, reluctant to leave all the sleeping children with Ayeleen.

A lyra player appeared and, along with Uncle Kuríllos on his *baglama*, performed the wedding melody and led the procession all the way back to the harbour. The priest – wearing his finest regalia – followed, then Sofía walked between Mamá and Babá. Word spread faster than gossip. People rushed out of their houses calling, '*Bravo! Bravo!*' and clapping boisterously as the procession passed. The women pretended to spit three times at the bride to ward off evil spirits while Sofía fought the urge to grin at everyone. This was a serious walk, not the time for merriment. However, her heart sang. At last, she would be married to her darling soldier.

'Mamá!' Sofía cried, coming to a sudden stand-still when two Italian guards, clutching rifles, stepped between the bridal procession and the gangplank.

'Halt!' they ordered. 'What's going on?'

Everyone froze.

CHAPTER 21
OLIVIA

Castellorizo, Greece, present day

'We were just looking for a way into the house without causing more damage,' I say to Greg. 'It seems impossible. The floor's not safe and the landslip at the back blocks the way in.'

'Anyway, you must be busy,' Rob says. 'Don't let us keep you.'

Greg ignores Rob and turns to me. 'Go through the toilet window, behind the lemon tree.' He nods at the pollarded tree. 'Here, let me cut it back for you, I've got some tin-snips that'll do the job. Be careful, lemon tree thorns are vicious.' He reaches for a pair of pliers hanging from the toolbelt, then pulls on leather gloves. I find I'm smiling, though I can't explain why. Greg's biceps flex and ripple as he works. I remember Andrew who was proud to keep his corporate body honed and toned in the gym.

Rob drags the branches away. A strong lemony scent fills the air around us and once again, a magical feeling about the place warms me.

While Greg works, I walk over to one of the sawn-off fir trees at the edge of the patio and sit there, looking out over the harbour below. There is a slight breeze, the little boats bob about and remind me of my uncle's paintings. Sunlight sparkles off the turquoise water and I wonder how that must appear to the stoic turtles on the bottom. I give my uncle another call, but there is no answer and although I realise there's probably a perfectly reasonable explanation, I'm worried.

'Hey, Livia, come on. We can get inside!' Rob calls.

I return to the side of the house and see a small window about a metre and a half from the floor, previously hidden by the shrubbery.

Greg lifts the shutter away. We see there's no window-frame and I'm relieved we don't have to break any glass. He stands with his legs astride, thumbs tucked into his toolbelt and studies the situation. 'Listen, Rob, I'm too big to get through there. Step into my hands, then on my shoulder and you should be able to go in through the window.'

Rob looks horrified. 'What if I get stuck?'

'Then you'll die quite a horrible death. Thirst and starvation, though the rats will probably get you first.' He throws me a wink.

Rob looks as though he's about to vomit and I'm struggling not to laugh. 'Not funny!' Rob says. 'You go, Livia.'

'No. You're the one who's desperate to break in.'

Greg squats and interlocks his fingers. 'Come on then, I've got work to do. Can't mess about here all day. Step up, Rob.'

Rob steps into Greg's hand, Greg straightens and Rob reaches the window. 'Now, step onto my shoulder and you should be able to get through easily,' the electrician says. I can't take my eyes off Greg's flexing muscles, his bronzed shoulders are glistening with sweat.

It goes to plan until Rob's hips slide through the window. 'Watch out for the toilet!' I call.

'I can't feel any toilet and it's too dark to see,' Rob shouts just before his balance falters. He see-saws for a second, then his upper body dips inside and his feet flip up on the outside. He slides in head first.

'Toilet?' Greg says. 'This place is old. I'm sure it's just a *ka-ka* hole in the floor.'

'Aaaaagh!' Rob wails from inside.

'Oh God, do you think he's OK?' I ask Greg, then notice he's doing his best not to laugh. 'You knew? You devil! Poor Rob.'

'Let's see if we can clear more of the back window,' Greg says.

We go around the back where the landslip is not as intense as the other end. Although scree covers half of the door, one shuttered window is almost clear, but we can't see inside.

'Do you think we'll get in, Greg?' I ask. 'We need some tools and a torch. I don't suppose you're an experienced burglar?'

He grins. 'I have a bolster chisel. Let's see if we can shift some muck with it.'

'Shouldn't you be working? I'm so grateful for your help.'

His eyes peer into mine. 'Before I forget, eight o'clock at the taverna, OK?' He starts scooping loose slurry clear of the window. 'We'll talk about your electrics over dinner.'

'That would be lovely, thank you.' Loud banging comes from the other side of the shutter. 'Listen, Rob's made it inside the distillery.'

'Good, let's nail it closed and run!'

I realise my mouth's hanging open and snap it shut.

Amusement shines in his eyes. 'I'm making a joke,' he says.

'Of course you are.' I feel a little stupid for thinking otherwise.

'Let me see if I can lift this shutter off.' He knocks his bolster chisel under the woodwork and gives it a thump, gets his fingers around the shutter and lifts it off the drop-on hinge.

Rob, on the other side of filthy glass laced with cobwebs, manages to open the window. 'Right, that was a job and a half, I nearly fell down the crapper. Can you lower yourselves in through this window?'

Greg shakes his head. 'Me, no, no, no. Not until we've had the dogs in – the place will be teeming with snakes and I can't stand them.'

Rob's eyes bulge. He stares down towards his feet and visibly shudders.

By now, I have the measure of the electrician – at least I think I have. 'Stop it, Greg! Rob, he's kidding you. I'm coming in. Here, let me pass you the torch first.'

'Snakes!' Rob cries, launching himself out of the window. I step back, lose my balance on the soft earth and fall against Greg. His enclosing arms steady me and – for a second – I imagine wonderful things.

'Oh,' he gasps. 'No need to throw yourself at me, Miss Olivia.'

'No . . . I slipped. I mean . . .' I stutter. He grins again. Why do I feel so unbalanced in his company?

The Australian clambers through the window. 'I hate snakes!' he mutters.

'What?' I say. 'After we've finally got you inside the property, you're not going to take a look around?'

'You can't please some people,' Greg says quietly. 'Is there anything else I can help you with, Miss Olivia?'

Rob decides to answer for me and shakes his head. 'No, I think Livia's right, we'd better check with the lawyer that it's all right to just bust our way in. What if we end up in prison like those plane spotters, remember? Perfectly innocent guys accused of being spies. It was even in the papers back home.'

'OK, it'll be going dark in an hour or two, so why don't we leave this until tomorrow? Let's go back to the port and find someone to fit proper locks. I'd never forgive myself if kids went inside playing hide-and-seek and fell through the floor.'

'We need a builder,' Rob says. 'We should get some idea of the cost of renovation, so we know what's what before we even consider claiming the property.'

So, he's still considering claiming the property. *A little slip there, Rob.* I should ask him how long he intends staying. 'Good plan.' I decide to humour him. 'Let's discuss over a beer at Eleni's.'

'I've just got a small job to do, then I'll meet you there at six, OK?' Greg says.

*   *   *

After a quick shower, I put on a red Fifties-style dress with a Bardot neckline and button front. I hurry to my usual table at the water's edge. A turtle swims right up to me. I peer into his eyes and wonder what he's thinking of me and I guess he's doing the same. How wonderful it would be if we could read each other's minds – if there were never any misunderstandings between friends, lovers, siblings, politicians. So captivated, I don't notice Eleni until she speaks.

'He's D'Artagnan, the most big turtle in the bay and the boss of all the others. He likes to eat calamari,' Eleni says. 'You look very nice tonight. Like a film star.'

I'm flattered. 'Calamari, mmm, me too, Eleni, but right now, I'd just like a nice glass of very cold Chardonnay to keep me company while the sun goes down.'

'Good choice.'

'Excuse me while I phone my uncle again. I'm rather concerned,' I say, pressing the redial button. Still no answer.

What if he's having another heart attack? Perhaps at this very moment he's on the carpet clutching his chest? If I can find the neighbour's phone number, I'll ask her to check on him. Molly, I remember, has a key. *Breathe*, I tell myself. He's possibly out with a friend, someplace where he has to turn off the phone. The theatre, the cinema . . . the hospital? *Calm down, give it an hour then call again.*

'You look worried, is everything all right?' Eleni asks, approaching the table with bread, a few dips and my wine.

'Wonderful, except I'm a little concerned about Uncle. I've just called him for the fourth time, but he's not answering. Also, I'm meeting Gregoris just now. He's going to give me an idea of costs to connect electricity to the house.'

Eleni nods and smiles. 'Gregoris is a good boy.'

I remember he's her son. She is clearly on my side, so I think it's time I put her in the picture. 'You know my grandmother Sofía and her sister María owned the house and distillery?' Eleni nods. 'Well, María was Rob's great-grandmother and I might as well tell you, he's come here to claim the very same property that I'm trying to sort out and now he's talking about a hotel or a nightclub.'

Eleni's eyes widen. 'Oh, *Panagia mou!*' She crosses herself three times. 'Then we all have a problem. I tell Dino and we will help you.'

'You're very kind, Eleni. Thank you.'

Half an hour later, I phone Uncle again, but his automatic message unsettles me: *'The subscriber is unobtainable, he may have turned off his phone, please try later.'*

My trepidation grows. Where can he be? I scroll through my saved numbers to see if I have a contact for Mum's neighbour. At least she can knock on his door and use her key if there is no answer. Worst-case scenario . . .? I don't want to think about it. Then I remember the caretaker, an overweight Irishman in faded blue overalls. He always carries a sink plunger in his left hand, a hammer in his right and most importantly, has a bunch of keys hanging from his belt. However, I don't have his number. I call directory enquiries and eventually get the caretaker's number and dial it.

After a lengthy explanation, Big Dave promises to check on Uncle. 'If there's no reply at his door, I'll let myself in – just to make sure there isn't a problem, so don't be worrying your pretty head.'

The minutes stretch out. Rob turns up at the table. 'Everything all right?' he asks.

'No, not really. I still can't get hold of my uncle. He seems to have disappeared. I'm rather worried.'

'Probably a simple explanation,' he says, staring up towards the cliff, which tells me he's thinking about the house.

'How's your mother?' I ask, but before he can answer, my phone rings. I snatch it off the table, relieved to hear Big Dave's Irish accent.

'I'm in the apartment, Olivia. No sign of your uncle. Bed's made, no dishes in the sink, fridge is empty apart from an unopened carton of long-life milk. I guess he's at the super-market. I'll check again in a couple of hours, when I knock off. Call me when I finish at nine.'

'Thanks, I will. To be honest, I'm starting to worry. He's just recovering from a heart attack. It's tempting to call the hospital. In fact, that's what I'm going to do. I'll give you a ring at nine.' I remind myself that's eleven o'clock local time.

Rob watches me while I call the hospital, give my uncle's name and explain my concern. Though it is against hospital policy to give out such information over the phone, when I say I'm in Greece, the woman adds, 'So, I need to make it perfectly clear, it's against the rules for me to tell you that there's no Konstantinidis in this hospital right now. Do you understand?'

'Thank you, that's a weight off my mind.'

'Good news,' Rob asks.

'Well, he's not in hospital, so I guess that's a yes.'

'I'm going for souvlaki and chips – you want to come?'

'Ah, thanks, but I've got other arrangements tonight.'

CHAPTER 22
SOFIA

Castellorizo, Greece, 1943

Sofía, dressed in her extravagant wedding finery, whimpered as an Italian soldier stopped the procession.

'What's going on?' the guard yelled again.

Mustafa stepped forward, towering over the stocky Italian. 'Good afternoon, my friend. Allow me to explain. This beautiful young woman is my sister-in-law, Sofía. She is about to marry one of my gallant sailors. We are leaving port shortly and there is an urgent need for the wedding to take place before we go.' He glanced down at the soldier's belly, then back to his face. 'If you get my meaning, Officer. We'd be honoured if you good fellows could join us for food and wine this evening.'

The Italian seemed to deflate in the big Turk's shadow. He squinted at Sofía, then at her belly, then at the priest. After a short discussion and a carton of cigarettes – miraculously produced by Uncle Kuríllos – they nodded for the small party to pass up the gangplank. Immediately, a deck-hand raised the drawbridge. Two of the deck crew slackened the mooring lines and the ship eased away from the quayside until a couple of metres divided ship from shore.

This did not stop the astute people of Castellorizo from celebrating. Church bells pealed. The lyra player delivered traditional tunes on the quayside. Someone started singing and calls of '*Opa! Opa!*' filled the air. As the early September sun slid towards the horizon, shadows lengthened and scarlet hibiscus wrapped their wide petals around each other in a sleepy hug.

People gathered on the promenade where MSV *Barak* remained secured a little way off. Men and women, old and young, each with their hand on their neighbour's shoulder, waited for the appropriate music. One of Mustafa's sailors slid effortlessly out along the ship's bowsprit, the polished wooden pole gripped firmly between his thighs as he played a merry tune on his squeezebox. He accompanied the lyra player's *syrtaki*. As the wedding procession disappeared into the ship, the locals came together on the quay and performed the steps of Zorba's dance.

Sofía's heart was bursting. All this for her and the Englishman she loved.

Suddenly, Babá raised his hand. 'Wait! The groom must ask me for my daughter's hand.'

Everyone agreed. In the space outside the captain's salon where the walls, doors and ceiling were highly polished golden oak, the scent of beeswax was overpowering. Sofía knew she would always associate that perfume with her wedding day. All this excitement was clearly too much for the half-starved girl. Mamá slipped an arm around her shoulders.

'Don't worry, you have our blessing,' she whispered. 'Your father just likes to be the centre of attention.'

Everyone stared in silence at the heavy oak door until two minutes later, it opened. Babá, a great one for drama, glared at each person in turn.

His face was stern as he finally spoke. 'The soldier asked for my daughter's hand in marriage. I said . . .' He paused, looking

191

around again. Sofía whimpered. Babá started again. 'I said . . .' the pause was long, 'Yes!'

Kuríllos stepped out onto the deck and cried, 'Babá said yes!'

They say the cheer was so loud that the shepherdess on the other side of the island heard it. With even more fervour the music and dancing continued. On the ship, everyone followed the priest into the spacious salon.

Sofía found Jamie in the exact spot she had left him, as if he hadn't moved since the moment she'd turned away. He gazed at her, taking in the opulently embroidered costume.

'You're back, beautiful as ever,' he said quietly.

'My father said yes,' she replied. 'I would have married you anyway.'

She could see he was nervous; at least she had her family around her. He was so alone that her heart went out to him.

'I've never known a wedding take place under such unusual circumstances,' she said. 'I have no idea what will happen next.'

'What do you mean?'

'Well, sometimes Turks and Greeks marry on the island, but then both sides have the support of their families. You, my poor darling, have no family to support you at your own wedding. Also, I'm an Orthodox Greek, marrying a British Roman Catholic. Very odd, really. Yet, I believe we'll survive more obstacles than this together.'

'The priest said our marriage will be binding in Greece and once we're married by the captain of the ship, Mustafa, our marriage will be binding in the United Kingdom too. It's maritime law.'

Jamie reached for her hand.

'No, no!' the priest ordered. 'You no touch her until you married, OK, you understand?'

Jamie nodded. Sofía lowered her eyes, remembering the touch of his hand on her breasts behind the church. All those confusing emotions, she now understood, were simply her natural longing for him.

The ceremony began.

* * *

'Now you're almost married,' Babá said when it was over. He shook Jamie's hand fervently. 'Treat her gently, or I will set Kuríllos on you.' They all turned to look at Sofía's uncle who ran his thumbnail across his throat, leaving no doubt of the consequences of being a bad husband. 'We go to celebrate the wedding of our daughter while you make your marriage bed here on the ship. MSV *Barak* is leaving at midnight to take Jamie back to Rhodes.'

The groom appeared a little embarrassed, but slipped his arm around Sofía's waist and pulled her against him. 'Yes, sir. Thank you!' he said.

Mamá stroked Sofía's cheek. 'My child has gone forever. Goodbye, child . . .' Her poignant words trembled on her lips and her eyes filled. 'I'll see you tomorrow.' She kissed Sofía's forehead then hurried away.

Uncle Kuríllos took Jamie to one side and had a quiet word before he turned and left the ship. Later, when they were alone together, Sofía asked what he had said.

'He told me if I ever hurt you, he'll break both my legs, then drop me into a barrel of burning oil.'

Sofía smiled. She wanted to say something funny, or clever, to lighten the threat. *No, he won't, because I'll do it first,* but the words wouldn't come, she was so emotionally charged. Jamie's eyes widened in mock horror until Sofía started to laugh and fell into his arms. The tension and intensity of their last kiss behind the church came back to her. It seemed so long ago and yet here they were, married.

'What are you thinking?' he asked, leading her to the captain's bed.

'I'm remembering the last time we met, behind the church. You told me you loved me and that you would come back for me. I didn't believe you and cried for days after you'd gone.'

'And now I have to leave you at midnight, like you're my Cinderella in your amazing clothes.'

'What if you stay? Please stay, Jamie. This is not right, to rush our wedding night like this.' With a sweep of her hand, she indicated the bed.

'If I'm not back at barracks tomorrow, they'll come for me, court-martial me and I'll be shot for desertion the following dawn.'

She gasped and – as if keeping up with her emotions – the music and singing on the quayside gained in intensity. 'Listen to your family and friends. It sounds as though they're having a smashing time. Shall we go and join them?'

Sofía's spirits sank again. He would rather join the party than take her as his wife? Her disappointment was so intense, she felt hot tears trickle down her cheeks. 'You don't *want* me ... want my body? Do you find me ugly, Jamie?'

'No, oh no! Sofía, don't cry. Please don't cry, I can't bear it.' Love shone from his eyes and his voice trembled with restraint. 'You can't imagine how much I want to make love to you – but slowly, gently – not in a rush like this and then abandon you and perhaps not see you for another six months.'

'Then why did you marry me now?' she whispered, fighting sobs, her hands clasped in her lap, elbows pressed in against her waist to stop herself trembling.

'You're so beautiful, how could I leave you at the mercy of your fellow islanders? I'm sure they *all* want you for their bride. I can't believe how terribly lucky I am to have found you.'

'Even though I almost killed you?'

He touched his head, smiled, then placed his hand against her cheek for a moment. 'My lucky day, to be knocked unconscious by my future wife.' He traced her jawline and with the lightest touch, followed the line of her chin, then his fingertips slipped south, stroking the contours of her neck. She willed them onward, her spine arching, her body aching for the want of him. He stopped to unwrap the long silk shawl that kept the traditional, richly embroidered *popazi* on her head. Next, he removed that colourful pillbox hat. She closed her eyes and embraced every movement of his hands. She heard his gasp as her hair tumbled around her shoulders and that one small sound said more than any words. Her mother's voice came back to her.

One glance at those lustrous tresses and you will become irresistible to him.

He slid the fur-lined scarlet coat off her shoulders and kissed the side of her neck, then whispered, 'At last, darling Sofía, you're my wife. I've waited so long for this moment.' Sofía's clothes fell around her as he spoke and she helped to remove his, tugging and tangling, clumsy amateurs in the art of lovemaking, until they realised the strange sensation of being naked together for the first time. He took her in his arms again. 'My universe begins and ends with you, Sofía. No ships or wars or countries could ever keep me from you because in the end, every path leads right back to your beautiful body.'

He turned down the oil lamp and pulled her into the captain's bed.

'My sister gave me a little oil, to make things easier,' she whispered, glad he could not see her flaming cheeks.

* * *

They made love, made plans, made love again, then a knock sounded on the door.

'The time has come for me to leave you again,' Jamie said.

Sofía gasped. 'Already, no, Jamie, no, it's too soon.' She could hardly deal with the confusing and painful emotions going on inside her. 'Promise you'll be back as soon as you can.' She would cling on to that knowledge and use it to protect her heart from the weeks and months of pain and loneliness that lay ahead. 'I wish I could stay by your side through the storms of war, Jamie.'

He held her close, his breath on her ear and she would recall it every time the breeze whispered. He would be like a ghost, always by her side giving her strength, patience and hope until the day of his return.

He turned up the lamp and drew the sheet back. 'Let me look at you while I dress, so I remember you as you are now, the most beautiful sight on earth.' He pulled on his clothes, then took his army knife to her. 'I want a little of your hair to take with me. Wherever I go, this will be next to my heart.' He cut a lock and put it into his top pocket. She dressed hurriedly, then followed him onto the quayside where they kissed to the applause of the wedding guests. Jamie returned to the vessel and the gangplank was raised.

'Goodbye, my darling wife,' Jamie called as she waved from the quayside, tears brimming and her mother's arms holding her tightly.

CHAPTER 23
OLIVIA

Castellorizo, Greece, present day

'Will you be all right here, by yourself?' Rob asks, glancing around the harbour as if it's a place of gang warfare. 'I'm quite happy to keep you company.'

'You're very kind, but isn't that why I came? To be alone with my thoughts and my cookery book ideas. You've been very helpful with the house, Rob – climbing in like that, so thank you. Now, I'm meeting Greg for dinner, which means I'll probably be gone by the time you've finished your souvlaki and fries. So please, enjoy your food and the sunset and I'll see you tomorrow.'

I pull out my notebook to confirm I am working. 'Have a super evening!' I fix him a smile and for a flicker of a second, he seems confused. Then he bids me goodnight. What a relief to see him walk away. Of course, he means no harm, but I feel trapped in his company.

I settle into my spot reserved table on the quayside. Eleni comes over and offers to teach me how to make *dolmades* with grapevine leaves. A loose-limbed woman in her late thirties strides enthusiastically along the quayside clutching a basket of greens.

'Oh, no – here we go,' Eleni says.

'*Kaliméra!*' a strange woman yells with a coarse Australian accent. 'Would you like some wild greens from my plot, Eleni? They're amazing. No chemicals, really good for the colon and liver.'

'I'm fine, thanks, Dorian,' Eleni says, turning to me. 'I'm busy helping Olivia. She's researching for her next book.'

'Good show. Written a book already, have you?' Dorian asks. 'I've written a book too. What do you write, romance? I like a bit of romance. Haven't had any for a while but that's because I'm fussy.'

I blink at her, not sure why I feel insulted. I like a good romance and they certainly sell more than recipe books. 'No, I'm doing cookery, based on ethnic Greek food.'

Clearly, there was no way out of not taking it without being rude. 'Thanks,' I say, taking the fading foliage. 'How much do I owe you?'

'Only four euros!' she cries like a market seller.

Eleni rolls her eyes. I scrabble in my purse for change. 'Sorry, I've only got a five.' I lift the note. 'Perhaps Eleni's . . .' Before I can say more, Dorian whips the money from my fingers.

'No worries, mate, I'll take it off your next bunch.' She turns and continues along the front shouting '*Fresh hórta*!'

I look down at the green slime in my hands as Eleni shakes her head.

'Well at least the *hórta* appears to be free of snail-lime and greenfly,' I say passing the bunch to her.

'That's because of the donkey piss,' she mutters, returning to her kitchen. I hear the clang of a peddle bin and guess that is the end of my organic greens.

I actually can't think of a thing to write and sit there gazing over the water. Something makes me look around and I see the electrician in a white linen shirt and jeans, approaching my table.

'*Kalispéra*, Olivia,' he says, smiling down on me. 'Are you ready for an adventure and something to eat?'

I almost gasp at the beauty of him without all the hair. 'Good evening, Greg. That sounds intriguing. What did you have in mind?'

'A surprise, but you'll have to trust me.'

I see Eleni and Dino at the back of the taverna, both looking my way. Greg holds his hand out, 'Come with me. I'm taking you out in your uncle's boat.'

I take his hand and, conscious of being watched, glance Eleni's way to be met by two beaming grins. 'Your parents seem very happy this evening,' I say.

'Let's give them a wave, then.' We do and Greg chuckles. 'Don't be alarmed, but my mother is probably designing our wedding cake in her head right at this moment.' He laughs at my startled look. 'You should start planning your escape.' He leads me to the swim ladder where *Sofía-María* is moored. 'I'll go first, you follow when I say.' He unties the boat, slips the rope around one of the rungs, then grips it tightly. 'Right, come on down.'

I'm glad I'm wearing flat pumps and a full skirt. He leads me to a bench behind the console and I sit. With the press of a button, the vintage boat – its glossy blue, yellow and red livery gleaming – surges away from the quayside, pushed by a high-powered modern engine. Joyously, I pull my phone out and take a few seconds of video for Uncle. I imagine Sofía sitting with her younger brother, going out to catch fish, the breeze fresh on her skin, as it is on mine.

'You like?' Greg calls over the noise of the engine.

I nod, thanking God I'm wearing waterproof mascara. We head out, past the string of little islands I saw from the ferry on my arrival. My hair whips about my face and my skirt fills and lifts and he laughs and slows the boat. 'Sorry,' he calls. 'I'm eager to get to the taverna.'

'Where are we going, exactly?'

'To one of Turkey's best beach taverna's, just outside Kaş.' He grins again. 'We'll be there in thirty minutes.'

Sea and time fly by in equal measure. Soon, we reach the opposite coast and Greg cuts the engine. We are in a small bay with a curve of pale sand. At one end, a cement wharf juts into the water. Just beyond the beach, I see the taverna, its bamboo walls draped with yellow fishing net and enormous seashells. Storm lanterns hang from the ceiling and candles in jars stand on gingham tablecloths. A fish-shaped sign says: THE WORLD'S BEST FISH TAVERNA. The place appears deserted.

'And for you, the best table in the house,' Greg says, pulling a chair out.

A large olive-skinned man with a full smile and sparkling eyes rushes at Greg with his arms spread. '*Ela*, Gregorius! I think you have forgotten your old friend. Where have you been? And who is this beautiful woman you bring to my humble taverna?'

They hug and slap each other's backs, then Greg introduces me. After the formalities, they exchange a few quiet words in Greek, or Turkish, I'm not sure. Greg turns to me.

'This man is Simonos. His grandfather and great-grandfather were both great friends of your family. They were also the best fishermen on the island of Castellorizo.'

'I'm eager to learn about my family and what happened to them. Why did they leave Castellorizo, Simonos, do you know?'

The two men exchange a glance then stare at the floor. 'Now that's a terrible story, not to be spoken of on an empty stomach,' Greg says. 'So come on, let's order our fish. What's your favourite?'

We study the menu, order, then stroll barefoot along the sand while the food is prepared. He takes my hand. It feels comfortable and I relax. As dusk falls, the lights of Castellorizo twinkle in the distance.

'It looks very different from here, doesn't it?' I say. 'Now I can see just how small the island is.'

Greg nods, scoops my arm up so that it's linked into his. 'They say, if all the Castellorizons come home, the island will sink.' He laughs. 'Can you imagine 30,000 people disembarking all at once? Of course it's impossible.'

'I'm still trying to find out why my family split up the way they did. My great-grandparents and all María's family emigrated to Australia, while Sofía and George went to England.' I look him in the eyes. 'Do you know?'

He hesitates, glances away, then nods towards the rocks at the edge of the cove. 'Look at that!'

A huge bat-like shape shivers its outstretched wings. It appears to be watching us. I gasp at the satanic shape and clutch Greg's arm. 'What on earth is it?' The looming apparition seems menacing in the falling light.

'Don't worry, it's just a cormorant on an old mooring pole, drying his wings after diving for fish. Their roost is just around the rocks.' He tucks his elbow in, trapping my hand between his arm and his torso. I feel the warmth of an inner smile, then curse Andrew for coming into my mind and spoiling the moment. I wonder where he is . . . who he's with. Not that I care.

'The cormorants have chicks so they must feed them. The birds' feathers are slow to dry now the sun's gone down. In an emergency, they wouldn't be able to fly from danger very quickly. But parents take risks to protect their children, don't they?' He stares at the bird. 'Castellorizons will risk their life to save those they love, particularly children. It's been proved, hasn't it?'

I shake my head. 'I don't know . . . has it?'

'Well, yes, with the fire. So many people died saving others.'

There it is again. The fire. Was this the same fire that Uncle mentioned? I try to remember exactly what he said: *The fire, drowning, the submarine.*

201

'Do you have children?' he asks before I can question him.

'No, I hope to one day, but my divorce has just come through after seven years of marriage, so I'm feeling a little emotionally battered. You know what I mean?'

'No, I never got that far. I was engaged, but she ran off with an Italian film producer.' His eyes narrow and he mutters, '*Bastardo!*' under his breath.

'Hard luck, but perhaps it's for the best. At least, that's what I keep telling myself. It's still terribly painful, though. All that love, gone to waste.'

He drops his head slightly to one side and peers at me. 'You really understand.'

I smile sadly and nod. 'Better not to be married than married to the wrong person.'

A whistle comes from the taverna and we both look up to see Simonos waving his arms above his head. 'Come, the food's ready,' Greg says.

* * *

'Thanks for a wonderful evening. It's been very special to eat with the sound of lapping waves as background music.'

'I agree,' he says. 'Can I kiss you before we return?'

Goodness, nobody's ever asked me before. How charming. I don't even answer, just step closer and turn my face up to meet his. My first kiss since Andrew and how wonderful it is. I find myself leaning into his embrace, losing myself in the kiss.

When we finally break apart, he whispers, 'We'd better head back or I shan't be responsible for my actions.'

CHAPTER 24
SOFIA

Castellorizo, Greece, 1943

MAMÁ DISHED OUT THE FOOD. Chicken-flavoured rice and cactus pads. Sofía's mind was on Jamie as she spooned food into the toddler Emre's mouth. Maria was with child, after having five boys in a row: Zafiro, Fevzi, Panayiotis, Emre, and, earlier in the year, little Mikali. Sofía imagined how it would feel when she had her own children. She longed to become a mother. Jamie had been gone for two days and already she ached for his arms around her and longed for his child in her belly.

Uncle Kuríllos barged through the door, shattering Sofía's daydream.

'The *maláka* Italians have changed sides!' Kuríllos yelled. He crossed the room with a striding limp, then threw himself into his chair opposite Babá.

Little Mikali hollered, deafening everyone, and Emre spat out his food.

'What's that?' Babá asked, pointing at an oddly shaped piece of wood in his brother's fist.

'Ah, a gun. I made it for Georgikie.' Young George came running at the sound of his name. 'Here you are, sport. Now you can be a soldier.' George grinned gleefully.

Sofia put Emre sitting up on the big bed and started mopping up the spilt food. 'Does that mean the British will come back, Uncle?' she asked, glancing at the door, imagining, hoping.

Kuríllos chortled. 'Perhaps, Sofía. Who knows? If you're lucky, your soldier might return sooner than you expected, eh? In fact, he might be here already.'

'Babá!' Mamá cried. 'I told you we should get the house made bigger, ready for Sofía and the soldier. You and your *What's the hurry?* You never listen!' She turned to young George who marched up and down the room with an enamel colander wobbling about on his head and the crude gun against his shoulder. 'Georgikie, put that dish back in the cupboard, if it falls it will chip and I'll be angry.'

'Nooo, it's my helmet, I'm a soldier, Mamá!' He pointed the weapon at his mother and cried, 'Ka-ka-ka-ka-ka!'

'Georgikie, you can't shoot your mother,' Babá called. 'Who'll cook dinner if you shoot her?' As is usual with boys, young George continued to do whatever he wanted and the adults looked on, smiling, proud of their offspring. George shot his mother, father, uncle and all the icons, then went outside to shoot his sisters, grandparents and the trees. It was a grand massacre and he had never had so much fun.

* * *

María, pregnant with her fourteenth child, worked on a new perfume order in the distillery with Mamá.

Sofía, surrounded by her sister's children, wondered why everyone in her family had to shout. She longed for a little quiet space to enjoy her daydreams and perhaps even write some poetry. She settled the younger children on the big bed for their nap, then sat on a footstool and knotted a row of tufts in the elaborate carpet. With only one metre left to tie, she hoped to have it finished by the time she and Jamie set up home.

This – the grandest carpet on the island – had simple, symmetrical figures telling the story of their family and its business. Mustafa's schooner was there and the three enormous copper *kazánni* that distilled precious oils. There where myrtle bushes, frangipani and sandalwood trees, bergamot fruits, jasmine flowers and so much more. The magnificent carpet would never lie on a floor. The epic story, depicted in the finest threads, would hang on a wall. In truth, a house would be built around the carpet and word of its magnificence was destined to travel far and wide.

Most of the children were sleeping, the rest played out on the patio. Ayeleen held the end of a rope secured to one of the pine trees. The other girls lined up behind her, taking turns to skip into the turning rope, sing the verse, then run out and join the back of the queue in the shade of the tall tree.

Pretty little butterfly, flitting in the sky so high,
Skip the rope, yes you must try,
And if you trip you mustn't cry.
One, two, three, out.

The two grandmothers looked up from their crocheting and smiled. Five boys in a row meant they were currently up to date with their dowery linen. With everyone's recent hunger satiated by Mustafa's sacks of dried beans and chickpeas, contentment hung in the air.

Babá and Uncle Kuríllos sat outside, playing poker. 'What happened last night, have you heard?' Babá asked. 'There was some shooting, but we guess the culprits were soldiers being soldiers – shooting at bats and rats – nothing unusual.'

'No, you're wrong. At three this morning, the British landed and seized the Italian garrison. Caught the *malákas* off guard.'

205

Babá, silent while he drizzled a little olive oil and salt on a thick slice of cactus, finally shook his head. 'Then why aren't we celebrating? I've a bad feeling that no good will come from this. Remember last time the British landed in '41? What a catastrophe!'

*　*　*

When it came to her living accommodation, Sofía had already thought things through. The next day, she chose a moment when her father and uncle sipped their morning coffee, quiet with their own thoughts. After trimming a row of tufts back with the carpet shears, she gave her mother a sly wink, then approached her uncle. She was his favourite niece and knew she could get anything she wanted from him, if she put her mind to it.

'Uncle, I need to ask your advice.' She plopped herself onto his lap and flung her arms around his neck. 'I'm in a quandary and really don't know what to do. The thing is, you know everything and everyone, so I think perhaps you can advise me.'

He grinned, his one eye sparkling, his other crinkling like a brown paper fan. 'You're a married woman now, Sofía. Is this the way to behave? What are you after?'

'Uncle, shame on you, what makes you think I'm after something?' He opened his mouth to speak, but she quickly slid her hand over it. 'As it happens, I do need your help, darling Uncle.'

'There, what did I tell you?' he said to Babá. 'She's a cunning one, this daughter of yours. You see what educating women does?' He frowned, but there was laughter in his voice. 'I'll bet this little devil in a skirt is still writing in Greek. She'll get us all shot in the end, you watch.' He turned back to Sofía. 'Now, spit it out, what do you want?'

'It's about a house for me and Jamie. So many people are leaving for Australia, I was thinking, perhaps somebody might like their house looked after in case they don't like it on the other side of the world. You know, we could live in their house, rent free, in return for taking care of the place. We'd have a contract drawn up to say we would move out the moment they returned. What do you think, Uncle?'

Kuríllos laughed. 'You have a good business head, Sofía. That's a fine plan. Let me think about it. I'll ask around and find out who's going next.'

'Don't forget the family house, too,' Babá suggested.

'I don't understand, Babá.' Sofía looked puzzled.

'The house that collapsed in the earthquake when you were born,' Kuríllos said. 'We could build you a house there.'

Sofía couldn't believe her luck. 'You are the most terrific uncle!' She kissed his cheek, leapt off his lap, then hid her hair under the brightly embroidered black scarf the married women wore. 'I'm going down to the *plateía* to look.'

'Just be careful – there are disgruntled British and nervous Italian soldiers everywhere. A twitchy man with a gun is a dangerous thing.'

As Sofía opened the door a pistol fired somewhere nearby. She hesitated, glanced around, then hurried down the back streets towards the port.

* * *

She kept her eyes wide, careful to avoid trouble and she succeeded until she reached the back of the square. Just as she turned the second to last corner, a strong hand caught her arm.

'Here, you're a pretty little miss, ain't you!' a coarse voice stated in English. 'Give us a kiss while there ain't nobody lookin'.' He swung her round hard.

As she slammed against his body, her scarf fell about her shoulders and she found herself staring into his pock-marked face.

'Get off!' she said. 'Get off or I'll call my father and he'll shoot you!' She tried to push him away, leaving no doubt to her objection but he had a fistful of her long hair now and she couldn't break away.

''Ere, can't you speak English? I ain't got no clue what you're blabbin' about.'

She could speak English, but in her distress, she couldn't understand his rough accent.

'Stop playin' hard to get, yer little peasant. I 'eard you island girls love it, so pucker up, an' give us a kiss.' His groin gyrated against her but as his round face came close, she stuck out two fingers and jabbed him in the eyes, ducked under his arm and ran.

'Bleedin' cow!' he yelled. 'I'll get you for that!'

Close to tears, Sofía raced around the corner and headed for the square, at the same time trying to retie her scarf. There were British soldiers everywhere. They all looked the same, but she was sure if her Jamie was there, she would recognise him immediately.

'Sofía!'

She swung around hopefully, but it was her uncle.

'Are you all right? You seem upset?' he asked.

'I just tripped, almost fell. Have you seen Jamie? Please, Uncle, I'm so excited, where's the house you told me about?' She wanted to forget the pig who'd accosted her.

'Just there, look. Most of the rubble has gone. It wouldn't take much to build a modern house in its place. Come, let's have a coffee together and talk about it.'

* * *

They sat at a harbourside café table. Soldiers swarmed over the port. Sofía wondered if her new husband was among them. A grey battleship sailed around the point. Beneath a Greek flag, the dull metal monster slid towards the quayside mooring. Locals straightened their skinny bodies and pointed at the vessel with pride and hope in their hearts. The warm autumn air buzzed with excited voices.

'What's happening?' Sofía asked her uncle.

'I don't know. It seems we're being invaded by more British soldiers. Let's hope they do a better job this time.'

He turned to the *kafenzies*. 'What's going on here, sport?'

'The Italians have joined the Allies, so our garrison's about to be reinforced by the British. Gossip says perhaps there are a thousand troops aboard the *Admiral Koundouriotis* – there . . .' He nodded towards the warship. 'I can't say I'm happy about it. Not one bit.'

'What! After all this time under that fascist bastard, Mussolini, you're unhappy. Why? What do you want, blood?'

'Oh, there'll be blood all right,' the *kafenzies* said. 'If you were Hitler, angry because the Italians joined the Allies, then you heard a couple of thousand of those Allies were standing on a tiny, defenceless lump of rock in the Mediterranean, miles from any military support, what would you do?' Kuríllos shrugged and waited for his friend's opinion. 'You'd bomb the place off the face of the earth, that's what you'd do. Kill every soldier, wreck every ship, murder every man, woman and child. And you know what? We wouldn't stand a chance.'

As he spoke, Sofía watched two dull battleships – flying the French flag – anchor just outside the harbour entrance.

The *kafenzies* continued. 'Look, here come *Koundourioti*'s escort, anchored outside the bay in full view, just to make us an easier target for the Axis.' He shook his head. 'Makes you wonder about the mentality of those in charge. Have they any idea – any brains at all?'

Sofía and her uncle stared at the ships, then glanced up at the clear blue sky. Surely he was wrong?

The *kafenzies* coughed and spat. 'Thanks to the cement ship that unloaded at dawn, everyone's eating grey dust and cursing Churchill for wanting to turn our homeland into a refuelling station for his fleet. Look at all the military here, we're overrun! Who's going to feed them? So many ships have run out of fuel on their way to Cyprus recently, the Allies have decided to build bigger fuel silos for their navy, right here at the port. We'll be living on a bomb! Look, here comes the convoy. Why don't we just surrender, save the bloodshed and the sunken ships? Or we could send Mein Führer an invitation? Or – I know! – we could save him the trip and all just shoot ourselves in the head!'

Sofía sipped the coffee and peered at the soldiers, hoping to catch a glimpse of her new husband, yet secretly terrified that she might not recognise him.

She glanced around, remembering how she used to play with other children, on the quayside, before the war. Plump children, boisterous and noisy with laughter. Fat Nathaniel with his dimpled knees, sticky-fingered Sonia, the baker's daughter, always sharing her sweet treats. Naughty Manno with a wedge of Castellorizo pie stuffed into his pocket, making a greasy patch on his short trousers. Everyone had a little glass bottle of water with a blob of white sugar paste floating around and when it was empty, they'd fill it from the local tap. Happy carefree days filled with laughter.

She blinked the daydream away. Now, a very different scene surrounded the port. Fat Nathaniel, now lean and strong, was in the Greek army but his younger sister, five-year-old Doris, sat listlessly on the kerb with no energy to play. Dark circles under her eyes and a pot belly protruding from under bony ribs told of the malnourishment in her family. Sofía decided to take them a bag of rice later.

'The people are starving to death, Uncle,' she said. 'I can't stand to see it. What can we do to help little Doris over there?'

He shook his head, the mischief falling from his face. 'Her father's gone to Australia to find work and set up home for his family. The sooner he sends for them the better. Things weren't so bad when he left. He doesn't know what his family's going through now.'

'Why doesn't his wife write to him and tell him?'

Kuríllos shrugged. 'Because, like half the women here, she can't read or write and neither can he. Also, I'm not sure that she knows where he is. They say Australia's more than a hundred times bigger than this place. Besides, the boat takes six weeks there and longer to come back. I doubt Doris will last another month, do you?'

'Thanks for the coffee, Uncle. I must talk to Anastasia, see if we can't help the illiterate adults. Will you keep an eye out for my Jamie?'

Kuríllos roared with laughter. 'I will, don't worry.'

'Do you think he might be here? You can't imagine how much I hope he is.' Suddenly, she was full of tears, her heart breaking so violently she could hardly speak. 'Each day, I wonder where he is, what he's doing, if he's in danger and so on. Mostly, I imagine he's with me, by my side. But what if he never comes back?' A sob escaped. 'Each morning, I think of him when I choose which dress to put on. I imagine him in my bed, looking at me and liking my clothes and it's so important that he does,

211

because, you see, each day I pray: this will be the day my Jamie returns home.'

'You are in love, Sofia, and love is never easy.'

She blinked at him, realising he understood. 'This seems really stupid; I hope he likes what I sing while I'm working, because I'm singing for him. I even talk to him in my head. I must do that, you see, to get through another day without him. Mikró Yiayá says love is a worm in my heart and it will eat me up from the inside and drive me mad. Do you think she's right, Uncle? It certainly feels that way.'

His laughter faded, his face softening. 'I think it is perfectly lovely. He's an extremely lucky young man to have a beautiful wife who cares so much.' He stared out over the sea. 'I understand how you feel, Sofía, because it was the same for me.' He turned and looked into her eyes, hesitating for a moment. 'I loved my beautiful black-eyed Isabella with her dark hair as straight and glossy as waxed silk. We were betrothed when she was fifteen and were to be married when she was sixteen.'

'You were? I didn't know this. What happened, Uncle?'

Kuríllos turned his attention to the ground at his feet. 'Her family would not let their perfect and very beautiful daughter marry a one-eyed-man, of course. So, after the dynamite accident, her father cancelled the betrothal. I could get over losing my eye, but losing Isabella, no way! We planned to run away together, but her brothers found out and came to visit me. They explained with their fists and a length of lead pipe that Isabella wasn't allowed to marry a man who was less than perfect.

'Foolishly, I said nothing would keep me away from her – me and my big mouth. They broke both my legs.' He slid his hands back and forth over his knees for a second and frowned. 'They'd already sent her to live with an aunt in Crete. She would be married there to an upstanding Cretan with two eyes and no limp. It was a year before I could walk without sticks again. I went to find her – planned to run away with her; we loved each other so much.'

After a silent moment when he seemed lost in his thoughts, Sofía asked, 'What happened then, Uncle?'

He looked up, seeming slightly startled to be pulled out of his thoughts. 'I was too late. Clearly, she was with child already. I stayed hidden and watched her from afar.' He sniffed hard. 'She seemed happy enough.' He stared into the distance, silent again. When he spoke next his voice was heavy though he wore a smile and his eye shone brightly. 'So, you see, I like the ladies a lot, Sofía, but there'll never be another true love for me. Isabella took my heart with her and I was glad to give it.' He glanced at the sky. 'Unfortunately, she died in childbirth not too long after I saw her, but one day I know we'll be together again.' He lifted his head and stared at the horizon. 'So when I die, promise you will celebrate for me, Sofía, because I will be happy in the arms of my Isabella once again.'

She nodded. 'I promise, Uncle, but what a sad story.' Sofía felt his pain in her heart. After sitting with him for a while, she set off for the teacher's house in the next bay.

CHAPTER 25
OLIVIA

Castellorizo, Greece, present day

I CHECK THE TIME WHEN I get to Eleni's for morning coffee and see it's too early to call Uncle.

'You want to meet with the lawyer now?' Eleni asks, pulling a chair out and sitting at my table. She has a quizzical look in her eye that makes me laugh.

'That will be great, Eleni. And it's no good looking at me like that, I'm not telling you anything about my lovely evening with your son.'

She tries to flatten her smile, but fails. 'So, you had good times. The lawyer, he's coming to eat here.' She glances at my notebook which lies open on the table. 'I'll leave you to your work.'

Remembering I had a plan to write a recipe every day, I realise I haven't decided on a pudding selection for my cookery book. The *galaktoboureko* comes to mind and I start writing about this delicious, syrupy, egg-custard wrapped in crisp, golden, filo pastry – but I lose my concentration and end up gazing over the water once again.

Eleni's voice bursts my bubble. 'Olivia, excuse me, here's our lawyer. Andoni Rodakinos. He speaks perfect English and will give you plenty of help.'

I look up and offer my hand. 'Pleased to meet you, Mr Rodakinos. Please take a seat.'

The tall, wide-shouldered man is a little older than me. Horn-rimmed glasses, handsome in your typical, brown-eyed Greek way. Olive-skinned, with dark hair and long lashes. He sits opposite me.

'I'm pleased to help you, madam,' he says formally. 'We have too many abandoned houses on this beautiful island. I feel it's my duty to connect those properties with their rightful owners.' He smiles a practised business-like smile with no sign of joy or amusement. 'It's very satisfying to see houses restored and occupied again. Slowly, over several generations, life is returning to Castellorizo.'

'Please, call me Olivia.'

Eleni brings two glasses of ouzo, a jug of iced water, and a little dish containing four dips: tzatziki, hummus, fava, and taramasalata. She also produces a small basket of finger-sized, home-made, olive-bread sticks.

We chat for a while – about my first time in Castellorizo, beautiful weather, amazing turtles and so on – enjoying the ouzo and dips as we do so. Soon, we both feel comfortable tackling the subject of buying property on the island.

'From what I've been told, it won't be easy or cheap to establish ownership. Is that true?' I ask. 'I've limited funds. By the way, thanks for coming to meet me like this. I could have made an appointment with your office.'

'My office is in Rhodes, where I live. This island's too small to warrant a full-time legal office. I'm only here on vacation.'

'And I've interrupted your holiday, oh dear, I'm sorry. I'm in Rhodes next week, I can come to see you there.'

'Thank you. But tell me which property you're looking at?'

'It belongs to the Konstantinidis family. The big house with the distillery at the back of the town.'

'I see. It's suddenly drawing considerable attention. Do you know of any conflicting interest?'

'My second cousin is here and I believe – though I don't know for sure – he has claim to a very small fraction of the property and I have agreed to buy that part from him if possible.'

'This is not the information he gave to me. He's claiming the property outright.'

'What?' I find myself wide-eyed and blinking rapidly. How dare he mislead me? I explain to the lawyer: 'As far as I know, the property was left to two sisters, María and Sofía, and their brother George. Sofía was my grandmother and she made a will leaving all her property to me as her only direct descendant. I believe Uncle has also bequeathed his property to me. I'm trying to get hold of him at the moment to confirm this. If my theory's correct, the remaining third goes to María's sixteen children, who in turn have had many children themselves, so I have offered to buy that share. A total of one-third of whatever the property is valued at.'

'According to the gentleman, the entire property belongs to María, as she was the eldest daughter. He does have legal documents from all her immediate living descendants giving him power of attorney in this matter of property inheritance.'

My jaw drops. All this time, Rob has deliberately deceived me. I feel sick to my stomach. 'How many descendants of María Konstantinidis are there, do you know?'

'Yes, we do have a list. Although some of her children died in the tragedy—'

'Tragedy? What tragedy?'

'Ah, you don't know, some lives were lost in 1945. It's a big story. Well, besides that, the Castellorizons are renowned for having big families. Currently, the average is five children, but

Maria, well, that's another story. The first of María's sixteen children was born in 1930 and in turn María became a grandmother in 1949 and a great-grandmother 1969. Now, it appears there are a total of 1,026 Australian descendants from María.'

Once again, I realise my mouth is hanging open. 'Good God! It's hard to imagine so many children.'

'Yes, it is, however, they do have their own website, so you can actually contact them yourself.' He glances at my phone. 'I'm sure they'd love any live video you upload while you're here.'

'Good idea, thanks. So it's me against all of them?'

He nods. 'One other thing: if you insist on staking your claim to the property through the courts, your second cousin tells me he's going to press for expenses. With so many people involved, that bill could far exceed the value of the property. The easiest solution is to work on an agreement with him and have it registered with a notary. In fact, I'd do that before trying to proceed with the property. I'll suggest the same thing to him.'

* * *

Seething, I storm past Eleni. She calls me over. '*Ela*, what's going on? You look like you will kill somebody.'

'I could do just that! Rob is a snake and he's determined to open his nightclub or hotel using the property that belongs to my family!'

'Do not get upset. The people of Castellorizo will not allow it, Olivia.'

'I could kill him! I'm so furious I can't even think straight. I'm going to run up those steps to the top of the cliff, to vent my anger, before I phone England or confront Rob. At this moment, I really do want to kill him! I'll see you later, Eleni.'

She pats my shoulder placatingly and says, 'Remember the turtle.'

* * *

Back in my room I change into shorts and tee, then pull on a pair of trainers. I head for the cliff at the back of town. The sign claims it takes an hour to reach the top via zigzagging steps. Breathless by the time I reach a plaque that tells me I'm halfway, I stop for a breather.

Below, the small town is less than a square mile of picturesque dolls' houses divided by a wedge of harbour. To the right, I gaze upon the dilapidated castle flying its statement Greek flag. Nearer the water a red-domed mosque has a startling white minaret that points to the sky like a new candle. Further to the right lies the bay of Mandraki, shallow and turquoise with clumps of waving sea-grass and sun-sparks flashing off the water. There is an empty curve of beach. A gallery of picturesque images, so perfectly peaceful one could weep with joy. On the far reach of Mandraki lay the cemetery with its iconic little chapel and beyond that, a short promontory that I know to be Nifti Point.

I must say goodbye to my mother. Sadness replaces my anger. I haven't thought about her for a week. Her urn stands in the bottom of my wardrobe and I ache for one of her hugs. I grip my own shoulders and pull on them, imagining her tight embrace. Suddenly overcome by grief, a howl of sadness escapes, taking my soul-destroying desolation with it. Breathless and sobbing I remember her kindness above all else. 'I'll always love you, Mummy,' I whisper. 'I wish you were with me, here on the island of your ancestors.'

I realise this is the perfect place to clear my head and decide on a plan. I glance down at the amazing view once more. The light has sharpened, giving a clean sparkle to everything. I notice the birdsong, away from the town and only now realise they are silent in the heat of midday. Feeling in harmony with my surroundings, I sit on the steps and take stock of my situation.

* * *

'Olivia!' On hearing my name rising from the bottom of the steps, I swing around and catch sight of my great-uncle below me! Breathless after jogging down the steps, I throw my arms about him.

'Uncle, what are you doing here? I've been calling you.' I give him a gentle hug. 'I've been so worried. How are you?'

'A bit shaky, but OK. Help me go up to the next turning. I'd like to see the view again.'

'If you're sure you're up to it so soon. Perhaps we should wait a few days?'

He shakes his head. 'You have to trust me to know what I'm capable of. After all, I don't want to die either.' He grins at me, and I see he's right. We link arms and ascend a few steps.

'That's enough,' he says. Resting his forearms on the rail, he peers out over the harbour. 'The view's magnificent. Did you go up to the top?'

I shake my head. 'Tell me about this place.' I wave my hand, indicating the town. 'What do you remember?'

As he stares over the harbour, his face pales and his skin seems to tighten, then his hand trembles as he puts his fingertips to his lips. 'All those poor souls; what a terrible thing to

219

happen. The warmongers have a lot to answer for, Olivia, and most of you people don't know the half of it. Don't know and don't care. Actually . . . without wanting to sound too unkind, it's ironic that I've come to love that country of yours, after everything that it did to mine. But it was wartime and one can only believe people were doing their best.'

'How do you mean, what did the British do to Castellorizo?'

'They used it as a refuelling port between Rhodes and Cyprus. To be fair, if they hadn't, the Germans would have. We were destined to be occupied. At least the Brits got us off the island once the bombing started – and they were on our side. Their brave young men were fighting and dying for Greece.'

I can hear sincerity in his voice and deep sadness. I'm tempted to interrogate him, but sense it wouldn't be appropriate now, so I stand with him and stare across at the port. He glances at the Turkish coastline, then back to the harbour again, but he isn't admiring the view. He is staring into the past and putting the events of history in place. His eyes narrow and his chin trembles.

'One third of the town – all that side—' he gestures with his left hand '—was flattened by two days of German bombing. Those Stukas made the most awful screaming sound – terrified us all. We helped our neighbours sift through the rubble for bodies and valuables, not that there was any treasure. The Castellorizons were starving to death and had already sold all they could to buy basic foods. Women keened as the dead were uncovered and carried to the cemetery over there, in Mandraki.' He waves his right hand, indicating the direction. 'A terrible time.'

After a moment's silence, he continues. 'Five or six days later, a British ship came to shuttle us to Cyprus in three groups. Men with houses still standing nailed their shutters and doors closed

220

to keep out animals and squatters. The sound of hammering echoed all over town. Though I was only a child, I remember the hard expressions on everyone's faces. You knew not to mess with grown-ups when they had that look. Some had lost children or parents in the bombing . . . that awful bombing . . . The place was in ruins. In my nightmares, I still hear the scream of the fighter planes and see the blind terror in everyone's eyes as they peered up, fearing for their precious families. And poor Sofía, out there in the thick of it.'

'My grandmother was out in the bombing? I can't imagine how awful it must have been. How many people lived here then?'

'I don't know, more than a thousand, less than two. We were in the first group to be taken off the island. The day our ship left for Cyprus, I was so tired. We seemed to have been at the port forever. Nobody told us that ship would only leave under cover of darkness. Fear of the bombs had kept me awake most nights. It had been almost a week since the first bombing. I went through to the distillery and lay on a sack of myrtle leaves. I was only five or six years old, but I remember not wanting to go on the big boat.

'Everyone on the ship – children and some adults, too – were shouting or wailing. Others were still rolling bales of clothing or bedding towards the port. María had a baby on her breast and one on her back and we realised later there was one in her belly too. Sofía had a blanket full of pans and utensils on her back and used one hand to balance a sewing machine on her head. Can you believe it? A sewing machine! I recall thinking the weight might snap her neck.

'Some women were hysterical, trying to find their children. Everyone was herded onto that grey metal ship. Ayeleen was crying loudly until Mamá slapped her face, then hugged her. We were on the ship most of the day, though it never moved. I remember how much I wanted to stay at home.' He blinks, gasps and returns to now. Seeming surprised to realise where he is, he ends the story. 'Anyway, it was so long ago, I must be boring you.'

'Not at all.'

'Let's go and drink coffee. I have some catching up to do with my friends.'

CHAPTER 26
SOFIA

Castellorizo, Greece, 1943

SOFÍA WAS THINKING ABOUT WHAT to suggest to Anastasia, her greatest friend, about teaching local adults to read and write. She felt herself glow with pleasure at the prospect of seeing her outside school time. Anastasia had shown Sofía such respect and given her the opportunity to become a part-time teacher. If Anastasia had been a man, Sofía might have fallen in love with him before she'd met Jamie Peters.

Despite the sad circumstances of Doris and her starving family, which was the reason for her visit, she was pleased to have something important to discuss.

British soldiers swarmed everywhere, but when she searched their faces, looking for her Jamie, they all got the wrong idea. Her cheeks were set aflame by winks and wolf-whistles and impolite remarks. Some rubbed the front of their trousers and shouted, 'Come, come, I've got something for you.' How she hated them and wished she had an older brother at her side.

She arrived in Mandraki panting, greased with sweat and almost in tears. Her heart thudded as if trying to beat its way out of her chest and just as she hurled herself at the teacher's door, Anastasia opened it.

'Sofía, look at you . . . what on earth . . .?' She spread her arms and Sofía threw herself into them and broke down. 'Come on, let it all out,' the teacher said softly after kissing the top of her head and hugging her affectionately. 'Tell me, who's upset you?'

'The soldiers! I hate them, *malákas!*' She swore for the first time in her life, instinctively ducking in the expectation of a swipe from her mother or father, though they weren't there. It felt so good! '*Malákas, malákas, malákas!*' she crowed.

Anastasia laughed heartily, pulled away and cried, 'That's the way to do it!' With their hands on each other's shoulders, they skipped a polka in front of the cottage. Around and around they went, crying the swear word, which meant *wankers*. When dizziness got the better of them both, they collapsed onto a bench against the front of the house and laughed real tears.

Anastasia took Sofía's hands and stared into her face with sparkling eyes. 'Better?'

Sofía, exhausted yet cleansed, gazed at the teacher and said, 'Yes, thank you. I love you, miss.'

'I know,' Anastasia said quietly, squeezing her shoulders, then smudging a tear from Sofía's cheek. 'But it will pass when your soldier returns.' She smiled sadly. 'Now, come on, tell me why you came over.'

Sofía related the story of little Doris and all the adults on the island who could not read or write. After a short discussion they decided to provide a free letter-writing service, under the disguise of adults helping their children to learn the Greek alphabet, which had been against the Italian law. Through this pretext, adults could come to the school with their heads held high.

'You've reminded me. I've got some rusks that I don't need, Sofía. If you wouldn't mind, hurry back to the port while she's there and give them to Doris, for her mother. I fear the poor woman has nothing for her children today and it's almost two o'clock already.'

'Of course, I'll be happy to. I could go home with her, actually and explain that we can find a way to help her to write to her husband.'

* * *

Sofía was on the highest land in the port area, with the teacher's cottage behind her in the little bay of Mandraki and the commercial harbour, spread out before her. The family home and the distillery were against the cliff to her left and the ancient castle, the mosque and the lighthouse to her right. There seemed far fewer soldiers now and she thought perhaps they were eating, though she could not imagine what.

October was one of Sofía's favourite months. The summer wind and stifling heat had subsided and a recent shower rinsed the dust off buildings and vegetation. The sky, blue as it could be, was reflected in the calm sea. The water added its own painterly hues including every delicate shade of green in the distance through to sparkling turquoise in the port. She stopped and gazed about, enjoying the beauty of her homeland. War or not, surely Castellorizo was the nearest one could get to heaven on earth.

She heard a distant hum, at first thinking a wasps' nest may be near her feet. The noise turned into a drone, then a deep and menacing rumble that stirred unease in her chest. She scanned the sky for planes, then the sea for warships, but nothing appeared to be moving.

Near the castle ruins, a British soldier manned the anti-aircraft gun. He, too, seemed suddenly alert, swivelling the long-barrelled apparatus on its gimlet. A soldier next to him raised a pair of binoculars and scanned the sky. They both pulled on their tin helmets and something about their tense stance told Sofía of their unease. She scanned the sky again, her eyes watering because of the bright light. The menacing rumble grew louder and louder until it filled her head, making it impossible to think, although now she was sure the noise came from approaching planes.

She prayed they were British aircraft, but then recalled the *kafenzies* and his forecast of an apocalypse. A small movement seemed to come directly from the sun's dazzling centre and in a single moment, everything changed.

Like angry hornets, the planes suddenly thundered into view over the clifftop. They swarmed over the port with a petrifying incessant shriek. Sofía's blood curdled and her feet remained rooted to the ground. The unbearable screaming shattered into deafening blasts of exploding bombs. She pressed her hands against her ears, but so intense was the noise, she could not block it out. The air was shredded with such violence that everything quivered. Sofía was stricken by fear.

Below, on the other side of the harbour, a line of buildings dropped like dominoes. One after the other, they disappeared in clouds of dust and rubble that lifted on the warm air and then hailed down like machine-gun fire. Trembling, unable to move, aware that urine gushed down her legs, Sofía stared at the devastation. A plane screamed past her, so closely she could see the pilot in his leather flying helmet and goggles, on his approach. The vibration of the Stuka engines ran through her like a dropped stitch in a knitted blanket. A Stuka U-turned straight back up towards the sun. A second later, another bomb wreaked havoc perilously close to her home. A great slice of the cliff behind her house fell, perhaps onto the distillery or even the house, she couldn't make out exactly for the instantly rising dust.

All our children! Oh God! The children, my family!

The urge to get back, irresistibly powerful, meant she was running so fast her feet never touched the ground. In her mind, she flew towards her home, towards those she loved, towards her family that depended on her. Yet, the awful shock came in a blink – her feet, in fact, had not moved. Sofía found herself paralysed by shock and terror. Dust from the bomb had dissipated, revealing bodies scattered on the opposite quayside. Over the loud whistling in her ears, she heard the soldier who was staffing the anti-aircraft gun hammering missiles into the sky, as another plane approached.

Movement on this side of the harbour caught her attention. Little Doris, hysterical, ran in a circle, her scream primal and without words, yet she was clearly calling for her mother in the most basic way known to all creatures. The soldier with the binoculars, twenty metres to Sofía's left, had also seen the child. He leapt down, bounding over walls and skidding down stepped streets until he scooped her up. She clung to his neck, still screaming. He put his tin helmet on her head and ran towards the mosque.

With the next explosion, rubble and grit flew at Sofía like bullets. Blood trickled into her eyes, blurring everything. Her left eardrum burst and she lost her sense of balance. The chaos around her became stony silence for seconds with only the bone-shaking vibrations assaulting her senses. Then, her other ear compensated, picking up the smallest noise with great sensitivity. She slammed her hands against the sides of her head again. Her mouth filled with the coppery taste of fear at the same time as the chicory coffee decided to leave her stomach.

A plane screamed through the air at terrifying speed, so close it spun Sofía around before the downdraught threw her to the ground. She moved her hands over the back of her head and squeezed her eyes tightly closed, trying to block out the image that, in a split second, had stamped itself into her brain. An image that would sear itself onto the backs of her eyes and never leave her.

No! No! No!

Yet she saw it again: a flickering horror movie repeating the same scene over and over as she spun around. Anastasia was running out of her cottage as if the devil himself were after her. Her beautiful face contorted with fear. She waved both hands over her head as she mouthed, 'Get down, Sofía! Get down!' Though the words were silent over that distance and in the din of the rampant assault, the urgency hit Sofía and she understood the teacher's fear.

The next instant would also leave its indelible mark. Sofia collapsed in tears of sadness, whimpering, '*Anastasia . . .*' In that screaming, howling, instant – that belch of fire and a deafening explosion of rocks – that direct hit which blew Anastasia and the cottage from the face of the earth forever.

All that remained were Sofía's heartfelt words hanging in the dust. *I love you, miss.* And the ghost of Anastasia's fingertips brushing Sofía's tears away as she whispered, *I know.* This nightmare was more than Sofía could bear. She lay on the ground, quaking in terror as Castellorizo exploded all around her. She heard nothing but a high-pitched whistling and felt the stickiness of blood on the back of her head as she sank into a black abyss.

* * *

Who could say how much time had passed before Sofía drifted up from that murky silence? Her first conscious thought was that perhaps she had died. In the darkness, she peered around, searching for the light of God, which she was certain would be waiting for her when the time came. Then, the pain that radiated from the back of her head told her she was very much alive. A buzzing sensation in her ears and distant, muted sounds as if she were swimming under water raised her suspicion of deafness. To open her eyes had been a struggle. Within the mumble of sound, she recognised the distraught wailing of her mother's voice, dull and distant as it was. She cupped her hand around her ear to try and orient herself and in doing so, realised her ear was bleeding.

Anastasia . . . Oh, Anastasia . . . I love you, miss.

Sofía didn't know if she was crying or not, only that her heart was broken and her soul was sobbing for the teacher. She pulled herself onto her hands and knees and found herself facing where the teacher's cottage had stood. The dull sounds that she picked up were from her family and friends who knew she had gone to see the teacher – pierced by the most heart-wrenching howling from her mother.

'Sofeeea! Sofeeea!' Mamá screamed as she lifted gigantic slaps of masonry and rocks, tossing them aside as if weightless. Then a man's voice, her father, she realised, boomed through the night, 'Sofía, damn it! Sofía!' followed by a cry of anguish. Both figures were silhouetted by the silvery sea like some gothic shadow theatre.

Sofía couldn't bear to see her parents in such distress. She tried to call them, but couldn't marshal her voice.

Mamá screeched, 'She's here! God and all the angels! Her hand, oh, the blessed hand of my dead child! I've uncovered my daughter's hand!'

'I'm here!' Sofía tried to shout. 'That's Anastasia's hand, Mamá!' But her sobbing wouldn't allow her to say anything, let alone call out over such a distance. Desperate to end her parents' grief, she pushed herself to her feet, but the world tilted and she immediately fell back to her knees. Her eyes, now accustomed to the dim, dust-thick light, caught a rope hanging against a wall to her left. The little chapel of Saint Nicholas's bell rope, she realised, grabbing it to haul herself up. The bell clanged above her. She pulled again, repeatedly. Someone shone a torch in her direction, people were shouting, 'Miracle! Miracle! Jesus, God and all the saints, it's a holy miracle! Saint Nikolas has snatched Sofía from heaven's gate and brought her back to us!'

People rushed around the narrow bay, then scrambled up the slope until Sofía found herself surrounded by family and friends, crossing themselves and muttering prayers of thanks. Babá kissed his daughter's face, squeezed her shoulders and arms though she winced with pain. Hardly able to believe what he saw, he gazed at her from his tear-streaked face. When they realised she'd lost her sense of balance, Babá and Uncle Kuríllos slung her arms around their shoulders and walked her home. Mamá, assisted by the other mothers who were helping to search, followed, all crying their thanks to God.

Word spread like lightning. Before the family reached home, Kiki, the cobbler's wife, rushed up to Mamá while tearing her hair and screeching. '*Kiriea! Kiriea!* Please! Pray for my son, Pavlo. God listens to you! Please, Pavlo is missing, my dear Pavlo. My only boy.' She fell to her knees at Mamá's feet, kissing the hem of her skirt and rocking back and forth. Tears streamed down the distraught woman's face. 'Please, *Kiriea*, please! They say the bomb fell on him. I'm begging you. Ask God and Saint Nikolaos to send him home. He's seventeen – just seventeen, the same as your Sofía! What would the Almighty want with a seventeen-year-old? Ask Jesus Christ to send him back, like your Sofía, while I go and toll that same church bell.'

Mamá opened her arms and took Kiki to her bosom. The two women cried on each other's shoulders, the one with relief, the other hysterical with desperation.

'She's a saint,' somebody cried. 'First she stopped the earthquake, now she's stopped the bombing!'

* * *

The funeral bell tolled all night, the dull, monotonous knell beating time for the lives lost to the bombs, that afternoon and evening. Many more were seriously injured. Two dozen family homes had disintegrated to rubble and a great number were seriously damaged. Six Stukas and two escort planes had executed the attack and the British expected them back.

Through the hours of darkness, the powers-that-be made decisions that would irreversibly affect every one of the Castellorizons. As dawn broke, the heads of the army came up one side of the port, informing householders of the decision and the mayor and town council, including Babá, came up the other side, knocking on doors and reiterating the government's plan.

'We fear another attack from the Axis. Pack your valuables and gather your family. For your own safety, a ship is coming to take you all to a safer place, probably Cyprus if they can accommodate the whole island until this war is over,' the officials stated.

Naturally, people asked, 'How long will we be away?' expecting the authorities to answer the impossible question with certainty.

What they received was a non-committal shrug. 'How can we know? Until the war's over. We've the Italians on our side now

231

and Churchill says the Americans are coming. We hope the war will end tomorrow. Surely, it will end soon,' they said. 'But we want you safe. This devastation must never happen again, so pack all your essentials and valuables – all you can carry – and close up your houses.'

Men consoled their distraught wives and children by saying they would not be gone for long, and, being hopeful for the end of the war, convinced themselves this was so. Yet livestock was set free, or killed and the meat salted; and tools of their trade such as farriers' irons and cobblers' lasts were packed along with the doctor's bag and the barber's apparel.

Bedding bails and bundles of clothes piled high on the quayside. Sack-trucks were trundled down from plots and chicken sheds to move cauldrons full of kitchenware. Mamá poured all the dried corn, beans and lentils into pillowcases and hurriedly stitched them closed. Questions ran like rivers. Did they need winter clothes? How could they secure their houses when most didn't have locks? Did they have to go to Cyprus or could they head elsewhere if they had another place of safety? Many locals owned a small farmhouse and land in Kaş, for example, and most of those left for Turkey immediately, filling their small boats with their chattels and children, fearing another raid.

The British said it was easier for everyone if they stayed together; however, it was a free country and if they had somewhere else to go, that was permitted.

* * *

At ten o'clock the following day, the terror returned when twelve Junkers Ju 88s wreaked havoc on the island with a repetition of the heavy bombing. The entire Konstantinidis family

232

hurried into the cellar, praying their goods, already lined up on the quayside, would not be blown to smithereens.

Many houses collapsed under this fierce and persistent bombing and more lives were taken. Hundreds of soldiers and residents suffered injuries and the death toll rose to thirty-eight. Some families sailed over to neutral Turkey while they waited for the British boats. Others put their faith in God, choosing to postpone their departure from Castellorizo until the evacuation to Cyprus.

The first transporter arrived five days later, on 23 October. This gave the local families more time to assemble and pack possessions and organise the closing-up of their houses. The strongest men banded together to help their neighbours whose homes had been demolished. Rubble was shifted and meagre valuables and sentimental treasures were recovered. Grateful women wept to have their traditional costumes returned to them from beneath the debris.

The dead were hurriedly buried, taking all the available space in the local cemetery. Prayers said and tears shed didn't distract from the mourners' nervous preoccupation with the sky and their exposed situation. People stacked all their belongings on the quayside. After four fearful nights they were ready for the British ship that would save them from further raids.

The following day, the island was unusually quiet. Everyone's ears strained towards the sound of aircraft. Grieving families uttered prayers for the dead and more chattels were added to the gathered heaps at the water's edge. People peered out to sea, hoping to spot their rescuing vessel approach, bringing certain salvation.

CHAPTER 27
OLIVIA

Castellorizo, Greece, present day

UNCLE SITS OPPOSITE ME AT a harbourside table. He's occupied with his Greek coffee and his sketchpad and pencils. There's a contented silence between us. A turtle pops its periscope head out of the water as if to greet the morning, then drifts carelessly past. I'm suspicious that the serene stillness is too good to last. Yet I sense it has always been like this. With less than a dozen vehicles on the island and no industry, the air has a special quality. It's more than clean, perfumed by nature, the trees, earth and abundant flora. An island of contrasts, of tradition and of values. I realise that silence is one of the greatest commodities on earth, unfortunately nearing extinction in the larger towns and cities.

The dull-grey navy vessel on the opposite port side breaks the peace. A shrill whistle sounds, an anchor chain rattles noisily, everyone stops to watch. About to make space for the Rhodes ferry, at the island's only large anchorage, the battle-ship manoeuvres with precision. The vessel reverses towards the harbourside church, then steams ahead out of the port. I find the contrast of this dull-grey warship a poignant contrast to the small wooden fishing boats in their vivid livery. Drawn to the magnificent church, Saint George of the Well, I see Uncle check his watch as the bell clangs ten o'clock.

'The ferry's early,' he mutters. 'Pleasing to think another glut of tourists will grace the island for a few days. Their hard-earned cash is welcome.'

'What draws them here when there are so many other unique Greek islands, Uncle?'

'The food, quaint rooms and trips to the blue grotto cave. Also, we have two museums worth a visit, the clearest water, the turtles, the challenge of the cliff steps – and no discotheques.' He smiles to himself. 'They come thinking four days will be enough, but when they leave, most have only ticked one or two things off their list, so they come back, again and again, mostly to be at peace and stare out over the water.

Discotheques – there's a word I haven't heard in a while! The turtle returns, glances a tired eye at Uncle, then continues along the quayside.

'Ah, you're still here, D'Artagnan, old man. I'm glad to see you. It's a little early for calamari, my friend.' Uncle smiles at the turtle, who continues to ignore him. 'Come back after noon and you might get lucky.'

A miniature dark-wood schooner, mirrored perfectly in the surrounding azure water, tootles its hooter to hurry tourists booked for the famous blue cave.

A couple of giggling girls in skimpy shorts and bikini tops jog along the quayside waving and calling to the trip boat, 'Wait! We're here!' They stop, cuddle up for a wide-eyed, pouting, Snapchat-selfie, then hurry on.

Old Castellorizo men hold their little coffee cups and stare with glazed eyes at the young women, admiring the curve of their buttocks and swell of their breasts. They recall the magic of their youth when loose-limbed girls – encumbered by traditional skirts and petticoats like a bundle of washing – fluttered their eyelashes and swung their hips provocatively. Mature Castellorizo women also watch the girls and smile. If only the two tourists realised the power they had at that age.

A big Blue Star ferry glides into view and turns into the harbour. An air of delicious bedlam fills the moment, yet at the same time, a sense of total control and organisation. Unseen on the seabed, the eighty-year-old turtle and its numerous descendants observe everything with stoic acceptance.

'I'd like to visit the house with you, after our coffee, if you don't mind,' Uncle George says. 'It's been so long, I can't wait to see it.'

'Of course, that will be lovely. Is there anything else you'd like to do while you're here?'

'Play *tavli* with my friends, sit in my boat one last time, swim in the harbour, eat octopus hot from the charcoal with a glass of ouzo over ice and watch the sun go down.'

I smile. 'I'm sure all these things can be arranged.'

'I packed some photos for the new album, so we can continue to work through your ancestors' past. Also, I found a few photos of my own and some newspaper cuttings of the disaster.'

'Disaster?'

'Well, some of them. There've been several catastrophes here in my lifetime. Didn't your grandmother ever tell you about them?'

I try to recall, then shake my head. 'Not that I remember. Tell me.'

'For Sofía, the British invasion in '41 was probably the most wonderful thing. She met Jamie, the love of her life, but it set off a chain of events that changed all our lives.'

'Jamie . . . my grandfather?'

Uncle hesitates, then nods. 'That was when the British tried to take the island off the Italians. They failed. The next catastrophe was in '43, when the British occupied the island and we had two days of bombing from the Luftwaffe. Those screaming Stuka aircraft were terrifying! I slept under my bed all the following week. A third of all our houses were destroyed.' He lifts a hand and indicates one side of the harbour. 'All that area, flattened. I've got the newspaper articles. You wouldn't believe the state of this town. At that time, Sofía was writing *The History of Castellorizo*. A jolly good job she did too. From her, I developed my love of history.'

'Sofía sounds as though she was quite a character. It's odd, but you never imagine your grandmother being anything other than your grandmother, do you? It never occurred to me that she had a history . . . a life of her own. Were you spoilt, being the youngest and a boy?'

'I'm not sure I was spoilt, Olivia, though I did get away with a lot. María was always busy with her children and the precious oil. Sofía was teaching in the morning, cooking and sewing and at everyone's beck-and-call through the afternoon and she worked in the distillery in the evening.'

I glance around the harbour of the isolated town. 'It's difficult to imagine life without TV, never mind all the instant entertainment we have today.'

'It was very different, but we entertained ourselves. Babá and Uncle Kuríllos played *tavli* or poker most evenings. Sometimes Kuríllos played his *baglama* while María sang – she had a wonderful voice. Everyone enjoyed watching Rosa practise her ballet. Rosa was so talented, everyone knew she was destined for great things. The grandmothers crocheted, Mamá liked to embroider . . . and so on.'

'And you – what did you do to entertain yourself?'

'Me? Well, I've always been on the arty side. My early childhood was filled with fantasy and as the island had soldiers, I imagined I was one too. I'd leap out from behind bougainvillea to shoot old women with my wooden gun.' He stops to chuckle. 'I felt the back of my father's hand for making Mikró Yiayá wet herself with fright once.' A full-blown laugh escapes him. 'When I was five or six, I had one of those pretend daggers with a rubber blade that disappeared into the handle, so it really looked like you'd stabbed somebody. Wouldn't be permitted these days, of course. Anyway, I imagined myself an assassin, out to kill the evil Russian queen. I hid in the grandmothers' wicker craft-basket and when I saw them sit on the dowry chest to start crocheting, I leapt out and stabbed them both to death.' He rocks back and forth, laughing. 'You never heard so much screaming in all your life! People in the street rushed into the house. I was so proud of myself. Goodness, I couldn't sit down for days for the belt weals across my backside.'

'Really, you were that naughty?' I find it hard to stop laughing.

He raises his eyebrows and laughs some more, nodding proudly. 'Uncle Kuríllos would take me fishing sometimes, but there was another boy I didn't like very much – Zak, he was a bully who would go out with his father at the same time as us. They had a bigger boat and always got the best of the fish. He would rib me about our small boat and nicknamed me Tiddler.

'Everyone was waiting for the sardines to arrive. I heard someone say they were expected at dawn the next day so, that night, I went out and tied an olive sack to the back of his boat by a length of strong twine, then I buried the sack in the sand. We were both moored in Mandraki. We beat them to the shoals because they were unaware of the dragnet they had to pull along too. But my laughter gave the game away and in the end I had to tell Uncle what I'd done.' He wipes his eyes. 'I thought I'd get the belt again, but Uncle Kuríllos kept our secret, though I had to promise never to do it again.'

'You really *were* a naughty boy then. I would never have imagined it.'

'I wasn't the only one, Fevzi was a bit of a devil too. We got up to a lot of pranks together. Now, how about a walk up to the house?'

I push my coffee cup away and stand.

CHAPTER 28
SOFIA

Castellorizo, Greece, 1943

THE DOCTOR HAD SHAVED THE back of Sofía's head and stitched a wound the length of her middle finger. Hearing returned to her right ear the next morning, but the doctor said it would be a few weeks before her left eardrum repaired itself. María and Mamá cleaned her wounds and the Papas, the local priest, paid them a visit asking Sofía many questions about what she remembered of the bombing and its aftermath, which was little.

'It's confusing, Papas. I remember Anastasia sending me back to help little Doris and me telling Anastasia I loved her. I don't know why I did that . . . the words just came, with no help from me.' Sofía battled to keep back her tears. 'The planes came . . . a huge explosion . . . then I remember looking down on little Doris, knowing she was in danger and asking God to keep her safe.'

His mouth fell open slightly as he blinked at her with a curious glimmer in his eyes. 'They found her in the mosque,' he said. Leaning forward, he clutched the crucifix that hung around his neck. 'When you say, you asked God to keep her safe, what do you mean exactly?

'It's a little mystifying, like when a kitten gets in the wool box and tangles all the yarn.'

'Do you remember anything else – hearing voices, or perhaps a bright light?' He gazed at her expectantly. 'What made you ring the church bell?'

'Me, ring the church bell?' Sofía closed her eyes, weary from it all. 'As I recollect, there was a bomb heading for our house.'

With her eyes still closed, she lifted her hand as if to push the missile away. 'I was afraid for my family and prayed. In my mind I . . . well, I sort of made it miss. Although it seems I was wrong. The bomb hit the cliff behind the house instead.'

When she drew back from that awful moment and opened her eyes, the priest appeared slightly alarmed. He crossed himself and continued asking his questions until Sofía interrupted him.

'Anastasia . . . she's dead, isn't she, Papas?'

'She is, child, dead and in heaven, but it was so sudden she wouldn't have known anything about it.'

Sofía shook her head and a sudden deluge of sadness washed over her. 'She knew, Papas. We were together at that moment. Her only fear was for me. She didn't want me to die.'

'I'm told your mother had hold of your hand. She prayed for God not to take you and the next moment, you were alive, on the hill next to the chapel and the bell was ringing.'

'Well . . . it's all a little confusing, father. All I can say is: I was with Anastasia, she told me to go and take care of little Doris . . . then I was falling, as if from a great height. I saw Doris running wild on the quayside, completely terrified. I wanted to help her. I wanted to do what Anastasia had instructed – it seemed very important at the time. Suddenly, I hit the ground so hard it knocked the wind out of me. Mamá was screaming my name, but I was deaf and she was all the way across Mandraki, so I don't know how I heard her. Quite unexpectedly, I found the bell rope in my hand and I knew I had to pull on it. All the time, I was asking for God's help. *God help me, God help me.*'

'It's a miracle, that's what it is, child. A real miracle. We must all thank God for reminding us that there's always hope.'

* * *

The back of the distillery was impassable. The bomb had brought down a wedge of scree, blocking the way. For the first time ever, Babá and Uncle Kuríllos passed through the house door and helped to bottle precious oils, ready for transporting to France. Mustafa would take care of the sales when he returned. The brothers scoured the stills and emptied the hoppers and, although nothing was said, they both realised and appreciated how hard Sofía worked in the distillery.

Departure day arrived. The first of three ships – once belonging to the Italians – tied up to the quayside at daybreak and dropped its huge tailgate. Priority went to those families who had lost their houses in the bombings. Then, it was those with the most children. Naturally the Konstantinidis family headed that list with twenty family members. The family surged forward, carrying chattels and herding children, everyone fretting about something. Taut nerves were apparent, eyes turned to the sky fearing another raid when they gathered on the ship.

The bombed houses on the other side of the harbour were reflected in the still, metallic water, doubling the atmosphere of devastation.

Eager to load their family, then their belongings, they gathered on the quayside at siesta time, hoping to keep the children awake until they were safely aboard. One of María's daughters, Bebe, started tugging at Mamá's hand and bawling for her ragdoll.

Babá picked her up and slung her onto his shoulders, but she continued to wriggle and screech irritably because of her disrupted routine.

'Hey, little one, don't you cry,' one of the soldiers said. 'You'll be back home in a day or two.'

Bebe continued to grizzle. 'Bebe! Did you hear what the soldier said?' Babá yelled, his patience worn out. 'Listen to me, Bebe! The soldiers said we'll be back home in a few days, isn't that perfect? We're just going on an adventure for a couple of days.'

His words were picked up by other families and passed around, the adults sceptical; for how could they possibly come back and risk being bombed again before the end of the war? However, almost every family had lost somebody in the catastrophe and the awful fear that things might get worse made the less astute clutch at any hope and repeat the rumours. The men's desire to pacify their wives and family overruled common sense. Consequently, they allowed the women and children to believe this nonsense of returning in a few days because, by this stage, all the men wanted was to get off the island and keep their family in relative safety.

Everyone knew they couldn't return to Castellorizo until the war was over. Besides this, two days of heavy bombardment, first by six Stukas, and then by twelve Junkers JU 88s had almost flattened the town with their payload of malice and bombs.

*　*　*

Once on the ship, Babá and Kuríllos organised everyone.

'Come on, let's get settled,' Babá insisted. 'We still have to load all our possessions and then secure the house. Ayeleen, go and tell the grandmothers to get on board. They can talk as much as they like on the ship! Fevzi, Zafiro and George, you take care of each other now. Sofía, Mamá and Ayeleen take care of the girls, keep them all together. María, you look after the babies.' He stood with his hands on his hips for a moment, surveying his enormous family, then George ran past him. Babá caught the boy by the back of his collar. 'Where do you think you're going, young man?'

'I left my gun, Babá.'

243

'Well, it's too late now. If we see it when we close the house, I'll bring it for you. Now be a good boy and stay with Fevzi and Zafiro.'

'But I want my gun!' he shouted, stamping his feet and clenching his fists.

Mamá snapped and slapped him across the back of his legs. 'Now you just stop that! Haven't we got enough to deal with without you behaving like a bad boy?'

George stared at her for a moment and then burst into tears. Rosa took him to one side and gave him a cuddle. 'Come on, Georgikie, don't be naughty now. Babá will get your gun when he goes up to close the house.'

Babá nodded, approving of the place Mamá had found for the children to sleep; near the stairwell of the middle deck. It would be the most stable place in the event of rough seas. He watched the women spread their blankets, then organise food for everyone. The ship was to set sail after dark and the last job for Babá and Kuríllos was to return to the house and nail the shutters and doors closed. They realised that rumours of a rapid return were simply to pacify the women and children. They didn't expect to see the place again until the war had ended. Although they had their most valuable possessions with them, they didn't want gypsies or refugees moving into their home.

'Everything except the donkey!' Babá complained as they hefted bundles of clothes, pots and bedding for twenty people.

'Ssh! If one of them hears you, they'll have us going back for the beast. Our mother's not well, do you know?' Kuríllos replied.

'What? No, What's wrong?'

'Blood when she coughs. She's so weak she can hardly walk.'

'Why didn't she say? Give me a minute.' Babá hurried to the two grandmothers and addressed Mikró Yiayá. 'Mamá mou, what's wrong? I hear you're not well.'

'I'm all right, mustn't worry. Perhaps my time's up, I don't know,' she gasped.

Babá took her small hand in his, then placed his other arm around her bony shoulders. He was shocked to realise the thinness of her. 'For how long have you been seeing blood, old woman?'

'Ah, your brother has a big mouth. Tell him I'll haunt him if he doesn't behave!'

Babá laughed, despite his concern. 'As soon as we get to Cyprus, I'm going to bring a doctor to you. We'll have you better in no time, I promise.'

'Don't make promises you can't keep, son. Let me say I'm proud of you and the fine family you've brought into the world. I couldn't have wished for two better sons. Tell the family I love them all, that I love them to heaven and back.'

'And we all love you, Mamá mou. Trust me, once the doctor has seen you, you'll feel much better.'

* * *

By mid-afternoon, the family had settled on the ship. Babá cast a weary eye over them all. The children were sleeping, the grandmothers crocheting and Mamá, María and Ayeleen all closed their eyes for ten minutes, then woke with a start, afraid a calamity had taken place on their watch.

Babá and Kuríllos, also exhausted, set out with nails and hammers to secure the house.

'You think we'll have time for a last glass of ouzo, before we leave our homeland for God knows how long?' Babá asked his brother.

'I can't think of one reason why we shouldn't,' Kuríllos replied. 'There's an hour and a half before the ship leaves. Ten minutes is plenty time enough to nail a few shutters closed.'

The steps up to the house were half concealed by fallen bracts of bougainvillea. In the past few days, local women had had more important things to do than sweep their street clean. Delicate as vermillion confetti, the drifts of colour reminded them of the *kafenion* near their house. They glanced at each other, sharing a thought and hurried onward and upward.

They noticed a game of *tavli* taking place outside on the patio. The contestants – the town's two best players: the owner of the general store against the blacksmith – had been rivals for decades. Each year, the *tavli* tournament started on New Year's Day and ended at midnight the following Christmas Eve. Whoever won the most games gave a live sheep to the other. Winning was an honour, losing was lucrative. Ten men surrounded the players, under the shady pergola laden with bougainvillea. Although gambling was forbidden by law, bets were taken and both the Konstantinidis men placed a few liras on the blacksmith, then they settled down with a well-deserved glass of ouzo to watch the game.

They both backed the right man, the farrier was destined to be a clear winner. The game, almost over, came to a halt when the ships foghorn vibrated through the air.

'*Poutana!* Whore!' Kuríllos mouthed. 'The ship!'

'*Maláka!*' Babá muttered, not bothering to compete with the thunderous clamour. 'Come on!' he mimed nodding towards their home.

They raced around to the house, hammered in the nails making sure the property was secure. With the klaxon still howling they sped back down to the ship. The stevedore signalled the ship's bridge and the foghorn stopped.

'I wouldn't want to be in your boots when your wife gets hold of you,' the stevedore said gleefully. 'She's going to kill you with a blunt knife.'

Babá turned to his brother. 'Let's get our story straight. It was a leaking pipe to the pump, OK? We had to get some lead from the blacksmith and fix it before we closed the house up, all right?'

Kuríllos nodded. 'Didn't want a flood, did we?'

The brothers hurried on board and moments later, lines were hefted off the stanchions. As the ship slipped her mooring, the sun slid below the horizon. Under a sky the colour of glowing embers, 400 residents of Castellorizo stood at the ship's railings and waved goodbye to their island and the dark silhouettes of their friends and neighbours who hoped to join them soon.

Mamá and Babá hurried everyone below decks to settle down for the night.

* * *

'Do you mind if I stay at the rail a little longer, María – can you manage without me?' Sofía asked.

María smiled and kissed her sister's cheek. 'You stay as long as you like. You're missing him terribly, aren't you?'

Sofía nodded, unable to speak for the pain in her throat. She battled rising tears and sighed. 'Sometimes I feel we will never be together again. I miss him so much.'

María always understood. She opened her arms and gave Sofía a warm hug. 'I remember how sad I was when Mustafa first went away for six months, I also feared I would never see him again.' She rubbed Sofía's back. 'I was heartbroken, but look at me now! I don't even know how many children I have,' she joked. 'Or when I'll see their swashbuckling father again. So, stop worrying. Now I'm going to see what my unruly mob are up to. You take as long as you like up here.'

'Thank you,' Sofía managed to whisper.

Once she was alone at the stern rail, Sofía allowed herself the luxury of tears. She watched Castellorizo, now bathed in silver moonlight, drift towards the horizon. Her whole life had taken place on that small rock. She admired Anastasia because she had travelled and experienced many different lifestyles and cultures. Could Sofía step into the teacher's place when they all returned to their island? This was a frightening thought, yet she knew Anastasia would want her to. Everyone would miss the teacher – and Sofía would never forget that last visit to the cottage. Tears spilt down her cheeks for Anastasia and then for Jamie. How she missed him and longed to lie in his arms. Would they ever be together again?

Her thoughts were broken by the emergency drill announcement. It was time to learn how to put on a life jacket in the event of an emergency. She smiled to herself. How could a ship this size possibly sink?

* * *

By nine o'clock in the evening, everyone was exhausted. They had spent four days packing and moving their valuables and essentials down to the port.

The sea took on a swell and Sofía noticed the children becoming unruly. They'd finished the food, a pot of flavoursome *kouneli stifado* – rabbit stew – that seemed to have more small bones than usual. Her uncle had gone down to the hold, to check on his prized breeding pair of mink. Much to Uncle Kuríllos's annoyance, the stevedore had insisted he left the creatures in the hold. Her father – from whom her sensitive nose had picked up the slight scent of ouzo – was asleep and snoring loudly. Sofía's mother and sister, exhausted from the day's tribulations, were trying to stay awake. Their eyelids slid down, heads tipped forward, then they jerked back to consciousness bearing a look of fear. Deciding to quieten the children the best way she knew how, Sofía gathered them around her for story time.

'Mamá, María, Ayeleen – why don't you get a little sleep while Rosa and I entertain the little devils?'

Rosa, who idolised Sofía, nodded rapidly. 'I can dance for them.'

'And I will tell them a story,' Sofía added.

'That would be wonderful. To be honest, I'm dead on my feet, Sofía,' María said.

'Me too,' Mamá said letting her eyes close without resistance and the tension leaving her face. Ayeleen had already curled her body around Mamá, her face soft and luminous and her eyes closed.

'I promise to wake one of you when I need to sleep,' Sofía said, then she turned to the little ones. 'Come on, boys and girls, settle down. First, Rosa is going to dance for you. Watch carefully, because one day your sister will be a famous ballerina. She will dance before royalty in the grandest theatres and kings and queens will throw roses onto the stage in her honour.'

Rosa tucked her skirt into her knickers and made a low bow. Sofía led the children in applause and then smiled to see their amazed faces when her niece started to dance. Surely Rosa's dream would come true. Uncle Kuríllos always said anything is possible if you want it badly enough.

By the time the dance was over, Mamá and María were asleep. Sofía claimed the children's attention. 'Now, I'm going to tell you a terrible story about a war. A scary tale, the legend of a great fight that took place before earth existed.' She glanced at her mother and had a fierce urge to kiss her cheek, but she turned back to the children, lowering her voice into an ominous whisper. 'Listen – if you're brave enough – to the story of "The Gods and the Giants". The beginning of all things as we know them today.'

The children loved to be scared by Sofía's stories. They sat around her, cross-legged, wide-eyed and already quiet. Sofía thought how lucky her parents were; things had worked out perfectly for them. Thank God Mamá had a son the third time around. She couldn't imagine her mother going through pregnancy as many times as María. She looked around specifically to bestow a smile on her amusing little brother . . . but where was he?

'Fevzi, Zafiro, where's George?' Sofía asked.

Zafiro shrugged. 'We haven't seen him for ages, Aunty Sofía.'

Mamá, instantly awake, picked up on the conversation. 'Has anyone seen George?' She stared about: a wild, disbelieving look grew in her eyes as her grandchildren shook their heads. 'Georgikie!' she called getting to her feet and shaking Babá from his sleep. 'Babá, where's George?'

'How should I know?' he mumbled.

'Did you get his gun and give it to him when you came back?'

'Gun? Ah, the gun. No, I forgot about it. Haven't seen him since I left to close up the house.'

Mamá shook him roughly. 'What if he got off the ship? Wake up, you buffoon! What if he fell overboard? What if he got on a different ship after we left? We have to tell the captain to turn around or we may never see him again!' Mamá cried, already verging on hysteria.

CHAPTER 29
OLIVIA

Castellorizo, Greece, present day

'I was so worried about you, Uncle. I couldn't imagine where you'd got to. I even phoned the hospital and got Big Dave to check the flat. Nobody knew where you were.'

'I'm sorry. I should have let you know. Mind you, it's not the first time I've been in trouble for disappearing.' He smiles to himself and I sense there was another story in him. I will remind him as soon as we relax later.

The walk to the house and distillery takes two hours. Every pensioner we pass has heard of Uncle's arrival and, after much handshaking, each insists, in turn, that he sits with them for a short chat. Only after sincere promises to return will they allow us to continue our journey. I am relieved by the short stops. Although he claims to feel better than he has for decades with the stent fitted, I'm being cautious. His friends' interest in me is a little unnerving, especially when one sprightly sixty-something asks if I'm married.

We finally reach the house. The moment it comes into view, Uncle stops and stares, a look of wonderment on his face. 'It's exactly as I remember leaving it,' he whispers. 'Needs new windows, shutters, balconies and doors, but apart from that, it's perfect. Can we get inside?' He steps towards the front door.

I try to imagine how he feels, returning after all this time. 'The lock's just some wire threaded through the keyhole and around a nail in the frame,' I say. 'I'm hoping to find a locksmith today, to make the building secure.'

Suddenly, I realise there isn't enough time to organise all the things I want to do. My week in Castellorizo is racing by.

'Last time I was here, without my family around me, I was a young boy, quite sure the Bogeyman was going to get me. My family had no idea where I was. My poor parents were out of their minds with worry. I had literally *missed the boat* you see.'

'Where were your family?'

'All on board a ship to Cyprus. It became so dangerous to live here, the British offered to take those who had nowhere else to go to a safer place. We were on a big ship in the port for a whole day. It started as an adventure – I'd never been on a real big ship before – but by late afternoon, the novelty had worn off.' He laughs and I know there is another funny story coming. 'I saw a row of seagulls on the harbour railings, near the mosque and thought it would be fun to shoot them, but I'd forgotten to bring my wooden gun, so I decided to sneak home and get it. After all, it was growing dark and so I guessed the ship was staying in port until the next day. Anyway, Babá and Uncle Kuríllos had gone back to the house hours before.'

'You were a rascal, weren't you? So you got off the ship?'

'I did. But there was no sign of Babá at the house and the door was still open, so I hurried through to the distillery where I remembered I'd last had my gun. There were sacks of some kind of leaves, all stacked four high, like a bed. The smell of them made me sleepy and it was so nice to be there, in my home, with no screeching babies for once.'

'Don't tell me you fell asleep?'

'You've guessed it. When I woke it was pitch dark and there was an awful howling that terrified me. Then, loud banging that sounded like someone was trying to knock the front of the house down. I hid myself behind the sacks clutching my gun, ready to assassinate the Bogeyman. Eventually, the banging stopped and then the howling ended, too and I guess I fell asleep for a while.'

'Poor thing – how old were you?'

'I don't know, around five or six, I guess. Anyway, when I woke it was still dark, but then I saw light coming under the front door and I realised it was morning. I tried to get out, but the door and windows were stuck closed. There was no food or water in the house and I was trapped. What a palaver. I shouted and hollered but everyone was busy taking their valuables down to the port for the next ship and as you can see, we are right at the back of the town. Nobody was coming past.'

I twist the wire off the nail and push the heavy door open. 'It's infested with mice, I'm afraid and as you pointed out, the floor's probably unsafe.'

'I'm not surprised about the mice. They were straw mattresses.' He nods towards the bed. 'I guess we could put some poison down, but be prepared for a hell of a stink later. In the old days, they'd put a couple of hungry leopard snakes in – that would clear the house instantly.'

I shudder. 'I'm not so sure about that. Let's stick with the poison or traps, Uncle.'

He chuckles. 'Your house – your choice.'

'Ah, there's a subject we need to discuss. Is it really my house?'

'Of course it is. What makes you ask?'

'There's a guy here, from Australia, who claims to be María's great-grandson. He says the entire family have given him power of attorney to claim that the house is legally his. He's been to see the lawyer already.'

Uncle's eyes narrow. 'Has he indeed? Well, we'll see about that. Now, let's have a look inside. Throw a few stones in first, will you, to scatter the mice.'

'Look, I'm concerned about the safety of the floor and it's half twelve already. Let's go and get some lunch and, while we're at the harbour, we'll ask at the supermarket about mouse poison.'

'Good plan, I'm a bit peckish myself, to tell the truth.'

'Hey, Olivia!'

We both turn and see Greg ambling towards us. I try to dampen my smile, but it's not working.

'This is Gregoris, the local electrician. He's preparing an estimate of work for us.' I introduce my uncle and invite Greg to join us for lunch at Eleni's.

* * *

Eleni throws her arms wide. '*Ela*, come and eat and tell me all your news. Everyone is talking about you, George. You want a menu?' Next, Dino comes running out of the kitchen.

Uncle hugs and kisses them both and eventually we settle at the table. 'Tell me what's the special today?'

Greg knocks the side of my thigh under the table in a bit of secret attention-seeking. We smile at each other, then smile in opposite directions, trying to fool the world.

'I have a list of jobs that need doing as soon as possible, but I don't know where to find the right people,' I say. 'Can you help us, Greg?'

'Anything for you,' he says, his eyes narrowing, then his lips part slightly with a smile. I have a terrific urge to kiss him and I am sure he knows. My heart patters with the memory of our kiss on the return from Kaş.

'I need proper locks on the door and window shutters. A water supply and electricity as you know. Also, some support under the ground floor, until we can establish how safe it is. The roof needs repairing, too.'

'Leave it with me. I'll get the builder to put some shoring props under the floor beams – today if possible, so that you can go in and investigate.'

'How can I ever thank you?' I say without thinking. He gives me such a naughty smile I feel slightly breathless, gaze into his eyes, then look away quickly.

'Olivia!' Uncle says so sharply, I jump and everyone laughs. 'What would you like to eat?'

'Surprise me, Eleni. Whatever you suggest will be fine.'

She stands taller and shuffles her shoulders. 'I have carrots *el Grec*, fresh from my plot, with macaroni I made myself, to go with a traditional dish of chicken and wild greens. Is very good! The best. For the pudding I have home-made apricot ice cream with toasted almonds and borage flowers.'

Uncle and I exchange a glance and say, 'Yes please!' together. I glance around, expecting Rob to appear any minute, but so far, there is no intrusion.

As if on cue, my uncle says, 'Why don't you tell me about this young man from Australia? You say he's my sister's great-grandson and he's claiming the house. Or is he saying both the house and the distillery belong to him?'

'This is the odd thing, he didn't seem to know about the distillery. With such a monumental history, you'd think he'd know about the building.'

Uncle purses his lips and frowns. 'I see. I look forward to meeting him. White wine and soda, Olivia?'

I grin and nod. It's going to be lovely having my uncle here.

CHAPTER 30
SOFIA

Between Castellorizo and Cyprus, 1943

UNCLE KURÍLLOS SUGGESTED THEY SEARCH the ship. 'Perhaps Georgikie's found a more comfortable place to sleep. We all know what a monkey he is. Perhaps he's hiding, so calm down everybody. Or perhaps he's fallen asleep with one of his friends in a cabin. We'll explore all possible locations and question everyone on board.'

This logical suggestion calmed Mamá. Sofía kept María's children occupied by telling more stories, while the adults helped to search the ship. As midnight approached, it became clear the boy was not on board. Mamá, panic-stricken again, went with Babá and Kuríllos to the bridge to ask the captain to turn the ship around.

The captain understood neither Greek nor Italian, so Mamá – now in tears of fear and frustration – fetched Sofía. María took her sister's place guarding the rest of the children, most of whom were asleep by this time. A long conversation took place between the captain and Sofía, while – ignorant of the language – her mother shuffled impatiently from one foot to the other. Eventually, Sofía addressed her parents and uncle.

'The captain says he can't do anything until daylight as they have to maintain radio silence through the hours of darkness, for fear of enemy submarines.'

The worried Greeks started making suggestions, loudly as possible, in their native language.

The captain appeared startled, probably imagining every U-boat in the Mediterranean listening to the noisy Greeks. He turned to Sofía for a translation, then explained. 'Tell them, at first light I will call Castellorizo and order the soldiers to do a thorough search. If the little boy is there, we *will* find him. Now, I must remind you we are trying to keep as much silence as possible, so as not to attract U-boats. I suggest you all get some sleep. You'll have a long day tomorrow.'

'My father wants to know if you're going back to Castellorizo tomorrow? If so and if there's no news, can he go back with you to search for his son?'

The captain scratched his forehead, then nodded. 'I don't see why not.'

*   *   *

María and Ayeleen took the next shift with the little ones, relieving Sofía and Rosa. Sofía ached to be alone, to cry her sorry heart out. She longed for Jamie and was reminded of him every time she saw a soldier's uniform. After only a couple of hours together as man and wife, she had not seen him, had not felt his arms around her and had to be content with hugging herself. Now, the ship was taking her further away and she discovered her prayers had also gone unanswered. She was not pregnant.

Exhausted from the day's events, she finally fell into a deep, dreamless sleep, only to be shaken awake again.

'Go away,' she muttered, imagining one of the children wanting a story, or a cuddle, or a drink of water.

'Sofía, wake up,' begged the voice of Megáli Yiayá. 'Come quickly, Mikró Yiayá has gone. She's gone and I don't know what to do!'

Sofía opened her eyes and saw the pale face of her big grandmother. The distressed old woman had tears on her cheeks and

257

a defeated look in her eye. There seemed to be an urgent situation, yet she didn't want to disturb anyone.

'Where's she gone?' Sofía whispered.

'She's in the chair. It looks like she's asleep, but she's gone. We must tell the captain before anyone realises that she's died.' The old woman was crossing herself and sobbing quietly.

'Died . . . She's dead? Mikró Yiayá? Dear God!' Sofía knew she had to make a plan before grief hit her. She couldn't allow herself to think about how much she loved the old lady; how she made her laugh when she was sad. How she had dabbed her grazed knees, removed splinters and brushed her long hair when she was a child. All the cuddles Mikró Yiayá gave her whenever María and her latest baby claimed everyone's attention. *They might not notice how hard you work for us all, but I do, my princess,* she would whisper as she wrapped her bony arms around Sofía and kissed her cheeks.

Sofía felt even more emotional to see Megáli Yiayá weeping quietly for her lifelong friend and companion. She kept peering about, watching the shadows as if expecting Mikro Yiayá to step out and explain it was all a mistake.

She had to act before emotion got the better of her. 'Come on, let's make sure she's doesn't slip out of the chair, then we'll find the captain. Depending on what he says, we'll wake Mamá and Babá. They've had such a difficult time, it's best to let them sleep for as long as possible. I've a feeling there's a big day ahead without this happening.'

Megáli Yiayá dabbed at her tears and nodded. Together, they went to see the captain who informed them they would have a sea burial before they reached Cyprus. Two sailors came with a stretcher and took Mikró Yiayá away. Thankfully everyone was still sleeping. Sofía and Megáli Yiayá leaned against each other and slept for a few hours. As dawn broke, Sofía woke and decided it was time to tell her father and uncle that their mother had gone to God. This was the hardest things she had ever done. With an arm slung around Mamá, her father slept soundly. As Sofía looked down at them both, she felt the closeness of their relationship. She put her hand on her father's cheek and whispered into his ear.

'Babá, wake up. I need you.'

He stirred, chewed some invisible food and screwed his eyes open and closed. 'Sofía, is that you . . . what now?' he muttered.

'I need you to wake up and come with me. It's urgent, Babá.'

'What? Have they found Georgikie?' He squinted at her, then slipped his arm from around Mamá.

'Please, don't wake anybody,' she whispered.

He shrugged out of Mamá's embrace and got to his feet. 'What is it, Sofía?'

'Not here, come out on deck, Babá. Where's Uncle Kuríllos? I need to tell him too.'

'He's sleeping on the floor behind the chairs. I'll get him.'

'I'll wait for you outside.'

Out on the deck, daybreak bruised the sky into a dull dark red. Her mouth dried as she looked at her father and uncle, the men who always made her feel special. Could she live up to their expectations right now and ease the blow she was destined to deliver?

'What is it, Sofía? You look upset. Has somebody behaved badly? If they have, I'll break both his legs,' Babá muttered.

Sofía thought of Kuríllos and the woman he had loved and what that woman's brothers had done to her uncle. She wanted to hold her father while she told him, but then poor Uncle Kuríllos would be alone, so she took both of their hands and tried to be strong and brave it out.

'No, Babá, it's your Mamá. Mikró Yiayá . . .' She struggled to keep her voice even, but a sob broke through. 'Oh, Babá, she died. Mikró Yiayá died in her sleep a few hours ago . . .'

259

Her father and uncle stared at her in stunned silence. 'Are you sure, Sofía? Where is she?'

'The commanding officer has her taken away. I didn't want to wake anyone, so I went straight to him on the bridge. He said once the ship's doctor has written the death certificate, she'll be lain to rest in the cabin they use as a chapel. They'll bury her at sea this morning, before we reach Cyprus.'

'It's all taken care of then? I must go and see her,' Babá said.

'Me too,' said Kuríllos.

'It's almost time to feed the children,' Sofía said. 'I must console Megáli Yiayá, she's very upset. They were closer than sisters, you know?' The two men nodded. 'Will you be all right?' she asked. They both nodded again, then hung their heads.

'I'll go and see the captain and remind him to send the message home,' Sofía said. 'Perhaps someone saw Georgikie get off the ship before we sailed. They could search for him. He can't be in the house, or you would have seen him when you were fixing the broken pipe, wouldn't you?'

*　*　*

At 10 o'clock, the ship's engines stopped. Sadness hung in the air. The captain called, 'All hands to bury the dead!' The ship's flags were lowered to half-mast and the crew, in uniform, assembled and stood with their feet apart and hands behind their backs. As everyone stilled – the silence broken only by the slop of waves against the side of the ship – a bugler played a few mournful notes. Four bearers brought Mikró Yiayá on deck, wrapped in a sailcloth shroud and covered by a white sheet. She lay on a narrow board which they lowered to the deck with her feet overhanging the side of the ship. She looked so tiny, Sofía thought, remembering the woman's big heart and sense of humour that lifted feelings even

260

in the worst situations. What would she say now? Sofía wondered, remembering her naughty smile and how her bony shoulders would jig up and down with her childish giggles.

'I love you, Little Grandma,' Sofía whispered as her tears broke free at last. She reached for her father's hand and squeezed it as hard as she could. Mamá and Megáli Yiayá were crying noisily, as was fitting. The commanding officer read the start of the 23rd Psalm.

The Lord is my shepherd; I shall not want.
He maketh me to lie down in green pastures:
He leadeth me beside the still waters.

Everyone stared at the sea for a moment, then the officer called, 'Firing party present arms!' They fired three times into the sky, which made most people look up. At that moment, the board tilted and the shroud containing Mikró Yiayá slipped smoothly into the Mediterranean.

* * *

Babá and Uncle Kuríllos went to the rear deck and stared out over the sea. Sofía felt her own sadness, so squeezed between them and held both their hands. At last, she felt able to cry for the fun-loving old lady.

'Do you think she knew how much we all loved her?' she sobbed, looking down at the water. Just at that moment, the flat sea boiled and heaved startling Sofía so much she slapped her hand over her mouth to stifle a scream.

Babá sniffed hard. 'Don't worry, it's just the engines starting.'

'How stupid of me. For a horrible moment I thought . . . well, it was Mikró Yiayá coming back to us.'

261

Uncle Kuríllos made a sad smile. 'She'll be chuckling her little head off at that one,' he murmured, glancing up at the sky. 'Always liked to have the last laugh, didn't she? We're going to miss her. Did you bring that bottle of raki, brother?' Babá nodded sadly. 'Then fetch it and bring my *baglama* too.'

The ship's engines built up to a vibrating rumble. The three mourners at the stern rail stared at the agitated sea that foamed powerfully before the ship set off again. Mikró Yiayá, Sofía imagined, would be resting on the seabed by now. At peace and, as her son said, probably smiling.

* * *

Two hours later, the ship berthed at the wide, deep harbour of Famagusta which buzzed with military activity. Jeeps rushed in and out of the security zone. Cranes loaded ships with the paraphernalia of war, while others were unloading supplies for the army bases. Whistles blew, horns honked and orders shouted above the din and the dust. A squadron marched mechanically back and forth, put through their paces on the quayside by their drill sergeant.

While María breastfed the baby Evdokia and Mamá bottle fed the one-year-old Mikali, Sofía found a length of red twine and tied loops into it.

'Gather round children!' she called. 'Now, I'm going to give each of you a loop to keep hold of. Do you understand?' She held up the twine. 'Nobody goes anywhere without holding on to their loop unless I give them permission, all right? We are going to stay together at all times.'

Fevzi stuck his hand in the air. 'What if I need to do a big stinky pooh, Aunty? Will they all have to come with me?' He grinned, displaying a chipped tooth gained from falling out of the big tree outside their house. A house, Sofía feared for a second, they might never see again.

Everyone voiced childish noises of disgust, holding their noses, blowing raspberries and nudging each other. Their giggling reminded Sofía that the children had all inherited some of Mikró Yiayá's mischief. She smiled despite the tears that sprang to her eyes. 'Then you'll come and tell me that you need the toilet, OK, Fevzi?'

'Aunty, please don't make us go with him when he makes a big yucky smell!' one of the little ones begged, while Fevzi and Zafiro nudged each other, making grunting noises and grinning with delight.

'Settle down now! Everyone take hold of a loop and let's have a practice around the deck.'

'Aunty, there's one empty loop at the end,' Zafiro said.

'That's for George when he comes back – and that's why you must all keep hold of your loop and if you see an empty one, you should tell me right away. We don't want anyone else getting lost, do we?'

'What if he never comes back, Aunty?' Zafiro asked, staring at the floor. 'What if he's been eaten by wolves?' A deep frown creased his young face while the rest of the children looked horrified.

'I don't want to be eaten by wolves,' Bebe cried, her lips trembling as she hid her eyes behind her hands, believing nobody could see her if she couldn't see them.

* * *

Babá accompanied his family to a line of Cypriot buses that waited to transport 400 Castellorizo residents and their chattels to Dhekelia military and refugee camp. Soldiers threw the bundles of belongings onto the roof, then a stout net held everything down securely. The rest of their things would arrive in a truck the next day. Sofía noted how wise the island's women had been to sew all their belongings into pillowcases and embroider the family name on the outside. She could imagine the chaos of bundles coming untied and squabbles over belongings if such sensible action hadn't been taken.

Everyone watched sadly as Babá kissed Mamá goodbye, not something usually done in public. Sofía noticed him glance at the sky and she suspected he was asking Mikró Yiayá to watch over them all. Her heart ached and, before she could do anything about it, she found herself running towards him with her arms outstretched.

'Babá, stay safe! Bring little George back to us on the next ship and please, can you bring my jewellery box back with you? All Jamie's letters are in there and I miss him so much.' She took a deep breath, hoping it would blow the tears away. 'And could you post this? It's a letter to him and there might be one to collect for me.'

'Of course. You look after everyone and I'll be back on the next ship with your little brother and your letters.'

'And could you bring Rosa's ballet books, please, so she can practise? It will help to take her mind off things.'

Babá smiled. 'You're always thinking of others, my lovely girl. Now, I'm leaving before you think of anything else,' he teased. 'I love you all very much. Keep them safe for me, Sofía.' He turned sharply and walked back to the ship. Sofía watched him go on board. He turned just before disappearing inside and gave one final wave. She waved back, then turned to face her family and saw they had all waved too. A fitting goodbye, she thought. He would be back in a few days and find out where they were and they would all be so pleased to see little George again.

CHAPTER 31
OLIVIA

Castellorizo, Greece, present day

'ARE YOU ALL RIGHT?' I ask Uncle across the table. 'You seem very deep in thought.'

'Sorry, lost in the past for a moment – and I'm almost nodding off. The warmth, the full belly, the wine, the pleasant company. Goodness, that was terrific food, don't you think? I'm in need of a nap, Olivia. Would you forgive me if I abandon you for an hour?'

'Suits me. I'd like to work on my cookery book. That meal was definitely a show-stopper.'

He smiles wearily. 'Then we agree. I'll meet you here at four thirty?' I stand to accompany him to his room. 'Stay here,' he says. 'I can manage perfectly well.'

I watch him walk towards his ground-floor room facing the harbour, reminding myself he's recently had heart surgery. I wonder if he flew against the doctor's advice. Still, I find myself smiling as he disappears behind a blue-painted door. *Stubborn old sweetheart.* I hope I'll be as independent at his age.

I order iced coffee, then get my notepad out and start work on the cookbook. I'm struggling to find a subtitle I like. *Fascinating Flavours of Greece: Traditional Greek Food from the Islands.* With tips on presentation that bring centuries-old village recipes to five-star presentation standards. Most importantly, there'll be astonishing flavours and unbelievable colour. From the most delicate deep yellow courgette flowers, stuffed with rice and aromatic herbs, to the mind-blowing taste of charred aubergines with sweet, sun-ripened tomatoes and salty feta cheese.

I sit back in my chair, imagine prepping food for the photos and smile to myself. Lost in a little bubble of pleasure, I find myself gazing over the harbour when Eleni comes to my table.

'Everything all right?' she asks, pulling out a chair and sitting next to me.

Reluctantly, I drag my eyes away from the water and glance her way, only to see her transfixed by the turquoise millpond harbour too.

'I'm working on my cookery book.'

'I see,' she says and we both smile.

'The pasta was amazing today. Did you use a machine?'

'Machine? Machine? No machine!' She sounds insulted, yet I know she's play-acting. 'No, I roll it out myself. Why a woman has hands if not to cook, to feed those she loves? Machine . . . bah! The machine is cold, steel. Real pasta, it needs cool hands and a warm heart. It needs to be kneaded by strong but gentle hands that care for others. The only ingredients are the flour, the fresh eggs and the love; nothing more.'

Eleni uplifts me. She has a way with words. 'I might have to quote you, Eleni. Anyway, you and Dino are certainly going to be in the acknowledgements.'

She grins. 'I have a booking this evening – fifteen peoples – so I must help Dino now. You want anything, you come get me, OK?' She returns to the kitchen with a definite shimmy in her shoulders and swing to her hips.

I glance around the harbour and wonder why I haven't seen Rob yet. He's bound to show up soon and I feel sure there will be trouble. Nevertheless, I have an ally in Uncle and look forward to returning to the house this evening. Perhaps Greg will have some news for me later. Tomorrow, I hope we will move forward with the lawyer, too, now that I have my great-uncle on board.

*　*　*

I write about the macaroni, about the salad and about the ice cream. Two hours have flown by and I still can't think of a suitable subtitle for the book. I should walk, but not far because I want to be here when Uncle returns.

'I'm just going for a stroll around the harbour and perhaps over to Mandraki, Eleni. I'll be back when my uncle returns, OK?'

'Is no problem, I put a reserve sign on your table.'

'Thank you. You spoil me.'

Something in the light changes as the sun passes its peak. The pale turquoise water turns a shade or two darker, yet it becomes more transparent without the glare. I can see small flitting fish nibbling at green algae on the underside of fishing boats. Someone has thrown a whole pitta bread into the water and so many fish are frantically pecking at the edges, it spins like a discus on the water's surface. Suddenly, a grey torpedo shape dashes up from the depths and dozens of tiny fish leap a foot into the air in a great flashing silver arc. They splosh back into the water with no sign of their marauder. Such drama pulls me to a halt. Within seconds, the scene repeats itself. The pitta bread spins, a hundred little sprats nibble and I suspect their predator waits in the depths for his chance to grab another mouthful of the little guys.

I think about Rob with an uneasy feeling. Where is he? What is he up to? I glance over my shoulder. He is staying in the only modern purpose-built hotel, so perhaps he's lying on a sunbed, adding depth to his tan. Perhaps he's as fed up with me as I am of him? Who can know? This is a weird situation. When he pesters me, I wish he would go away. However, now it seems he has gone away, I feel unsettled.

I continue around the bay, past the mosque, following the path. Up and down stone steps, stopping often to take in the view. I pull out my phone to take pictures of breathtaking scenes and ask myself: is this the place for my mother's and grandmother's ashes? Such an area of peace and beauty. I feel serene just standing here. *Oh, Mummy, what made made my grandmother take you away from Castellorizo, never to return?*

CHAPTER 32
SOFIA

Cyprus, 1943

Sofia had a child on her lap and two in the seat next to her. The hot and dusty bus bumped its way over rough ground to Dhekelia military and refugee camp. It seemed they would never get there. The younger children were grizzling; hungry, tired and thirsty. The journey seemed to take forever. They heard gossip of another air raid on Castellorizo and that now there was hardly a house standing. Sofía wondered how anyone could know this and suspected it was propaganda, spread to make them glad they'd left. She fretted for little George: he would be terrified, all alone if he was still on the island. But, where else could he be? Surely one of the remaining families had taken him in.

The bus came to a halt. Most of the children were crying. Parents took one look at the long rows of tents and the high wire fences and many of them battled with tears too. They got off the bus, desperate for food and water, but their ordeal was not over.

Sofía always had one eye on the news for information to go into her history book. Suddenly, she recalled rumours of how the Nazis tricked Jews into what the Germans called work camps – but there were whispers of awful things happening there. Could this be one of those diabolical places? They said it wasn't just Jews; they were interning anyone less than perfect. What if the Allies were doing the same? How could they know? She stared at her mother's pale face, then at María, who caught her glance and shrugged in reply. She saw fear on most adult faces. Their belongings, thrown off the roof of the bus, garnered anxious glances, then a truck filled with the remainder of their chattels pulled up next to the bundles and started unloading the rest.

'What are they going to do with us?' Sofía asked a soldier who was herding them together.

'You'll be processed, showered and disinfected while your clothes are fumigated, then we'll feed you and allocate the tents,' he said. People had crowded around her to listen.

'Can we have some water, please? The children are fainting with thirst,' Sofía asked.

'I'll find out. Don't look so afraid, we'll take care of you. Now, follow me.'

He led them through the rows of tents until they reached three tables, behind which sat two men and a woman, all in uniform. The occupants of the buses and trucks had to queue in family groups, have their details taken and to be allocated a tent. After disappearing for a few minutes, the soldier returned with a bucket of water and a couple of tin mugs.

'You – what's your name?'

Sofía glanced either side to make sure he was talking to her. 'Me? I'm Sofía.'

He handed her the bucket. 'You seem the sensible sort. Take this to the front of the queue and start giving everyone a drink while I get more and join you. Can you manage that, Sofía?'

'Yes. Thank you,' she said humbly. Passing the end of the string with loops to Ayeleen, she warned the youngsters to behave, then started dishing out water. The young soldier joined her and together they worked their way along the hundreds of arrivals from Castellorizo. Occasionally, the soldier caught Sofía's eye and smiled. Everyone gulped the precious liquid down, some pouring a cupful over their sweating red-faced babies' heads.

* * *

That night, Sofía took to her bed with a full belly for the first time in years, as did everyone else. The meal of mashed potatoes, boiled carrot and swede and bully beef in gravy, was the same food that fortified the troops. The Castellorizons had never eaten the likes of it before and claimed this was surely food for babies. A person didn't need a tooth in their head to eat it, yet unanimously, they found it delicious.

Another anomaly the women noticed immediately was that these British soldiers – from the army that would save the world from Nazi tyranny and communist evils – wore little boys' trousers! The Castellorizo females blinked at the sight of bare knees and tight suntanned calves. They quickly diverted their eyes, glancing at husbands and children, before sneaking another peek. An observer might notice an occasional look exchanged between the women when eyes narrowed slightly and soft smiles fell on silent lips.

After an exhausting and emotional week, the Konstantinidis family slept from dusk until dawn feeling safe and secure. There was no lantern in their tent, so darkness was absolute. Even Mamá, who generally kept her feelings to herself, let her worry for Georgikie go. As her eyes closed, she imagined his small body curled against her, his arm slung around her neck and his head on her shoulder. She recalled her joy on the day of his birth

271

and this memory renewed her strength and fortified the faith she had in her husband.

Babá would find him. Georgikie was the light in her husband's eyes.

*　*　*

The next morning, breakfast consisted of bread and jam, all washed down with stewed sweet tea. Warmed milk satisfied the babies and infants. The refugees from Castellorizo had never eaten refined white bread before, or tea that didn't consist of herbs that grew wild on their own mountain slopes.

They collected their food from a row of trestles set in the middle of the camp and then ate in their own tents, which contained only beds. Everyone was grateful for the food and also for the peaceful night's sleep that had put them all in a good mood.

Officials came around and explained they had forty days' quarantine in the camp with nobody allowed in or out. The next task was to find their belongings, organise their tent and wash all the children before lunchtime.

*　*　*

Four days later, the ship returned with a fresh batch of Castellorizo refugees. The moment Mamá heard, she and Sofía rushed to the three tables where the newcomers lined up for registration.

'Babá! Georgikie!' Mamá called, running along the row of tired and thirsty new arrivals.

'Kyría, they're not here,' one of her neighbours called. 'Here, I have a letter from your husband.'

Sofía raced to her mother's side, wanting to read the letter at once. Mamá whimpered as she tore at the correspondence. 'Oh! They still haven't found my boy!' She shook her head slowly. 'Where can he be?'

'What does Babá say, Mamá?'

'He can't find Georgikie, nobody's seen him. I'm out of my mind with worry, what's happened to him? Babá says he won't leave the island until he's found his son. Can you imagine what your father's going through? To lose his mother and his only son in a matter of days.' She sniffed and rubbed her eyes. 'We must do all we can for the rest of our family, Sofía. Things can go wrong so easily. Let's make sure everyone is safe and sound when your father gets back.'

The sun beat down, the air so still it was an effort to breathe. Sofía peered down the long line of sweating adults and distressed children and remembered her own anguish on arrival. With her heart breaking for her husband, she tore her thoughts away and concentrated on the new Castellorizo refugees. She went to the table and spoke to the woman there.

'Excuse me, could I give them some water? The children—'

'Are you with them?' the woman barked.

'Well, no, but—'

'Then go away!'

Mamá tugged her arm. 'Haven't we got enough trouble without this?'

There was a sudden bunching up in the queue, a child cried out, people were bending over, then Sofía realised one of the mothers had fainted and lay on the ground.

She turned back to the woman in charge. 'Please! They are collapsing with thirst.'

'For God's sake! Go on then.'

Sofía grabbed her mother's hand. 'Come on, see if we can find the bucket and tap before somebody else collapses.'

A few minutes later they were handing out beakers of water to the thirsty Castellorizo refugees. Sofía kept an eye on her mother who asked friends about her son. Occasionally, she caught her mother's voice. 'Are you sure you didn't see him?' Suddenly, overcome by grief, Mamá fell into her friend's arms and cried, 'Why did I have to shout at him and smack his legs? What if I never see him again and it's my fault because I made him run away? My only boy.'

Sofía tried to think of a way to ease her mother's pain while she handed over another mug of water. The recipient seemed to look past her and grin. A pair of hands slipped over Sofía's eyes and she knew immediately. Everyone heard her squeal of delight. 'Jamie!' She spun around and leapt into his arms, wrapping her legs around his hips and her arms around his neck.

'Sofía, please!' Mamá called disapprovingly and hurriedly moved further up the queue with the water bucket.

He kissed her fiercely. Their teeth clashed together because they couldn't stop grinning. He grasped her shoulders and pulled back.

'I'm not the only one who's missed you,' he said. 'Look who's here.' He stepped aside and there stood George.

'Mamá!' Sofía called. 'Mamá, Georgikie's here!'

Her mother turned and with a yelp, shoved the bucket at somebody and ran to her child. She scooped George up and felt him all over as if testing for broken bones. Tears came to her eyes as she kissed his cheeks.

'Are you OK? Are you hurt? Tell me. Oh, dear child, I could kill you. Where've you been? Blessed Virgin give thanks!' She prattled on, holding him, stroking his limbs, hugging him as if to reassure herself he was real. With sudden startling clarity, she remembered Babá. Staring at Jamie with mad eyes she yelled at him: 'Does Babá know his boy's safe?'

Jamie appeared puzzled. 'How can I know? They told me you'd all left Castellorizo. When I found George, I asked permission to bring him to you but I was held up because they made me sail back to Rhodes, then fly to Cyprus.'

'How did you find him?' Sofía asked, already yearning to lie in her husband's arms, recognising the mutual longing in his eyes.

Jamie grinned at the boy still squirming in his mother's arms. 'I was on the ship that waited outside the harbour for your vessel to leave, though I didn't know you were on it at the time. We had six hours' leave while the ship refuelled so I raced up to your house, shocked to see the town almost flattened. We heard you'd come under fire from the Luftwaffe, but I had no idea it was that bad.' He slipped his arm around her waist. 'Let's go somewhere more private.'

'Help me dish out the water first, they're fainting with thirst.'

'You're a saint,' Jamie said, the love-light shining from his eyes.

He picked up Mamá's bucket and together they hurried up opposite sides of the queue, making sure everyone quenched their thirst. The adults knew the couple's situation and congratulations were as common as thanks until eventually they reached the end of the 300-plus line of people. They hurried to the back of the kitchen, disposed of the buckets and mugs, then slipped unseen behind the administration building. They found an empty shed and in that shady corner, they fell into each other's arms.

* * *

'You never finished telling me how you found George,' Sofía asked later as she rested her head on Jamie's shoulder, her voice conveying her quiet contentment.

'After seeing most of the houses in ruins after the air raids, I hurried up to your home. You must understand, it was very dark that night. I knocked on the door, but nobody answered. I was afraid for you all and tried to enter, but the door seemed jammed shut. I shouted, *Sofía!* and that was when I heard this crying, *Mamá, Babá!* I realised a distressed child was inside. I didn't want to make him more afraid so I called, *Don't be afraid, it's me, Jamie, the soldier that married Sofía!* and he called back, *The one that guards against Bogeymen?* which made me laugh – but the little chap was serious and I remembered his fear.'

'I don't understand.'

'When I hid behind the carpet that first night – almost unconscious – it was George that kept my presence a secret and gave me milk. He asked if I would guard him from the Bogeyman. So, you see, we knew each other already. Anyway, I closed the house back up and took him down to headquarters. My sergeant's a good man. Realising my new wife was in Cyprus, he organised for me to sail back to Rhodes then fly with George to Cyprus.'

'Do you have any news about the war, or what will become of us?'

'No, only that they are moving you all to the town of Xero after your quarantine. You'll find it's much better. The old copper mine has closed now, so they're going to put you in the workers' houses. It's near the sea, not too bad at all. Most importantly, you'll be safe. *Cyprus* means copper in Greek, did you know?' Sofía shook her head. 'At one time, this island was the largest producer of copper in the world.'

'Really? You know so much. So long as we're safe, I don't care what the island is famous for. María's pregnant again. If you see Mustafa, will you tell him?' she said. 'Also, we have to decide what to do about the oil production. Should we sell the recipe, or keep producing the precious oil ourselves? A third of the business is mine, you see.'

'How can you produce it if you're not there?'

'We have a few barrels maturing right now, but we'd have to go back every month or so, when the time is right for certain oils. Mustafa says we could do it in Turkey and so long as it stays out of the war, we'd be safer there too.'

'Surely it would be too difficult and take time, to move those stills?'

She nodded. 'Difficult, yes, but there are quiet times between seasons. In winter and early spring, we harvest the citrus fruits, flowers and leaves which we get from Fodele in Crete. May and June, we make oil from the myrtle and mints. June, July and August, we harvest the fragrant frangipani flowers and blend them with oil from the vanilla orchid and rose petals, for the most luxurious perfume in the world. It matures for two years, so we have stock to last us for some time. That's the recipe they want to buy. We all hope the war ends soon and we can go home to start work again.'

Jamie peered into her eyes. 'Your whole face lights up when you talk about the oils. I know you love teaching, but I fear you miss the distillery too much.' He kissed her again.

'There's something magical about the scent of each precious oil. It's as if the very smells themselves seep into my body and control me.'

'I don't understand.'

'When we make a blend using ginger, my appetite grows and my mouth waters, until I just have to go and eat something.

277

Cinnamon makes me warm and sleepy; it turns my skin to velvet and I could almost purr with contentment. Myrtle and eucalyptus are cleansing and purifying and make me feel healthy. They ward off winter colds, yet they also remind me of Christmas and winter days, for no reason I can think of. The citrus peels, leaves and blossoms have me zinging with energy and I feel sparkling clean and complete. Of course, everyone has their own unique perfume and it says so much about them.'

His eyes opened wider. 'Me too?' She nodded. 'Tell me about my perfume,' he said.

'You, my gorgeous lover, smell of the forest after heavy rain. Earthy scents of pine, sandalwood and ferns.' She pushed her face against his neck and inhaled deeply. 'Oh yes, I smell the woods, cedar and patchouli, too, and roasted chestnuts, my goodness . . . you make me feel hot. You make my own scent change from fun-loving honeysuckle to the rich and heavy perfume of a fully blown rose. Intoxicating, giddy feelings whir around my head and an exciting tingling in certain places that I can't mention.' She half closed her eyes, feeling his body harden against her and hers responding, yielding, wanting.

'I need to investigate exactly what you mean,' he whispered. 'Where is this magical tingle that you mention – can I touch it?' His eyes sparkled, gazing into hers as he kissed her again. 'As your husband, it would be my duty to deal with the problem.' He spoke into the crook of her neck. She laughed, gasped and almost fainted as the heady scent of desire enveloped them both.

* * *

'Fancy María being pregnant again. I can't wait to have our own family,' Jamie said, straightening his uniform and then smoothing her hair. 'After the war, I'm going to take you to England for a month and see where you would rather live and wherever you choose will be our permanent home and the home of all our children. Then we shall visit the other place for our holidays.'

'Oh, Jamie! I love you so much.' She frowned for a second. 'All our *four* children – you promised, remember?'

'For the moment, I think we should just concentrate on the first one, don't you?' He slid his arm around her and pulled her against him.

* * *

Everyone was happy at Xero camp. Basic food was plentiful and the locals were kind and helpful. However, the two Konstantinidis sisters missed their husbands. Jamie returned to his camp in Crete and Sofía feared she would never see him again. She hoped and prayed she was pregnant, but two weeks later, wept with disappointment. However, María felt the stirring of tiny limbs in her belly and started praying for another boy.

Christmas passed without incident, but on New Year's Day, word spread to start packing.

CHAPTER 33
OLIVIA

Castellorizo, Greece, present day

'I HAD A WONDERFUL SIESTA,' Uncle says. 'Now, I'm ready to tackle anything. Let's buy a couple of torches and walk up to the house.'

I'm pleased to see him so chirpy. 'I've had a most productive afternoon creating a reader profile for my cookery book.' Her uncle frowns. 'I've worked out who my target audience will be.'

'Ah, I see and who are they, exactly?'

'Mature women with style and a strong sense of place. Greek-o-philes who adore the traditional, wholesome foods of this country, but also like a twist of sophistication.'

'Sounds intriguing. If you'd rather carry on . . .'

I shake my head. 'I'll just pop into my room and pick up my camera on the way.'

The shadows are longer now, making the walk pleasant. Elderly people shake Uncle's hand and welcome him. I learn that his last stay on the island was forty years ago. We stop a few times and sit outside people's houses to sip iced-water and chat about the past. With great pride, they feed us *katsimara*, the local pie which takes the form of a large spiralled croissant sprinkled with cinnamon and sugar.

My excitement is building. Perhaps today I will learn the secrets of my family. I'm sure they are connected to the distillery. I feel at peace and at home. Uncle is a real soulmate, a super-trouper I know I can depend on. But yes, I sense his reluctance to fill in the blanks of my family history.

We're both glad to reach the solitude of the house where we sit on the sawn-off pine trunks and admire the view. Some building materials and scaffolding poles lie on the patio.

'Looks as though somebody's started work already,' he says.

The perfume of night scented jasmine and honeysuckle waft about us and the scent of lemon still lingers from the cut branches. I inhale deeply.

'I love the wonderful smells of flowers, especially at dawn and dusk,' I sigh. 'They seem so much stronger here than at home.'

'It's in your blood,' he says softly. 'Also, it's because there's no industry and hardly any traffic here.' He glances over his shoulder, towards the house. 'That's what it's all about, Olivia, the scent.' He stares at me intently. 'The scent was the cause of it all, you see. It wasn't that anyone was wrong, or evil, they just fell under the irresistible spell of the perfume.'

I wait, hope he'll continue, but his shoulders drop and he seems to fall under a cloud of depression, staring glumly over the town. 'It's important that you understand this fact, so that you don't blame anyone for what happened.'

Oh, the frustration. I want to remind him: *But I don't know what happened! Nobody will tell me!*

'What do you think you'll do with the property when it's in your name?' he asks, changing the subject.

'Well, first, I'll restore it. Take it back to basics. A solid wood front door and new shutters in the same geometric style. Double-glazed windows, of course, but sympathetic. And those balconies, wow! Big, boxy and bold. I'll have plenty of time to think about it while the building's being restored. I need to earn a living, so I might run cookery holidays, or – depending on the distillery – learn about precious oils and do something along those lines. I'd like the idea, I guess it's in my blood, as you say, but I don't know where to start. I feel the building is a historical time capsule, a living museum – though I've hardly seen inside. It's most important for me to keep as much of the original building and the way of life, as possible. I do wish I could see inside.'

'Then let's try. Come on.' Age falls away from him in an instant and enthusiasm shines from his eyes. I feel the urge to give him a hug.

* * *

We manage to push the door open and I give the mice a few seconds to scatter before I peer inside with the torch.

'Look at all those cooking pots on the wall, Uncle. What a great place to give Greek cookery demonstrations! I can imagine great pine scaffolding planks on trestles down the centre of the room and people who *really* love food, discovering new incredible gastronomic delights in this very place.'

'Marvellous!' he exclaims, catching my enthusiasm.

'You say there's a cellar, too? Oh my – there's just too much to think about.' I am almost breathless with excitement. 'What's all that mess at the back?' I turn the torch to the rear of the room.

He squints into the gloom, then suddenly brightens. 'Goodness me, I'd forgotten. That, my dear child, is Sofía's dowry carpet, still on the loom.' He steps inside. 'Right, here we go, then. I'll go to the back door via the hearth, as that's where the driest joists will be. It would be foolish to try and walk straight across the room. Wish me luck.'

'Be careful, Uncle,' I say. He sidesteps around the room and we hear a few warning creeks from the floorboards. Then he disappears behind the tattered carpet. I hear creaking door hinges.

'It's open!' he calls gleefully. 'Follow in my footsteps if you want to see the distillery. Mind you don't touch the carpet; it's likely to disintegrate into a dust cloud, then we'll both choke to death.'

I step gingerly around the room, keeping my feet as close to the wall as possible, until I slip behind the ropy remains of the carpet and through the adjoining door. Here, I am pleased to remember, the floor is solid; however, it is pitch dark and the torch throws black shadows everywhere.

'Can you turn on your phone's torch as well?' Uncle asks. 'Shine it under the counter. We used to keep some storm lamps and matches under there in case the electric went off while we were working.'

We? I don't want to pry, but curiosity gets the better of me. 'Can I ask, what made you leave here, Uncle?' I can't make out the expression on his face in this gloom.

'My partner died,' he says flatly. 'Once Sofía and Jamie were settled in Brighton, we came over and kept the distillery going. However, much as I loved it, I couldn't manage the business on my own, so I locked up and went to England to join Sofía.'

'So you were the last person in this workshop?'

'I guess I was. Seems a long time ago now.'

A match flares, then the storm lamp comes to life, bathing everything in yellow light.

'Look at that, first strike! Army matches, you know, were dipped in wax so that even if they fell in water they would strike on anything rough and dry. Anyway, I digress . . . about the distillery. I'll bet my old contacts are still going strong . . . so if you

283

want to start up the precious oil business again, I'll help you to get it started. It would be something quite unique.'

This is a lot to take in. 'So, you actually made perfume, or precious oils, yourselves?'

'Certainly did. Well, I personally only invented one precious oil blend. The rest were simply continuations of Sofía's and María's recipes.' He pulls a wooden drawer open and takes out two enormous ledgers. 'I was afraid, for a moment, the mice might have had these, but they seem OK. One is the—' He stops speaking, distracted by voices coming from the house.

'It's Rob and the lawyer,' I whisper.

Uncle shuts down the storm lamp while I turn off the torches. We both listen.

'Someone's opened the door – look. Kids, probably,' Rob says.

'It looks bigger from the outside. What's around the back?' the lawyer asks.

'No idea, more of the same I guess. Don't you know?'

'Me, no, I'm from Rhodes, not here. Are you sure she'll fall for this?'

'Hundred per cent, mate. She already suggested we should come to some sort of arrangement. So that's your job. Work out a good deal and you're in for twenty-five per cent. She gets the building, we get the dosh, everyone's happy.'

'What if she can't come up with the cash?'

'She will. I checked her out. She has a property in the UK that must be worth almost a million euro. Silly money. She can get a mortgage on it.'

'OK, I've seen enough. I need a *topograph* – a survey – and a list of all the people in this family you supposedly belong to. I can arrange the *topograph*, then I need a Greek tax number, mother's name, father's name, and a long list of papers, all officially translated. Also, someone who'll swear you're who you say you are. The mayor will do it for 500 euro.'

'Not going to be easy then?'

'It takes time and money, but we'll sort it out, Rob. The hardest part is proving legal right to the property.'

The bastard! I want to leap out and confront him but Uncle senses my agitation and places a hand on my arm. Once Rob and the lawyer have pulled the door closed, we wait a moment, just to be sure they've gone.

'After hearing that, I'm not even sure he's a relation,' Uncle George says. 'What do you think?'

'I'm pretty sure if we did a DNA test, we would find he was family. He has the short thumbs, you see, like my mother. I know it's a very rare distinction. I don't have it, neither did Granny Sofía, but Mummy said that several of María's children had it and it could reappear in my own children.'

Suddenly I have the feeling I've touched a nerve.

'I've just remembered something Granny Sofía said, long ago, that puzzled me, but she got so upset I couldn't ask her to explain. I said, *Having short thumbs is hardly a life-threatening disability.* To which Granny replied, *Unless people's lives depend on you being able to turn off a paraffin stove.* What did she mean, exactly?'

Uncle gasps, then places his hand over his mouth and stares at nothing. 'Did she say who she was talking about?' I shake my head. He says, 'It must have been Katina or Athena. Dear God, now I understand,' he whispers. 'Poor Sofía, she knew all along. She guessed the girls were trying to warm some milk for their seasick mother. What a terrible thing to live with.' As his eyes meet mine, I see they are full of heartbreak.

I think a change of subject will settle my uncle. 'Shall we take the ledgers with us?'

'Good plan,' he says, yet I feel his mind is elsewhere.

'You were going to say something before we were interrupted – about the old books.'

'Ah, it's gone . . . old age, you know. I'd forget my head.'

Again, I have come to a dead end. Will I ever find out what happened?

'I'm not sure I can handle another big meal this evening, Uncle. How about we ask Eleni for some home-made soup and bread and eat it in your apartment?'

'Good idea. If I eat too late, I get awful indigestion. Besides, there's something I want to show you.'

* * *

We lug the books down to Uncle's room, then have a cup of tea while we wait for Eleni to bring our takeaway. An exhausted sun with all the heat washed out of it threatens to slide behind the headland. The harbour water is so flat and dark it mirrors the scene perfectly, duplicating the mosque, minaret and port police building. Above everything, the gigantic Greek flag atop the ruined castle descends for the night. We gaze in reverence, silent, like everyone else.

Eleni appears with a pan of soup, a crusty loaf topped by toasted sesame seeds and a bottle of white under her arm. 'Here, you bring the pan back tomorrow. No leave in the apartment, OK?'

'Thank you, Eleni. This is wonderful.'

'Is chicken-egg-lemon soup with rice, I make it myself this morning. Is very good. Wait, now – I have something else for you. Is gift from me, you no pay. Is *loukoumades*.' She produces a tinfoil bundle from her big apron pocket. I laugh to see Uncle pout as his eyes light up. 'Small doughnuts soaked in honey and sprinkled with toasted sesame seeds. Still warm,' Eleni explains.

'I love cake!' Uncle states. 'I'd better swim tomorrow morning or I'll be as fat as a barrel by the time I go home and that won't do my heart any good.'

We sit inside with the front and back windows open creating a delicious draught. While we eat, he talks about the two books. One is the business accounts and the other contains the recipes for the oil blends.

'I kept the recipes of each mix up to date, once my sisters had gone their separate ways and my partner did the accounts. David was very meticulous about this, that was one of the things I loved about him. He was also a good negotiator when it came to sales. It was David who made the big deal with the French fashion house for our precious oil blend, once the first contract had ended.'

The way he says, 'David', with such affection and sadness . . . everything falls into place.

'María's husband, Mustafa, had already negotiated with the French. Anyway, it was a deal that changed all our lives. After ten years, the contract was up for review and by then, David and I were running the distillery.'

CHAPTER 34
SOFIA

Middle East, 1944

ON 4 JANUARY, THE REFUGEES were moved again, transported in army trucks from Xero camp to the Cypriot port of Famagusta.

'Does anyone know where we're going, Uncle?' Sofía asked Kuríllos. 'All anyone will say is that they are shipping us out.'

He shrugged. 'We'll go wherever they want, we don't have a choice. Everyone's complaining, of course – it's our nature – but at least our starving children have meat on their bones at last and there's a doctor who has enough medicine to treat the sick. We must be grateful for these things. They'll take us to another camp and when the war's over, they'll return us home.' He squeezed her shoulder. 'That's the thought to hang on to . . . we *will* go home.'

'When will I see my husband? You can't imagine how badly I want to go back to Castellorizo.'

'Patience, Sofía. You have your whole life ahead of you.'

At the port, the Konstantinidis family and all their neighbours boarded a ship headed for the Middle East port of Haifa. After one difficult night in the muddy military camp of Atlee, they were packed into a train and travelled to their destination, Nuseirat camp, an hour north of Gaza in the desert.

'God help us!' Mamá cried, relieved to reach the journey's end. 'Sofía, will you stop writing your letters and get the older children to do their lessons?' She turned to her other daughter.

'María, there's warm milk being dished out for the under-fives. Give me a hand to get them all together. Where's George?'

Almost everyone was asleep before Sofía got a chance to write to her husband with the latest news.

Dearest darling Jamie,

I know you are hoping, but it is with great sadness I must tell you I am not pregnant. I tell myself we have plenty of time and it would be wiser to start a family after the war. But still, my heart is sad.

On 4 January we embarked for Haifa, then on trucks to a military camp called Atlee where we ate boiled potatoes and bread. We slept in huge tents with many other people. They gave each of us an army blanket, but still we were cold because of torrential rain all night.

The next day we were on the move again. It was heartbreaking to see the very young and very old up to their knees in the mire. They herded us onto trains where the only toilet facility was a bucket in the corner behind a sack. Really it was quite disgusting. Still, we managed despite a lot of complaining by the usual ones. The rest of us were glad to be safe, away from the war and any further attacks from the Luftwaffe.

How quickly people forget the danger and dereliction we left behind on Castellorizo. With few houses standing after that awful two days of bombing, we're all lucky to be alive. But perhaps it's better that people remember our homeland as the beautiful town it was before the war. I'm sure if there was no danger, the Allies would be glad to send us all home and be done with us and our eternal moaning. With our constant peevish attitude and the vast drain on their resources, we must appear so ungrateful. Houses can be rebuilt, but lives cannot be given back, so we must primarily stay safe and be glad for our rescue.

We arrived at our final camp, Nuseirat. They say it houses many thousands of Greek refugees. First, we were registered and given a number, written onto a label, threaded on string and worn around our necks like a goat bell! Everyone had to shower and have a medical examination while they disinfected our clothes to stop the spread of lice and such. They say this procedure will take place once a month while we're here.

We're divided into municipalities depicted by our island of origin: Castellorizo, Chios, Kalymnos and Samos. Each community is surrounded by sand dunes. Our camp has four huts dedicated to other things. A school, where I hope to teach the little ones, also a church, a medical centre and one hut for ablutions. For the children there are organised games such as football, girl guides and boy scouts. We collect our cooked food three times a day and eat in our own huts. It's really not so bad.

I'm pleased that I brought my sewing machine. I came across another woman with one and she said she has too much work. I'm meeting her tomorrow to discuss how we can start a little sewing enterprise in the camp.

Rosa has made friends with another ballet dancer, Zoe, from Chios and is learning more steps. They dance beautifully together and there is talk of a show.

I'm very tired after this crazy day and really must get some sleep. So, that's all my news for now, my gorgeous lover. Please write back as soon as you can. I love you to the end of the sun and stars and back again.

Forever your faithful and loving wife who longs, oh yes, really longs to be in your arms again,

Sofia XXX

Four weeks passed before Jamie's reply reached her.

My beautiful wife, Sofía,

There is hope, my darling, just stay strong and pray to God that we will be together soon. I'm in heaven and wishing you were with me.

We think Frederick will be leaving soon. Once he's gone, we will concentrate on starting a family. I have decided to come to live on Castellorizo when I can. That way, I will feel like I'm a real member of your family. Then later, you must come and try England. Our lives together will be a big adventure to start with. I can't wait to lie by you all night and wake to find you beside me in the morning. I long to hold you close, kiss you passionately and feel your head resting on my chest, so you can hear my heart beating with love for you. I miss you so much, my precious darling.

Darling Sofía, I love you so fiercely it's painful. I lie awake at night missing the warmth of your body and the sound of you whispering my name. Though we are far apart, my thoughts are only of you. It's like my soul is continually calling you and will only silence when we are together once more.

Tell your father about Frederick.

Write back soon.

Sending my eternal love,

Jamie XXX

Frederick was their code name for the enemy. Letters were censored by the military, so they were careful not to mention war or politics. Sofía hurried to Babá and passed on Jamie's news.

'Babá, Jamie says he's in heaven – that's Chania, in Crete. He says he thinks the war will soon be over. He's heard that Frederick – that's the Germans – are about to leave the island with their tails between their legs.'

'For God's sake, keep your voice down, Sofía!' Kuríllos said. 'You'll get your husband shot! How can he possibly know what's going on between Churchill and Hitler?'

'It's probably just hopeful gossip put about to hike up people's morale,' Babá added.

'Or put about by the enemy so that people lower their guard,' Kuríllos said.

Before she could comment, Babá spoke again. 'Listen, your mother needs help. María's gone into labour and George has a terrible bellyache. She wants you to take him to the doctor, to make sure it's not food poisoning or appendicitis. Also, as soon as the baby's born, we're meeting with the Rhodini family about Ayeleen's betrothal and dowry. She's sweet on their eldest and they're a good family. So, I've agreed to the marriage on her sixteenth birthday.'

Sofía grinned. 'A wedding, just the thing to lift everyone's spirits.'

Yet, as she walked away from her father and uncle, Sofía's smile turned to a frown. Money had become a big problem for most people. Nobody had any and the Castellorizo people were a proud lot. Her neighbours made frequent trips into Gaza on the pretext of simply having a day with friends, but on her first visit, Sofía noticed a neighbour, Polyxena, carrying a large bundle, which was stashed with several others on the roof of the bus. The true mission, she guessed, was to sell something of value. No one discussed the situation, even when they recognised Castellorizo bits and pieces for sale by stall holders. A silver filigree button from the traditional costume, a gold ring or locket, a grandmother's gold chain and crucifix. Also, the people of Castellorizo loved their gold coins, especially sovereigns and half-sovereigns, placing the same value on them as the Arabs did on gold teeth.

One by one, as the months passed, family treasures were traded for cash in the Gaza bazaars. When nothing remained, the highly prized Castellorizo costume with its mink-lined coat garnered more necessary items and a little cash.

Sofía found George hugging his belly. 'Come on, Georgikie, let's get you to the doctor,' she said, trying to sound cheerful despite her concern. 'He'll give you some medicine to make the pain go away. Have you eaten anything you shouldn't?' He shook his head, but then glanced at her sheepishly. 'Come on now, tell me the truth. What have you eaten this morning?'

He drew his knees up and rocked back and forth. 'Fevzi's hiding, but he's got the bellyache too.'

Eventually, Sofía found the underlying cause of her little brother's discomfort. Cook had sat by the kitchen window, peeling sour apples all morning for pies. The boys, seeing the apple peel come flying out of the window towards the bin, had intercepted its journey, catching it and stuffing it into their mouths with great glee.

A good dose of Epsom salts from the doctor sorted out the gurgling intestines of both little rascals.

Next, Sofía went to see how her sister was getting on with her latest confinement but – to her dismay – she found her mother crying her heart out behind their hut.

'Mamá! What's going on? Is María all right?'

Convulsed by sobs, Mamá could hardly speak. 'They took her away to be buried . . .'

Sofía slammed her hand over her heart. 'María?'

'No, María's fine, just upset. I mean the baby; *Loulouthi*, Flower. She opened her eyes, took one breath, then closed her eyes forever. 'They took her away, straight from María's arms.' She broke down again and Sofía had never seen her so devastated.

'Oh, Mamá, I'm sorry. Please don't get so upset.'

She sniffed hard, smudging tears from her cheeks. 'You don't understand . . . and how could you? Loulouthi was my granddaughter – my darling granddaughter – a part of me born through my daughter. I never got to hold her. Not for one second did she lie in my arms. She never even saw me. But that does not matter. I had all the love of a lifetime inside me, to give her. As María held her, I saw her perfect baby face, her thin eyelids closed, her cherub mouth, perfectly still when there should have been a cry. I *ached* to hold her to me – my granddaughter – but she stayed with María for as long as possible, then was suddenly whisked away by the priest. In that moment I lost the only chance I had to hold that tiny infant of my own heart. And all the love I had for her . . . that love is trapped inside me with nowhere to go.'

Sofía tried to imagine. 'And you feel cheated?' she asked quietly, struggling to understand the grief her mother would be feeling.

Mamá dropped her face into her hands and nodded before she gave free rein to her sadness. 'How can anyone understand what it's like to be a grandparent, unless they're one themselves?'

'Stay here a moment, perhaps it's not too late,' Sofía said.

She rushed around to the converted church, but it was empty. From there, she hurried to the administration building and told them what had happened.

'You need to see the doctor,' they said. 'He'll have to establish the cause of death.'

Why didn't she think of that? She hurried to the surgery and found the doctor writing out a report.

Back at Mamá's side, feeling all her mother's grief, she placed her arm around her shoulders. 'Come with me if you want to say hello and goodbye to your grandchild,' she said softly.

Overwhelmed, Sofía struggled to contain her own emotions. Together, they walked over to the medical centre where Sofía knocked on the door.

Inside, Doctor Ishmael indicated a baby crib. 'I will leave you alone for a few minutes, *Kiríea* Konstantinidis.' He made a short bow and left the room, exchanging a kindly glance with Sofía as he did so.

Sofía nodded and mouthed, 'Thank you,' as her mother headed for the crib and her tears overflowed.

* * *

In bed that night, Sofía tried to imagine how her sister must be feeling. She guessed it made no difference how many children a woman had: to lose one at birth must be terrible. How she longed to experience being pregnant. Sometimes she imagined the moment she would tell Jamie. His joy would be beyond measure. Building a home and starting a family was their ultimate goal, the thing they dreamed of above all else.

* * *

Mamá, María, Sofía and Ayeleen were getting the little ones ready for bed when Popi and Martha came rushing into the hut.

'Have you heard the news? The King of Timbuktu's coming to visit,' Popi said.

'They say he's looking for a beautiful woman to make into a princess and marry,' Martha added, swishing her long tresses over her shoulders.

'Well, he'll have to look hard to find any beauty around here – I haven't had time to brush my hair for three days!' Mamá cried with a weary grin. 'Anyway, who wants to be Queen of Timbuktu? Doesn't exactly roll off the tongue, does it?'

'I do!' cried Popi.

'And me!' said Martha.

'I wouldn't mind being Queen for a day,' Ayeleen said, waving her arm around the room. 'Just imagine: *Who are all these children? Off with their heads!*' She giggled.

Bebe's eyes widened and she started bawling. 'I don't want my head off!'

'Tut! Now look what you've done,' Mamá said, putting the dampers on a smile but her shoulders were still jigging. 'It was a joke, Bebe; don't fret, my precious. Your sister's being silly and you're overtired. Be a good girl and you can get into my bed for half an hour.'

* * *

Later, Babá came home with more accurate news. 'The camp's about to receive a visit from Prince Peter of Yugoslavia. The mayor's ordered the women to wear their Castellorizo costumes.' Every family had one, proudly passed from mother to daughter.

'Mamá, help me find my costume, I must wear it for the prince! Where is it?' Sofía cried staring at the bundles that lined one wall of their hut. 'This is the most exciting thing to happen for ages!'

Mamá's face paled. 'It's under the mattress, along with your father's suit,' she said.

Together, they lifted the bedding to one side and retrieved Babá's best suit and Sofía's costume, last worn for her wedding. Sofía rejoiced at the thought of wearing it again.

'But Mamá, two of the silver brooch-buttons are missing. There're only three *boúkles* closing the blouse.'

'We've been robbed, like so many others,' she said dully, glancing at Sofía with guilty eyes.

Sofía considered that her wonderful jewellery box, containing all Jamie's letters, had not been disturbed. If thieves had been afoot, wouldn't they have taken it? She stared at Mamá, saw her cheeks flare and her eyes fill with tears.

'Mamá, what's happening? Did you take the silver *boúkles*?'

Mamá's tears overflowed. 'Don't tell anyone, Sofía. I needed the money so badly. We've never been short of money before, but now we're in the same situation as everyone else. I heard of a souk paying good money for the silver *boúkles*.'

Sofía stared around the hut. 'But what did you need the money for?'

She swiped at her tears. 'I couldn't allow them to toss baby Loulouthi into a pauper's grave, in a foreign country.' She made a determined nod, justifying her actions. 'So I bought her a little plot with a bit of marble on top.' She turned to Sofía, her resolution crumbling. 'It's so small, so very, very small, but it covers her two minutes of life with dignity.' For a moment, she battled against more tears. 'I don't know why this has upset me so much . . . it's just that, well, after the boys, I desperately wanted María to have another girl. I do love the girls so. Please, forgive me, Sofía. I'll replace the *boúkles* as soon as I can.'

'There's nothing to forgive, Mamá. I'm pleased you did it. One day, you must show María the grave.'

Poor Mamá, Sofía thought. Such a good woman with a strong sense of right and wrong. How difficult it must have been for her to take the brooches and sell them.

Apparently, Mamá was not the only Castellorizo woman who needed money. Quite suddenly, many families claimed their tents were slashed open by thieves and their valuables taken. Everyone wore their flamboyant costume for the visitation, although most had a missing brooch or two.

The Prince remarked on the great beauty of the Castellorizo women and the intricate detail of their needlework. After his departure, crates of knitting wool and needles arrived with a request for the women to knit gloves, scarves and socks for the troops.

Ayeleen discovered the United Nations Relief and Rehabilitation Administration were opening a clothes distribution centre in the camp.

'Mamá! We can get free clothes!' she cried, dashing into their hut. 'And they're employing twenty-five women to manage the centre. Let's all go and see if we can get a job!'

'And who will look after the children?' Mamá said.

'Babá and Uncle?' she replied, which made Mamá laugh.

Sofía came rushing into the hut. 'They're going to train women to be social workers, Mamá, can I apply, do you mind? The pay's good and they'll teach me about the welfare of the children.'

'As if you don't know already.' Mamá saw the excitement in her daughter's eyes and knew Sofía needed a challenge to take her mind off her husband. 'I guess we can manage without you for a few hours each day.'

Sofía put her name on the list of applicants and, because of her language and teaching skills, was accepted immediately.

* * *

The officer of the camp, Major Galway, saw Sofía and her friend Kiriaki with their sewing machines set up in the shade of the clothing store. He nodded at the women, then, unable to speak Greek, he pointed his swagger-stick at the machines and spoke to his aid.

'Who are these girls and what are they doing?'

'Sir, I hope we're not breaking any rules by helping people,' Sofía said in English, glancing into his eyes.

'Ah, you speak very well, young lady. Tell me how you help people?' the Major asked.

She summoned her courage to converse with such an important person. 'Well, you see, UNRRA are very good to us, sir. Without them, how would we clothe our growing children? But sometimes they don't have the correct sizes. So, we alter things for them.'

He frowned at her. 'And do you do this for money, or goodwill?'

'Being honest, we would like to do it for money, sir, because we don't have any. But mostly, we do it for goodwill. Who could see a child with his trousers falling down when we can make them fit in a few minutes?'

'Very noble. Do many women have this skill?'

'Practically every family on Castellorizo owns a sewing machine, but only two of us brought ours along, on account of them being heavy.'

'I see. Well, carry on, ladies.' He walked away, talking to his aid in a low voice.

* * *

Three days later, while Sofía and Kiriaki were working behind the clothes store again, the Major reappeared.

'Good morning, dear ladies,' he said with gusto. 'Please answer some questions for me.' The women nodded. 'Good show! Now, If I had more sewing machines delivered and the equipment you'd require, could you manage a small sewing factory?'

They both stared at him, then each other, then nodded furiously.

'That's the ticket. You'll be trained and well paid.'

Before the month's end, a large hut was erected behind the clothes store. Twenty Singer treadle machines arrived and a total of twenty-five Greek women were trained as machinists. Before three months passed, the sewing factory dealt with vast bundles of cut-out uniforms at an exceptional rate. The workers treadled into the night to keep up with demand.

CHAPTER 35
OLIVIA

Castellorizo, Greece, present day

'So, here's the thing, darling girl. The news that will change everything,' Uncle says, then hesitates. 'But no, first we must finish the food. Rip open that tinfoil and let's hope there's a little warmth left in the *loukoumades*.'

'You're such a tease, Uncle!' I say, putting a plate under the foil to catch any dripping honey as I tear open the packet. We stab them with our dessert forks. 'Oh my God! They're so delicious!'

We eat until we can't swallow another mouthful. Even then, our forefingers slide over the foil scooping up warm honey and toasted sesame seeds.

'Best meal ever!' I laugh at the lunacy of enjoying soup and doughnuts so much.

'I need to wash my hands before I show you my next surprise,' he says.

'OK, me too, I'll use the kitchen sink, you've got the bathroom.' I quickly clear the dishes and wash my hands.

We regroup with the ledgers and a couple of glasses of wine. 'Go on, then.' I'm impatient.

'Right, well . . . if you do decide to re-open the precious oil business, I'll sign it over to you on one condition.' I nod, so he continues. 'The first perfume that goes into production is this one.' He turns to the last recipe in the ledger.

I stare at the title: ROSA. I've heard the name before, but where? 'I can see it means a lot to you. Would you care to explain, Uncle?'

'I will, but later. We've a lot to get through this evening.' He goes to his open cabin bag on the sofa and pulls a stack of A5 envelopes. For a moment he hesitates, then places them on the dining table. 'I took the liberty of sorting out the album. I've put the photographs into groups and have written a little of their history on each envelope.' He stares out of the window for a moment, deep in thought. 'We've been through the first ones: the earthquake at the time of your grandmother's birth. That's when the house was moved and rebuilt in front of the distillery. Most of the pictures are from newspaper archives, but they help tell the story.'

I pause to take in his words. 'Just a minute, you said, rebuilt . . . where was the house before the earthquake?'

'On the square.' He catches my frown and explains. 'You know, that space when you go to the bakery. Where the enormous, wide-trunked rubber tree is?' He stops and smiles. 'My grandmothers loved that tree's predecessor, because of its dense shade. Sometimes they'd sit on its surrounding wall all day, crocheting and gossiping with passers-by.'

'I'll see it in a new light tomorrow,' I say.

He smiles. 'Later, my sister married Mustafa, the trader with a beautiful ship. Mustafa was an incredibly handsome and generous man. The gifts he brought were treasured.' He shakes his head. 'He bought my Uncle Kuríllos a camera and bought little Rosa a book on ballet and later pumps and a tutu. He had a knack for giving people exactly what they wanted most . . . even if they didn't know their own desires. Uncle Kuríllos loved that camera and he took a picture at every important occasion, so, recorded the lives of the Konstantinidis family right up to his death . . . and oddly enough beyond.' He takes a sip of wine and stares into the distance, then laughs. 'Though he missed my greatest moment. And what a moment that was! However, I have a sneaking feeling my uncle saw it all from afar.' He stops again, lost in a memory, then comes back to now. 'Nevertheless, it's imprinted on my brain and one of these days I'll put it to canvas.'

I laugh. 'Uncle, I have no idea what you're talking about.'

He grins. 'You will. I have so much to tell you.' He pulls two old black and white photographs out of an envelope and passes them to me. 'The first one's the whole family apart from Babá, my father. He'd come back to Castellorizo with the other men, to help get the town ready for the women and children. Kuríllos got one of the stevedores to take the picture on the quayside at Port Said. In the background, you can see the ship that was about to bring us all home, HMS *Empire Patrol*. We were just going to board. That was the very last time we were all together for a photo.' Suddenly, his face drops and I see nothing but sadness. 'Oh my dear. Give me a moment, will you?'

I study the photograph and give him another glass of wine. He doesn't respond and when I look up his mouth is tightly compressed and fat tears roll down his cheeks. Unable to speak, he shakes his head slowly and then pulls out a big white hankie. 'Oh, Uncle, I'm sorry! I didn't mean to upset you like this.'

He dries his face and blows his nose. 'No . . . it's me, dear girl. Sometimes it all comes back too clearly. I hope I haven't embarrassed myself.'

'Don't be silly. Do you want to talk about it?'

He shakes his head. 'Nobody wants to talk about it. That's why you don't know . . . and that's why it's so painful. Let's leave it for the moment and go on to the next photo.' I study the waiflike ballerina on points. A slim, beautiful woman beside her with a finger under the child's chin and a hand under her elbow, guiding her into the correct position. The picture was taken outdoors and the light was low, to the side, throwing a long shadow across the ground. 'Oh dear, I seem to have them in the wrong order. This was taken before we left Castellorizo . . . before the bombing.'

'What a beautiful artistic picture. Who is it?'

'The girl is Rosa, María's second child. The woman is Anastasia, the local schoolteacher. Your grandmother adored her.' He pauses for a moment. 'More than that, now I think back, I believe Sofía loved her.'

'So, the perfume recipe was named after Rosa? Or, Rosa was named after the perfume?'

He smiles and nods, which only adds to my confusion. There's been so much to take in today, along with the relief that my uncle seems to be making a rapid recovery, I try to suppress a yawn. 'Sorry, I'm intrigued and want to know more, but it must be all this fresh air and good food. I really must go, or it'll be lunchtime before I even wake!'

Later, in my bed, on the very brink of sleep, I recall something Uncle said: the news that will change everything. He hadn't elaborated. Clearly, the photographs and the emotions they brought to him had wiped the important news from his mind. I must remind him about it tomorrow.

* * *

After a good night's sleep, I prepare to meet the day, and then set out for our reserved table.

'*Kaliméra!*' '*Kaliméra!*' '*Kaliméra!*' The greeting comes from all sides. I realise this 'good day!' is not a greeting but a statement. It *is* a good day!

304

I find Eleni and Uncle in deep conversation at our table, but the moment Eleni sees me she jumps up.

'I bring you coffee, yes?'

'*Ef-har-is-tó*,' I try. She laughs, clearly delighted. I turn to my uncle. '*Thank you* is the most difficult word to say, Uncle.'

'Then let me help. *A fairy's toe* will get you understood and appreciated and if you remember it's not a pixie's foot – it's a fairy's toe – you'll never forget it.'

'Clearly, you were a great teacher. Thanks.' I feel a warm sense of pride. My family were an incredible lot. 'Now, what's planned for today, Uncle?'

'I think it's time we confronted this Rob. According to his claims, he's family too. I want to know who his parents are.'

'Do you really think he's a Konstantinidis descendant? I thought he might be an estranged in-law who found out about the house, but he has the family thumbs. It's not something one can fake, or hide.'

Uncle appears slightly uncomfortable. 'Yes, you're right about that, dear girl.'

'And, by the way, what is the news that will change everything, that you talked about yesterday. I'm intrigued. Does it have anything to do with our Australian friend?' I look up and mutter under my breath. 'Bugger, speak of the devil.'

'G'day, Livia. How's it going, mate?'

'Hi, Rob. Not so bad, you know. Let me introduce you to *O Theios mou*,' I say, proud to use the Greek for my uncle.

They shake hands. 'Nice ta meet ya. Are you from here too, mate?' Uncle nods. Clearly, Rob hasn't made the connection. He turns back to me. 'Mum's got the all clear to travel, so she's booking a flight as soon as possible. Can we meet with the lawyer this arvo and sort out the property deeds?'

I nod. 'Why not?'

'Great, say five o'clock?'

'Sure, suits me fine.'

'OK, then we just need to find somewhere quiet to hold the meeting – he's from Rhodes, you see. Hasn't got an office on the island.'

Uncle sticks his finger in the air, then points at his room.

'*A fairy's toe,*' I say seriously.

Rob blinks at me. 'Sorry, I thought you said . . . never mind. I didn't know you speak Greek.'

'My mother was Greek, remember. *O Theios mou* is offering us his apartment for our negotiations, which is very kind.'

'Ta, mate. Good on ya,' Rob says amiably.

Dino rushes out of the kitchen and yells at Uncle, gesticulating wildly. They seem to be having a huge row and for a moment I fear they may come to blows.

Rob's eyes widen. He steps back, staring at the two men. 'Right, I'm off to see the lawyer now. See you this arvo, Livia. OK?'

'Very good.' I turn to Uncle. 'What was the argument about?'

'Argument?' Uncle blinks at me. 'What argument?'

'You and Dino, all the yelling and arm waving.'

He laughs. 'Nothing! He's inviting me to a fishing competition, sunrise tomorrow, in my own boat. We always have this rivalry – the catcher of the biggest fish pays for dinner tomorrow night.'

* * *

We decide to take a slow walk up to the house and I have an overwhelming sensation of walking home. The small town has worked its magic on me. Everyone we pass knows who we are and the strong feeling of belonging is wonderful. Several people – mostly mature locals – invite us for coffee. A woman rushes out of her house and gives each of us a ripe apricot. 'Fresh! Fresh!' she cries and Uncle grins at me as if to say, 'See, it's wonderful here.'

The house is as we left it. Solid and promising, yet at the same time, ramshackle and deserted.

'Leave the front door wide open and perhaps we'll get some light in the back,' Uncle suggests.

We creep gingerly around the edge of the floor again, then we hear a man shout.

'*Ela, Kyrie Yeorgo!*'

'Who's calling me now?' Uncle says, slightly exasperated, turning to peer at the silhouette in the doorway. 'I'd better go and see.'

The figure starts to walk across the floor. 'No! Stop, stop! It's not safe,' my uncle shouts.

A great creaking sound comes up from the boards.

'Go back slowly!' I call, too late.

We watch – unable to move – holding our breath. The centre of the floor drops a metre. I scream. The man falls and lies spreadeagled, unable to move. The floor is still groaning, threatening to collapse completely.

Greg rushes into the doorway. 'Stay back, Greg, the floor's collapsed. There's someone stranded – in danger!' I cry.

Greg shines his torch on the poor guy, then laughs. 'I'd like you to meet Fannes, the local locksmith.'

'*Ela, maláka!* Get me out of here. I daren't stand in case I fall through the floor!' the poor guy shouts with an Australian accent. 'It could drop at any moment.'

Greg has a coil of cable over his shoulder once more. 'I'm going to throw you a line. Wrap it around your chest and I'll pull you up, OK?'

Soon the locksmith is out and shaking hands with Greg. We do the hokey-cokey around the room again until we stand outside the front door.

'Hi, I'm Frank,' the man says. 'The locals call me Fannes.' He shrugs. 'I've come to do your locks.'

'Good grief, Olivia, that was close! He could have broken his neck,' Uncle says.

A shout comes from behind us. 'Hello!' Another man appears. Short and wide, with biceps like a footballer's thighs, he strides towards us with an arm extended. 'I am the builder, Manno, I come to fix your floor, OK?'

Greg grins, strong white teeth displayed in a mischievous smile. I remember the meal in Kaş and his kisses after and my pulse throbs.

Oh my! Don't be silly! I'm not the sort to be impressed by . . . Jesus in heaven . . . such good looks. I mean, he belongs on the cover of a cheap romance!

Uncle clears his throat and I realise I'm staring and chewing my lip.

'*Yiasas,*' Greg says, shaking hands with my uncle.

Manno explains, 'As soon as I have light and electricity, I can replace the floor. You tell me when you want.'

Greg turns to me and I can't think of a thing to say. 'My cousin lives below here,' he says. 'We will plug the cable in his house, then you get light in the house of yours, so the builder can start right away – yes, is OK? Have you met my cousin, Andoni? He looks like me.'

There are two of them? Honestly, I need a swim.

I might have been staring. From the grin on his face, you'd think he'd just invented electricity.

Uncle beams at me, then him, *then* goes into a huge discussion that sounds as though World War Three has just broken out, but I am getting the hang of this now. The louder they shout, the more they like each other.

The cable is lowered over the edge of the patio to the street below. Unfortunately, the bulb at the other end only reaches the front door. After much hollering, a couple of two-metre extension leads are brought up by children, then a roll of cable on a spool. Greg joins everything together and I have a *déjà vu* moment, feeling sure I've seen this happen in an old cowboy film at some time.

'*Ela!*' the electrician yells over the edge of the patio and, hey presto, we have light in the house. A crowd gathers. Kids punch the air, women smile and nod at each other and men shake hands and call out, 'Bravo!'

'Very good! I'll start on the floor now,' Manno says. 'Everybody go!'

Uncle slips his arm around my shoulders. 'You can't imagine how much I want to see my home restored, dear girl.' He sighs wistfully. 'It reminds me of a time, long ago, when the entire Konstantinidis family longed to return to this very same building.'

CHAPTER 36
SOFIA

Returning to Castellorizo, Greece, 1945

MAMÁ PUT DOWN HER EMBROIDERY. 'Sofía, I wish we could go home and take all we have here with us.'

The year had flown by. Ayeleen and Mamá took part in the knitting and sewing enterprises which became a regular source of income for the Castellorizo women. The Greek refugees had not sat idly waiting for war to end. Small business emerged over the first few months, restoring pride and self-esteem in the displaced Greek people. The *kafenion* was most popular with the men. A tailor's and a bread shop stood next door. Proudly displayed to the front of the bakery were traditional Greek delicacies such as halva and the Castellorizo cinnamon and sugar pie, *katoumaría*.

Sofía worked hard and saved all she could, dreaming of the day she and Jamie would be together. 'I can't believe April is almost over,' she said sadly. 'Do you think we'll ever go home, Mamá?'

'Isn't that what I just said? I know you're missing your husband, Sofía, but let's not forget what we left behind. Our island was almost destroyed. We were all half starved. Here, the children are healthy, everyone has a little money in their pocket, clothes on their backs and food on the table.'

She gave Mamá a hug. 'I'm going to see if there's a letter from my husband.'

There was no mail for her, but the mailroom buzzed with excitement. She listened to the gossip, then hurried to find her father. Outside, most were taking advantage of siesta time. Cicadas sawed monotonously in the warm still air. Sofía hurried to the coffee shop and brazenly interrupted her father's game of *tavli*.

'They've executed Mussolini, Babá! Can you believe it? He's dead, the Duce is dead. They say we'll all be going home soon.'

'Where did you hear this thing about the Duce, Sofía?' Uncle Kuríllos asked, pausing with the dice in his fist.

'In the mailroom, everyone's talking about it.' She lowered her voice. 'They say it was on the radio.' She stared from one to the other. 'Do you think they'll assassinate Hitler? If someone did that, the war would be over for sure and we'd be able to go home tomorrow.' Her eyes narrowed. 'Given the chance, I'd do it.'

The two men exchanged a glance. 'For God's sake, Sofía! Keep such thoughts to yourself,' Babá said. 'You don't know who's listening. Besides, we can't simply pack up and go home, even if the war does end tomorrow.' Sofía blinked and recognising her confusion, he continued. 'Remind yourself why we left. On 17 October 1943, six German Stukas bombed our small town to smithereens.'

'I know . . . of course, I know.'

'But like everyone else, you forget! You've a romantic picture in your head – our perfect island – happy families. The famine's forgotten. The painful truth is, most of our people were half starved, there was little food, no money, no work. Most wanted to leave for Australia. Also, houses don't rebuild themselves – a third of the town's in ruins after the bombing,' Babá said. 'I know you want to go home – we all do – but you must get these rainbows out of your head and remember the truth! People were killed on that first day of bombing, our own neighbours, British soldiers, your friend. *You* were almost killed and many homes were destroyed!'

Sofía felt her jaw stiffen and a painful lump rose in her throat. Like everyone else, she didn't want to remember. She had no wish to recall the devastation they'd left behind. Her grief for Anastasia came back so suddenly sometimes, it caught her unaware and she wanted to scream.

'Babá, don't be cruel, how can I forget that day?' She swallowed hard, determined not to lose control. 'Those bombers took my friend's life, right in front of me. The vision . . .' She panted, swallowed, then managed to continue. 'The memory still torments me when I try to sleep . . . well . . .' She ran out of words, saddened to her soul.

'But you don't realise *how long* we've been struggling. We're a proud lot and would never admit our problems, even to each other. Listen, when your mother was pregnant with you, I was desperate for a son. I needed silver to make a *tamata*, a pendant, to hang under the Blessed Virgin in the little church. You see, they said she was capable of miracles. Word got about, that I was buying silver. The town's mothers and grandmothers, desperate for money to buy provisions, implored me to buy the silver brooches from their treasured Castellorizo costumes. They begged with tears in their eyes and tales of their starving babies. What could we do? We ended up making so many *tamatas* to hang in the church, it's a wonder that you turned out to be a girl after all.' He smiled and reached out to touch her cheek. 'But to tell the truth, I wouldn't have it any other way. So, when you see a costume with three of the elaborate silver brooches holding it closed, instead of five, you know why and you say nothing, OK.'

312

Sofía stared at him for a moment, digesting all this information. She closed her eyes and visualised her hometown. After a moment, she sighed, overwhelmed by her heavy heart. 'You're right. When I see Castellorizo in my mind it's perfect, I'm incredibly happy and so eager to go home. I really have to force myself to remember the place as we left it, after the bombings.'

'It's the same for everyone here,' Kuríllos said.

Sofía continued. 'But if I force the truth and see it as I did from the ship's stern rail when we left, I just want to cry. It's too awful! What are we going to do, Babá?'

'It seems clear to me that the men must go back first and start rebuilding and the women and children follow when things are ready for them. What do you think, brother?'

Kuríllos nodded. 'I've been thinking about this,' he said. 'Sofía's right: with Mussolini gone, I believe the war's drawing to a close. We should be prepared for that time and not just take our families back when they'll be far better off spending another few months here. I mean, we've become complacent. Our children are strong and well fed. Those who want work are earning money. The sick have a doctor and medicine at hand. For most people, this is pure luxury compared to our little, war-torn Castellorizo.'

'Let's think this through and call a meeting tomorrow night,' Babá said.

* * *

Fifteen days later, Uncle Kuríllos came rushing into their hut. 'Hitler's dead! Killed himself and his *poutana*, whore.'

'Language!' Mamá called back. 'There are children in here!'

313

Sofía grabbed her mother's hand. 'Surely this is it. The war must end now.'

Just a week later, Kuríllos burst into the hut again and Sofía knew by the wild joy on his face, the announcement they were all waiting for was imminent. 'Germany's surrendered and Churchill has announced Victory in Europe!' She ran into his arms and they danced a mad polka of happiness until they collapsed, breathless and laughing onto the bed.

'You're both mad,' Mamá said, grinning wildly. 'Where's your father? Somebody had better bring him home before he gets steaming drunk.'

Fevzi, Zafiro and George also came racing into the hut. 'We're going to be torch bearers tonight, Mamá, there's over a thousand of us. We're going to march around the camp and sing our great songs of war and victory and our Greek anthem!'

'Then you'd better go to the shower hut and scrub that grey neck of yours or you won't be allowed anywhere. Take the carbolic and off you go right now! I'll find you some clean clothes.'

Excitement buzzed through Nuseirat refugee camp. Everyone with a musical instrument – trumpet, trombone, squeezebox or harmonica – came out that evening and played. Anyone who could play the spoons, drums, or tissue paper and comb, joined in. Babá and Kuríllos got so drunk that Uncle played his *baglama* before they both fell off their chairs, laughing and crying and trying to pull each other up.

All the women put on their Castellorizo costumes and danced the *Kalamatianó* in elegant circles, nodding and smiling aloofly. Men, so inebriated they could hardly stand, suddenly found their feet and danced *Zebetiko* with amazing grace, waving their arms over their heads like seagrass and prancing lightly on bent

314

knees. Great feats of bravery were demonstrated for the first time since the outbreak of war. A bottle of raki was poured in a circle on the dance area and set alight, then braved by barefoot Heféstus, the blacksmith. The man – more like a bull of bulging muscle – rolled up his trousers and danced gracefully through the flames to loud cries of '*Opa!*' as the hairs on his club-shaped calves shrivelled to nothing. People threw plates and saucers to smash around him and they all knew he would be plucking ceramic splinters from his feet for weeks.

Two chairs were balanced one atop the other on a table and Simonos climbed to the top, demonstrating his dance skills and balance, until the whole thing toppled. To more loud cries of '*Opa!*' his friends caught him and slapped him on the back while shouting, 'Bravo!'

Women knelt around the edge of the dance area, proudly clapping time for their exhibitionist men. Megáli Yiayá smiled broadly, sipping a glass of plum brandy as she watched and recalled her younger days.

The music changed to *tsifteteli*, the belly dance. Men sat as women gathered on the dance area, swinging their bony hips and gracefully beckoning them with scrawny arms. The camp women who'd sacrificed everything for their families, were skin and bone. In other circumstances, their voluptuous forms would have supported ample hips and heavy breasts and complemented the slow sensual melody.

The music picked up speed until the dance area was a shivering display of flaccid bosoms and flat buttocks, yet the watching men became a little puffy-faced and glassy-eyed, for they saw what they dreamed of and what they loved. Older women grinned at the helpless males who had fallen under the sly spell of female allure.

Someone brought a cauldron of oil under which a fire was lit. Smiling mothers appeared with fermenting pots of light dough. Others, adept at making doughnuts, scooped small handfuls of the glutinous mixture, squeezing their fists until a ball slid from between thumb and forefinger, to be dropped into the oil. Once the doughnuts had puffed up and turned golden, crisping as they bobbed to the surface, they were scooped out, dropped into a tray of honey-syrup and sprinkled with toasted sesame seeds.

'Everyone, take! Take!' the women cried, rejoicing at the basic Castellorizo custom of pleasing their friends and neighbours, celebrating the imminent prospect of leaving for home. The joyous hysteria mounted through the night until weary, happy people dragged themselves back to their huts as the sun came up.

'We're going home!' wine-warmed Mamá cried as she hugged George. She stared around the room and made plans to start packing. 'I can hardly believe it, after all this time. Just to think, in a few weeks we might be making precious oil, earning proper money, instead of having to sell bits and pieces on Gaza market. Oh, to sleep in our own beds!'

* * *

The next afternoon, bleary-eyed adults gathered outside the *kafenion* to discuss the situation. Women still insisted they were going home first. The mayor suggested they meet in the sewing factory as the elderly could at least sit down there. That evening, after sundown when the air had cooled a little, almost a thousand people tried to cram into the hut behind the UNRRA clothing store.

'This is ridiculous!' the mayor shouted as more people tried to squeeze inside and a scuffle broke out. 'Right! Two people from each family . . . everyone else, OUTSIDE!'

316

The outcome of the meeting produced other plans, a vote and a decision made.

'So, we are all agreed,' the mayor cried. 'Women and children and those over sixty-five will stay here until their homes are rebuilt.' The husbands nodded calling, 'Hear! Hear!' bringing tears of protest or vicious swipes from their angry wives. 'Does anyone have anything to add?' the mayor continued.

Sofía had run around the outside and secured herself a place at the open window. Now she leaned in, waving her arm in the air. 'Sir!'

'Yes, miss.'

'My husband is a British soldier and he was on Castellorizo recently. He explained that the fuel dump exploded, killing two of his fellow soldiers and igniting anything flammable in the area. This means, not only must the houses that were bombed in '43 be rebuilt, but also new windows, floors and doors need making for most of the other houses. I wondered if a carpenter should be with the first shipment of men returning to the island and also a consignment of seasoned timber be shipped to the island with them.'

'Good thinking, young lady! Any other comments?'

* * *

With the knowledge that three ships were to return to their island, the Castellorizons voted for a committee to decide on the order of departure. The mayor and an inspection team, plus the strongest men and those with homes in the most damaged area would be the first. Next, those men with the skills needed to prepare the town for the women and children: the baker, doctor, storekeeper and so on. Lastly, the elderly, disabled, and the women and children would return to their homes.

Babá managed to get himself on the first list, whereas Kuríllos failed, despite using his charm and resorting to bribery. His one eye and gammy leg had always served to get him out of physical work but now went against him and put him in the last group. Babá said he was glad to know his brother would be taking care of the family.

Three hundred men, including Babá, headed for Castellorizo in early July. Jamie had checked the Konstantinidis house and to their relief, he found everything intact. The house miraculously escaped damage from the fire and the bombings, apart from the landslide at the back of the building which Babá would try to clear when he had time.

Two weeks later, the second group left for Castellorizo, eager to prepare for the wives and children.

* * *

Sofía could not remember such fevered excitement. Once the men had gone, everyone, from Megáli Yiayá to the youngest toddler helped to prepare for their departure from what had become the Konstantinidis family hut.

'Don't let me forget my sewing machine, Mamá.'

'How did we manage to collect so much stuff in a year and a half?' Mamá cried as she strung another bundle and attached a label describing the contents. 'We've never had so many clothes before.'

Ayeleen helped María with her younger siblings, while Rosa and Popi folded clothes and added them to neat piles.

'Here,' Mamá said passing the ball of twine. 'Wrap them in a small blanket, string them up and write the contents on a label, OK?'

Popi nodded. 'I'll write, you wrap,' she said to Rosa.

* * *

At the end of September, Mamá sat on the edge of the bed and looked around. 'At last, we're leaving. I've grown rather fond of this hut, but I'm looking forward to getting on the train for El Shatt and the Dalmatian Refugee Camp.'

'I hope it's light when we go through the Sinai Desert, Mamá,' Sofía said. 'I really rather like Egypt.'

However, after a week in the Egyptian refugee camp, everyone was impatient.

'Why are they holding us here?' Mamá cried. 'What are they up to? I don't feel safe without our men. Sofía, you must remind me to never tell your father to, *Go away and leave us alone*, ever again.'

Sofía laughed. 'Patience, Mamá! We've endured almost two years of camps, a few more days makes little difference.'

Three of María's children, Athena, Kristina and Bebe, were chasing each other around the tent.

'For goodness' sake, you're making me crazy!' Mamá shouted, lifting her hand and making slicing movements through the air. 'María, control your children!'

Panayiotis coughed raucously. María looked up. 'Are you OK, son?'

'My chest hurts, Mamá, and my throat's sore.'

María placed her hand on his forehead. 'You've got a temperature. Come on, let's take you to see Doctor Ishmael.'

They passed Kuríllos as he entered the tent. 'I have some good news, everybody,' he said. 'We're leaving for Port Said tomorrow.'

'Hurrah! Wonderful! At last!' everyone cried.

319

Mamá turned to her daughters. 'María, you can help me with our chattels, when you come back from the doctor, there's more than I can manage. Sofía, you and your rope loops are in charge of the children. Please, keep a special look out for George. I can't stand the thought of him going missing before we get on the ship again.'

* * *

The refugees found Port Said in darkness when they arrived.

'I'm so excited to be going home at last. Isn't it amazing?' Sofía said. 'I wonder if Jamie is still in Castellorizo. I haven't had a letter for two weeks.'

'Don't get your hopes up,' Mamá said. 'The island is still a mess, remember.'

Everyone spoke in whispers so as not to wake the children. Bleary-eyed toddlers were slung over their mothers' shoulders and babies suckled discreetly at the breast. Every happy step towards the ship was one step closer to home. Sofía, with her length of string like a fishing rig that captured small children, made mental notes, eager to record every detail of this important day in her history book later.

Mamá checked where was George, worried that he would wander off at a crucial moment again. She found him holding her mother's hand, telling her he would be the captain of a ship when he grew up.

There were almost 500 women, children and the elderly; and nearly twice as many bundles of belongings. The sun broke the horizon, lighting the sky in peachy warmth. Adults smiled at each other. United in their elation, they all knew this would be the perfect day. War had ended and, at last, they were returning to their homes and their men.

A chain gang unloaded many wooden boxes from the hold, which somebody in earshot claimed was army ammunition left over from the war.

'Stand back, children,' Mamá said, pushing George behind her, concerned about the consequences of a dropped box of explosives. 'They're coming to collect our luggage now.' She frowned as Panayiotis started coughing again. 'We'll get some oil of eucalyptus on that chest as soon as we get home, don't you worry. You'll feel better in no time.'

Everyone's bundles were taken on board and the queue of Castellorizons shuffled closer to the table of forms to be filled in before embarkation. Once they were ready to board, Kuríllos produced his Box Brownie and gathered them together for a final photograph before they returned home.

'Come on! Smile, everybody. You're about to start the happiest day of your life, look as though you're enjoying it!' he said to his nieces and nephews. Then he handed the camera to a docker and gave instructions, before getting in on the last frame on the roll of film. He carefully rewound it, scribbled his name and 'Castellorizo' onto a slip of paper and gave the little canister along with a monetary note, to the stevedore who promised to send it for development.

CHAPTER 37
GEORGE

Castellorizo, Greece, present day

UNCLE OPENS HIS WALLET TO pay Eleni for breakfast. He stops for a moment, gazes at a photograph in the wallet's little cellophane window and recalls when it was taken. On the dockside at Port Said. He still has the original negative. It was reprinted many times until, in the new millennium, a nice young man in the photo place in downtown Brighton put it on disk for him. He ran his thumb over the silky plastic window and stared at the last photo ever taken of his entire family, apart from Babá. He guessed most had passed on now. How badly he'd wanted his father to love him . . . show how proud he was of him. But in life, it seemed George only managed to disappoint him.

The love he had had for his father was fractured when Babá took his belt to him, determined to turn him into a *real man*.

'My only son, not married at twenty-one! What's the matter with you? Why are you refusing to take Cilla for your wife, you fool? She's not bad-looking and she comes from a good family with the largest fishing boat on the island.'

'I don't love her . . . in fact I don't even like her. She smells of fish and her mother's a bully with too many warts. Her daughter will turn out to be just the same and so will any children she manages to produce.' Although he towered over his father, he wouldn't raise a finger against him. 'Let's face it, Babá, I'm not your cave-man sort. I can imagine a lifetime of nagging with that one and I'd rather die than make babies with her.'

'Well, if you don't want to marry just yet, become a priest, for God's sake.'

'Just one small problem there, I don't believe in God.'

'Well, pretend like everyone else! People are going to start making accusations. I'm not having anyone whispering about my son! Christ Almighty, the shame!'

'Babá it's 1959, I'm twenty-one. The world is changing. America and Russa have sent satellites into space, a nuclear submarine has reached the North Pole, Communists have just about taken over Greece and you want me to get married and have children, in this crazy world?'

'This is Castellorizo, none of those things will affect us here!' He swiped his belt and caught George across his arm.

'I seem to remember you saying something like that in the Second World War. You mustn't judge people the way you do – and if you swing that belt at me again, it will be the last time you ever see me!'

Babá threaded the belt back into his trousers. 'I'm trying to knock some sense into you. Anyway, we leave for Australia in three months. You'll feel differently when we get there. They say the women are very beautiful. I'm looking forward to it myself.' He sucked in his belly and threw his shoulders back.

George had no intentions of going to Australia. Sofía needed his help. She had given her entire life serving the family and now they had ostracised her and her baby, just when she needed them most. He loved his two sisters more than any other women in the world and he knew it would always be that way.

* * *

323

George studies the other picture in his foldover wallet. A treasured photograph of David. He remembers their wonderful life together and their beautiful home. He looks up, peers across the harbour and into the town square. He will walk over there when he has a quiet moment alone. Sit on the wall under the rubber tree and remember. Perhaps see old ghosts as his memory revisits the happiest time of his life. He has the house key in his pocket.

He glances across the table. Olivia has stopped writing in order to watch the Blue Star ferry. It pulls away from its mooring and raises its tailgate at the same time. The massive propellers churn the water as the ship turns, its bow and stern almost touching the sides of the harbour. The ferry sounds its baritone horn, warning small fishing vessels to get out of the way as it heads out towards the open sea. Shortly, the ferry is replaced by a navy patrol boat that ties up at the same Castellorizo berth.

Olivia turns and smiles at him. 'I'm quite sure Rob doesn't realise who you are. I wonder what he'll have up his sleeve this afternoon.'

'Whatever it is, you can bet it involves us giving him money.' He chuckles. 'He has such a high opinion of himself, it won't occur to him that we know what he's up to. Shall we go up to the house again tomorrow morning and see how the builder is doing with the floor? Perhaps you'd like the electrician to come along, too and give you an idea of his costs.'

She nods, smiling. 'Actually, I've already asked him. All right, I know what you're thinking, Uncle. Is it so obvious?'

He can't help laughing. 'Two good-looking, intelligent, single people of about the same age are bound to be attracted to each other, aren't they? Now, dear Olivia, if we're all ready for the meeting, I want to take a swim to cool off first. There's a ladder into the harbour, see.' He points to the quayside near his room. 'They make it easier for us old fogies to get in and out and I know what you're going to ask . . . The answer is no, the turtles aren't bothered at all.'

'Is it all right to swim, so soon after your operation?

'Dear girl, it wasn't so serious. I had a stent fitted to keep an artery to my heart open. It saved my life, but these days, it's not a big procedure, I didn't even have a general anaesthetic. According to my surgeon's instructions, I could have gone for a swim yesterday, so I'm quite safe today.'

*   *   *

George dresses carefully for his swim. He wears a straw Panama-style hat, a white tee and a pair of madras-check shorts. He keeps the hat on, climbs down the ladder and swims a few strokes. For eighty-something, he knows he's pretty fit. Eleni has a word with Dino who comes to the quayside with a kid's boogie board.

'*Pámme, Yeorgo!*' Let's go, George! Dino calls. 'One more time, for the submarine!'

Olivia is watching him. She looks a little concerned as he laughs and pulls himself onto the brightly coloured Styrofoam board. He lays belly down then paddles, furiously, with his hands.

Locals hurry to the harbourside and call, '*Opa! Opa!*' '*Pámme, Yeorgo, pámme!*' '*Bravo!*' '*Ela! Ela!*' They laugh, clap and cheer, then hook their arms in the air and egg him on. He's laughing, enjoying every moment.

Quite suddenly, the atmosphere changes. Faces fall, eyes fill and women hug each other then cross themselves. The air is suddenly silent and seems charged with sadness.

Two of the bigger men help Uncle up from the water. He feels a little breathless and slightly overwhelmed like everyone else who remembers the past. The fun and laughter have gone, replaced by emotion. Eleni brings him a towel and drapes it around his shoulders. The crowd drift over to the big church and enter, although it is noticeable that they came out again after only a minute or two.

'What's going on?' Olivia asks after walking over to join him. 'I was feeling all your glee and mischief, then everyone's mood changed.'

'Ah, sorry, I forget that you don't know? It's about the fire,' he says.

Olivia sighs. 'There it is again, the fire that I don't know about. Promise you'll tell me later. But please explain – why are they going into the church?'

'They are lighting a candle for every person they lost.'

She mutters, thinking aloud. 'But dozens of people have . . . surely, it's not possible that . . .' She links his arm and walks back to the table with him. His white tee is drying rapidly in the sun.

'And the boogie board?' she asks.

'Ah, a long story involving me, a plank and a submarine,' he says. 'I *will* get to tell you, don't worry.'

Dino and a few other men come over. They shake his hand and slap each other on the back like brothers.

'Those days, my friend,' Dino says. 'They never leave us, do they?' He pinches the bridge of his nose and stares at the water.

Uncle lowers his eyes sadly. 'Lest we forget, they say. But how can we forget?'

'My father still talks about that night, it's so fresh in his mind.'

'Your father – you mean my friend Demetriou – is still alive? I thought . . .'

326

Dino smiles softly. 'He's still alive, but very frail. Would you like to see him?'

'But of course. Can we eat together this evening?'

'He will like that. He's in a wheelchair, but I have an old table I cut to fit. I'll bring it down. He hasn't been out of his room for a year.'

George's eyes fill. 'So there's no chance of getting him into the boat tomorrow morning?'

'I doubt it, but I'll think it over and see if I can come up with something.'

George turns to his great-niece. 'Right, enough of this nonsense, my dear girl. A short sleep for me and then we'll meet with the young man and his lawyer.'

*　*　*

By the time George gets to his room, his clothes are almost dry. More exhausted than he will admit, even to himself, he eases down onto the bed and closes his eyes. The little pantomime earlier woke a bunch of memories. The boogie board pressing against his belly felt just like the shelf of wood that saved his life, so long ago. It has all come back so vividly. Poor, dear Rosa.

He tries to relax, let it go, remember how happy they all were, standing on the quayside at Port Said. With nothing but joy in their hearts, they had stared at the great ship that would take them home, the *Empire Patrol*. He thinks about Olivia, surprised to realise she knows nothing of the fire. He must tell her . . . but he is afraid. The one thing that might tear his heart asunder would be to recollect the events of that trip home.

CHAPTER 38
MAMÁ

Aboard HMS Empire Patrol, *1945*

EVENTUALLY, THE KONSTANTINIDIS FAMILY BOARDED, found their bales of clothes and goods and settled in a corner of D deck, in the centre of the ship. They made claim to the area by spreading their belongings about. Once they were all together, they went up top to enjoy the fresh air. Mamá commented to one of the UNRRA women on a distinct smell of petrol below, but was assured it would disperse once they were underway.

Uncle Kuríllos claimed the ship had transported tanks of fuel and it took some time for the stink to go. 'Just remember, thanks to this old ship, we'll all be home soon,' he said.

The doctor, who was travelling back to Castellorizo with them, found Mamá. 'I have a cabin for your grandson with the bad chest, your elderly mother and your daughter – María, isn't it? It's next to the medical room, so I can keep an eye on this young man.' He ruffled Panayiotis's hair. 'A big sea's forecast, so your grandmother will be more secure in a smaller space.'

* * *

At daybreak on 29 September, Mamá and Sofía checked the children, then Sofía took her book up to the top deck and watched the urgency surrounding a ship preparing to depart. She made notes on what people wore, the weather, the atmosphere of excitement. When word spread that they were about to toss the warps, everyone hurried up top to wave Port Said goodbye.

'Look, look!' George cried, pointing at a submarine. 'What's that? It looks like one of Uncle's big cigar tubes.'

Mamá laughed, happy beyond words. 'It's an underwater ship.'

'Nooo, a ship can't go under water, Mamá!' George cried. 'It would sink!'

'It certainly can, young man,' a Greek-speaking sailor interrupted. 'That's HMS *Spark*, one of the finest submarines in the British navy.'

'Wow! Did you hear that, Mamá?'

'I did. Now come on, let's wave at all the soldiers, Georgikie.'

With whistles and hooters sounding, HMS *Empire Patrol* slid away from the quayside. All the refugees cheered. Mamá felt an old hand slide into hers and was surprised to see tears in Megáli Yiayá's eyes when she looked around.

'Are you all right, my dear old mother?' she asked softly.

Megáli Yiayá squeezed her hand. 'I can't believe we're going home, child,' she said. 'I feel Mikró Yiayá is with us in spirit and now I can die happy on my own soil.'

Sofía, standing between Mamá and little George, breathed a great sigh. 'We're truly on our way back to Castellorizo. The next time we meet land, Georgikie, it will be in our own harbour.'

She turned to Mamá. 'I'm pleased María has a private cabin next to the medical centre, Mamá, and I think Megáli Yiayá will be better off there too.' She lowered her voice. 'The doctor has told me he will give her a strong sleeping pill to make her more comfortable. María can keep a close eye on young Panayiotis and his bronchitis, too.'

Mamá nodded. 'I'm going down to finish getting the little ones changed. I know it's early, but I'm longing for a few hours' sleep, it was such a long night.'

'I'll be there in a minute,' Sofía said. 'I'm just completing my notes.'

When she returned to help Mamá with the children, Sofía found them all laughing hysterically.

'What's going on?' she asked.

Rosa answered. 'Uncle Kuríllos helped to get the little ones ready while we were up top and now Bebe has her dress on back to front and her shoes on the wrong feet.'

Athena and Katina, ten and eleven, were hugging each other in a dramatic fit of giggles. 'Men!' the inseparable pair exclaimed together. 'They're all useless.'

This was one of Mamá's favourite sayings, but it sounded much funnier coming from the youngsters. Athena and Katina were so alike with their brown curly hair and short thumbs, people often thought they were twins.

Bebe, caught up in the hilarity of it all, blew a noisy raspberry into the palm of her hand.

The boys deliberately mistook the noise, pointing at Bebe and crying, 'Phew, phwah, she blew a bottom cough! Stinky-pinky!'

Sofía and Mamá exchanged a grin at the madness of their family. Everyone seemed over-excited at the prospect of going home. She noticed the UNRRA nurse dishing out beakers of warm milk for the children and babies. 'Settle down now, there's milk and biscuits for all those who behave themselves. Come on, head up, arms folded. No talking until you've finished eating and drinking.'

The boys performed silly antics, trying to eat and drink with their arms folded, while everyone else giggled.

María appeared. 'Panayiotis was awake most of the night, coughing. Poor little man. I'm exhausted. He's asleep now so if everything's all right down here, I'm going to catch some sleep.'

'Everything's fine, María,' Mamá said. 'Get some rest while you can. There's a lifeboat drill at ten thirty. Is my mother all right?' María nodded and blinked slowly. Poor girl, Mamá thought, she's worn out.

María appeared for the lifeboat drill and explained that Megáli Yiayá was fast asleep and Panayiotis wasn't well enough to attend. By eleven o'clock the drill was over, but the sea had taken on a heavy swell and soon most of the refugees were suffering from sickness and didn't want lunch. The crew rolled barrels onto each deck for those who had to throw up, then spent their time swabbing areas after those who didn't make it to the barrels.

The *Empire Patrol* ploughed into steadily increasing seas. The captain announced a fire drill for the early afternoon. Everyone groaned.

'Let's remember, we'll soon be home,' Mamá said. 'And at least the very young don't seem to be affected by the sea. Will you keep an eye on everyone, Kuríllos, while I go and check on Panayiotis, María and my mother?'

'The only eye I've got,' Kuríllos said and laughed.

* * *

Mamá passed the UNRRA nurse on the stairs. The woman was coming to D deck with warm milk and biscuits instead of lunch. Nobody had the stomach for food.

Bad luck to pass on the stairs, Mamá thought, glad war was over and there was no chance of a torpedo or bomb, in which case she'd be blaming herself forever for tempting fate. After finding the three occupants of cabin 26 asleep, she returned to D deck where the nurse called, 'For those who can't face the milk, there'll be warm water with a little milk of magnesia shortly, to settle your stomachs.'

Sofía was not badly affected by *mal de mare* and Rosa and her dance friend were not ill at all. They decided to put on a little show for their captive audience to take their minds off the turmoil. 'Rosa, put your shoes on. If you get a steel splinter in your foot, it could travel to your brain – and then what?'

'She'll have to walk around for the rest of her life with a spike sticking up from her head,' Zafiro said. 'Like a unicorn!'

'Ha-ha, don't worry, Mamá,' George cried much to the delight of Fevzi and Zafiro. 'It's never going to find her brains; she hasn't got any!' He poked the side of his head with his forefinger.

Rosa stuck her tongue out and with her thumbs in her ears she wiggled her fingers at Zafiro – then turned to Mamá. 'My shoes are too tight now, I've grown out of them. A ballerina has to take very good care of her feet, you know, so I try to go barefoot as much as possible.'

'Poor girl.' Mamá remembered the little money she had left from Loulouthi's gravestone. 'I'll get you a pair of new shoes as soon as we get home, that's a promise.'

Like a true ballerina, toes out and arms held in an oval shape before her, Rosa ran gracefully to Mamá and threw her arms around her neck. 'I love you so much! Now, are you ready, shall we begin?'

Mamá smiled proudly and nodded. Rosa made a low, dramatic curtsey to a young man who folded a square of shiny Izal toilet-paper over a comb. His friend had a pair of spoons which he clattered across his fingers and up and down his thighs and arms when Rosa said, 'Maestro?'

The boys made a fine noise as they played a recognisable rendition of 'Boogie Woogie Bugle Boy', while the girls performed a mix of ballet and jive, much to the entertainment of D deck. Even the sailors came in to watch. Mamá was so proud of her granddaughter she had to blink back tears. She swore to herself she'd ask Mustafa to find Rosa a new pair of ballet shoes.

Everyone clapped and cheered and Uncle Kuríllos used his finger and thumb to make great ear-splitting whistles. The boys stared at him in admiration. Rosa flushed with delight, her eyes sparkling as she lived her dream. Some of the sailors threw small coins, which the girls raced to pick. Then they held hands and took a low bow together.

Tears now trickled down Mamá's cheeks. At that moment, she felt all the trouble and strife in her life had been purely to arrive at this place in time. After seeing such a performance come from her granddaughter, she would die happy.

Katina and Athena said they were going to see if their mother wanted some milk.

Uncle Kuríllos whispered into Zafiro's ear, after which the boy called to Rosa, 'Here, I'm going to be your manager. Thirty per cent, all right!' He held out an open hand.

'Go away, silly boy!' Rosa cried, understanding the situation and squinting a warning at her uncle. 'I'm saving for ballet school. One day I'll dance with Margot Fonteyn before kings and queens. You just watch me.'

'Oh yes, well—' Before Zafiro could say more, a heart-stopping scream ended the teasing. Everyone held their breath in a fight-or-flight moment. Nurse put down the pitcher of milk and, followed by several others, hurried to the staircase.

'Fire!' the nurse cried. 'Everybody up top!'

Over 300 refugees on D deck stopped talking and stared at her for a second. An almighty rush for the stairs followed.

Mamá and Uncle Kuríllos exchanged a glance, picked up the youngest two, Evdokia and Mikali, and called for Sofía, Ayeleen and Rosa to gather the rest. Sofía snatched her rope-rig for keeping the children together and glanced around furtively to see the family made their way to the stairs.

'Sofía, bring everyone up top!' Kuríllos called. 'Stay together, now!'

'I can't find Katina and Athena,' Sofía said.

As the crush moved towards the staircase on D deck, they were all choking on the dense smoke that billowed down from C deck. With absolute horror, they wondered if they could pass. Then Sofía gasped as a shocking scream sounded from above. On and on it went, but the worst was, both Sofía and Mamá recognised the agonised the voice of María.

'Help me!'

* * *

Still clutching two-year-old Evdokia, Mamá bustled her way through the crush on the stairs and screeched, 'María! Oh my God, that's my María. Let me through!' Then, looking back at the turn in the stairwell, she shrieked, 'Sofía, Kuríllos, take care of everybody. I'm going to María.'

The moment she reached C deck she saw the UNRRA nurse dragging María towards the dining room. María was only recognisable by her half-burned clothes and voice. Her arms, legs and face were a mass of huge, water-filled yellow blisters.

'María! María!' Mamá cried, passing Evdokia to a neighbour. 'Give her to a Konstantinidis!' She begged. 'I must find my mother and my grandson, Panayiotis!'

Evdokia held her arms out stiffly, screeching, '*Yiayá*! I want my *Yiayá*!' and viciously kicking the poor recipient as she was carried away.

Mamá took hold of María's legs and together with the nurse, carried her into the dining room. As the nurse put butter on María's burns, Mamá asked, 'Where's my mother, the old lady? And my grandson, Panayiotis?'

The nurse shook her head. 'I don't know. The room was ablaze when I heard this one. She was in the corridor, her clothes and hair on fire, screaming hysterically, so I pushed her up to B deck, but she collapsed before I could treat her.'

'She's María, my daughter,' Mamá said.

'Wait, she's gone into shock, I don't know what to do. Let me think,' the nurse said. 'I remember . . . We must raise her legs a little and loosen her clothing. Pass me those cushions in the corner.' Mamá did. 'Look, there's nothing you can do here,' the nurse said. 'I swear I'll do everything I can for her. Go up top and find your mother and grandson . . . and please, get everyone to put on their lifebelts.'

Mamá wanted to kiss María, hold her close and tell her everything would be all right. Her unconscious daughter looked so terrible, her hair gone and her skin raw. Mamá's heart squeezed. She'd buried Mikró Yiayá and Loulouthi, she didn't want to bury her first child as well. After thanking the nurse, she hurried into the corridor where two men with fireman's hoses almost knocked her over.

'Go up top, lady! Put your lifebelt on!' they shouted, eyes red-rimmed and squinting through the smoke.

'Did you see anyone else in there? A boy, two little girls and an old lady.'

'The boy has some burns, but someone's taken him upstairs. The woman saved him, but she's in a bad way.'

'And the others?'

He shrugged. 'Nobody could survive that.' He nodded towards cabin 26.

* * *

The refugees continued to surge upward. Only one more flight of stairs to the open deck, but where was her mother and Panayiotis? Was María so badly burned because she was trying to get her son and her grandmother out of the cabin? Mamá, almost mad with anguish, feared the very old and the very young were still in there, alone, fighting the flames. She pushed against the tide of refugees, desperate to get down to C deck.

The refugees were panic-stricken. 'The boilers will explode!' a male voice exclaimed. 'We'll be trapped and drowned in the sinking ship!'

Everyone pushed, a woman fell on the stairs, screamed as others trampled over her. The smoke and heat increased, then flames cracked through a plywood wall just as a burning beam fell across the stairwell. Everyone screamed and backed away but clothing and hair caught fire and it was only the quick thinking of a crew member with a hose that saved them. While dousing the medical room, he heard their screams and turned his hose onto the burning passengers. Everyone changed direction and raced up the corridor to the bow of the ship.

* * *

Cabin 26, where Megáli Yiayá, María and Panayiotis had slept was in a short blind corridor now engulfed in flames. Fire leapt out of the door and up the walls. Three spent fire extinguishers rolled about in the corridor as the ship rocked and pitched. The two men with hoses tried to douse fresh flames that licked the low ceiling, but all seemed futile. The inferno roared. Mamá prayed to God her family had escaped that hell-hole.

Everyone ran along the main corridor, hoping to find another staircase to the front of the ship, but they were out of luck. Someone noticed a hatchway and ladder that took sailors to the top deck. They could only go one at a time and though they hurried up the rungs to gulp blessed fresh air at the top, the fire approached screaming people at the rear. Old people found it difficult, but they managed, slowly, slowly to get up to the open deck.

Mamá realised the ship's engines had stopped. Flames were roaring up in the middle of the *Empire Patrol* and blowing straight towards them, but then the ship turned, so the wind was hitting the side of the vessel, rather than blowing the fire towards the front. Realising her feet were getting hot, she looked down to see flames break through part of the deck. Some people rushed to the lifeboats and scrambled in, many without a life-belt. While they were attempting to launch themselves, ropes caught fire and one boat broke free of its rigging and fell from a great height into the sea. Mamá couldn't see what happened to the occupants. She stared around for her family. There must have been 200 people at the bow of the boat, most were women and children. Smoke was coming up through the floor now. If the wooden deck burned through they would all drop into the inferno below. Some men with children in their arms had the idea to leap overboard.

'Sofía! Ayeleen! Kuríllos!' Mamá shouted, but no one replied.

CHAPTER 39
OLIVIA

Castellorizo, Greece, present day

I move into the shade outside Uncle's room. The little patio to the front has striped loosely woven rugs, a couple of cane chairs and lots of Turkish-style cushions. Absolute peace and quiet falls over the town at siesta time as the locals sleep and the tourists sunbathe. I pull out my notebook and look up all things related to the beautiful borage plant. Then, I write about Eleni's home-made apricot ice cream with toasted almonds and fresh borage flowers.

Quite lost in my cookery book, I jump when Rob calls, 'G'day! Sorry, did I startle you? I'm a little early, hope that's OK.'

'Sure, no problem,' I say. The lawyer is standing behind Rob, eyes unreadable behind black aviator glasses. I nod at him. '*Kalispera.*' Then to Rob, 'Good afternoon. Let's go to Eleni's, shall we? *Theios* is still sleeping.'

We stroll along the quayside, then sit at Eleni's and order drinks. A beer for Rob and water for myself and the lawyer whose name I've forgotten.

Eleni gives me the sisterly look: if I needed help, she is there for me. I pat her arm and nod when she brings the drinks to let her know I understand and appreciate her concern. However, I hope Uncle wakes up soon because although we haven't had a minute to talk about a strategy, I trust he has one. I keep glancing at his front door, which is just about visible from where we sit.

Small talk will stall the situation. 'How's your hotel, Rob?'

'Ah, you know what, it's not the Sydney Palace, but it is fair dinkum for the cash. At least it's a stretch from that church bell. Don't know how you stand it up there.' He nods towards Saint George of the Well.

'Actually, I quite like it. It's only through the daylight hours, you understand.' I smile and say, casually, 'I'm curious to know what you'll do with the house once it's in your name. Do you think you'll come and live here for part of the year?'

'With so many interested parties, I'm sure somebody will. Pity it's not nearer the water, though. However, if you choose to buy my share, I doubt anyone will come once Mum's . . . you know.' He stares sadly at the floor. 'What were you going to do with it?'

'Ah, look, the door is open. We can get out of this sun with our drinks.' I get the impression the lawyer isn't too happy. 'What do you say, Mr . . . sorry, I've forgotten your name.'

'You can call me Filippos. Yes, let's get out of the sun and draw up this agreement, then we can all get back to our holidays.'

Uncle steps out of his apartment and waves an arm. Rob picks up his beer and stands. Eleni comes over.

'We'll be back to eat, Eleni. Would you put the drinks on my bill?' She nods at me

'Good on ya,' Rob said with a grin. 'My shout tomorrow.'

Everything changes in Uncle's room. The table is empty, save for four sheets of lined paper each with two pens on top, four glasses and a jug of ice and water in the centre.

'You don't have to stick around, mate, if there's somewhere else you'd rather be. Coffee with your friends?' Rob says to Uncle.

'Really? Thank you, but actually, I'm very interested and would like to offer Olivia my support. Besides, I'm finding it very warm today.' His eyes flick to mine. 'Please, everyone, take a seat.'

I remember Uncle's instructions. I must put my phone on record if he mentions the heat of the day. We exchange a glance as I comply.

Rob nods at the table. 'This is very professional of you Mr . . . Theios, is it?' My uncle nods and we all sit at the table. 'Can I ask what you did before you retired?'

'I taught history in England, actually. You, what's your profession, Rob . . . Robert, is it? And your family name? As my interest is history, I'm fascinated by genealogy.'

'My surname is Riganos, but my mother was a Konstantinidis.'

'Was?' I cried in alarm. 'Oh no! I thought she was getting better?'

'No, no, you don't understand. She is better. I meant to say – was, until she married Michael Riganos.'

The lawyer speaks for the first time, addressing Uncle. 'May I ask what made you leave here and go to work in England?'

A slight frown furrows my uncle's brow. 'Sorry, terrible table manners. Let me give you some water, it's so warm today.' Uncle fills everyone's glass. I press record, sensing things are about to happen.

'Can I ask why you've called this meeting, Rob?' I ask. 'I mean, it seems quite formal to have your lawyer here too.'

'I'm here on holiday, Miss Olivia, but if you have any questions, do ask me. I believe our property laws are quite different from those in England or Australia.'

I smile at him. 'Thank you, you're very kind.'

'So, what do you propose we do about this property, Olivia?' Rob asks.

'What do you want to do about it, Rob?'

'Well, it seems to me we have two choices. I buy your share from you, or you buy my share from me. My share would in all fairness be more expensive because of all the costs of my family, but I'm prepared to simply split the value straight down the middle. What do you say to that?'

'That sounds very generous,' I say. 'You say you have power of attorney for everyone on your side, Rob?' He nods. 'So how much would you want for your half?'

'Just the going rate. I had the property valued at 200,000, so, say 100,000 and the place is all yours, Olivia.'

The lawyer slides a sheet of paper my way.

I peer into his eyes but he looks away. 'That's a lot of money.'

'It's still a massive bargain. The thing is,' Rob continues, 'it will have to be transferred before I go back to Oz at the end of the month, so I've instructed Filippos to prepare the transfer deeds which I can sign the moment you're ready to complete. Then, dear cousin, the house will be all yours.'

'You mean the entire portfolio that belongs to the Konstantinidis family, of course?' I ask, to which he nods without hesitation. 'But you're giving me less than two weeks to save my family home?' The panic I feel is apparent as my voice waivers. I glance at Uncle who pats my wrist.

He turns to Rob. 'Young man, I suggest you go back to your room, right now and pack your bags. There's a ferry to Athens this afternoon and if you're not on it, this document and an account of how you tried to defraud Olivia will be released to the press, not just here, but in Australia too. As there are over a 150,000 Castellorizon descendants living in Melbourne alone and you're sullying their reputation with your fraudulent attempt to grab a property here, you won't be very popular when you get back home.'

Rob frowns. 'Look, it was very kind of you to let us use your room, but, in fact, you don't know what you are talking about and this is none of your business.'

'But you see it *is* my business because I own all of the property.' Uncle drops a folder of papers in front of the lawyer.

Rob turns to me. 'You sold it to him?'

I shake my head, but before I can speak, Uncle interrupts. 'My sisters, Sofía and María, signed the property over to me when they left the country.' He turns to the lawyer. 'It's all recorded in the land registry of Rhodes in my name, George Konstantinidis. I'm very surprised you didn't check.'

The lawyer looks shamefaced. 'I'm here on holiday, sir.'

Rob's mouth hangs open for a moment. 'You're George Konstantinidis?' he stammers.

'Yes, I am, your great-uncle. For the record, I've printed a copy of the deed of sale, for the three properties. The deed was completed and registered in 1949, so you understand this is irreversible.'

'Three properties?'

'The big house, the distillery and the house on the square by the port.'

'By the port . . .?'

'None of this property has anything to do with you or your family. Though if you had been more honest, you may have benefited. But it's too late for that. Now, I'd like to show you both the door, if you please and I trust we will never have to set eyes on you again, Rob. Oh and regards to your mother, whom I happen to know is in very good health, don't try that cruel trick again.' Uncle opens the front door. 'Goodbye,' he adds musically.

'Wow!' I say when they've gone. 'You really are a dark horse.'

He shrugs. 'I believe it's time to crack open a celebratory glass of fizz, dear girl. What do you think?'

'You won't have to twist my arm, Uncle. I can hardly believe how you handled that.'

'By the way, save that recording, just in case we need it in the future. Now, come on. Time to celebrate with Eleni, Dino and Dino's father, my old friend, Demetriou. He's the same age as me. We were in school together and he was on the *Empire Patrol* with me.'

'The *Empire Patrol* . . . what's that?'

'Oh dear, I keep forgetting that you don't know. Tomorrow morning, I'll tell you everything. I'll start at breakfast and continue until you've heard it all.'

'No, you're going fishing in the morning, remember?'

'Ah, I forgot. OK, tomorrow afternoon then. Unless of course you are out with somebody far more attractive.' He grins and bobs his eyebrows.

While Olivia cleared the table, George closed his eyes and remembered that terrible day on the ship.

CHAPTER 40
SOFIA

Aboard HMS Empire Patrol, *1945*

A SHIP'S OFFICER APPEARED, SHOUTING at them in English. They didn't understand anything except for the words SOS. 'Thank God!' Mamá said, shaking so violently she could hardly stand. 'We're in a shipping lane and war is over. Someone is bound to come to our rescue at any moment.'

The officer started shoving people towards the flames and gesticulating they should run to the rear of the ship, but the heat of the fire was too intense. Mamá was so desperate to find her family, she came forward and ran the gauntlet of the up-wind rail. Her lips and nostrils burned and the soles of her feet became unbearably hot even through her shoes. She knew her feet had blistered when she ran over a section of metal deck and felt her rubber-soled shoes sticking to it. Yet, she made it past the inferno and some passengers followed.

'Oh, my family!' She fell into Kuríllos's arms, then grabbed Sofía. 'I was afraid I'd lost you!' They both had children in their arms. 'Where's María?' she asked, frantic for news.

'She's in the lifeboat down there, Mamá. Panayiotis is with her, and some others with burns, and also little Emre.'

'And my mother, my mother,' she sobbed. 'Has anyone seen Megáli Yiayá?'

The family gathered around her in a huddle. 'I'm sorry, Mamá,' Sofía said. 'She had sleeping pills. The nurse thinks she was overcome by smoke and never woke up. We're all very sad. It's such a tragedy. But she would not have known anything about it. She simply went to sleep and woke in heaven.'

Mamá sobbed into her hands. 'My poor mother, with her big heart and fine sense of humour.' She crossed herself and looked at the sky as the family gathered around her. 'How many dowry chests did she fill with her fine work? How many times did she make us laugh when we were down?' She sniffed and smiled while the tears continued. 'We'll miss you so much, my darling mother. Thank you for sharing your life and your big heart with us.' She crossed herself again, then peered at each of her children and grandchildren. 'Has everyone got a lifebelt on?'

'Yes, apart from the little ones,' Sofía said. 'And I can't find Katina and Athena.'

'Oh no! No! Not them too!' she sobbed. 'Listen, everyone, we must get into a lifeboat.' She looked around and saw people were panicking. Some tied ropes around themselves and leapt over the side. Most of the Castellorizo females couldn't swim and the majority had small children or babies in their arms.

* * *

Kuríllos, at the stern of the ship, was also assessing the situation. He spotted two aeroplanes circling over the ship. It would not be long before their rescue. He took off his lifebelt and put it around Evdokia and Mikali. 'There, if you end up in the water, you'll be fine, so don't be afraid, children, OK?' He took stock, told everyone to stay together at the back rail and assured them the rest of the family was safe at the bow of the ship. He went to the sailor staffing the lifeboat winch.

'My family need to be in the next boat. Can you fix it?' He tugged at the heavy ring on his middle finger, his prize possession, a priceless gold Venetian ducat. 'Here, it's a gold sovereign for you, if you can get my family into a boat and safely over the side immediately.'

'Get in this one,' the sailor said. 'Hurry, it's the last lifeboat and the deck's almost burned through here.'

A sailor pulled a bucket of seawater up and slewed it over the decking. It became vapour immediately.

Kuríllos dashed back to the Konstantinidis family. 'Come on, everybody, quickly, follow me and do as you're told!'

They did, until flames speared through the wooden decking, then half the family backed up. 'Come on, run onto the metal part, it's safe there.' He straddled the smoking decking and lifted them over to the metal plates, where the sailor then lifted them straight into the lifeboat. Mamá leapt over, then only Rosa and George were left. Kuríllos glanced at Rosa's bare feet and knew she must be suffering. 'Come on, Rosa, you'll be fine once you're in the lifeboat.' He lifted her slim body over the smouldering wood. Shocked by the weightlessness of her, he put her down on the metal plate, eager to collect George next. He hadn't noticed the iron deck now glowed red. As he swung around for George and put him next to barefooted Rosa, she screamed and her knees buckled. He tried to lift her, but she seemed stuck, then he realised her feet were frying on the metal plating. Horrified, he tugged her free then tossed her featherweight body towards the sailor who placed the unconscious child in the lifeboat.

George, his own shoes smoking and unbearably hot, stared at the soles of the ballerina's feet still sizzling like rashers on the glowing metal deck. The sight was more horrific than the young boy could take. Pushed by pure horror he hurled himself over the stern-rail.

Uncle Kuríllos had no choice but to go after the boy. Reluctant to dispose of his beloved soft-leather Cretan boots, he dived over the side with them on. During the long drop down, he cried out, suddenly afraid he would land on the boy and kill him.

*   *   *

George went into the sea feet first. He descended, down, down, into the darker depths. At the start, he was sure his direction would change at any second, he'd dived off the rocks at home often enough. He kicked to change course, but the daylight continued to move further away and the weight of the water crushed his chest. His lungs needed air. He had to go up but his skinny legs were making no progress against the pull of the deep. Frantic, he wanted to scream, when some huge mouth bit into his shoulder. His heart banged. He turned to fight, punch the monster on the nose, but then he recognised his uncle who gripped his collarbone and dragged him upward. The semi-darkness and underwater deafness burst into a crescendo of light and clamour as man and boy sucked in air on the surface.

Heavy ropes hung down from the deck. Kuríllos grabbed one while George, lungs still screaming for more breath, scrambled onto a hatch cover.

'There's a lifebelt!' Kuríllos said, swimming for it, then tossing it onto the hatch cover. 'Can you fasten it around yourself, lad, while I tie your raft to this rope?'

'Yes, Uncle.'

'Look what's coming down for us. It's the lifeboat with everyone safe inside,' Kuríllos said. 'Hang on to the rope until the boat's afloat, then we'll get aboard.'

No sooner had he uttered the words when the heavy rope he hung onto, snaked down and crashed into the rough water around them, almost upending George's hatch cover.

'*Maláka*! Hang on, boy. The deck must be on fire. The rope's burned through.'

George looked up and saw the side of the ship glowing red.

'We need to get away from here,' Kuríllos shouted. 'The boilers will explode and fire shrapnel at us.'

George couldn't wait to get into the lifeboat, only two metres above them, but suddenly it lost its bow rope and his family were tipped, screaming and flailing, into the heaving sea.

'Mamá!' he yelled, knowing his mother couldn't swim, hoping she had her lifejacket on. Someone above had the sense to release the stern rope so the vessel fell into the sea too. Although upside down, it floated. George lay belly down on his hatch cover and paddled towards Fevzi, who was nearest him.

'Hang onto here, Fevzi!' he shouted, propelling himself towards the lifeboat. Fevzi hung on and kicked and, in a few seconds, he was gripping one of the rope loops around the rim of the lifeboat. Mamá was there, too, a hysterical look in her eye as she stared around at the chaos.

'Where's Sofía?' she shrieked. 'Sofía's got the little ones on a string!'

*　*　*

Kuríllos ducked under the water and saw Rosa out of reach. Her eyes were open and her face serene. Toes pointed down, arms gracefully over her head as she pirouetted in the maelstrom.

Kuríllos lunged for the surface, gulped for air, then dived after the waiflike dancer, but she was too far below him, her long hair streaming upward. He kicked for all he was worth, but the distance between them grew and he realised the point of no return loomed. Just before Rosa disappeared, her hands fluttered as if waving him goodbye. His tears added to the salt water as his mind screamed, *'Rosa! Sweet, ballet-dancing Rosa!'* But the painful truth was he could do nothing to save her.

Before he drowned in his own sadness, he remembered the others and kicked for the surface. Sofía, where was Sofía! She had Kristina, Bebe, Mikali and Evdokia tied to her string. He wished he'd left his soft, Cretan boots behind now. They dragged, heavy on his legs, constantly pulling him down.

He broke the surface and yelled at Mamá. 'Where's Sofía?'

'She went under with the little ones!'

Minutes had passed since the boat fell, surely nobody could survive so long under water. With hardly enough air in his own lungs, he ducked beneath and stared around. Poor visibility – impaired by all the kicking going on – meant he couldn't see far. Sofía and the little ones had disappeared, surely into the deep. His heart ached for his favourite niece. How often he had imagined her looking after him in his old age. She was the daughter he wanted so badly but never had. She even had a look of Isabella.

He had let his brother down so badly.

I'm sorry! I'm sorry I couldn't save them, brother! he yelled in his head.

Babá's wife, children and grandchildren – entrusted to him – were mostly drowned or burned. Weighed down by grief and his Cretan boots, he allowed himself to sink slowly. One last look towards the sun, he thought, tilting his head back and peering upward.

He saw it quite suddenly, not believing his eyes. Legs hanging below the lifeboat, on the opposite side to Fevzi and Mamá and

George on his hatch cover. Was this real – or a cruel trick of his oxygen-starved brain? Exhaustion left him as he pushed at the water with all his strength, lungs bursting, until he came up in an air pocket under the upturned boat. For a few seconds, he couldn't speak and brayed like a donkey, so desperate was his need for air.

'What's happening?' he asked squinting into the dark space. 'Are you all here? Is anyone hurt?'

'I think my ankle's broken,' Sofía said. 'We're so tangled up. I think the cord is caught on something behind me, but I can't check without pulling the little ones underwater.'

Kuríllos pulled the Cretan knife out of his belt. 'Can you hang on, Sofía? I'll cut them free one at a time and take them to Mamá.'

'Yes, do it.'

Kuríllos got to work and with Kristina's arms around his neck, he ducked under the water, then back up beside Mamá. 'They're safe,' he said. 'I'll be back in a minute.' He passed the child over, then turned to George. 'See if you can find any more lifebelts floating around. Bring them back here. But mind you don't go too far.' He dived under the rim of the lifeboat again and back up into the air pocket.

'Come on, Bebe, you're next,' he said as cheerfully as possible. 'Let's go up to Mamá and put a lifebelt on you.'

'I don't want to go! I want to stay here with Sofía!' she cried petulantly.

'There's a good girl,' Sofía gasped, clearly in great pain. 'Go with Uncle Kuríllos. You don't want to be left down here, all alone, do you?'

'I'm scared!'

'Don't be scared. I'll tell you a secret that not many people know . . . Uncle Kuríllos is a guardian angel. It's his job to keep

350

little girls as safe as they can ever be. So trust him and perhaps if you are very lucky, you'll see his wonderful angel's wings on the way.'

Bebe stared at Kuríllos with her wide and trusting eyes. 'Can you fly?' she said with an amazed voice that made him want to weep.

'Well, there's no room for flying in here, is there? I can't even spread my angel wings. So we're going duck out and then fly straight into the arms of Mamá, OK? It's an adventure. Put your arms around my neck, hold tight and take a deep breath.'

Clutching her in one arm, he summoned all the strength he had to duck under the rim of the boat and pass her to Mamá. George had managed to find another lifebelt and together they fastened it around Bebe.

'You're safe, stop making such a racket,' Mamá said. 'What's the matter?'

'I forgot to keep my eyes open so I didn't see Uncle's angel's wings!'

Mamá laughed and Kuríllos heard a tinge of hysteria in her voice, but she kept her head up and dealt with the children quite sanely. Mikali and Evdokia were next. They still had their lifebelt on, but it would be better if they had one each. A great splash beside them made everyone jump.

'Don't panic, it's a raft,' Kuríllos said. 'Let's get you all onto it before I go down for the others.'

Five minutes later, they were all on the raft, apart from George who insisted on going after another lifebelt. Kuríllos ducked under the lifeboat for the penultimate time, but Mikali and Evdokia proved more troublesome. Eventually, he had to tug them under the water by brute force, hoping they would automatically hold their breaths for the few seconds it took to

351

reach the outside. Weary to his bones now, he shoved them onto the raft.

'Tell George to get on the raft now,' he said to Mamá. 'I'll be back in a moment with Sofía.'

Kuríllos pushed himself away from the raft and went down for Sofía. 'They're all safe on a raft. Before we get you out, can you hang on while I search for the lifesaver box?'

'Yes, don't worry. I just can't swim with this ankle,' Sofía said. 'By the way, I do think you're a guardian angel. You've been so wonderful, Uncle, and I love you to heaven and back.'

For a moment the weariness was gone. He grinned at her in the dark, his heart bursting with love. 'I love you too, Sofía.' He knew she had heard the smile in his voice and his heart sang for a second. 'Did you notice a tin box anywhere?'

'Yes, it's in a net nailed to the back end.'

He used his knife to prise it free. 'It will have some flares and drinking water inside. Just what we need. Can you keep a grip on it while I cut you free and get you to the surface?'

'Only if you promise to use you angel's wings, Uncle.'

They both laughed, but Kuríllos knew this was going to be difficult. 'I'm going to put you over my shoulder, but it might be a bit awkward and take longer than I estimate, in which case, drop the box and save yourself. I know you're not a great swimmer. Do you understand?'

'We'll manage, don't worry. Just cut me free, let's fill our lungs and go for it.'

Kuríllos slashed through the twine, then pulled her over to the other side of the boat. 'Right, all we're going to do is duck under the rim, then I'll grab the rope around the outside of the lifeboat, OK.'

'And we'll take it from there,' Sofía added.

In a few seconds, through a rush of water, they were on the outside of the lifeboat, but to Kuríllos's dismay, the raft had floated some distance away.

'*Maláka poutána!*' he muttered, making Sofía grin.

'*Maláka poutána!*' she whispered back, remembering her last moments with Anastasia, swearing and dancing away all her distress.

Give me strength, Anastasia. 'Come on, we can do it, Uncle. I'll hold on here while you take the box to the raft. Then you can come back and escort me to safety, like the gentleman you are.'

'You're sure you'll be all right?'

'Go, Go! *Maláka poutána!*' They grinned at each other.

* * *

The swim to the raft seemed endless. On the way, Kuríllos picked up the end of a floating rope. With his arms and legs getting heavier by the second and dreaming of a sip of refreshing water, he eventually reached his family.

'Zafiro, you're in charge of the emergency tin, OK?' Even speaking was a gargantuan effort. 'Inside you'll find a flare, some wax-covered matches and some drinking water. They're all precious and need to be kept dry. I'll be back with Sofía soon.' He tied one end of the rope to the raft, then set off with the other end, towards the upturned lifeboat. He longed to let go, allow himself to sink to the depths. The big sleep called his name and resisting was almost impossible. He heard his older brother's voice: *Come on, you troublemaker, don't let me down now!*

Kuríllos kicked until he could not swim another stroke, then he rolled onto his back and frog-legged until partly recovered.

It took half an hour in the rough sea before he found himself at Sofía's side again.

'That took some time, Uncle.'

'Because I'm pulling the raft with me. We don't want to go too far from the ship.' They both turned towards the *Empire Patrol*. When the swell lifted them – though it was difficult to judge – they had drifted over a kilometre from it. 'It's a shipping lane, so the distress signal will soon be answered and we'll all be saved. Now, what next?' It was as if his brain wouldn't work and despite his effort, the words came out slurred.

'A nice cup of proper coffee, what do you think?' Sofía said, directing some humour at her weakening uncle.

'Or the best whisky on earth . . .' He untied the rope from his belt.

'Both! I've never tasted whisky, so let's make a pact: my first one will be with you.' She sensed his spirit lift a little. 'You saved all our lives, Uncle.'

'I'm just going to see if I can turn the lifeboat over. Can you hang on a bit longer?' He slung the rope over the upended keel. 'I'll tie it to the opposite rowlock, then come back to this side and pull on the rope with my feet against the side. You hang on to the pointy end in case it flips over suddenly. Don't want you having a cracked skull too.'

After several attempts, Kuríllos was exhausted. 'It's no good. Let's get to the raft.' He untied the rope from the lifeboat and tied it under Sofía's arms. 'Just lie on your back and relax,' he said. 'Look – there's an aircraft carrier on the horizon. I do believe it's coming to the *Empire Patrol's* rescue.'

Sounds carried over the water. Distant voices, mostly women, called for help. Children cried, someone screamed and the thrum of the aircraft carrier increased bringing hope to everyone. Yet despite all the distant noise, Kuríllos felt incredibly alone. He wished his brother was with them, then he longed for the skinny arms of his mother whose big heart and irrepressible mischief would find something humorous even in this diabolical situation.

You were the best mother a boy could ask for.

On and on he swam, occasionally rolling onto his back to get his breath. The muscles in his arms and legs burned, sweat greased his brow and stung his eyes, but he glimpsed the distant raft and his journey shortened inch by inch. Then the cramp struck. Every muscle he needed spasmed into the tightest knot that had to be torn open with the next stroke. His legs contorted in agony, his fingers stiffly rolled against each other, even his heart seemed to squeeze in a tight fist. Yet Sofía, his favourite niece with her broken ankle, depended on his determination.

'*Maláka poutána*, I'm done for,' he muttered, taking Sofía by the hips and lifting her high out of the water so that she fell onto the raft.

'Sofía!' Mamá cried. 'Thank you, God. It's my precious Sofía!' Mamá's joy rang like church bells, making Kuríllos smile before the water closed over his head and he surrendered.

* * *

Down and down Kuríllos Konstantinidis went, peaceful in the darkness, relieved to let go of the painful cramp. Relaxed now, as if on the verge of a wonderful dream, then, in the distance, he saw her. His heart pattered, then stopped in awe. Could it really be . . .? Yes, it was! How long he had waited for his beautiful black-eyed Isabella with her long dark hair as straight and glossy as waxed silk. 'My love!' he cried in his mind, his chest exploding with love.

CHAPTER 41
OLIVIA

Castellorizo, Greece, present day

'I'M EXHAUSTED,' GEORGE SAYS, REMEMBERING his one-eyed uncle.

'Why don't you sit here and relax for half an hour and I'll go and pop the fizz into Dino's chiller?'

'Sounds like a plan, dear girl. Thank you. Perhaps I've been overdoing it, climbing up to the house and then the swim.'

'We don't even have to go out this evening. I can bring food in.'

'Except that Dino's going to bring his father down. I haven't seen Demetriou for half a century. Oh, we had such times. He was the most handsome man on the island and the girls loved him . . . you wait and see. He'll charm you too.'

'Right, you relax, Uncle. I'll be back to make you a cup of tea and put you in the picture.' His eyes are already closing. I grab the champagne bottle and head for the taverna.

On the quayside, a voice comes from behind me. 'They'd throw you in prison, in America, you know.'

I turn and see Greg catching up with me with his loose, long-limbed stride. 'How come?' I smile.

'Walking down the street with a bottle of booze in your fist, you'd be classified as a wino.'

'It's champagne!' We stroll side by side.

He smiles. 'OK, a very posh wino.'

I laugh, then realise I'm batting my eyelashes. 'I'm just going to pop this in your father's chiller. He's promised to bring your grandfather down later, so the two old men can get together again.'

'Good plan, I hope Pappoú is up to it.' He catches my confused look. '*Pappoú*, pap-poo, Greek for grandfather.'

'I like it. How're the electrics coming on?'

'I can't do more until the mice are definitely gone because they strip cables. Also, I need the floor in. Then, I'll be done in a day. What are you doing later?'

'You tell me,' I say with an internal smile. From the corner of my eye, I catch his grin. 'Look, Dino's brought your grandfather's table down, so he can get his wheelchair under. Why don't you join us for dinner? Make it a family affair.'

'I'd like to, thanks.'

* * *

I find Uncle asleep in his chair when I return. Poor thing must be exhausted. I put the kettle on and sit at the table while I wait. The numbered envelopes with the photographs lie before me. I long to investigate, but feel it would be cheating my uncle out of his great exposé. He's snoring softly, so I turn off the kettle and go to sit outside. The soft light of early evening dims the reflections on the water. All eyes around the harbour turn towards the castle ruin as the enormous Greek flag slides down the flagpole. Although the atmosphere is calm and serene, there is an underlying sense of defensive patriotism. I glance down the quayside and see Dino and Eleni, side by side, facing the flag. He slips his arm around her shoulders and I wonder what thoughts they share.

I wish we had more time on Castellorizo, because the longer I'm here, the more I sense Uncle's story is too big to cover in a few days. I'm still gazing at Dino and Eleni when I notice Greg appear from the taverna. His mother speaks to him, he grins and then he ambles my way.

'My mother has sent me to ask what time you would like to eat.'

'Do you always run your mother's errands?'

'Only when there are beautiful women involved.'

'That is so corny!' We both laugh. I feel an intensity between us that I've been trying to ignore since the first time we met. 'I sense the whole island is watching me, waiting to analyse my next move.'

'Then let's leave the old ones and escape from prying eyes to the Best Fish Taverna in the World.' He nods towards Kaş. I stare over the darkening waters and remember that kiss.

'It's tempting ... but what about my uncle and your grandfather?'

He looks slightly startled. 'You want to bring them along too?'

I laugh. 'What a wonderful idea, but no. My uncle has just had heart surgery and I'm afraid he's overdoing things.'

Greg blows through pursed lips. 'Phew, that's a relief. OK, I'll ask my mother to make sure Uncle gets home all right.'

The door opens behind us. 'Speak of the devil,' I say. 'Did you have a nice nap, Uncle?'

'I did. I'm just going to see if my old friend is about. See you in half an hour.'

* * *

I hurry to my room for a shower and change of clothes and return to Eleni's in my best white linen outfit and carefully applied make-up. I guess the old man sitting in the wheelchair next to Uncle is Demetriou. He is painfully thin, pale-skinned from a year indoors and slightly lopsided. His big eyes twinkle mischievously from within his cadaverous face, and he has a wide smile that would melt anyone's heart. I'm still standing when my uncle introduces us.

Demetriou tries to lift a hand to me, but I stoop and kiss his cheek.

'You're still a devil with the girls then,' Uncle says to him. 'How do you turn on that charm? But this is my niece, so no hanky-panky or I'll have to challenge you to a fist fight.'

Demetriou grins and winks at me and I sit next to him and take his hand.

'I might have to take you on, Yeorgos,' he says in a small, squeaky voice. 'She's very beautiful.' Everyone laughs. 'Anyway, I heard about your underwater dash in the harbour today, old man. Wish I'd been there. It's still painful to remember, but we survived, didn't we?'

'I've heard so much about it over the years, I feel as though I witnessed it for myself,' Dino says.

I lift a finger. 'Excuse me, I have no idea what you're all talking about.'

'The fire, the ship sinking and your crazy uncle,' Demetriou says.

Just then, Greg arrives by boat, ties it to the swim ladder and joins us. I try not to look his way, because everyone is watching every move we make and I sense Greg is aware of it too. Dino and Eleni disappear into the kitchen and return with six champagne flutes and the bottle of Brut in an ice bucket. I suspect Dino has given it a shake, because the cork flies out and he expertly catches the foam in the first glass.

We all cheer, clink glasses and laugh, then drink a toast to life, love and a successful result with the house and distillery.

'So go on, Mr Demetriou. You were going to tell me about my crazy uncle.'

The old man rolls his eyes. 'He was, I don't know, seven or eight years old – leapt twenty metres off a burning ship – then tried to gather lifebelts for all those who didn't have one. Should have had a medal. Then, he . . . well, it's better if he tells you himself.'

'It's so long ago, I'm not sure I can recall everything,' Uncle says. 'I remember pulling myself onto a hatch cover that someone had thrown in for those that had jumped. Then, I paddled furiously, refusing to be beaten by a lifebelt that bobbed out of reach. I wondered how far I'd gone. Thought perhaps I ought to give up and return to the raft where my family waited to be rescued.' He puts his hand over his mouth and shakes his head, thinking back. 'At the peak of the next swell, I looked over my shoulder and saw the burning ship. It seemed miles away.'

'You were very lucky and brave, my friend,' Demetriou says with all due severity.

'I knew I should turn back, but before I had a chance, the water ahead began to agitate and boil. What was going on?' His eyes widened, staring into the past. 'The sea lifted in an enormous grey hump, splitting into white foaming barrels. I thought it was a whale or the Greek god of the sea. Old whatshisname?'

'Poseidon?' Greg asks.

'That's the one.'

I am aware of Greg's grin. Our eyes meet for a second, then we both look away and try to smother our secret smiles.

Uncle continues. 'I remember thinking, It's that *poutana*, Poseidon. Well, he needn't think he's going to upend me,

361

maláka! I must explain. My Uncle Kuríllos was the greatest swearer on the planet and I admired him so much. When I was alone, I took every opportunity to say as many of his swear words as possible, though I had no idea what they meant, only that they garnered a clout if Mamá heard me say them.' Everyone laughs. 'So, I gripped the sides of the hatch cover and stared, ready to challenge the god to a swearing competition. Then, I remember wondering if Poseidon ate small boys.'

Everyone laughs again.

'As my Greek god rose from the sea, the most remarkable thing happened. A hatch opened in the top of Poseidon's head as it came clear of the water and then a man got out . . . two men . . . four men. They were shouting and pointing at me.' Uncle beams at everyone, seeing his audience is captivated and again I imagine he must have been a wonderful teacher. 'Then I realise as more of the vessel rises from the swell, it was the submarine! The cigar tube I'd seen in Port Said when we left. What had the sailor called it? Ah, submarine *Spark*, yes, that was it. The vessel seemed *much* bigger, close up.

"*Boy! Boy!*" they shouted. "*Come this way!*"

'I didn't understand their language, but the way they hooked their arms in the air made it clear they wanted me onboard. Perhaps they would take me prisoner and feed me bread and water. I hoped it would be the delicious white bread we'd had in Nuseirat camp. Perhaps they'd give me a go at driving the submarine to the centre of the earth like Captain Nemo. Anyway, I was tired and hoped they had some cake. I've always loved cake.'

Demetriou chuckles. 'Remember when we stole that cake off Kyria Popi's windowsill? Mamá slapped the backs of your legs and sent you to bed.'

'Yes, but I still had half the cake in my pocket, which I enjoyed in the comfort of my own bed.'

'I'm seeing a whole new side to you, Uncle!' I say, laughing.

'Anyway, I paddled towards the submarine. Each time I dipped into a trough and then rose on the next crest, they were closer. One of the men tied a rope around his own waist and jumped into the water. The sailor was calling foreign words as he swam towards me. I listened very hard for anything that sounded like *cake*.'

We all laugh together.

CHAPTER 42
SOFIA

In a rough sea near the burning ship, 1945

BACK ON THE RAFT, SOFÍA couldn't bear the pain in her ankle, it flared with the smallest movement. She managed to lie next to her mother with the little ones huddled about them. Darkness fell as they drifted further away from the blazing *Empire Patrol*. The biggest ship Sofía had ever seen towered next to it, taking people aboard, she guessed. A plane flew over and dropped flares onto the sea, but they were too far away now. When the raft dipped into the troughs, they were invisible. If only the sea would calm down. She wondered when she should set off the flare. They only had one chance to use it. Where was Uncle Kuríllos and George and Rosa? She couldn't figure out who was on the raft and decided to check.

'Listen, everybody. I want to know who's on this raft so I'm calling names, like at school, all right? Answer me good and loud, because I have water in my ears.

'Mamá! Are you here?' Of course she was, but Sofía wanted to set an example to the little ones.

Mamá, realising her daughter's plan, called out, 'Yes, I'm here, Sofía!'

'OK, well done, Mamá. Next is Uncle Kuríllos, are you here, Uncle?'

After a moment's silence, Zafiro answered. 'He was here. He gave me instructions for the flare. I saw him lift you out of the water. I was coming to help him, but he went back under.'

Bebe's trembling voice came out of the dark. 'He flew away on his angel's wings. All the way to the stars.'

'I thought you kept your eyes closed and didn't see his wings, Bebe?' Zafiro said.

'That was after, when he brought Sofía, see,' she said petulantly. 'He lifted her up, then he flew away into the night. I saw him waving at us from way up there, by the stars. Then he was gone.'

Sofía had such a pain in her throat, she couldn't speak. She could hear the heartbreak in her mother's voice when she said, 'Don't worry, he's probably gone back to the lifeboat because the raft is quite full. Who's next, Sofía?'

'That would be María, but we know she is in the other lifeboat with the doctor and they'll be taking good care of her.' Sofía's voice cracked. Poor beautiful María, so badly burned. She recognised her mother's hand, squeezing her shoulder quite fiercely. For a moment, they shared their devastation in silence, each understanding the other. Sofía took a breath, then continued. 'So next is Ayeleen. Are you here, Ayeleen?'

'I'm here, Sofía, but I'm so very cold and tired now. Do you think I could snuggle up to Mamá and have a little sleep?'

'Don't go to sleep yet, Ayeleen. I need you to dish out the drinking water in a few minutes.'

'The next person is Rosa . . . are you here, Rosa?'

'Rosa's gone,' Zafiro said. 'Uncle went after her, but she was unconscious already. Her feet were too badly burned.'

A moment of abysmal silence fell over them all until Sofía said, 'Let's say a prayer for our darling Rosa who will be watching us from heaven right now. Dear God, please welcome our beautiful Rosa into heaven where we all hope to join her one day. We love her very much and know she would have been the best dancer on earth. We believe she will be a prima ballerina in heaven too. Everyone say, Amen.'

'Amen.'

Mamá whimpered, sobbed, then said, 'God bless our beautiful Rosa. Amen.'

'Do they have cats in heaven?' Mikali asked.

'I believe they do,' Sofía told him.

'Rosa always wanted her own kitten, but she was afraid if she kept one as a pet, everyone else would want one too. You think God will let her have a kitten, Aunty Sofía?'

Sofía swallowed hard, but still couldn't answer for a moment, then her mother's hand found hers and squeezed tightly. 'I'm quite sure God will give Rosa her very own kitten, Mikali. She'll be very happy. Who's next? Popi. Are you here, Popi?'

'I want to go home,' Popi cried. 'I want to go back to Castellorizo and go to school with my friends. I told Babá a long time ago but he said this was an adventure. I don't like adventures, Aunty Sofía. I really don't! Please don't let anyone else give us an adventure.'

'You just need to say, I'm here,' Fevzi said. 'There's no need for the dramatics.' He sighed. 'Girls! They're all the same.'

'Fevzi, she might be older than you, but she's still afraid,' Sofía said quietly. 'We're all afraid. It's just her way of dealing with it.'

'After Popi, we've got Martha. Are you here, Martha?'

'I'm here, Aunty Sofía.'

'Very good. Now, Katina?' Silence. 'Has anyone seen Katina?' Silence again. 'Who was the last person to see Katina?'

'Please, Sofía; Katina and Athena went to see Mummy in the sick room, just before the big fire. Athena was crying because she spilt her warm milk and Katina said not to worry, she would try and get her some more.'

'Is that you, Kristina?'

366

'Yes, I'm Kristina,' the quietest family member said. 'I wanted to go and see Mummy too, but Katina said we could only go one at a time because Mummy was very tired. And I'm nearly sliding off the raft now. My feet keep falling into the water.'

'Who's nearest to you?' Sofía asked.

'Zafiro.'

'Zafiro, you're in charge of Kristina. Can you pull her further onto the raft and keep a hold on her? Now, Bebe, Zafiro and Fevzi are next to me and Mamá is holding Mikali and Evdokia, so everyone is here apart from Uncle Kuríllos, Rosa, Katina, Athena and Panayiotis – am I right?'

'George,' Mamá said. 'Where's Georgikie? That boy is always wandering off!'

'He was collecting extra lifebelts for everyone. Perhaps he got into one of the other lifeboats,' Zafiro said. 'Can we open the tin now? I'm thirsty.'

'Me too,' cried Kristina

'And me,' said Mikali.

'Listen, it's only one sip of water for everyone, all right? And, no drinking sea water or you'll die, understood?'

'I swallowed some . . . I'm going to die. I don't want to die!' Bebe was crying.

'No, Bebe, you have to drink an awful lot for it to kill you, so you're safe, I promise.' Sofía reminded herself to be more careful when talking about the dangerous situation they were in. 'OK, Zafiro, can you open the box. Mind to keep everything dry and don't let anything fall out.' She had some night vision and could see everyone huddled around Mamá. 'There should be a metal flask of water.'

'I've got it.'

'Right, pass it over and close the box up again.' He did. 'Listen, everyone. One mouthful each, no more. And whatever you do, don't drop it.' The bottle went round to everyone, but was empty before Ayeleen, Mamá or Sofía got a sip.

They'd drifted so far, the *Empire Patrol* was nothing but a slight glow on the horizon, only visible when they were lifted by the crest of a wave. Planes had stopped dropping flares and the sounds of other distressed passengers from the big ship had disappeared. Sofía was cold, very cold and she guessed everyone else was too. Time lost its meaning as they huddled together, constantly lifting and dropping on the waves. How long could the darkness of this endless night last? Surely after another hour or two, the morning would come with light and hope. Sofía prayed that dawn would arrive with the purpose of revealing the Konstantinidis family to their rescuers. She wept silently, hoping everyone could hang on a little longer. The pain in her ankle seemed to have grown to reach her knee.

'Zafiro, what else was in the tin, do you remember?' she asked forcing a sensible tone into her voice.

Silence. Were they all asleep? Although tempted to let them rest, she knew they should stay awake and alert. 'Come on, everybody! Wake up now. We need to look for a ship and light the flare or we'll never be rescued. What else is in the box, Zafiro?'

Everyone budged around a bit to give Zafiro elbow room. 'A torch!' he said. 'Aw, it's not working.'

'The batteries might be separate to keep them dry. Perhaps they're in wax paper, or an oilcloth wrapping. What else is in there?'

'A tin of biscuits.'

'Give everyone one biscuit, Ayeleen.'

'Ah, I found the batteries!' Zafiro continued. 'I'm not sure we should use the torch, except for signalling. When I went fishing with Uncle Kuríllos, he told me it takes time to get your night vision and one spark can destroy it. We can all see each other now, yes?'

'But you need to read the instructions for the flare, Zafiro. We need to be ready for when a boat comes near,' Sofía said.

As they crested the swell, a distant light swept the water. 'There, look – they're still searching for us. Light the flare!' Mamá said. 'Quickly!'

'Can you stand in the middle of the raft if we hold on to your legs, Zafiro?' Ayeleen suggested.

'Quick! Read the flare instructions! Somebody! Find the matches,' Mamá said.

'Everybody shout together,' Sofía ordered. 'On three. One, two, three: *Help!* And again. Have any of you girls got a petticoat on? I need it now, take it off.'

'You can have mine,' Mamá said. Everyone bobbed around as she struggled to get out of her underskirt while in a sitting position in the centre of the raft.

'Ayeleen, you're the tallest. If I grasp your ankles, can you stand and wave this?' Sofía said lifting Mamá's slip.

Zafiro managed to light the flare and stand in the centre of the raft with it raised above his head. The sky was lightening, but once they lit the flare, nobody could see anything for the orange brightness of burning sulphur. A blanket of panic fell on them. As soon as the flare died, Ayeleen stood and flapped the underskirt over her head. Everyone hung on to Ayeleen's legs to keep her upright on the undulating sea. They cried, 'Help!' until their throats burned.

'Why did we bother?' Mamá said, half an hour later when the attention-seeking palaver was over.

Sofía looked around at the sorry state of her family in the dawn light. 'Listen, everyone! Babá will have heard what happened on the *Empire Patrol*. He'll be worried sick. We have to draw attention to ourselves. Is there another flare, Zafiro?'

She had only just uttered the words when a plane swooped out of the sky. 'Ayeleen, wave the flag, girl! Wave for all you're worth!'

They were hanging on to Ayeleen's legs when the plane circled, then came over even lower. 'They must have seen us!' Popi cried.

'There's another flare,' Zafiro said. 'Shall I light it, Sofía?'

'No, if he saw us, he'll send someone to pick us up and we'll need to tell him exactly where we are then. Make sure you keep the matches dry and be ready to signal when we can see our rescuers.' Everyone's eyes were wide with hope. 'Now, I think we could all have another biscuit for our breakfast.'

* * *

According to the ship's log on HMS *Mermaid*, it was 7.23 when a flare caught the lookout's attention. A large signal lamp, used as a searchlight, played across the water and eventually fell upon the bedraggled and desperate occupants of an open life raft. Nine children and two women had braved the night, waiting to be rescued. The *Mermaid*'s rescue craft had already picked up thirty survivors from the *Empire Patrol*. This would be her final salvage and the crew hoped for a good result.

Once on board, Mamá and Sofía collapsed in tears of relief. The refugees gulped down beakers of hot sweet tea. After bathing, small wounds and burns were cleaned and painted with iodine. Sofía's ankle, dislocated not broken, was reset. Clothed in fresh, ill-fitting outfits, the survivors devoured a most welcome meal of boiled potatoes followed by bread and jam. Five hours later, the Konstantinidis family were back in Port Said refugee centre searching for their missing family members.

Through the next days, news came that another raft or lifeboat had turned up. Everyone waited for names convincing themselves their missing family members were safe at last. A week after that, a raft washed up on a Cyprus shore and miraculously delivered more barely alive refugees. Although none of the survivors were from the Konstantinidis family, it gave everyone hope.

* * *

Uncle Kuríllos's body was never recovered, nor was Rosa's. Sofía feared her uncle had perished right after saving her. Sometimes, she felt his hands on her hips, lifting her and tears sprang to her eyes. She never told anyone, for it seemed stupid. She would always love Uncle Kuríllos.

The whole family went to visit María and Panayiotis in Port Said hospital. Poor María, all her beautiful hair burned off and her face and limbs badly seared. When her dressings were changed, the intense pain meant that high doses of morphine had to be administered, making her incoherent. Her incredible beauty was stolen by the fire and her bravery was destroyed when she learned her ballet-dancing daughter and her two sisters and her grandmother, had certainly gone to God. Sofía sat on María's hospital bed, her distress intensified because she could not wrap her sister in her arms while they wept together.

'Poor Rosa,' they both whispered.

* * *

As María started to recover, her greatest fear was that Mustafa would abandon her and the children, for she was under no illusions about the fact that he had fallen in love with her great beauty. Now, her angry red scars meant she would wear a hijab for the rest of her life and she would make sure he never saw the brutal reality of her withered and scarred naked body.

'We have to get home and start the distillery again, before we lose our French clients,' María told Mamá and Sofía.

'But what about your operations?' Mamá said. 'They must do skin grafts over the burns, they told me. Then there'll be plastic surgery.'

'Look, the scars will always be there, Mamá. What's the point of going through any more pain? I'm tired of suffering, really. Just let me heal and then I can hide the ugliness so as not to offend anyone. It's enough for me that I managed to save my little boy. Have you heard anything about the enquiry?'

Mamá nodded. 'They say it starts on 9 October, here in Port Said. You're not to worry about it. Just concentrate on getting better. Shall I bring the little ones to see you tomorrow?'

'God, no! I don't want them to see me like this. They'll be terrified.' Her brimming eyes appeared strangely vacant without their lashes.

Sofía wanted to take her sister's hands, but they were both bandaged to splints to stop them curling into claws as they healed. 'What about Panayiotis? Will they do skin grafts on his back?'

'No, they say, although the scars look big now they're only second-degree burns, so they'll shrink. Anyway, they'll look smaller as he grows. Poor little chap. He's been so brave. He'll be OK,' María said, then, in barely more than a breath, she whispered. 'You can't imagine . . . To see your child on fire . . .

what could I do but smother the flames and shield him from the inferno with my own body? If the sailor hadn't emptied a fire extinguisher on me when I was on fire, we'd both have perished. It's a nightmare that never leaves me.' Her shrivelled lip curled as tears ran into the bandages around her head. 'I saw Athena . . .' She sobbed loudly. 'I saw the girls. My poor girls! I was so seasick. They said they would look after me, I should sleep. I just wanted to lie there with my eyes closed. And then . . . when I opened my eyes, oh, the terrible fire. The dreadful screams of my children . . . sounds that came from a place of horror, appalling beyond description. We were surrounded by flames. Surrounded, I tell you. What had they done?'

A nurse came over. 'Sorry to break up the party,' she said with a kindly smile. 'Our patient needs her morphine before we can change the dressings. Would you like to come back tomorrow?'

Before she could say more, a white coated doctor with a stethoscope around his neck came into the ward. 'Do we have any members of the Konstantinidis family from Castellorizo here?'

María gasped and Sofía lifted her hand, a sudden explosion of hope in everyone's heart. 'Yes, we're Konstantinidis.'

'Good. I have someone to discharge into your care.' He stepped back into the corridor, then returned with a child holding his hand.

CHAPTER 43
OLIVIA

Castellorizo, Greece, present day

'YOU ARE VERY QUIET TONIGHT, Olivia,' Greg says as we walk along the sandy cove outside Kaş.

I take his hand. 'Sorry, I'm a little overwhelmed. It's the older generation. What tremendous lives they have led. I had no idea my uncle went through so much and I still don't know a great deal about his life. I'm ashamed to say, I only thought of him as an elderly gentleman who used to teach kids history and that he paints in his spare time.' Greg slips his arm around my waist as we walk. 'Now I discover that when he was only eight years old, he paddled around the open sea collecting lifebelts for his family and friends. I'm seeing him in a whole new light.'

'It is remarkable, I know. My Pappoú was only ten and that fire cost him a lung. He crawled around finding people who were trapped or unconscious and pulled them up to the fresh air. Five times he went back into the inferno and led people to safety, until he collapsed from smoke inhalation.'

'They should get medals.'

'What about Uncle's sister, María? Such bravery, to stand fast – actually burning alive, using her own body to shield her son! It's difficult to imagine.'

I stare at him. 'I don't know most of the story. My uncle is trying to tell me, but it's so painful, he can only manage a little at a time.'

'That's because it still haunts him.' We turn and head back to the taverna. 'I could tell you what I know, but perhaps Uncle *needs* to do it, you know, to purge himself of the nightmare.'

'There is so much I don't understand. Why did the family split the way they did?' She meets his eyes. 'Why are you looking at me like that?'

'I'm trying to decide how to change the subject. I can tell you to shut up. I can kiss you and hope it makes you forget everything else. Or, I can rent that room for the night, over the taverna.' He brushes my hair away from my face and kisses me gently on the cheek. 'What would you suggest?' He stops just short of the taverna, waiting for an answer.

I bite my lip for a moment. Is it too soon? 'My grandmother said, *Never do anything on an empty stomach*, so let's eat before we make any decisions.'

* * *

'Hell, it's six thirty! I promised Uncle I'd see them off on their fishing trip and take pictures!' My hair is stuck to my face, the room is stifling and our clothes are . . . all over the place. I scoop them up on my way to the shower then realise my fat and very naked bottom is on full view.

Then I hear what I can only describe as a giggle come from Greg.

'I wish I could rewind that and play it again,' he calls. 'You're very beautiful!'

Nobody has ever said that to me before. I peer around the bathroom door. 'Sorry, could you repeat . . . I didn't quite catch . . .'

He beams at me. 'Simply beautiful! A real woman. Come back to bed.'

'No, I promised my uncle a photographic record of this morning. It's important to him, really important. We have to hurry and get back to the port!' I cry over the noise of the shower.

'Right, you'd better move over then, I'm coming in.'

'Don't be silly there isn't room, no, there isn't . . . ooh!'

Ten minutes later, we are racing down the jetty. He runs, then starts the engine. I'm the wrong shape for any kind of speedy athletics. I jog . . . well, walk quickly and gracefully. We speed over the water in the tubby brightly coloured boat. It's then the penny drops. We are in Uncle's boat! They can't go anywhere until we get back and they'll be waiting for us on the quayside. Oh, the embarrassment! They'll know everything. I try to brush my hair and put on some make-up, but this is a disastrous plan. My posh white linen clothes look like a bag of washing and if Greg doesn't stop laughing . . . I don't know what I'll do.

Twenty minutes later, we pull into the harbour. They are all on the quayside, waiting. A pick-up with some kind of small crane on the back has reversed to the edge. Next to it is Demetriou in his wheelchair. I can feel my cheeks burning as Dino offers me a hand and pulls me up.

'Good night, was it?' he says with a grin that seems to be passed around. Even Greg has a mile-wide smile.

There is a pile of fishing tackle on the quayside. Eleni rushes up with a small box of shrimp and calamari for bait. 'Olivia! Good morning!' she says with gusto, then bobs her eyebrows, winks and adds in a mischievous manner, 'Coffee?' The word is loaded with enquiry.

I want to say, *Yes, I did have sex with your son last night, more than once and it was great!* but I just shake my head. 'Must dash to get my camera.' I hurry back to my apartment. Inside, I pull my hair into a scrunchy, then apply a slick of lipstick and mascara. Back at the scene, I pray my battery will last and take a few shots.

When I return, I notice the water surface break a few metres away. A turtle sticks its head up as if watching the quayside pantomime.

The guy with the small crane attaches four luggage straps to the wheelchair, then loops them over the crane hook. He has a little remote-control gadget which raises the crane arm to its maximum. At this point, we all realise it's a bad plan to use bungee-cord luggage straps because Demetriou is still on the ground but, at any moment, he and his chair may catapult across the harbour.

The crane is lowered and, after a loud arm-waving discussion which surely wakes the town – though many have already gathered to watch – a mooring rope takes the elastic's place. Everything is held up for five minutes because, due to all the laughter, several of the elderly people have to use Eleni's bathroom. After a shaky start, Demetriou and his wheelchair lift gently and then descend slowly into the boat. A round of applause sounds for the happy crane operator.

I photograph everything, then take a video of them leaving. 'Not far . . .' they promise. 'Back by midday!'

'Right,' Greg says after finishing the mug of coffee his mother has put in his hand. 'I'm off see if Manno has finished your floor. The electrics should be ready after noon. Your main feed will stay plugged into my cousin's until the solar panels and batteries arrive.'

* * *

The men return at noon, thrilled with their small catch. Demetriou is hoisted out of the boat with no further complications and everyone is invited to a supper of Eleni's delicious fish soup that evening.

Uncle needs a sleep so I make him a ham sandwich and a mug of milky decaf and leave him in peace.

I decide to walk around to Nifti Point and find the best place to scatter Mum's ashes. Then I return to my apartment to catch up on some missed sleep.

* * *

At four o'clock I find Uncle awake and refreshed. 'Let's go up to the house and see how things have progressed,' he says.

We talk to lots of people along the way. All the chairs in the streets and the short stops are just the ticket for my uncle. It takes us almost an hour to reach the patio, where we find Greg and Manno packing up their tools.

'How's it going, guys?' I ask, suddenly realising the crowd of well-wishers have followed us up.

'All done. The ground floor is sound and you have electric lights and a few sockets,' Greg says. 'Perhaps while you're here with the builder, you should discuss what you want to do next.'

'Good plan, but first I need to see inside properly. We've only seen it once and that was by torchlight.'

'Right, come to the doorway then and turn on the light.'

There's a real sense of occasion about the moment. Uncle comes to my side, places his arm about my shoulders and together we throw the switch. Everyone cheers when the big room shines with unbridled light.

'It's so big, Uncle, I hadn't realised. Wow!' I stare at the vast space. To the right, the big bed is still there, although the rotten steps have been removed.

'That side is quite sound and the staircase, too, but the middle of the upper floors are rotten. That's everything below the hole in the roof. Mano suggests a roof repair as soon as possible. Now, the distillery . . .' Greg says.

We walk straight across the new floor, repeat the little 'turn on' ceremony, then all stare at the brightly lit factory.

The room – about sixteen metres long – has three enormous copper stills in the centre. Although they have acquired the green patina of age, the warmth of copper shines through adding to the pleasing bulbous shapes. They stand like exquisite sculptures, supported by brick fire-rings. I can imagine the heat they generate in that room, then notice the roof vents with chimneys over the stills.

More and more people come into the distillery and many bring foil-covered plates which they line up on the counter. The builder produces a lyra, sits down next to the food and starts playing. Bottles of raki and ouzo and small glasses are lined up next to jugs of ice-cold water. Women hold hands and jig to the music and Uncle grins and shakes hands with everyone.

It's all so surreal – just like my first day on the island. I can't remember feeling this happy, it's like a light has been turned on inside me too. Before long, the women lose control of their dancing feet and, with their hands raised to shoulder height, they trip around the stills, through the big room and out onto the patio to the rhythm of the lyra. The builder follows and as the music drifts down towards the port, more people appear with food and drink.

'Come, come!' the last woman in the chain of dancers cries. 'Is easy, kick left – kick right – step behind. Here, you look at my feet and do the same!'

I do and yes, it is easy. Holding hands, keeping the rhythm, being in harmony with them is kind of special. Dancing with the people of Castellorizo really makes me feel at home. I catch sight of Uncle who's sitting on a chair that somebody has brought up. His face is shining with happiness. Dino, red-faced and sweating, pushes Demetriou's wheelchair onto the patio and parks it next to my uncle. The wizened old man with his Gollum features is smiling broadly.

The music picks up speed, which draws my attention to the builder. I throw a smile his way and he winks back.

Greg's face comes down to mine, so close his nose is against my cheek and his lips brush my jaw when he speaks. 'Let's go to your room,' he whispers. 'Nobody will miss us.'

Oh gosh – does my heart patter! What's going on? I never even had such intense feelings with Andrew and we were married for seven years. I look away quickly, flustered and blushing.

I'm transfixed by the music, the rhythm and by the kindness of everyone. It occurs to me that this very scene probably occurs every time the builder plays his instrument. How many women have danced on a patio here, gazing at the man they love while their hearts go crazy?

'Later,' I say to Greg.

'Tonight?' he whispers back. 'Tell me I can come to your room.'

*　*　*

The party continues for three hours. The food is devoured hungrily as excitement always instigates an appetite. A great

380

pinwheel of spinach and feta wrapped in crispy golden filo pastry is cut into narrow wedges. There are tiny cheese pies; plump sweet olives; halved, hard-boiled eggs with bright orange yolks sprinkled with black pepper, herbs and olive oil; tiny cracked new potatoes; giant beans and stuffed vine leaves.

A few of the men sip raki, but most drink water.

Uncle chats with everyone, listens to family names until one connects with another. Eventually, in loud and triumphant moments, people find they are related and much back-slapping or cheek-kissing seals the genealogy.

One rotund elderly gentleman rattles a fork against a glass without caution. It seems to be a recognised conversation stopper. Even the music fades. The man slings his arm over Uncle's shoulders and bellows gleefully, 'Hey, listen, everybody! His aunt's second cousin in Australia – the woman doctor, you know? Yes, of course you do, well, she married my sister-in-law's uncle's boy, Manoli. Bravo! We're family! Bravo!'

'Bravo! Bravo!' the people add. The builder plays with even more gusto and I grin and kiss my uncle's cheek.

'This is madness, Uncle. I am fascinated by the way that everyone bubbles with enthusiasm but each conversation is nothing more than a long list of questions, searching for connections and an exchange of good wishes.'

'I know,' he replies, eyes sparkling. 'Everyone is crazy about finding their family. It's linked to the past, the terrible time when we lost each other. I remember that moment, after the submarine incident, when I was reunited with Mamá.'

CHAPTER 44
SOFIA

Port Said, Egypt to Castellorizo, Greece, 1945

'GEORGIKIE!' MAMÁ CRIED AS HER only son entered the ward. 'God and all the saints, my son's alive. Oh, my blessed boy. I prayed and prayed!' Choking on emotion, she ran her hand over her boy's face and body, stroking his hair and lifting his chin so she could peer into his eyes, as if to confirm he was real, living – and not just a dream.

George told of his adventures aboard HMS *Spark*, how they let him look into the periscope and call, 'Dive! Dive!' into the microphone.

'They took me to the big aircraft carrier and painted me purple, like my fingers after picking blackberries, except all over – and I do mean all over, Mamá!' He nodded emphatically. 'They said it would cure the burns. I'm going to be a sailor when I grow up, Mamá. Just so you know.'

* * *

Uncle Kuríllos, Rosa, Katina and Athena went on the list of MISSING. Two weeks later, a shorter list hung in its place headed, MISSING PRESUMED DROWNED. Poignant prayers were said for the dearly departed at a special Sunday service accompanied by much weeping and wailing from Mamá and the other bereaved women. Some tore their hair out by the clumps, others raked their nails down their faces, eager for real pain to help dispel the agony of their broken hearts. All the drama seemed to fit these tragic losses, especially considering the ages of those who had gone before, from a newborn to an octogenarian great-grandmother.

Sofía's heartache for the loss of her loved ones came in waves. In the middle of a normal day, she would suddenly find herself floundering in a wilderness of grief and real tears. Uncle Kuríllos, oh . . . She knew he would come back to her in every stranger's laughter, every wink of a mischievous eye, every dramatically exclaimed swear word. He'd always been special to her and she'd loved him dearly. Her uncle had spent the last moments of his life saving her. He would always be in her heart and she would live her life to the full, for him. Though her grief ebbed at times, it also caught up with her unexpectedly and hit her hard. She tried not to cry in front of the others, yet her soul screamed for justice. Somebody must pay! She needed to blame, to see the culprits suffer for what had transpired, but especially for what had happened to María. Her beautiful sister had to live with those terrible deforming scars for the rest of her life.

She could murder whoever started that fire.

In these moments of deep depression, she longed for Jamie's arms around her and the distance between them only exacerbated her distress.

* * *

The morning of the enquiry, Sofía was trying to spoon some rice boiled in sweetened milk into two-year-old Evdokia. The little girl decided she was having none of it and blew a mouthful all over Sofía's chest.

'You really are asking for a smack, you naughty, naughty girl!' Sofía cried, exasperated. Evdokia, who had never received a smack in her short life, laughed at her aunt. She blew a raspberry into her sticky palm and then plopped it onto Sofía's cheek. 'No, don't you try getting around me, you're still naughty and you must still eat your breakfast like a good girl, or you know what? We might be having baby soup for lunch!' she quipped, knowing the child would not understand her macabre sense of humour.

A pair of hands came from behind and slid over her eyes. 'That's a very wicked thing to say to an innocent child,' a man's voice said.

Sofía gasped, dropped the spoon and spun around. 'Jamie! Oh, Jamie!' In an instant, she was in his arms, his lips on hers. With barely a glance at her charge, she saw Evdokia tip the bowl of food over and run her hands through the mess. Enjoying every sensation, the infant licked her fingers and made cooing noises, then she attempted to suck up the spillage and, in doing so, got most of it in her hair. Sofía didn't care.

Jamie had stepped from the shadows of two years and stolen the sadness right out of her soul. She felt her body lighten so much, perhaps her feet left the floor.

'You came back in my darkest hour,' she said, tears flowing down her cheeks. 'I've missed you so much. You can't imagine how much I've missed you!' She melted against his firm torso and sensed his beating heart within. His strong arms drew her even closer. Her body shook violently, her soul crying for the missed time they could never recapture. 'Two long years, Jamie. Really, I thought I would never see you again.'

He pulled his chin in and smiled. 'Don't cry. Everything will be all right, I promise.' He wiped her tears away and the touch of his hand on her face brought her more pleasure than her heart could stand. He kissed her cheek. 'Mmm, nice, sweet. A bit sticky, though.'

Sofía gasped. 'Oh, the baby!' She pulled from his arms and swung around. 'Oh, my goodness, we are in a mess, aren't we?' she said to Evdokia, sweeping her up. 'Come on, miss, let's get you in the sink for a washing down before your grandmother sees you and has a fit.'

'Can I help?' Jamie asked.

'Why not? There's a communal laundry room, I'll wash her in one of the big sinks. Just let me gather some soap and clothes.'

In the laundry room, Jamie played the fool for Evdokia while Sofía washed her. She gurgled at his antics, trying to copy him and laughing when he crossed his eyes and blew his cheeks out. 'I can't wait to have our own children, can you?' he asked Sofía. 'It must be amazing, don't you think?'

She grinned at him. 'And it's rather enjoyable trying, you must agree.' He kissed her, hard.

Evdokia kissed the palm of her hand and made a raspberry sound and they all laughed.

'I have a week's leave – come to England with me? Meet my family.'

'Yes, oh, yes!' But as she swooped Evdokia up and wrapped her in a towel, her face fell. 'That would be wonderful – so terrific – but I can't, Jamie.' He asked why, so she explained. 'Three of my sister's children were killed on the *Empire Patrol* and my dear Uncle Kuríllos. We are all in mourning for twelve months. Also, María is so badly burned, Mamá will need all the help she can get to look after everyone.'

He hid his disappointment well and if it hadn't been for his downcast eyes and a little tension around his mouth, she would have said he didn't mind.

'OK, if that's the situation, I have no choice but to spend my hard-earned leave bathing babies and trying to find a little privacy so I can kiss my wife without her entire family gawping at us.'

'I love you, Jamie Peters,' she said, her heart as happy as a butterfly in spring. 'Now let's get some clothes on this little monster.'

* * *

María drifted in and out of her morphine-induced stupor. Sometimes she felt nothing when they changed the dressings, other times she felt everything as they eased the dressings from her raw flesh but was so doped she couldn't move or make a sound. In a vague middle distance, she heard nurses talking: *Poor woman . . . how many children? They say she was beautiful. She'll be hospitalised for months.*

* * *

The enquiry came to the conclusion that nobody could be held responsible for the *Empire Patrol* disaster. Everybody wanted to blame somebody, of course they did. Anger, grief, loss, all can make a person bitter. Some blamed the British for taking them away in the first place, or for not providing a better ship, or for not treating them properly. Nobody blamed their own county for abandoning them. However, the loyal Castellorizo people still gathered and sang their national anthem with great pride whenever the opportunity arose.

Due to the daily administration of morphine, María was found not capable of giving evidence and once the magistrate went to see her, he admitted she should not be put through further misery. Anyway, her testimony could not be relied on because of her medication.

A month passed before the surgeons completed María's necessary skin grafts, then they transferred her to Rhodes hospital and the rest of the family returned home. Each weekend, an adult and two children caught the ferry and went to visit her. They stayed overnight in the home of a distant cousin, where they slept on the floor. The next morning, they boarded the ferry for its return to Castellorizo. After another month – on 1 December – the doctors allowed María to come home at last, much to the joy of everyone.

* * *

Mustafa returned from his Christmas trading trip on Christmas Eve. As usual, he brought a sack of oranges and nuts and chocolate for the town which had reduced to little more than a small village. The majority had emigrated to Australia. The Turk also brought special gifts for everyone in his family.

Everyone was a little too cheerful, compensating for the absentees. Glances were made to the place where the olivewood chest stood, where the two grandmothers had sat and crocheted for as long as anyone could remember. On the windowsill that Rosa had used for her barre exercises, Mamà had placed a small vase of red roses. Nobody mentioned it was a lovely gesture, though everyone thought it. Sofía took one bloom and walked over to Mandraki. She laid it on the pile of rubble that was once the teacher's cottage.

When she returned, Mustafa was dishing out gifts. 'Sofía, here, I found this just for you!' he boomed, clearly pleased with himself.

Laughing, she tore open the package, then stared, tears welling, at an identical music box to the one that went down with the *Empire Patrol* with all her precious letters from Jamie. She turned the key and opened the lid and there ... the beautiful ballerina pirouetted, promising to remind everyone of lovely Rosa. Sofía looked up to see tears in the eyes of every person. She placed the open box next to the vase of red roses.

María, still swathed in bandages, blinked slowly then spoke to Sofía. 'I want to make a precious oil especially for a perfume called My Rosa. In memory of my ... little ...' She covered her gnarled lips with a scarred hand for a moment and took a heavy breath. 'Sorry, everyone. I still can't believe she's gone. She *was* destined to be a great dancer, wasn't she?'

Everyone lowered their eyes and nodded, then they realised they were staring at the floor where Rosa had danced her best. Where she had given them all so much pleasure. The room was silent until María spoke again.

'I want her remembered by a perfume, the rich scent of deep red roses. Velvety petals and enormous blooms. That's how I think of her. Where could I find such a shrub, Mustafa? Could we buy these petals to make a unique precious oil?'

'Holland grows very good roses, but perhaps there are better nurseries. I will put your quest at the top of my list, María. My homeland also grows amazing roses that perfume the scents of the east.' He stared at her for a second, his eyes bright with tears, then he turned and went out onto the patio.

Sofía felt her heart breaking for her sister and for Mustafa too. He loved his little ballerina so much. He also loved his wife, but because of the great beauty she had he could hardly bear to look at her now. The only thing that remained the same was her lovely voice. In the evenings, they turned off the lights while she sang Evdokia to sleep and as her sweet voice drifted through the house, they all saw her as the beauty she had been.

CHAPTER 45
OLIVIA

Castellorizo, Greece, present day

'Sit down, Olivia,' Uncle says. 'I realise how little you know about your family and I think it's time I told you what happened. I should have explained earlier, but I'm sure you realise, I find it difficult.'

The impromptu party has ended and everyone has taken their plates, chairs and leftover food home with them.

'So, what's changed to make you feel you can tell me now, Uncle? I mean, I'm longing to know what happened, but I'm also concerned about your heart. Perhaps we should wait until you're stronger.'

'I'm not sure what's changed. Perhaps being here with old friends, being reminded of their values, their sense of place and family and home. Seeing you and Greg together, trying to hide your feelings from the world and all the possibilities of a new beginning. That gladdens my old heart, I can tell you. Then seeing old Demetriou at the end of his very full life. It's made me realise that you need the blanks filling in, so I'm going to tell you all I know from the earthquake, onward. Feel free to record, or make notes, dear girl. I'm not too sure I'll get past the fire, but I'll try.'

* * *

An hour has passed and in the silence of his room, my darling uncle peers at me from a pale, emotionally drained face. Both his hands and his voice are trembling and I have tears in my eyes.

'I'm so sorry, Uncle. I had no idea that you'd been through so much.'

'Been through . . . dear girl, that was just the start.'

I am about to put the kettle on when I notice two of the old photographs on the side. I pick them up. 'These old photos are wonderful, Uncle. They're such a lovely record of the past, far more poignant than a digital image. Who are these beautiful people?'

His face suddenly brightens as he smiles. 'These are my sisters. The first is Sofía in her traditional Castellorizo costume, on her wedding day. The silks and gold thread were provided by Mustafa and the finest mink around the coat came from Uncle Kuríllos. The man beside her, in his British army uniform, is her new husband, Jamie Peters.'

'My grandfather! He was rather handsome, don't you think?'

Uncle gazes at the picture. 'They were so in love, look at them. Public displays of affection were frowned upon in those days, but look at the photo. They're standing quite stiffly side by side, but see how the backs of their hands are pressed against each other.'

I study the sepia photograph and wonder what happened to make them leave Castellorizo for good. However, I don't want to ask him now. He has already been far too emotional for his own good. 'It's a beautiful picture and they look so young. Can I see the other photo, please?'

'Ah, yes. This is a professional portrait of María that she had done for Mustafa. The original hung in his ship's cabin. Taken before the fire, of course. She would never have one taken after. Poor darling.'

'Gosh, look how the photographer has captured her beauty. So stunning. She has a look of that old film star in her prime . . . what was her name? Played Cleopatra, married a Welsh actor, more than once, I think?'

'Elizabeth Taylor? Yes, María bore strong similarities and you're not the first person to say so.'

'Absolutely beautiful. But you mentioned she was scarred in the fire?'

'More than scarred. So badly burned it was a miracle she survived. She put herself between her child and the flames and remained there, steadfast, burning, protecting Panayiotis, until they doused her and got the boy out. María had been the most gorgeous woman on the island, no doubt about it.'

I placed my hand on his shoulder. 'It sounds horrendous. No wonder you're finding it hard to tell me.'

My uncle runs his fingertips over the picture, caressing her face, lost in his memories. Then he says something I don't understand. 'Even after the fire and all its destruction, the perfume saved her, but at the same time, it completely destroyed our loving family forever.' His eyes fill. 'Forgive me. I have to stop a while.' He takes a deep breath in and blows it out slowly.

'I'm so grateful. Let me get you a drink. What would you like: coffee, ouzo, wine?'

'Bring me a good whisky from Dino.' A tear trickles down the crags in his old cheek and makes me want to weep too.

I hug him, kiss his forehead and hurry out. At our table with the permanent RESERVED sign, I sit and place my hand over my eyes to stop myself from crying. In a flash, Eleni is at my side.

'Is something wrong?'

'My uncle is so upset, he asked me to come to Dino and get a large glass of his best whisky.'

'*Panagia mou*,' she mutters, crossing herself. 'It must be bad. We're not busy, would you like Dino to take it to him?'

I nod. 'Good plan. He told me some of his story. From the earthquake to returning here after the war. It's really upset him and I'm afraid it's all my fault for pressing him.'

'Wait here,' she says and scurries to the kitchen. A minute later, Dino appears with a bottle of whisky in one fist and two glasses in the other. He looks my way and does the sort of nod that horses do, more up than down. Then he marches along the front to my uncle's room.

I sit with Eleni, watching as he goes in. I'm still staring in that direction when two things happen at once. In the far distance, the Blue Star ferry sails around the headland and heads for its mooring on the opposite side of the harbour. Then Rob comes scurrying out of the big hotel, where he's been staying. He rushes past us as if we aren't there and I see he has a rucksack on his back. Apparently, he's heading for the ferry.

'He's family and he didn't even say goodbye,' I say to Eleni, the disappointment clear in my voice.

'Good riddance, I say – the swindling whore without a conscience!' she mutters.

'I'm not sure the lawyer is such a bad lot, actually.'

'Anyone who is that easily persuaded to go along with something for the promise of a small percentage should never be trusted again. Believe me, I know what I'm talking about,' she says vehemently. 'What are you doing tonight . . . or shouldn't I ask?'

Damn it, I actually blush. 'I'd like another look at the perfume book with Uncle,' I say. 'And an early night because tomorrow, I want to get an architect, the builder, plumber, carpenter and of course my favourite electrician together, to make a proper plan for the house.'

'No architect on the island, Olivia. If George isn't up to it tomorrow morning, I'm sure it will be cheaper if I'm there,' Eleni says. 'It's three floors and a cellar, yes?' I nod. 'So you'll probably want three bathrooms, a kitchen of some sort . . . but first things first. The roof and front door are priorities. Then a basement tank for rainwater. Anyway, think about it.'

'Shall we have a sundowner?' I suggest. 'We've hardly had any time to ourselves, Eleni, and I'm so grateful for all your help.'

'I suspect we're not going to have any time now either. Look who's coming.'

Two burly port police have Rob by the armpits. They power-walk him back around the harbour. I hope they are going straight back to the hotel, but no, they stop in front of me.

'Livia, you've got to help me. I'm in trouble and we're family, right?'

Eleni spoke to one of the port police in Greek, after a short conversation she turns to me. 'He's accused of trying to leave on the ferry without paying his hotel bill.'

'I wasn't, honestly, I wasn't! My credit card maxed out and there's no bank here. I was just going to Rhodes to organise a money transfer. Tell them I wouldn't cheat anyone, Livia, please!'

'How much do you owe?'

He looks at the floor, then at me. 'One and a half grand.'

'What! Give me your passport. In fact, give me your wallet too!' He does. 'I'll talk it over with Uncle.' I turn to the port police. 'Meanwhile, he's all yours.' I hand them the passport and wallet.

'Livia, please!'

'You need to understand that you can't go around cheating people and expecting to get away with it, Rob!'

CHAPTER 46
SOFIA

Castellorizo, Greece, 1946

SOFIA TOSSED AND TURNED AS dawn's first light leaked through a gap in the shutters. She couldn't sleep. Jamie had gone back to his battalion with the disappointing knowledge that his wife was still not pregnant. She came down to the big room to get a drink of water and an aspirin for her menstrual cramps and saw the light on in the distillery. Concerned that one of the children might have gone in there, she hurried to investigate.

'Come on, who's in here?' she said quietly, not wanting to instigate a ruckus.

'It's me – María. Go back to bed, Sofía.'

'What's going on, it's four o'clock in the morning?'

'I'm working on something, just go back to bed and leave me alone!' María whispered sharply. 'Why do you always have to interfere? Go!' In the harsh light of the bare bulbs, María's face was a tragedy.

'Please, María, don't upset me. Let me help.'

'No! No! Just go, will you?'

Shocked, Sofía backed away. 'All right, I'm going. It's not my intention to upset you. I just wanted to help . . . to understand what was going on because I care, María. You're my sister and I love you and it hurts when you shut me out.'

María sighed and spun away from Sofía and the light. Her shoulders drooped like those of an old woman and were shaking with despair. Sofía sensed her sister's deep sadness.

'I'm trying to blend a new perfume, if you must know. A perfume just for me,' María said.

Sofía could not see her sister's face, but there was so much tragedy in those words, it made her want to weep.

Maria continued. 'I want . . . well, Mustafa will be home soon and . . . oh!' Suddenly, she dropped to her knees on a sack of rosemary and covered her ugly face with her hands. 'I want him to love me again, if you must know. I want to enchant him like I used to. I want a perfume so strong that he won't see the freak I am. Something so powerful and irresistible it's magical.' Her voice quavered with a plea that tore into Sofía's soul. 'Let me be adored just one more time, Sofía, that's all I ask.' She took a breath and then whispered, 'You can't imagine how much I long to lie in his arms again.'

Sofía felt her heart break for her sister. She gathered all her emotional strength and gave her as much support as she could, as she always had. 'Well, come on then, no use in snivelling about it, let's get going. How far have you got?'

María sniffed and dried her eyes on the sleeve of her nightgown. 'I've blended jasmine, vanilla and frangipani, with undertones of coffee. It's a start, but I'm missing some heat. I need a darker side – passion, even lust. Something rich and mystical and completely irresistible.' She sighed, tears bumping their way down the scars on her face.

Sofía's heart cracked open and bled.

María lowered her eyes. 'You must think I am crazy. I should simply let him go and be glad for the wonderful time we've had. There's no way I can keep him when I look like this.'

'Oh, do shut up and stop feeling sorry for yourself,' Sofía said, sharply. 'Let's try adding bergamot and what about a little myrrh, or musk to give it weight, or mandarin and almond – ooh, I love orange marzipan. Do we have any cocoa? I mean, who doesn't feel sexy after eating dark chocolate?' Perhaps she spoke a little too fast. Finding the right words to feed to her sister seemed urgent. Sofía's body was paying attention to the scents and a stirring sensation awoke inside her. 'Make a note of that, cocoa; goes wonderfully with the almond and bergamot.'

Dawn broke and one by one the children woke. 'Come on, let's leave it or our nose will be tainted. We'll continue this evening,' Sofía said.

'Listen, you never told me, why couldn't you sleep?'

Sofía sighed. 'Why can't I get pregnant, Maria? It's not for the lack of trying, I promise you. We're both terribly disappointed and I can't help feeling somehow it's my fault.'

'You know what they do on Rhodes?' Sofía shook her head. 'Instead of going to their doctor – the desperate, childless women climb Tsambika Mountain on their knees until they reach the chapel of Saint Tsambika at the top. Then, if they have a child in the next year, they must name the child after the saint.'

'Perhaps I should do it,' Sofía said.

'No, you will not, Sofía! It's a silly superstition and an arduous task and some women have died after getting sepsis in their wounds from the goat droppings. Really, think about it. What sort of a saint would want to cause that much suffering to women who are already devastated because they're childless? It's a cruel and silly superstition, nothing more.'

Panayiotis came into the distillery. 'I'm hungry, Mamá,' he said sleepily.

* * *

That evening, Sofía and María continued in their search for a perfumed oil so potent it made those who detect its aroma fill

396

with blind desire for the wearer. For seven nights, they worked in pursuit of this infallible concoction.

'I know!' Sofía cried with a sudden flash of inspiration one evening. 'Add some boswellia resin to increase the blood flow; after all, that's what we're looking for, isn't it . . . throbbing, pulsating, hard passion?'

María grinned, her top lip turning white and shiny with the stretch. 'Sounds perfect, but I'm brain dead with tiredness. Remind me, what's boswellia resin?'

'You know, frankincense.'

'Ah, yes, why didn't I think of that? I'm so excited. We must have the perfect ingredients. Now, we just have to get the quantities right.' She smiled at Sofía. 'I'm so grateful, darling sister.'

'Look, why don't we take the same ingredients each, go to opposite ends of the distillery and blend. We're so close, I'm sure one of us will soon come up with something, to use your own words: so powerful and irresistible it's magical.'

* * *

Another four nights of blending, writing recipes and testing – then, approaching midnight, the day before Mustafa's expected arrival, Sofía inhaled the scent of her latest blend.

The room seemed to close in on her. 'María,' she whispered. 'Come here.' She realised her voice was thick, as if she were half asleep, or drunk. 'My God, I do believe I have it.'

As María came close, she seemed veiled in a holy light that was only semi-transparent. Sofía's own body responded to the perfume. Her lips swelled and tingled, as did her nipples. But most importantly, her sex throbbed with desire.

'Oh my goodness. I'm breathless and my heart's pounding,' she whispered. 'María, I'm sure I have the recipe for your magical perfume and I have the name too. You must call it Desire.'

'You've really mixed the perfect blend?' María whispered. 'Please, let me try it.'

Sofía took a little cotton wool, dipped it in the oil and stroked a line across the inside of María's wrist.

Even while they are talking to each other, the scent rose and María whispered, 'Oh, this is the weirdest sensation, I feel as if I'm in a dream, floating, intoxicated, at the same time I'm filled with passionate desire and powerful eroticism. My vision is so blurred I can hardly see. Yet my other senses are increased a hundred-fold. I have a fire burning below and I long to press my body ... well ... I can hardly breathe for the want. But enough of this.' María realised she was trembling. 'I must wash this off to break its spell, before I burn up. I think we can celebrate a success, dear sister, and I certainly could not have done it without you. Of us all, you are the one who has always had that magical sense of smell.'

Sofía was filled with happiness for dear María. She slung her arm around her sister's shoulders. 'You're beautiful, María, as you always have been.'

'This is terrific, exactly what I was hoping for. You did write down all the ingredients and their proportions, didn't you?'

'Yes, of course. Look, it's almost dawn. You go and catch a couple of hours' sleep while I tidy up here. Babá is in Kaş for a few days, so when Mustafa arrives, Mamá and I will take all the children for a swim. You will have the house to yourselves.'

Since the *Empire Patrol* disaster, all the Konstantinidis children had learned to swim. Terrified at first, each eventually found the courage to lie on the water without a lifebelt and be guided, trembling, back onto their feet by a watchful Babá.

'Are you crazy? You need to sleep too. Go to bed, we'll tidy up later. And Sofía . . .'

'Yes?'

'Thank you.'

* * *

Sofía and María were on tenterhooks for nearly two weeks, waiting for the schooner to appear. At nine o'clock the following Sunday morning, Zafiro came racing into the house. 'He's here! Papa is here! I just saw the ship turn into the harbour.'

As the church bells pealed nine o'clock, they all rushed onto the patio and saw the great ship slide home. It had been six months and now María was terrified that he had come to say their marriage was over.

Sofía saw that fear in her sister's eyes and could have wept for her. 'Come, María, it's time to get ready. Don't let me down now.' She turned to Ayeleen. 'Get everyone to clean up and put on their best clothes. We must give your father a welcome like he's never known before!' She gathered the girls together. 'Ayeleen, Popi, Kristina and Bebe, make a real fuss of your darling Papa.' She turned to the boys. 'Right, you lot. It's time you started to behave like young men. Zafiro, Fevzi and Panayiotis, you make sure you shake hands with your father. Fevzi, pay attention! This is important, or I'm telling you all, you may never see him again, do you understand?' Their eyes widened and they all nodded frantically.

'Zafiro, you ask you father if you can work on the ship, next trip,' Mamá said. 'You tell him how much you admire him and that you want to be just like him, right?'

'But I don't want to work on the ship. I want to go to school,' Zafiro said.

'Don't argue with me, young man. Your father won't take you on the ship until you're sixteen anyway. So don't worry.'

Mamá, who never missed an opportunity to rib Babá now he was back from Kaş, ordered him to go wash and smarten up, then she sent Fevzi down to the butcher for lamb chops, 'And while you're there, get a litre of raki and a kilo of salted almonds.' She turned to Popi. 'Go into the field and pick a bunch of fresh *glystretha* for a nice dish of greens – Mustafa loves my purslane salad – and collect the eggs while you're there and put them on to boil. Now, listen, make sure everywhere is as clean and tidy as possible. Best clothes and washed hands and faces at all times! Sofía and I are going to help your mother get ready. Don't let me down now!'

Sofía had made a beautiful pale blue dress that hugged her sister's figure. Besides her singing voice, the only thing not spoiled by the fire was María's amazing body.

The family had just emerged from a year of mourning when black was worn by everyone, even the children. The new dress was button fronted with a deep elastic belt, which showed off María's narrow waist. The pencil skirt finished mid-calf and flattered her long legs and narrow ankles. The sisters had studied post-war fashions of Paris and London and had copied the most classic style.

The red, angry-looking skin grafts on the backs of María's legs were covered in theatre make-up, then a pair of proper silk stockings with seams up the back. Sofía struggled to control her tears, when she remembered why the back of María was so much more badly burned that the front.

A delicate white chiffon scarf – draped softly over her head and around her neck – kept her hair in place and hid her shrivelled ears. The doctor stated it was a miracle that her thick and lustrous tresses had grown back, but he doubted her eyelashes or eyebrows ever would. Meanwhile, the two sisters had become experts at applying false eyelashes and Mamá had wept the first time she saw the result. Sofía applied pan-stick make-up, then a fashionable shade of red lipstick and a dab of rouge. She stepped back and studied her sister.

'You look amazing, María!' Sofía trilled. 'He'll be swept off his feet. Now, apply a drop of the perfume, no more. Then later when you're alone, splash it on you and him, all right?'

'Yes. Oh, I hope it works, Sofía!'

'I'm sure it will. We've re-arranged the children's accommodation so you'll have the room to yourselves. I've also taken the light bulb out and left some candles, which throw a more flattering light.'

'Thank you. This means so much to me.'

Excited sounds and the aroma of grilled lamb chops drifted upward. They both heard a pattering on the stairs, then Ayeleen burst into the room.

'Papa's here!' Then a gasp. 'Oh, Mother, you're so beautiful . . . so beautiful, you look like a film star.'

María's tension fell away. 'Do you really think so, Ayeleen?'

'Let's all go downstairs, shall we?' Sofía said to her niece.

'I'll go first, then you follow me, Aunty Sofía, then Mother, so we'll have everyone's attention.'

'Good plan,' Sofía said.

'I'm feeling nervous,' María said.

'Honestly, Mother, you look terrific,' Ayeleen said.

'On second thoughts, just a dab of perfume behind your ears, María,' Sophia said with a wink.

They came downstairs and, as María appeared, Mustafa gasped, then stood blinking at her as if he wasn't quite sure she was his wife.

* * *

The evening was a huge success. Lamb chops in the twilight on the patio, then an early night for everyone. Mamá scurried the children off to bed, then almost dragged Babá up the stairs. Mustafa couldn't take his eyes off the wife he truly loved and María's confidence returned. She flirted with him, made it clear she wanted him and he found her irresistible. Before long, they were blowing out the candles.

* * *

Early the next morning, a rather dishevelled María woke Sofía. 'He's going this afternoon, please, help me get ready again. I'm not sure I could make such a good job of the make-up.'

'Was it worth it?' Sofía giggled.

María sighed. 'What a night. He loves me, Sofía, and he adores his children. I was foolish to worry.'

'Still, it's best to not leave anything to chance.'

CHAPTER 47
OLIVIA

Castellorizo, Greece, present day

'MORE CAKE, GEORGE?' ELENI ASKS.

He pats his belly. 'Tempting – it was so delicious – but absolutely not, thank you, Eleni. Couldn't fit another crumb in here.'

'Let's have the bill, Eleni, please,' I say. 'I think we're all in for an early night.' I'm thinking of Greg. 'We have a lot to do tomorrow, going through the house renovations.'

'First, will you join me with a small brandy, Olivia? Helps to settle the food while we make a plan for tomorrow?' Uncle says.

'Why not?' I pull my notebook out while he orders the drinks and pays the bill.

'Now where shall we start . . .?' He looks at me expectantly and I get the feeling he's testing me, so I voice my plans.

'First, we must secure the house, get the roof repaired and a new front door and windows installed. I'm hoping we can rescue the original shutters. Next, order the solar panels and batteries to produce our own electricity and while we're awaiting delivery, we do the first-fix plumbing. I think we should tank the basement. Two tanks with water pumps to bring it up, fitted before the rest of the ground floor goes down. At the same time, we must organise guttering and downpipes to capture the winter's rainwater.' I draw a line under my list. 'Once those things are done, we can look at the next stage.'

'Which is?' Uncle narrows his eyes; yes, I was right. He's testing me.

'New floors, walls, ceilings, all made sound; internal doors. Then, a ground-floor kitchen, bathroom and decoration.'

'You seem to have thought it through.'

'To be honest, it's not as simple as it sounds. I suggest just making the ground floor habitable to start with. Open-plan living room and kitchen, a bathroom and two bedrooms.' I peer into his eyes for a reaction, but he simply stares back, so I continue. 'That way, the money we save on accommodation when we come over can go towards the refurbishment.'

Now, he smiles and nods.

'Can we take the ledger and the perfume book home with us? I'd like to study them.'

He nods again. 'What are you thinking?'

'I'm not sure; just considering all options. I wonder if there's a market for cottage industry here. Precious oils, handmade candles and soap, ethnic cookery, flavoured olive oils, bee keeping, even painting and photography holidays. There's space for eight rooms in the current building and so many people with special skills here, yet it all seems a little . . . trapped in the past.'

'I'd love to see the distillery running again. So, we agree, tomorrow we'll concentrate on the building?'

'After you come back from fishing.'

'And you drag yourself out of bed.' He winks mischievously.

* * *

The next morning, I walk up to the house, hoping to be alone for a while. After a struggle to get the front door open, I sense the mice have vacated the premises. Probably a mass exodus on the day of the party. The floor feels solid as I walk across it. In the distillery, I come across a few handwritten notebooks in a drawer. I gather them up and return to the patio. They all seem to be variations of the same blend. Interesting. I wonder what they were aiming for as I drop them into my bag. It's time for a coffee, so I decide to return to Eleni and to work on my cookery book.

At ten o'clock, my uncle surfaces. 'What time do you call this?' I tease.

'Oh dear, I guess I missed the fishing trip? I've just come to realise I'm not as young as I was. Did they go?'

'You're recovering from a heart attack, dear Uncle, so you really ought to be taking it easy! No, they didn't go. Eleni says that Dino and his father overslept. Young Nathan was going with them. He waited until six o'clock then went out for a few hours alone.'

He grins at me. 'Good, I hope he catches something. Anyway, there's still time for a trip before we leave. Have you ever been fishing at dawn?'

I laugh. 'Dawn! Fishing at dawn – no, that's obscene. And I can't imagine I ever will, either. There's only one place I want to be at dawn.'

'Now there's a mistake, deciding you won't like it without giving it a go. You must let me take you out before daybreak one time, before we go home. I would like that very much.'

I realise he's had a smile on his face for most of the time he's been here and it's infectious; I smile too. Then a sudden heaviness in my chest makes me realise how much I don't want to go home. He turns to Eleni as she approaches with his coffee.

'Any of that wonderful cake left? Would make the perfect breakfast.'

'You're a hopeless case, Uncle,' I say. 'Perhaps we ought to have a day off today. Take a boat over to Turkey. Visit Kaş, just relax.'

'No, we have to get the builders organised,' he says. 'Even if we only get the roof and the front door sorted on this trip, it's a step forward.'

'All right, Mr Stubborn, have it your own way.'

'Cake for the overweight man with a weak heart,' Eleni says, sliding a portion across to sit next to his coffee, then pulling a chair out for herself. 'Have I missed something?'

'No. Clearly you know today is pick-on-George day!' he says.

Eleni and I laugh.

Dino staggers out of the kitchen. 'My Blessed Virgin, I'm not as young as I was, George. Dead on my feet today.' He glances over at me and bobs his eyebrows. 'I would suggest a fishing trip, George, but I'd be afraid that your boat may be kidnapped by the lovebirds again . . .'

Uncle nods wearily. 'How about a game of *tavli* instead, your father was one of the best on the island. Besides, that would leave the boat free, just in case anyone else has plans . . .' He winks mischievously at his friend and nods my way.

'You can both stop it, right now,' I say with humour. 'You're being too naughty!'

'*We're* naughty?' Uncle says, grinning.

I narrow my eyes in a threatening way, warning him to behave. I guess somebody saw Greg come to my room last night . . . or leave this morning.

* * *

By midday, we have an appointment with the electrician, the builder and the plumber. Eleni and Dino have gone back to the taverna to prep for lunch.

'Shall we have another look in the distillery now that we have light in there?' I suggest.

I find myself drawn to a row of demijohns above the heavy wooden counter and quickly make a note of the names and numbers on their labels.

'I'm sure I've seen all these in the recipe book, Uncle, apart from the one marked XXX. Do you know anything about it?'

'I know it's dangerous. That's the elixir that changed everything. Be careful with it.'

I climb down. 'Changed everything ... that sounds a bit dramatic. Also, I found some boxes of small bottles in the cupboards so I've decided to take a sample of each perfume home with me and get it analysed to see if the chemical balance has changed with maturity.'

Uncle appears alarmed. 'Listen, I'm warning you, Olivia, that perfume, XXX, is dangerous. Don't go near it.'

I laugh. 'Forgive me for saying so, but that sounds a little corny. Do you mean it's likely to explode – like nitroglycerin – or it's poisonous like cyanide?'

'Not in the way you think, but it's just as toxic. Mind you don't inhale that scent. Trust me!'

* * *

Uncle, happy but exhausted, has gone for a nap. I walk up to the house and find the place buzzing with activity. The builder is looking at replacing the second half of the ground floor but first he must build stone steps down to the cellar and dig out a

407

couple of window lights so there is natural daylight in the basement. Then there is all the rotting wood from the wall-to-wall bed to cut down and stack and the water tanks to get down into the basement.

'Why don't we just burn the wood?' I ask.

Manno is clearly shocked. 'What and set the whole island alight? No fires until after the first rain, Olivia.'

'I'm learning.'

Time is running out with only two days left on the island and I still have Granny Sofía's and my mother's ashes in the bottom of my wardrobe. After one last look around, I switch off the light and lock the door. As I turn, I see the electrician sitting on one of the tree stumps.

'*Kalispéra*,' I say.

'Good evening,' he replies, a smile in his voice. 'How are your plans coming along?' He stares out towards the sun which blushes as it slides into the sea. The harsh colours of the day soften and melt into each other, like a fresh watercolour.

'Plans are moving forward . . . just about.' The light is changing quickly – yet slowly and peace falls about us.

'Ah, that's how everything goes here. You'll get used to it.'

I sit on the next stump. The sea lies hidden under a cobweb of drifting heat-haze as the sky turns yellow through to umber. The Turkish mountains are hardly more than the pale flick of an artist's brush. I watch the last sliver of sun disappear and consider waiting for the stars but there is a lot to do – and where is Uncle?

'Thanks for your help with the electricity,' I say, turning towards him, shocked once again by the wide, enigmatic smile that waits for me.

'When are you leaving?' he asks, the smile fading a little.

'Day after tomorrow. But we plan to come back in September. To be honest, I don't want to go.'

'Then why are you?'

'Money. I need to sort some things out so that we can stay longer next time.'

'In September?'

I nod.

'Can I take you for a farewell meal this evening?' he asks. 'We have a lot to talk over.'

'The men are going fishing at dawn.' *Yes, yes, take me for anything you want this evening.*

'Then we shall return at midnight, Cinderella.'

'Sometimes you sound very English for a Greek.'

'That's because my mother was English. She died when I was ten. Eleni's my father's second wife.' He brushed my hair away from my face. 'You're not answering, so I guess you don't want to come for a meal.'

'I do, honestly, but there's just so much to do.'

'Nine p.m. until midnight. Can't you spare me three hours? OK, if you can't I'll have to accept it.'

I laugh. 'You drive a hard bargain. Let me talk to my uncle. I'm wondering if we can stay a few more days.'

I catch a look of restrained eagerness. 'Then we can get a lot more done on the house if you're here.'

I shake my head. 'No, that's the point; no money.'

'Ah, the curse of no money, I see. However, if you're coming back in September, will there be money then?'

'I hope so. I have some plans, but I must discuss them with my uncle first. I'll see you later – nine o'clock?'

'We'll eat far from our taverna.' He must have read the relief on my face because he smiles. 'Meet me at the end of Lazarakis' jetty at eight forty, OK? Flat shoes.' He nods at a taverna in the curve of the harbour. White tablecloths flutter in the breeze on tables set along a small pier.

* * *

I wear a multicoloured striped shift with my feet in pink pumps and my hair in a high ponytail. A clutch on a chain and a white pashmina completes the outfit. I've brought an evening dress, not knowing exactly what I am coming to, but it is destined to stay zipped inside its hanger-bag. I sit at the end of the pier, watching the quayside for Greg, when the owner comes to me with a glass of white wine.

'I am Lazarakis, pleased to meet you, Olivia,' he says making a slight bow.

'Thank you. How did you know . . .' I glance over at Eleni's taverna to see several people, including my uncle, wave my way. I wave back, then wish I had ignored them. Greg approaches in *Sofía-María* and helps me down into the boat.

'Thanks, Lazarakis!' he shouts at the taverna owner who hands down my glass of wine.

I sit in the prow, facing Greg at the wheel. We proceed slowly out of the harbour, past the dull-grey navy ship, past the mosque and around the bend. Several night fishermen speed by us in their colourful boats. We proceed to a tiny island about 500 metres away. It has a few tables on the beach and a little hut cantina. Our food is cooked on a barbecue by a local Greek. His wife, a beautiful Turkish woman, serves us. The food is amazing and the evening ends too soon.

* * *

'I've had a lovely time that's passed too quickly, Greg. Thank you.' I glance over at the church clock: 11.30. Pleased with my own restraint at not making menu notes, I have simply enjoyed the food: gilthead bream with salads, dips and home-made bread, washed down with my favourite chardonnay. We link arms as Greg walks me back to my room.

'I feel rather self-conscious sometimes. Am I imagining it, or does everyone watch us?'

'Yes they do, but it's only because they have nothing better in their own lives, so just make the most of being the centre of attention.'

His eyes narrow a little and I guess he's wondering if he can come to my room later. I'd like that. I've enjoyed his lovemaking, as he has enjoyed me.

'Leave me here,' I say when we reach the big church. Once again, I am struck by the handsomeness of him. 'My door will be on the catch at midnight, for fifteen minutes.'

He looks at the dark sky and smiles smugly. 'I'll be there.' He kisses my cheek and walks away.

I hurry to my first-floor room. From behind the muslin curtains, I watch him walk towards Mandraki. We have talked about many things, but mostly the building and how I will develop it. I step out and sit on the balcony. A full moon lights the harbour turning the water to liquid mercury. Apart from a night fisherman chugging out to sea, leaving a fan of silver ripples behind and a little distant music from the café-bar by the mosque, the place is silent.

I take a deep breath and close my eyes. How peaceful it is and that very tranquillity makes me ask myself: why did Granny Sofía leave with my mother, never to return?

'Psst! Livia!'

Oh for goodness' sake, Rob!

'I'm in trouble, can I come up?'

'No you cannot!' I peer down but can't see him. 'Where are you?'

'Behind the Coke fridge.'

I hurry down to the empty taverna below and find him. 'What's going on, it's almost midnight? I thought they were going to keep you locked up.'

'They don't want to man the station all night, so they kept my passport and I have to sign in each morning, so now I haven't even got a bed for the night.'

'Oh, no! Don't look at me like that. You're on your own, mate.'

'The thing is, you know my card's maxed out and I've just got my hotel bill . . . jeez, mate, you wouldn't believe it! What am I going to do? The police won't let me leave until the hotel bill's paid.'

'I hope you're not going to ask me for money.'

'Wouldn't dream of it . . . normally, but I called home and they've abandoned me. Said I should ask the hotel if I can work it off. Can you believe that? After all I've done for them.'

'It sounds like a good plan to me – and what exactly have you done for them, apart from take a free holiday at their expense?'

'I'll have to do a runner. There's a ferry that goes all around the islands, but it ends up in Athens. I'll have to sneak on it, because I've got no passport; then I'll catch my return flight home to Oz.'

'Rob, you can't do that! Firstly, even if you make it to Athens, they won't let you on the plane to Australia without your passport. Secondly, what about the family reputation? What about all those Konstantinidis people who contributed towards your fare? You'll blacken the family name forever, paint us all as untrustworthy, when we're not. No!'

Because we are tucked away behind the big chiller, Greg doesn't notice us when he walks past.

'Greg!'

He turns, startled. 'What's going on?'

'Rob's in trouble. Let's all sit down.' I explain the situation.

'*Maláka!* Wanker! What you think, coming here and behaving like a goat?' Greg says.

'I thought I was doing something good for the folks back home.'

'*Les psemata!* You liar! You think only of yourself.' He glares at Rob. 'How much you owe?'

He kicks the dirt and stares at his feet. 'One-thousand-five-hundred.'

'*Maláka!*' Greg says again. 'OK, I'll pay your debt, me and the builder and the carpenter and the plumber. You're an idiot, Rob! When's your ticket back to Australia?'

'Three weeks tomorrow.' A grin breaks over his face. 'You're a real mate, Greg! I knew you and Livia would help me out.'

I raise my hand in a halting gesture. 'Not me; I'd call the port police if it was up to me.'

Greg squints at him. 'You will work for us for three weeks, twelve-hour days, no day off, right?'

Rob nods, clearly relieved.

'In the morning, we will go to the port police and you will sign your passport, credit cards and phone over to me, right?' He nods, then Greg continues. 'I've got a lot of work tomorrow and need some sleep. Where are you staying tonight?'

He blinks at me.

'Don't you dare look at me. If you've got nowhere else, make use of a sunbed by the mosque. And go right now, Rob, or any chance of help is off,' I say.

413

'So, meet me at Eleni's at eight o'clock in the morning, Rob. Working clothes. Don't be late. Good night,' Greg says

Rob hurries away in the direction of the mosque.

* * *

Morning comes too soon. The builder, plumber and electrician turn up to have coffee with Uncle and myself at seven thirty. I explain the situation with Rob. Greg says Rob will labour for them all. When Rob arrives, the builder tells him his first job is to barrow the dirt from behind the distillery and tip it over the side of the patio. They leave together.

'Rob,' I call after him. 'You might want to buy a box of plasters and a pair of work gloves before you start.'

Dino and Eleni bring their coffee to our table and we talk about the restoration. The electrician and plumber ask questions, then go to measure the building's footprint and make plans.

'I was thinking about Rob, Uncle. I'm wondering what the little house on the square is like inside. Have you been in?'

'You're too good to that boy, Olivia. He tried to rob you of everything you have, remember?'

'I think you're right, but what can I do?'

He shook his head. 'You're a hopeless case, you know that? People will always take advantage of your kindness.'

'My mother once told me, *Mostly there are two types of people in the world, givers and takers. Make sure you recognise them*, and I believe she was right.'

'Tsambika was very wise, she got that from Sofía.'

'Can you tell me why they left Castellorizo, or what circumstances drove such a close family apart, Uncle?' I peer at him, wondering if I can force the issue, at the same time fearing

414

I might uncover something so awful, it might destroy the wonderful relationship I have with my uncle.

'You could say it was all of their own making, though that's a bit of a cryptic clue.' He stared out over the turquoise water. 'Where's D'Artagnan today? Bring me some squid, Eleni, before I start fretting.'

She laughs and goes to the kitchen.

I catch the fact that he's changing the subject. Following his eyes, I realise how different the scene is now from the steel-grey of midnight under a full moon. Now, the scene sizzles with colour. Mirrored reflections across the harbour seemed solid enough to walk on. All this under an unbelievably blue sky.

'I wish we didn't have to leave tomorrow, Uncle. I really want to stay another few days.'

'I know. Unfortunately, I have a hospital appointment. But you can stay, of course you can.'

'Not without you. I'm being selfish, letting my heart rule my head. Sorry.'

'Before we leave here, I will finish the story of Sofia and Maria, OK? That's a promise. It was Sofía's dreams and wishes that actually split the family in the end. María wanted to keep her husband at any cost, but she believed he could not love her once he saw her so badly deformed by the fire. She was wrong and that was her big mistake. Then there was Sofía who put her trust in superstition and myth when she should have trusted mother nature and common sense to take care of things.' He sighs, blinks slowly and shakes his head. 'What a tragic result, yet, from all that tragedy, came you.'

CHAPTER 48
SOFIA

Castellorizo, Greece, 1947

MARÍA'S LAST BABY WAS BORN three weeks before Christmas, a boy they named Mustafa after his father. Sofía peered into the baby hammock at the sleeping infant whose fist curled against his cheek. She touched it gently and the baby immediately grasped her finger and pulled it towards his mouth. Sofía laughed with pleasure. What a wonderful Christmas gift, a child. She stared at the baby's sweet little hands which were just like his father's. Mustafa had a rare genetic trait – most of his children had very short thumbs.

Sofía lifted little Mustafa from his baby hammock. Sometimes she imagined the baby was her own child, so desperate was she to start a family. She passed the baby over to its mother.

'I think he's the most beautiful of them all, María,' she whispered. The infant was her sister's sixteenth baby and she claimed her last . . . but she always said that.

Jamie was due to arrive in Castellorizo at any time. He'd written to tell her about his promotion from lance corporal to corporal, which also meant a pay increase. Not that they had ever been short of money. The promotion came when he signed up for another stretch in the army. She longed to see him again and her dreams came true at the start of Christmas week.

Jamie found his wife shovelling mandarin leaves into the copper belly of the *kazáni*, the still, ready to start a fresh distillation process.

'Darling Sofía,' he whispered after locking the distillery doors and taking her into his arms.

He led her to the holding pit and pulled her down onto the sacks of leaves, wishing they could be alone for more than half an hour. They made love with all the fervour of any couple that had not seen each other for three months.

'This reminds me of the first time we met,' Sofía said, plucking a leaf from his short hair and feeling so happy she believed she could fly.

'Oh no! I still have the scars,' Jamie joked. 'Listen, my darling, I have a month's leave coming up in June next year,' he said. 'I want you to come to England and marry me in the church. Let's start off with a proper wedding, Sofía. I love your family, but I can't relax with so many people in one house.' He slipped his hands around her waist and pulled her against him. 'I know they're your family and you love them all, but I have a family, too, and I haven't seen them for two years because every leave I have, I come here. My mother writes to say they are longing to meet you. They want to welcome you into the family.'

He kissed her. 'I fear if we are to have children, it will only happen in a more private place than this.' He placed his hand on her cheek. 'Don't be sad. I only have to look into your eyes and I'm home, no matter where I am, but my homeland is beautiful too . . . and I also love my parents, but they're too old to travel this far.'

'Actually, dearest Jamie, we do have a home of our own right here, we just have to build it.' She told him about the house on the square that collapsed in the earthquake.

'That's quite a story. Let's go down to the harbour later and you can show me – but please, say you will come to England.' At this point, Sofía realised he wasn't going to give up. 'Make me

417

the happiest man on earth. Ayeleen and Popi are old enough to take your place for a few weeks.'

Sofía felt a spark of panic. How would her family manage without her? María needed help with all her children. Fevzi was going through a rebellious stage and it seemed Sofía was the only one who could talk some sense into him. Mamá's lumbago had worsened, which meant Sofía and Ayeleen did most of the heavy work in the distillery and around the house. She was just back from taking Emre, the quietest of the boys, to Rhodes to have his appendix out. It was only luck that she got Jamie's letter before she left Castellorizo, or she would still be there. As it was, sixteen-year-old Popi had taken her place at Emre's bedside, nursing the boy in the Rhodes hospital.

On top of all this, Babá had stomach problems, but refused to go to hospital.

Sofía didn't want to visit England, but she loved Jamie too much to disappoint him. The best thing she could do was take his mind away from the subject. She doused the fire under the *kazáni*.

'What are you up to? I know that look, Sofía, you she-devil.'

'Up to? Nothing, honestly, Jamie.' She narrowed her eyes and pouted as she approached him. 'I've blended a new perfume and I'd really like to hear your opinion. It needs to age a little longer, really, but I still think it's quite powerful as it is.' She turned the simple glass bottle upside-down on her middle finger and dabbed it behind her ears. After repeating the process, she ran a loaded fingertip down from her chin, ending deep in her cleavage. 'Come here, lover. Inhale this perfume on me and tell me your impressions. What does this scent bring to you?'

Before she could say more, he was upon her, nuzzling her ear, then, following the scent, he pushed her dress off her shoulders.

418

His face became puffy, his eyes glazed and as he pressed himself against her, she felt his wonderful body harden.

'You witch, you make me lose control of myself,' he muttered, sweeping her up and laying her on the citrus leaves. 'What is this magic power you have over me that makes me want to love you in the middle of the day?' He tugged at her clothes, biting the side of her neck, thrusting against her. Driven by longing. 'I shall have you right here, outrageously, while you are supposed to be working. You turn my blood to fire and my head is spinning with desire.'

One hand pressed against her lower back, while the other was behind her head. He kissed her so passionately she feared he'd bruised her lips, yet she wanted him more than she ever had before. Almost fainting with pleasure, she suddenly realised they were both naked. As the heat of her body intensified, so the scent increased and wafted around them both with each movement until, intoxicated, they were lost in the lap of Aphrodite, drunk on the wine of Eros. Pan played a rapid rhythm on his pipes as the gods smiled down on the lovers. Out of control, each took their own pleasure from the other, which lifted their eroticism to new exquisite dimensions until all sense of time and place escaped them.

After, they lay panting in the pit of citrus leaves, silent and smiling and staring at the rafters. Sofía glanced around at the scattered leaves and the scattered clothes. She rubbed behind her ear and sniffed her fingers for any sign of the perfume, but it had disappeared without a trace. Just as well, she thought.

They stood. Kissing and laughing, they peeled leathery foliage off each other's body and found their garments. Sofía, so happy, was sure she had conceived. It was the right time and what could be more glorious? Yes, she convinced herself, a few days before the church celebration of the birth of Christ, she might have managed to get herself pregnant at last.

* * *

Christmas week passed with all the traditions of the season. Too soon, Jamie had to return to his battalion now stationed in Athens where the Greek Civil War had gained impetus. The conflict was fought between the army of the Greek government, whom Britain supported, and the Communist Party of Greece, the KKE (backed, everyone suspected but never said, by the Soviet Union). The world watched and twitched nervously as the Cold War gained momentum and the threat of nuclear disaster terrified the world.

* * *

On the last day of the year, María went into the distillery and found Sofía crying uncontrollably.

'Hey, Sofía, what's brought this on?' She put her arm around her sister's shoulders. 'Tell me and I'll see if I can help.'

'I'm not pregnant!' Sofía sobbed. 'I was so sure this time. It's not fair, María. What's wrong with me? We've been married for four years, yet we don't have a family of our own. People will think I'm barren ... that I don't have a womb capable of supporting life.'

'There's nothing wrong with you, Sofía. You may have been married for four years, but the fact is you've only been together for what, six months?'

'Jamie says the same. Now, he wants me to go to England for a month in June, but I fear you can't cope without me.'

'We can manage! You must go. Meet his family, be alone with him for a while. Ayeleen and Popi are quite grown up. They can take your place for a month; besides, it will do everyone good to see how hard you work.'

*　*　*

As the church bells rang in the new year, Sofía tossed and turned in her empty bed, trying to decide. When the dawn light crept over Castellorizo, she resolved to visit England and despite María's warning that the Tsambika Mountain legend was pure superstition, desperate Sofía decided to make the pilgrimage. She would do it the day before she flew to England from Maritsa airport, in Rhodes.

*　*　*

In June, just as Sofía was leaving Castellorizo, Mustafa returned from his travels. As always, the big Turk was delighted to see the latest addition to his family, the baby boy named after him.

Sofía was running late. Just about to leave for the ferry to Rhodes, she remembered her intention to take some of the intoxicating perfume to England, hoping the passion it instilled would help her to conceive.

'Go ahead, Zafiro. Take my case down to the ferry,' she cried. 'I'll be there in a moment.'

She hurried back into the house, ducked behind the unfinished carpet and through the stout door into the distillery. On the top shelf, out of the reach of children, a row of glazed stone demijohns with a tap near the bottom held maturing oils, each bearing the name and date of the content. She had to stand on the worktop to reach the one marked with XXX.

Trying not to inhale any of the scent's aroma, she stretched up, smiling to herself as she decanted a measure of the concoction into a glass aspirin bottle. It would be wonderful to lie in Jamie's arms again and she found herself remembering their last time together, over Christmas.

She didn't hear Mustafa enter the distillery. 'What are you doing up there, Sofía?' he asked.

She blinked at him, speechless for a second, not wanting to tell him about the power of the oil, or why she was taking it to use on her husband. 'Ah, I'm going to do the Tsambika pilgrimage, in Rhodes, so I'm taking a little oil to help my legs heal in case of injury. They say you can get some bumps and bruises.'

'Do you really believe putting yourself through such a terrible ordeal will help you get pregnant?' he asked. 'Surely that's lunacy?'

'I don't know, Mustafa.' She turned her eyes away, not wishing for an interrogation. 'But you see, I'm willing to try anything. I love Jamie so much, I'm desperate to give him a child.'

The big Turk gave her a withering look, shook his head and raised his hands towards her. 'Come on, let me lift you down from there.'

* * *

'What!' María shouted. 'She's going to climb to Tsambika Monastery on her knees before she gets on a plane to England? She's mad! The only miracle that might happen is that they allow her on the plane with her legs in shreds,' María shouted. 'Please, Mustafa, go after her. God knows what might happen. We might never see her again!' She pushed him towards the door. 'Go down to the port and talk to her, quickly, the ferry's due out in five minutes.'

Mustafa, always a martyr to María's wishes, called Zafiro. 'Come, my son, help me find your aunt before the ship leaves.' They hurried down to the port. The ferry trumpeted loudly as the last passengers rushed aboard with their bundles and boxes.

Mustafa and Zafiro separated and raced around the decks for a minute, with no luck, then Mustafa shouted from the top deck railings to his son, below.

'Zafiro! Go ashore, quickly! Tell your mother I'll be back on the next ferry from Rhodes.' The mooring loops were tossed off the yellow-painted stanchions as the sailors started to lift the ramp. 'Quick, Zafiro!' Mustafa yelled, then gasped as his son, on seeing the tailgate being raised, ran and made a flying leap, arms whirling, legs running through the air heading for the retreating quayside below, as the ferry pulled away.

For a terrifying second, it looked as though Zafiro might end up falling onto the ferry's propeller – and that would surely be the end of him. He landed on the very edge of the quay, teetered, fought for his balance right on the rim of the concrete, but then threw himself forward and secured his place on the dock. Mustafa grinned, proud as a priest at a baptism.

Zafiro punched the air, spun around and yelled to his father. 'Don't worry, Papa, I'll take care of everything while you are away!'

* * *

At last, for the first time in her life, Sofía could relax away from her family. She found it an odd sensation not to be at everyone's call and to have no responsibilities. Locked inside her tiny cabin, she lay on the bed and tried to imagine Rhodes. She'd never been

423

before. Even when María was there in the hospital, Sofía stayed home to take care of things while other children went with Mamá. She heard that Rhodes is an island of castles, palaces and beautiful buildings. With her love of Greek history, she longed to spend some time in the ancient city.

She had two days before her flight to London. Could the story about Tsambika be true? It seemed far-fetched, but her desperation made her susceptible to fables and fairy tales. Because of her secret belief that somehow the childlessness was her own fault, she would try anything to get pregnant. Perhaps the deal with Tsambika was that she had to believe – in that case, she would.

Sofía had been so exhausted when she embarked the ferry, she fell asleep shortly after entering her small cabin and woke to the sound of the ship's hooter as it entered Rhodes commercial harbour at five o'clock in the morning. Still under cover of darkness, she was one of the first to disembark the ship. The Castellorizo ticket office had booked a room for her near the Rhodes bus station. The travel agent told her to catch the Lindos bus and ask to be called at the Monastery of Tsambika. On the dockside, she took a waiting taxicab and, ten minutes later, was standing outside her room.

'Here's your key, miss,' the landlady said handing over a key with a brown label stating the number and address of the room.

'Thank you. Do you happen to know what time the first bus to Lindos leaves?'

The middle-aged woman smiled kindly. 'Every two hours starting at nine and the return is also every two hours starting at eight o'clock. It takes an hour and three-quarters to Lindos.'

'Thank you, but actually I'm going to Tsambika.'

The woman's face fell. 'The pilgrimage?' Sofía nodded. 'Alone?' the woman asked, concerned now. Sofía nodded again.

'Oh my goodness!' The landlady crossed herself. 'Where have you come from?'

'Castellorizo. It's my first time in Rhodes.'

'Listen, you can't go up Tsambika mountain on your own, you need the support of friends or family with you. Who will give you water? Who will wash your bleeding shins with salt water? Who will feed you words of encouragement, wipe away your tears and join you in prayer?'

'I'm sure I'll be all right, don't worry,' Sofía said.

'No, you won't. There's little shade and it's steep and gruelling. Please, don't go alone.'

Slightly unnerved now, she wanted to be by herself. 'Perhaps I'll just go and look. Thanks for warning me.'

An hour later, she found herself sitting on a street bench waiting for the first Lindos bus. She watched the driver get out of his cab, step on the front bumper and turn the destination roller until RHODES TOWN disappeared and LINDOS took its place. Then he climbed down and called, 'All aboard!'

She paid her thirty cents to the conductor who gave her a ticket, then settled back to enjoy the journey. After all, she wasn't forced to climb the mountain on her knees. She could wait until the last minute before she made her decision. On the seat in front of her, a woman was trying to control her two children. A doll-like girl of about three and her brother, a babe-in-arms. What would it be like, to have little ones of her own? She'd be the absolute best mother. Her children would be highly intelligent due to their early introduction to books and learning. They'd also be beautiful, with lovely manners and a kind disposition. She made many plans for their future and dreamed of the day she would have grandchildren too.

CHAPTER 49
OLIVIA

Castellorizo, Greece, present day

WE WALK OVER TO THE square, Uncle and I, arms linked. 'I wonder which house it is?' I study the buildings around the open space. To my right stands a travel agent, then the island's only supermarket, clearly family owned and fully stocked. There are spaces where dwellings once stood – the square foundations visible in the paving – but all other signs of the buildings have gone. I wonder if their demise was due to the bombings, or the earthquake that my uncle has mentioned. A majestic rubber tree dominates the space. Ahead, a small sign indicates the way to the island's only bakery.

Uncle stares around, seeming confused. 'I can't quite get my bearings,' he mutters, 'it's been fifty years, you know.'

Four elderly women in black sit shoulder-to-shoulder, crocheting in the deep shade of the tree. Uncle goes over to talk to them and comes back beaming. 'I guess by that smile, you found it?' I say.

'Yes, look, it's that one with two floors; burgundy walls with cream shutters, doors and balcony. I should have recognised it, but didn't because it's been painted. The house was white when I left.'

'I wonder if anyone lives there now?'

'It seems not, according to the ladies over there.'

* * *

We find the old priest and learn that seven men of the cloth have passed through since Uncle first handed over the keys, half a century ago. My uncle returns with the key to his old home, a notebook of expenses and a little bundle of blue bank books wrapped in an elastic band. Delighted to find the pages filled with almost fifty years of rent deposits.

'There's enough here to make a good start on the renovations,' Uncle says as we return to the house. 'I can tell you I'm quite excited about this, Olivia,' he says, turning the key to his old home. 'And a bit emotional too.' I catch the tremble in his voice.

The latch bolt resists, clonks and complains as it tumbles. With a loud protesting groan, the heavy painted door creaks open. We stand for a moment, staring into the gloom, feeling as if we are about to step into another dimension.

Uncle's hand covers his mouth and I can see he's struggling. I take his other hand and give it a squeeze. Sad for him, I touch his arm. 'Do you have a photo of David?'

He nods and without speaking, reaches for the wallet in his trouser pocket. He flips it open and hands it over. There is great declaration in the moment: a coming out, a display of bravery, as if dark secrets from a buried past find release and escape into the astonishing Greek sunlight right there on his doorstep. An odd sound comes from him, half gasp, half sob.

'Oh, David,' he whispers then turns to me. 'We were so happy here.'

We stand close together. I slide my arm around his shoulders and give him a gentle hug. Poor dear. I suspect he's been very lonely for a long time.

'It was different in those days, Olivia. People like us . . . well, we were attacked, thrown into prison, even killed, by self-righteous males and religious zealots, so we were very discreet. No shouting of our love for each other like Sofía and Jamie, or María and Mustafa. Just two businessmen who shared a house. But we loved each other more than life itself. You said there were two types of people in the world, givers and takers . . . well, David was a giver. He gave to the poor, the needy and the very church that condemned him. I never got over his death.'

I study the black and white photo behind a cellophane window in his wallet. The heads and shoulders of two handsome young men, very alike, smile back at me.

'Shall we go in?' I say, peering into the gloom. 'After you, Uncle, as it's your house.'

I follow him through the doorway. The shutters are closed. It is dark inside. He tries the light switch and with a click, the place dazzles in illumination.

'Oh my! It's another time capsule,' I say. 'Look at the place – 1960s–70s, all of it. My friends go crazy for this stuff.'

'Sofía and Jamie had rebuilt one floor, before baby Tsambika came along. It was enough for them. David and I added a second floor. The big house was too much for us. Besides, we liked being closer to the harbour. It's always been the hub of the island.' We gaze around the interior.

'Shall we open the shutters and let some natural light in?' I suggest.

My uncle goes around the room, touching things, smiling sadly, peering into space as if watching old ghosts. He opens windows, pushes at louvres, gazes, sighs and reminisces in his mind.

'After David's death, I fell into a bit of depression, so I went to England to be with Sofía. María, all her children and my parents had gone to Australia, you see. I'd always been fascinated by the past, something I got from my sister, so I went to teacher training college, studied history and became a teacher.

After a while, he says, 'Sorry, Olivia; I know what you're thinking, but I'm very reluctant to let that Rob – family or not – stay here.' He pulled a book from the bookcase and let the pages run through his fingers. James Joyce, I noticed. 'Just to think of him touching David's things, it's like sacrilege. You probably don't understand.'

I want to say: yet you didn't mind *strangers* living here . . . but I hold back. After all, I'd probably feel the same. 'Look, next time we come to Castellorizo, why don't *we* stay here? It would more than halve our expenses.'

'Seems like a plan,' he says. 'I'll tell the priest not to rent it out from now on. However, it's clear somebody's been coming in to clean the place. Perhaps we should keep them on. What do you think?'

I nod. 'We could get their phone number, inform them when we're coming and they can deal with fresh linen and so on. Right, back to the problem of Rob. Where shall we put him for three weeks? Please reconsider. We could photograph everything before he moves in and warn him of the consequences of a mess, breakages, or anything missing and we could ask the priest to look in on him every day. Anyway, think about it, no pressure, but you only have until tomorrow.'

'You drive a hard bargain, Olivia. All right, I'll think about it, but I'm not promising anything. Now, time's ticking on. We have the urns to deal with and a wake . . . which, I must tell you, is absolutely alien to the Greek way of thinking about death. Cremation itself an abomination to them. So, let's agree to keep quiet about scattering the ashes. OK?'

* * *

At sunset, Uncle and I stand at Punta Nifti, ready to empty our urns onto the sea.

'I want to remember all the people from this island, particularly all the souls from the Konstantinidis family who share this watery resting place,' he says. 'United by the sea in death, as they were united by family love, in life.'

'Amen,' I say.

Uncle has his sister's ashes and I have my mother's. We try to scatter them, tipping the urns, but the ashes blow back on us and we understand this is not going to work.

'We should have taken them out in the boat and tipped them over the side,' he says. 'Let's just toss the open urns into the water. Not very graceful, but they're only ashes and the urns are natural marble. It's not actually them, after all.'

Later, we sit on the rocks with our thoughts and watch the sun sink in a translucent sky, which turns deep red moments later.

'How beautiful,' I whisper.

* * *

We walk around Mandraki Bay with heavy hearts, silent and deep in thought until we arrive back at Eleni's. 'I'm ready for a sundowner, a G&T will go down well. How about you, Uncle?'

'Just the ticket, Olivia. A stiff drink. Shall we have a mezze night and invite all those who've helped us?'

'Good plan.' I can't help smiling when Rob appears on the other side of the harbour, inspecting the palms of his hands as he walks towards the chemist's. 'Look over there. Poor thing, I do believe he's suffering.'

'It'll do him good. Teach him a lesson. I suspect he's had it easy all his life, spoiled boy.' After a silent moment he continues.

430

'I've thought about what you said and if there's absolutely no alternative, he can stay in our house for the three weeks. But I want all the necessary threats and penalties in place, if he lets us down in any way. Otherwise, he can get a camp bed and stay at the big house.'

'Good, that makes life easier.'

'Oh, look, we've only just arrived and here comes the electrician ... what a surprise,' Uncle George says, bobbing his eyebrows.

'Stop it!' I say, feeling glad. 'I'll just to nip to the ladies'. Wash my hands, tidy up, you know.' He smiles mischievously and I realise how much I have come to love my uncle. In the bathroom, I quickly brush the tangles from my hair and dive into the bottom of my bag for a mascara and lip-gloss. What I pull out is a small bottle of the precious oil. I must have missed it when I returned to my room with the other samples. This is the bottle with the mysterious XXX on the label and I am just about to put a couple of dabs on my wrists when Eleni calls.

'Olivia, quick!' I rush out, my bag on my shoulder and see the most wondrous firework display going off over Turkey. A big wedding, someone says. We ooh and aah at the great pyrotechnics, then gather around the long trestle filled with *mezzéthes*. Olives, little cheese pies, tzatziki and various other dips including the famous pink taramasalata, crusty baguettes, feta in golden, crispy filo pastry and drizzled in honey, little meatballs, cheese balls, courgette balls, dolmades and so on.

Greg comes over. 'Hello,' he says, head slightly to one side, eyes curious, smile wide.

Bits of me tingle. Damn my blush! 'Hello to you too,' I reply softly, hardly daring to meet his eyes. 'Thank you again for a lovely meal last night.'

The builder arrives with his wife, the plumber too, with his. The electrician, always near, wears his contagious smile and makes me promise to go for a drink with him later. The priest arrives and informs us that the house cleaner will be along soon, so we can instruct her. We both admire Rob for turning up, though he can hardly walk and has badly blistered hands. I study the red-raw palm he thrust towards me.

'Looks sore,' I say.

'It's worse because I have this hereditary condition, short thumbs. Most of the people in our family have it. Comes from my great-grandfather, Mustafa.'

'Mustafa?' I frown, trying to work that out. 'Anyway, it can't be very rare, Rob, because my mother had it too. Mind you, she never had to heft a wheelbarrow, so it made no difference to her.' Before I can think about it, Dorian comes lolloping towards me. I try to sidestep out of her vision, to escape her attention, but she is onto me and so loud, I haven't a hope.

'*Yiasou*, Olivia! The Papas says you want to talk to me about cleaning the house. Is that right – your nephew, or is it cousin, might be staying there? What's his name? Rob, is it? He's a bit of all right, don't-cha think?' She pulls a coin from the pocket of her shapeless cardigan. 'Here's that euro I owe you. Don't want it said that I rip off the tourists, now do I?'

Why does she have to shout? Rob must have heard his name mentioned, because suddenly he is beside me. 'Did I hear right? You've got somewhere for me to stay? Good on ya!'

'Hi there, mate. I'm Dorian,' she butts in. I look up to catch Uncle folding his arms across his chest, following the conversation with interest. I guess he's having second thoughts about the house because he's shaking his head rapidly.

Dorian is still wittering on. 'By the way, Olivia, I found this bottle in the restroom, is it yours? Great perfume!' She whips

432

the top off the sample bottle and dabs the oil behind her ears. 'Yeah, really nice, try a bit!'

In a flash, she loads her fingertips and makes a swipe for my neck, but I duck behind Rob who receives the scented oil on his cheek. 'Oops, sorry, mate. It does smell amazing, though, don't you think?' She sniffs the side of his face. He catches the scent of her, slips his arm around her waist and pulls her against him. I stare disbelievingly, then look up to see Uncle with a hand over his mouth and his eyes wide. He comes over to us.

'You can keep the perfume, Dorian,' Uncle George says. 'But use it sparingly. They say it has magical properties. Changing the subject, perhaps you can help us out? Instead of cleaning the house, how about you give Rob lodgings for three weeks? I believe you live by yourself.'

Rob gazes at Dorian with a slightly glazed look in his eyes. 'Sure,' he says. 'That would be fine by me. But perhaps I'd better check the accommodation before I commit.'

'Right on! No worries. That's cool,' Dorian agrees, slipping her arm around his waist. 'Best do it now before we start on the food and drink, mate. What do you say?'

I blink disbelievingly at Uncle, who seems very pleased with himself.

'Let's leave the little house locked up, shall we?' my uncle says. 'By the way, it was there that Sofía was born in the chaos of the earthquake and – over two decades later – where she gave birth to your mother.'

I step out of the group and look over towards the little house and then at my surroundings. Apart from general modernisation, I guessed little has changed. A haze drifts into the harbour, enveloping fishermen who are already dismantling their rods, discussing the day in a clatter of Greek voices.

I really am going to miss this place.

'Are you packed?' I ask my uncle.

He shakes his head. 'I'll pack while you're out galivanting with your new friend.'

'Stop it!' I warn him and then glance across at Greg who is talking to Eleni.

CHAPTER 50
SOFIA

Rhodes, Greece, 1947

THE BUS CAME ONTO THE coast road near the port. Sofía gazed in awe at the old town, built by the Knights of Saint John. Sandstone city walls glowed golden yellow in the morning sunlight. Angled and castellated, the nearest buildings were separated from the castle of the grand masters by a row of pointed cypress trees appearing black in contrast. A tall minaret rose like a finger pointing the way to heaven. The war had taken its toll of the city, some of the fortifications were under reconstruction. She wondered if the same Stukas that devastated Castellorizo had bombarded Rhodes.

The bus bumped along narrow roads in need of repair. Sofía opened the sliding window as most of the men on the bus were smoking and the little pull-down ashtray in the back of the seat before her was overflowing. She gazed to her left and saw a dazzling display of colourful fishing boats. How she wished Jamie was with her, sharing the joys of the island. She hoped, one day, they would come to Rhodes on holiday and discover the island together.

Heading south, the bus entered villages to pick up or drop off passengers. The conductor called the names of hamlets and she tried to memorise them to tell her husband later. Each place had its individual charm. Koskinou had pretty, brightly coloured houses; then came Kallithea's medicinal springs, though nobody got off. Next came a fishing village named Faliraki which had an endless beach dotted by more colourful fishing boats, lobster pots and nets drying in the sun. Old men sat in groups with their shuttle and twine, carefully mending yellow nets.

The highway left the beach and snaked between lollipop-shaped olive trees and orange or lemon groves. Her sensitive nose picked up the scent of citrus and she smiled, reminded of home and the distillery. The bus twisted and turned along narrow lanes, around lush low hills, only meeting the occasional local who travelled by donkey. 'Afandou!' called the driver and some passengers alighted while others mounted the bus. She saw that like Castellorizo, Afandou was a place where women wove carpets. They worked at large wooden looms under makeshift shelters in the street. Others spun wool on a hand bobbins that hung, pendulum-like, twisting the yarn.

The bus returned to the coast and its next destination, Saint Benedict, another pretty village reached after driving down two kilometres of eucalyptus-lined road. A most impressive entrance.

'Next stop, Tsambika!' the driver cried, making Sofía's nerves skip. She gathered her things from the net luggage rack above her head: a wide-brimmed cotton hat, some caramels for energy and a bottle of water, then she moved to the front of the bus.

'What time is the last bus back to town, please?' she asked the driver.

'You must be here at six thirty, no later.' The vehicle bumped over a pothole, almost throwing Sofía off the bus before it stopped. She hoped this wasn't an indication of things to come.

* * *

Sofía let her tears run free. Sharp stones cut into her shins. HALFWAY, a sign read. She could do this, she could! The worst was over now. Her black embroidered scarf held the heat of the sun, sweat ran through her hair and dripped off her jawline. Shuffling forward, she tried to imagine what it would be like to hold her own baby. 'Please God, have mercy on me,' she prayed. An old goat with oddly twisted horns stared at her, its amber eyes glinting in a devilish way. Exhausted, she fell forward and placed her palms flat on the dirt, forcing herself to continue on all fours. Once she reached the three-quarter point, Sofía knew she would make it, the end would soon be in sight.

One more step, one more step, one more step.

Sofía remembered Uncle Kuríllos and his great determination to save them when all seemed lost. 'Help me, Uncle,' she whispered. 'Give me strength.' The sun beat down, burning the back of her neck and her hands and shins stung with every step forward. How much further could it be? A kitten appeared, mewling at her and keeping her company for a few metres, then leaving. She kneeled up and peered towards the top of the mountain. A glimpse of the distant white chapel almost broke her heart – it hardly seemed any closer. She recognised the impossibility of reaching the top.

'Please, God! Don't make this any harder for me. I'll never get up all that way without help.' She crossed herself and, still crying, continued. More goats appeared, then a collard dove flew out of a bush, startling her. She cried out, her voice echoing in the clean mountain air. Her heart beat hard, then a pain came to her chest, warning her to stop and take a rest, but she feared if she did she wouldn't continue. The palms of her hands grew hot as fire as the sharp gravel cut into them. She must keep going, onward and upward. Every step was a step closer.

'Sofía! What madness is this?'

She recognised the manly voice of Mustafa, yet she was so sore and exhausted she could not even twist her neck to look up.

I'm hallucinating, she suspected. *This ordeal has taken more out of me than I realise. What would Mustafa be doing up here, he's not even a Christian. I need to drink some water, then continue the last stretch to the top. If I can only complete the pilgrimage, I know I'll get pregnant.*

She ploughed on, muttering prayers, trying to ignore the pain.

'Sofía, stop!' the voice said again.

It's the devil, she thought. *He's trying to sabotage my journey, put an end to me completing the test.*

One more step, one more step, one more step.

Her body trembled violently. The chapel was in view. Nearly there. Her legs and hands were sticky with blood. 'God help me!' she called out, collapsing. Her face hit the ground, her cheek throbbing and grit grated the skin from her cheekbone. She pulled herself back up onto all fours and dragged her bleeding limbs the last few metres.

She touched the chapel steps. 'God be praised, I did it! Blessed Virgin and all the angels, thank you! All I have to do now is light the candle.' With the relief of completing the arduous task and knowing that she now deserved to get pregnant, consciousness rushed away. In a strange delirium, she felt strong arms scoop her up and with a steady, plodding motion, carry her back down the mountain.

Her senses filtered back with vague realisation that someone appeared to be taking care of her. Such was her relief, she turned her face towards the chest of her rescuer and wept with exhaustion.

At the bottom of the hill, he placed her in a motor car where, overcome by fatigue, she drifted into semi-consciousness. Later, sunlight filtered through her lashes. She was in her room, a wet cloth across her forehead. Someone was talking to her.

'Sofía, you silly girl. How can you go to your husband in this state? There's no skin on your shins and your hands are cut to ribbons.' It was Mustafa, she realised. 'It's a good job María sent me after you! Just imagine if you had lain up there, alone, after nightfall! Who knows what might have happened to you?'

'Thank you for being so kind, Mustafa, but how did you find my apartment?' she murmured with her eyes still closed.

'You had a room key with the address in your pocket. Now lie still and relax. I've cleaned your hands, so you can try and sleep a little while I bathe your legs. I must try to get some of this grit out of the wounds before you get blood-poisoning or lockjaw.'

He had big practical no-nonsense hands. His fingers were sensitive enough to feel the true quality of silk, yet his hands were strong enough to grip hemp ropes and haul heavy canvas sails up the masts of his ship.

'Your legs are cleaned as best as I can manage. Let's have a look at that graze on your cheek. We don't want it to leave a scar on your pretty face.'

Overcome by exhaustion, she drifted off in the good care of her brother-in-law, barely registering his words as he dabbed at her cheek.

'A good job I remembered you'd brought this oil. I'm just dabbing a little onto your wounds. Tell me if it stings.'

Oil? Not the special oil that could drive men insane with lust? The oil that gave María her husband back. The oil that got her sister pregnant.

439

Now, she feared, that same oil was working its irresistible magic on the wrong person!

Mustafa's hands slid gently yet firmly up and down Sofía's shins. On warming slightly, the oil exuded its hedonistic perfume. As the scent rose and swirled about them, licking their senses and tickling their desires. Sofía herself became intoxicated to the core, romanced by the magical touch of Mustafa. Delicious sensations enveloped her, layer upon layer, until they weighed so heavy on her, she could not resist rising to his touch.

'I feel very strange,' she whispered.

'Me too, I confess. I think it's the smell of the oil. Just close your eyes and relax, Sofía.'

* * *

'What harm can a little precious oil do, Sofía?' When she didn't reply, he stopped massaging the oil into her legs and looked into her face. Her closed eyes seemed to flutter slightly, as if she was dreaming. Her back arched, suggesting to him that she longed to be touched. Immediately, her beauty and appearance of pure innocence struck him. Her mouth drew his attention, so beautiful, he thought. Her luscious, tender lips were slightly parted . . . inviting him, it seemed.

He breathed in the scent that enveloped him. The noxious fumes seeped into his lungs, his heart and his brain, controlling his actions and instilling irresistible longing. He could not help stealing a kiss, just one sweet embrace. What harm could it do? Those lips were driving him crazy now. Desire burned in him. He had never tasted another woman since his betrothal to María, so many years ago and now, he felt the irresistible surge in his loins. He pressed his lips against hers, felt them yield under pressure. This is what wine must taste like, he thought, sweet and irresistibly intoxicating.

The scent coming from the precious oil grew stronger in the heat of the moment and now it seemed to have a slow, sensuous cadence to it, like a heartbeat. A pumping, thrusting, rhythm-of-life surge that throbbed through his body. He inhaled deeply, drowning in the allure of sensual possibilities. Could he seduce her into echoing his desire? Suddenly shocked to discover his hands were on her breasts and she arched and squirmed beneath them. She unbuttoned her blouse and as she did, he poured a little oil into the palms of his hands and gently massaged her breasts. Her groans excited him beyond measure, his entire body throbbed with pleasure which quickly turned to irresistible desire.

He kissed her breasts, rejoicing in her gasps of elation, then realising her hands were exploring his body. The oil, now on his own lips, tasted of sweet, bitter chocolate, bergamot and myrrh. The rich taste intoxicated him. He kissed her on the mouth again, sharing the taste of eroticism. When he asked himself later, he could not say how or when they became naked. The luxury of mutual self-indulgence and gratification drenched them equally in a plethora of pleasure.

* * *

In her teenage years, Sofía had wondered what it was really like for María to be married to such a big man, a boss, a controller of other men. Yet in his work, he was also a sensitive discerner of quality, of value; a negotiator and a persuader. A man with the power to entice others to want what he had.

Often those same men believed their submission was entirely an act of their own doing, their own business acumen and subtle negotiating skills. Like Uncle Kuríllos, she had found herself in awe of him on those evenings when she heard of his bargaining feats. She would sit at the loom, quietly tying off the carpet-pile while Mustafa, Babá and Uncle Kuríllos drank raki and talked.

This handsome buccaneer could have any woman he wanted, but even in her sister's darkest hour he remained loyal to her. There had been times when he held Sofía's hand, laid his arm across her shoulders, even kissed her cheek, but there was never anything more than affection in those gestures.

Now, as she lay on the bed, he dabbed the rich dark innocent-looking oil onto her cheek, leaning in close to make sure it didn't run into her eye. She felt his breath on her face, the perfume rose from the oil, engulfing them both at the same time.

'What is this?' he asked, his voice sounding thick and confused. 'I'm going dizzy from the smell of it.' He tried to joke about the effect it was having on him. 'What poisonous potion did you bring with you, Sofía, you witch?' His face came closer to hers, his eyes, narrowed suspiciously then widened with the horror of realising his wife's sister was kissing him, deeply, passionately.

Realising the danger, Sofía tried to push him away, but the perfume entered her mouth and nose, coiling its magical scent in tendrils that enslaved her heart and brain. Her arms disobeyed every command. Though she fought against her instincts, her hands tangled in his hair, gripping the strands of curls and viciously dragging his face closer to hers.

'If you have a soul, go away from me, now! Go now, I say, it's the devil in that magic perfume!' But even as she said the words, her body was arching, pressing against his. Her mouth seeking his, her tongue exploring the sweetness of him.

His hot breath tumbled over her face, his lips covered hers so that her last words were said straight into his open mouth. She bit hard, tasted blood, but even so, wanted his body in an explosion of blatant desire. Sensations she had never known before overcame her rational, level-headed demeanour.

She tried to pull back, her head swimming with her effort to resist him, yet her body disobeyed her commands and arched again to meet his. Wrapping her legs around his hips, her arms tugged at his clothes.

'It's the perfume! You won't be able to resist the perfume, believe me!' she sobbed. 'The yearning . . . It's a magical concoction that seeps into the blood. Its power is irresistible, Mustafa. Fight it if you will, but your body is helpless to resist.' She tried to make herself push him away, but found herself dragging his shirt off his shoulders and pulling him against her bare breasts. The tight curls on his chest were deliciously rough against her most delicate skin and she found the sensation irresistibly erotic and squirmed against his body. 'We're in terrible danger!' she cried. 'We must stop this.' But even as she uttered the words, she longed to feel him inside her.

The passion brought on by the scent reached dizzying heights. A fire raged inside her. 'You must go now, go!' she said, yet her arms pulled him down to cover her body, her legs wrapped around his hips, her hands tearing at his clothes. 'God give me strength, Mustafa, it's not me, it's the perfume . . . get rid of the perfume!' She swiped at the bottle in his fist, hoping it would fall to the floor, but it slipped out of his oily fingers and spun towards the ceiling, showering them both with droplets of the scent.

He stared at her, eyes bulging with madness. 'I can't help it, Sofía. Pull the knife from my belt and plunge it into my heart; stop me before it's too late. Don't let me do this, I love my wife and children!'

* * *

At some point, lost to them both, it became too late to turn against their ardour. In the frenzy that rose like a phoenix from the ashes, they became roaring flames that burned down their own defences. The simultaneous obsession with each other soared, before returning, spent, to ashes once again. In that hour, they had both lived infinite lifetimes of desire and lust and love and regret. Although they knew it was not them. The culprit, the perfume, had possessed them both and controlled their hearts and souls.

CHAPTER 51
SOFIA

Castellorizo, Greece, 1948

THE FOLLOWING SPRING SEEMED THE same as every year before it, except for two things. Sofía was heavy with child and when Jamie was home, they lived in the little house on the square, rebuilt by men that Babá had hired. They agreed, for the moment, to spend a month in England every summer and the rest of the time, while Jamie was in the army, in Castellorizo, where he would come home on leave.

The other unusual thing was that Mustafa had not come home for the Christmas of '47. This had happened before, when violent storms in the Bay of Biscay halted his return from northern France. María was saddened and missed him, but Young Mustafa kept everyone busy. The boy was the double of his father. Tall for his age with a thick head of hair, dazzling green eyes and the rare family trait of short thumbs. The boy, always bursting with energy, kept his sisters busy too.

Post-war trade for precious oils had trebled meaning they all worked extra hard in the distillery. María knew Mustafa would be home in July. She told Sofía she would depend on the magical secret perfume and Sofía's make-up skills to enchant him once again.

* * *

Everyone was surprised when MSV *Barak* sailed into port in February. Children raced up to the Konstantinidis house.

'Mustafa's back!' they cried, then hurried down to the port to be sure they were ready to receive the gifts he always brought. It was then that locals noticed the black flag at half-mast and the sombre faces and black shirts of the crew.

A large chest, dark blue with ornate, highly polished brass corners and straps and a domed lid was ceremoniously carried down the gangplank on the shoulders of six burly sailors. Headed by Mustafa's first mate, they marched, in step, up to the house and deposited the huge casket in the big room.

Confused for a moment, María pulled on her white hijab, hiding her deformed face, as the men approached. Most of the town followed in a silent procession and, in the street below the patio, they heard María's heart-wrenching howl.

'Mustafa!' she cried, throwing herself onto the chest, which contained only his belongings and gifts; and a letter for his wife and another for each of his children. Mustafa's body had been buried at sea, facing Mecca, at sundown.

'Madam,' the skipper said, bowing low. 'I made some promises to my noble captain which I intend to keep. Now is not the time, as you are burdened by grief, but with your permission I will return in three weeks and we will talk.'

'How did he die?' María asked between sobs. 'Tell me! How did my husband die?'

The first mate stood to attention next to the big chest. He felt nothing but sympathy for his captain's widow.

'His heart, madam, it simply stopped beating. They say the Turk always suffered from a big heart.'

'He did,' she sobbed. 'Mustafa had the biggest heart in the world.'

The first mate nodded. 'He was a brother to me, madam. He took me in when I was orphaned at fifteen. My captain knew his time was close and he prepared everything.'

He would keep his secrets, as commanded by his beloved captain. This was surely the kindest thing to do. He had loved and been as loyal as a brother to the big Turk for all his adult life. He had known something was wrong when he received a telegram from Mustafa while the ship was under his charge, at Castellorizo.

```
Bring schooner to Rhodes. Wait for me there.
```

* * *

The Mustafa that boarded the next day was a changed man. A heavy cloud hovered over him, his wide smile and effervescent mood were gone forever. Business was carried out with urgency, journeys undertaken at the greatest of speed.

The ship's clock had just struck midnight, when he heard the revolver's report come from his captain's cabin. The first mate found Mustafa at his desk, wearing his finest clothes, the pistol still in his hand.

A letter addressed to the first mate explained Mustafa's wishes, but not why he had gone to meet his God. He wished to be buried in that part of the sea where his children lay. The first mate was to take care of his family, teach any of his boys to sail and pass the ship onto them when he retired. Until then, it was his for the use of.

* * *

After three days of mourning, María opened the chest. On top of everything was a letter to her. With her heart breaking, she tore it open.

My Dearest Princess,

I have loved you since the first day I saw you. The fire changed nothing, you should not have worried. I have left you on your island, in charge of all our children; forgive me. They will make you proud, I know it. I hope I will be able to look down on you and our children and in some way keep you all safe, but I don't know. These are unchartered waters that I sail now. Keep me in your heart and tell my children I love them more than life. Forgive me for leaving you like this.

I sold the perfume recipe and the money is in the bottom of the chest. I suggest you divide it into three and go to Australia and start a new life. The sale makes you a very rich woman.

I love you so much, my precious Princess, forgive me for any wrongs I may have done. You are, always have been and always will be, my one and only love.

Mustafa

* * *

A month later, Sofía woke in the night, at first unsure what had pulled her from a deep sleep. She tried to get comfortable again, but her swollen belly and the heat of the room meant she lay on her back, staring into the darkness. The strangest sensation of a soft tingling cramp gently gripped her pelvis and she knew, rejoiced, that her baby was ready to meet the world. It seemed an age before it happened again, but so great was her joy, she woke Jamie.

'It's started, Jamie. Our little baby is on its way into the world. Promise you'll stay with me as long as the midwife allows, my darling?'

'Of course I will. Can I get you a drink? Is there anything you want? What about Mamá or María?'

'There's plenty of time.'

Their house on the square consisted of one large room with a wood-burning oven at one end and an enormous bed at the other. However, it had the luxury of an outside bathroom and toilet attached to the back. This extravagance had proper plumbing, a soak-away, buried under the building. Also, a huge tank in the yard collected rain from the apex roof in the winter and piped it to the tap of an outside sink. The house was enough for the moment. They both enjoyed the privacy after what felt like an eternity in the chaos of the Konstantinidis family house.

Another contraction faded. Sofía prepared for the day ahead, hoping they would be a family of three before it ended.

* * *

'Out! Out!' the midwife yelled, slapping Jamie around the head.

He staggered outside, passing Mamá and María on the way. Babá rolled up with a backgammon board and the neighbours provided a small table and two chairs.

'It's time you learned to play *tavli*, young man,' Babá said sitting in the same spot as he had twenty-two years earlier on the day of the earthquake. He glanced at the sky, then the ground, then at Jamie. Remembering his brother, the flamboyant Uncle Kuríllos, Babá looked towards heaven once more and crossed himself.

'Are you all right?' Jamie asked. 'You look a little peculiar.'

Babá blinked. 'What do they call it, *déjà vu*? I was sitting right here with my brother, Kuríllos, while Mamá lay inside there giving birth to Sofía.' He nodded at the door. 'That was the moment when the earthquake rattled this island.'

'I can imagine it must have been terrifying, but I'm sure we're not in for a repeat, Babá. Now, take my mind away from my wife's labour and teach me this crazy game, sir.' He grinned at his father-in-law.

'Concentrate now, because for every game you lose, you are bound to bring me one bottle of good Scottish whisky.' With that, he looked up at the sky again and winked and Jamie felt the mischievous smile of Uncle Kuríllos rain down on them.

Jamie was a little drunk by the time he won his first game against his father-in-law. Already in debt to the account of six bottles of whisky, the win was surely a great triumph and it was only moments later, when the neighbours' congratulations and back-slapping ceased, that the baby's cry made his heart leap. He dived into the house and when he didn't re-appear almost instantly, holding the child aloft, everyone knew it was another useless girl.

Inside, Jamie gazed in wonderment at his wife and child. 'You've made me the happiest man on earth, Sofía. I love you both so much,' he whispered.

'We must call her Tsambika, after the saint,' Sofía told him, her pale face luminous in the dim light.

'My daughter,' he said, gazing at the baby closely swaddled in a soft cotton shawl.

There was something unique, sacrosanct, about the moment. His life had reached its zenith and been worth living. 'I can hardly believe it,' he whispered. 'Wait until I tell my parents, they'll be so thrilled to have their first grandchild. Thank you, Sofía; I love you so much.'

The midwife took baby Tsambika to be washed, then dressed her in the traditional clothes; a flannelette nightgown, a bonnet, scratch mittens and bootees. Placed in her mother's arms, the infant slept soundly.

Overjoyed, Sofía thanked God for this special gift, her previously sceptical view of religion was now beyond reproach. She prayed every day, giving thanks for the miracle of a child. It was on the third day that the midwife returned to check that the umbilical was healing nicely. The little girl was a lively creature, kicking and boxing an imaginary foe as she lay unswaddled. One of her scratch mittens fell off with all the activity.

'Look at that,' the midwife said, taking the baby's tiny hand. 'Another one with short thumbs, like most of your sister's children. If I didn't know better, I'd have said this child was sired by the big Turk.'

The words played on Sofía's mind. The terrible thing that happened after her trip up to Tsambika Monastery had faded, as bad dreams do when never talked about. The next morning, when she had woken alone in the Rhodes apartment, she told herself that's what it had been, just a nightmare. A terrible nightmare brought on by acute exhaustion. She was woken by the landlady's knock and the woman had dressed her wounds and taken her to the airport.

'This is so kind of you,' Sofía had said, telling herself she was right, it had all been a nightmare. Mustafa had never even been there. She was exhausted, delusional, had imagined it all.

'No trouble,' the landlady said. 'Just doing my Christian duty.'

*   *   *

451

Jamie returned to the army after taking his fourteen days' leave. Once he'd left, Mamá and María came down each day to bring food, collect the washing and help with the baby. While Sofía had a much needed rest.

María missed having a baby to care for. Young Mustafa was just under a year old now and with the big Turk gone, María knew she would never have another child. As Sofía slept, María picked up the infant, marvelling at her beauty. For a second and for no apparent reason, she thought of her darling Rosa.

A rocking chair stood in the corner of the room and María sat there, content, rocking gently. The baby snuffled, pushing her fist at her mouth. It was feeding time. María glanced over at Sofía, who was still asleep and decided to try and give her a few more minutes.

'Come on, dear Tsambika, give your mother a little longer.' She eased the baby's fist away from her mouth. That was when the scratch mitten fell off.

María stared disbelievingly. The baby had Mustafa's hands! How could that be? She knew this was an extremely rare hereditary condition. Like a knife into her heart, everything fell into place. This was Mustafa's child!

CHAPTER 52
OLIVIA

Castellorizo, Greece, present day

I TOP UP MY UNCLE'S wine glass. 'I've been thinking – you know this thing with Rob's hands, the genetic thing?'

'Yes, the small thumbs?' Uncle George says.

'Is it really very rare?'

He nods. 'Yes, really very rare.'

'Well ... how come ...? I mean, if it's really rare, was Mustafa my grandfather, not Jamie? Did Sofía, you know, have an affair with María's husband? I find it very hard to believe. Sofía and María seemed so close by your accounts. On top of that, I can't believe Mustafa was a philanderer. It seems he adored María.'

Uncle nods again. 'This is all true. However, the perfume that María and Sofía made was ... still is, incredibly powerful. You witnessed for yourself, what it did to Dorian and Rob this evening?'

I laugh. 'Yes and a perfect couple they make too.'

'To be serious, when María realised Tsambika was Mustafa's child, at first she was devastated. She wanted to hate Mustafa and hate Sofía, but she couldn't because she loved them both. Once she was over the shock and the hurt, she realised what had happened was because of the perfume that she and her sister had made. However, it was an impossible situation.'

'How terribly sad.'

'María decided the only way forgiveness would come was for the sisters to separate. She didn't want them to be apart, they'd been together all their lives, but what else was there. Thanks to Mustafa selling the French perfume recipe, we three – me, Sofía and María – were rich beyond our dreams. However, I had met David, a London stockbroker who was sick of the rat race. He loved Castellorizo and neither of us wanted to leave. So he learned the logistics of making precious oil and we continued to produce and sell it. Sofía and María signed the distillery and all the family property over to me. They had no use for it, yet they both wanted to keep it in the family. Sofía and baby Tsambika went to Brighton, Jamie's hometown, where they bought the flat and were very happy. María went to Australia with all her children and Babá and Mamá. Jamie knew nothing of what had happened, he died thinking Tsambika was his child and he was also thrilled that Sofía had decided to move to his hometown. Sadly, María and Sofía never met again.'

'It is very sad that they were parted forever. It sounds as though María and Mustafa had such a strong love.'

Uncle nods. 'And Sofía and Jamie too, they adored each other.'

'What happened to Jamie?'

'Ah, he was killed in a car accident when Tsambika was a toddler. Icy road, fog. He was driving home on leave. Skidded into a tree, killed instantly, they said. He knew nothing of the turmoil that surrounded the parentage of the daughter he absolutely adored.'

'I'm glad he never knew the truth. What about Mustafa?'

'When I next met the first mate, he told me of Mustafa's distress when he picked him up from Rhodes. He confided that the big Turk was changed beyond belief – so unhappy, he had taken

454

his own life. I had already guessed the truth. It was the perfume, you see. It had driven him to do something so alien to his religion and his own morals, he could not live with the guilt. María was right when she said he always suffered from a big heart. I never knew such a generous man.'

'And the secret recipe, the magical one, was that ever sold?'

Uncle shakes his head. 'I haven't even had a chance to check if it's in the recipe book, though I'm sure it will be. My sisters were very meticulous. We need to go through both ledgers, very thoroughly, when we get back.' He pauses and looks at me closely. 'By the way, did you say you were going to move in with me, or did I dream it?'

'I'd like to. What do you think?'

'I'd like that too.'

'So one last question, Uncle . . . what happened to the ship, MSV *Barak*. Do you know?'

'There's a happy ending. Young Zafiro joined the first mate when he was a young man. Like his father, the boy developed an enormous passion for the sea. He went on to become a sea captain and steered great container ships between major trading ports around the world. As for Mustafa's beautiful three-masted schooner, when the first mate retired, MSV *Barak* made its last great journey across the oceans to end its life in Adelaide, Australia. The clipper became a waterside family restaurant. A grand Castellorizo reunion took place there for the Australian branch of the Konstantinidis family. I'm sure there are photographs in the album. However, eventually it fell into disrepair and was scrapped.'

The story is almost over but there is something else I feel needs to be understood. 'Just one *final* question . . . Did Mummy know?'

'You mean that Mustafa was her father?' My uncle shakes his head. 'There was no reason to tell her.'

Uncle George glances over my shoulder and smiles. 'Oh look, here comes your friend. I wonder if Greg does solar – could you ask him? Although we all have one foot in the past here, I do think we should have the other one firmly planted in the future, or rather, future generations.' His eyes narrow and sparkle with mischief. 'I mean, I sincerely hope there will be future generations.' He bobs his eyebrows in that naughty way that always makes me smile, then continues. 'What with global warming and all this sunshine, it would be good for the house to be off grid, don't you think?'

'Solar, yes, it would be a good plan.'

'Well, whatever you decide, I'll meet you here at eleven o'clock tomorrow morning. Oh and one more thing: I'd like to come back in a month, if you can spare the time to accompany me.'

'It's been wonderful, Uncle,' I say. 'Of course I'll come back with you.'

'That's good to hear,' Greg says as he appears at my side. I feel his fingers intertwine with mine and know we will be walking into the future together.

ACKNOWLEDGEMENTS

Thanks go to my editor, Sarah Bauer, and everyone on the team at Bonnier Books UK for their great work in bringing *The Summer of Secrets* to fruition. Gary and Jeff Coventry-Fenn for their hospitality, information, and tours of Brighton. Thanks to the residents of Castellorizo; I treasure every moment spent on that little Greek island. Thanks to Patricia Castle for introducing me to her friends on the island of Castellorizo (Patricia was an extra in the 1991 Oscar-winning Italian film, *Mediterraneo*, directed by Gabriele Salvatores, location: Castellorizo). Thanks also to the Mayor of Castellorizo who bears no resemblance to the mayor in the story (who was a figment of my imagination). Mayor Psapsakis Yeorgos was very helpful, as was the beautiful book he gifted me, *Kastellorizo*, by Michael N Sechas. This gave me good insight to the people of the island at the start of my research. Another book that helped me with the facts was the story of the HMS *Empire Patrol*, *Embers on the Sea* by Paul Boyatzis, a young survivor of the HMS *Empire Patrol* disaster. There are so many versions of the truth, which is hardly surprising as those who claim to remember what happened were young children at the time. Thanks to Heleny Karavelatos who, at four years old, found herself in one of the *Empire Patrol*'s lifeboats which capsized. Her earliest memory is of a large woman sitting on her, the lifeboat capsizing, then at some point a rope was tied under her arms and attached to the side of a float where she remained until her rescue. Thanks to Danae Korypas and her kind explanation and lovely photographs of the Castellorizo costume. Also, Castellorizo's oldest resident, ninety-year-old Maria Lazarus, one of sixteen children, for sharing her memories of the bombing of Castellorizo and all that followed. Thanks to Richard Fenn, a professional scent analyst who helped me to understand how our daily lives are influenced by the natural perfume of everything around us.

HISTORICAL NOTES

The History of Castellorizo

CASTELLORIZO IS THE MOST EASTERN Greek island. Only 7.3 square kilometres, this tiny island lies three kilometres from the Turkish coast. The turn of the century saw Castellorizo at the peak of its prosperity, under Ottoman rule. Nearby Turkish farmland belonging to the islanders, magnificent trading ships, and a thriving boat-building business in the bay of Mandraki, brought great riches to the community of Castellorizo. More than 9,000 people lived on the island, with another four to five thousand living across the water on the Turkish mainland in an area now known as Kaş.

A local revolution on the island in 1913 led to a disastrous period of self-rule when Castellorizo's prosperity dwindled. Along came World War I, when Turkey and Greece found themselves on opposite sides. In the years 1921 to 1945, Castellorizo fell under Italian occupation. Harsh restrictions were imposed on trade, shipping, and diving. The Castellorizons, under Italian rule, were exempt from conscription, yet they had no political rights and came under the Italian education system. Any reference to Greece or Greek was prohibited by law. Local church festivals were banned, and Orthodox weddings and funerals required special permission. The economy fell into further deterioration.

However, under Italian rule, a number of benefits came to light. All the Dodecanese islands were mapped systematically, maintenance of ancient and medieval monuments commenced and under public works programmes hospitals were built on Rhodes, Kos, Kalymnos and Leros islands. However, Castellorizo itself did not benefit greatly from the Italian occupation or its public works programme, but improved shipping connections with Italy and between the Dodecanese allowed interaction with other islands. Postal and telephone communications were improved. A massive exodus of the Castellorizo people took place, mostly heading for Australia. This book, *The Summer of Secrets*, starts on the 16th of March 1926 when a massive earthquake damaged or destroyed 361 houses and devastated the port area. Italian authorities mobilised aid from Rhodes and Rome, and the Turks came over to help with the rescue of buried people. Although the Castellorizons worked together in an enormous communal effort, recovery was difficult. Eventually, elegant buildings rose from the rubble, some of these were by designed by Florentino Di Fausto, one of Italy's greatest architects, whose amazing designs already graced the island of Rhodes.

Loss of trading opportunities and privileges, combined with the outbreak of World War II in 1939 contributed to the increasing migration to Australia. The population dropped to just over one thousand people.

Castellorizo in World War II

Castellorizo first felt the affects of direct combat in February 1941. The British Operation Abstention saw two British destroyers arrive off the coast of Casterllorizo on the 24th of February 1941.

Two hundred commandos from the British army disembarked into ten whaler boats (very large rowing boats) and headed for

Nifti Point. Only two of the boats (and about fifty men) found their destination. Some of the other boats ended up in the darkness of the harbour where they were fired upon by the Italian army.

At dawn, the first group of commandos approached the harbour overland but were discovered and fired upon by the occupants of an Italian patrol truck at Mandraki bay. After overcoming the Italians, the commandos proceeded to the harbour where they occupied the Italian transmission station and the Governor's house, both of which they found empty. The Italian garrison of approximately fifty had apparently fled.

The HMS *Ladybird*, a British gunboat, arrived in the port but was fired upon by the Italians at Cape Stefano and Paleo Castro. A battle ensued. The British triumphed and took the remaining Italian soldiers prisoners.

The Union Jack was raised over Castellorizo and the locals came out of their houses and sang the Greek national anthem in Greek for the first time in decades. The celebration was short lived as two Italian CR 42 bombers appeared overhead. The battle continued for days with the British coming under relentless fire from Italian torpedo boats. On the 27th of February, an Italian flame-thrower squad and the Italian Black Shirt Battalion arrived.

Without naval or air support, and desperately short of arms, ammunition, and food, the British withdrew. It was a resounding victory for the Italians and a humiliating defeat for the Allies.

The island suffered much damage. Twenty-nine Castellorizo locals who assisted the British commandos were charged and transported to prison in Brindisi, Italy.

Italy surrendered to the Allies on the 8th of September 1943. British military arrived on Castellorizo, on the 10th of September, anxious to occupy the island before the Germans took hold. Castellorizo suffered sustained German bombing throughout October and November 1943, but remained the only island in the region occupied by the Allies. Four hundred British troops were stationed there by the end of September, and a further nine hundred in October, resulting in almost as many British soldiers as Castellorizo civilians.

Heavy bombing by a total of eighteen Luftwaffe planes on the 17th to the 18th of October caused substantial damage to local housing and loss of life. In the following week, approximately 1,000 malnourished and frightened Castellorizons, gathered their valuables and children, nailed their houses closed, and boarded a British ship for free passage to safety in Cyprus. In a Cypriot refugee camp, they were showered, their clothes fumigated, then they were fed and quarantined for a month under medical observation before being moved to Nuseirat refugee camp in Gaza in March 1944. Here they remained safely housed, clothed, and fed until the end of the war in September 1945; a total of seventeen months. Some even managed to earn a living in the camp which contained another 14,000 Greek refugees from Dodecanese islands.

These refugee camps were supported by the international relief agency; United Nations Relief and Rehabilitation Administration (UNRRA). Founded in 1943 and supported by forty-three countries, the purpose of the UNRAA was to organise, co-ordinate and administer relief for war victims in any area controlled by the United Nations, such as the people of Castellorizo.

During its four years of existence, the UNRRA distributed approximately $4 billion worth of clothes, food, medicine, tools, and farm apparatus despite global shortages. Greece was particularly hard hit by starvation and political chaos through World War II and beyond. UNRRA also helped many thousands of displaced people return to their homes after the conflict.

Many dwellings on Castellorizo were destroyed in the severe bombings which continued into November 1943. Throughout 1944, the island was an important base for the allies and vast stores of fuel were held there. The summer of 1944 saw yet another tragedy strike the island. The weather was unusually hot and dry, causing a catastrophic fire. It is not clear where the fire started, but it is purported to have broken out in a petrol store later spreading to the ammunition dump. Any remaining houses that were left along the waterfront quickly went up in flames as the fire spread.

When World War II ended in 1945, the Dodecanese islands were left under British military control, but the citizenship of the inhabitants remained Italian. Castellorizo was in ruins but the British army remained on the island to help the evacuees return. The first fifty refugees came back in early July 1945, followed by 151 from Nuseirat a few weeks later. By the end of the month, almost 200 men had started rebuilding their homes with supplies and rations provided by the British. In September 1945, three months after the first working party had returned to the island, 494 refugees boarded the British vessel HMS *Empire Patrol* bound for home.

HMS *Empire Patrol* Fire, 1945

Soon after leaving Port Said on the 29th of September 1945, a fire broke out in a small room next to the medical room, Cabin 29. The room housed various medical stores and was also used to heat milk and water on a primus stove for toddlers and infants. The cabin was occupied by two children, Maria and her brother, Economou. Accompanying the children was their mother Christina Papoutsi and their grandmother, Katerina Palassi. The waves were particularly strong but the ship continued to plough through the rolling swell towards Castellorizo and everything seemed perfectly normal.

Just after midday, everyone was alerted by hysterical shrieks coming from the main staircase that connected B and C decks. Cabin 29 was ablaze and Christine Papoutsi, badly burned, was screaming in the corridor. Their grandmother, Katerina, dived into the burning cabin and managed to get the children out, but then collapsed with shock and probable smoke inhalation. One of the crew emptied a fire extinguisher into the cabin, but the beds and walls were already ablaze. Another three extinguishers were emptied into the room, to no avail. The fire took a hold of the ship and in minutes, the middle of the ship was ablaze.

The flames quickly broke through the wooden flooring, setting one of the lifeboats alight. The rigging burned through and the lifeboat, containing twelve refugees, fell from its great height into the sea.

The ship's master, James Taylor, hurried to the bridge and sent the following SOS message after stating the ships exact position: SHIP ON FIRE STEM TO STERN, TAKING TO BOATS.

His SOS was received by SS *Empire Glory*, thirty-three kilometres to the east, whose captain immediately radioed Port Said and passed on the message. SS *Empire Glory* could not attend the disaster as her cargo was explosives. The Naval Office ordered the aircraft carrier, HMS *Trouncer* to head for the *Empire Patrol*.

Meanwhile, the situation on the *Empire Patrol* worsened. Many jumped off the ship from a great height. Hysterical passengers on Lifeboat 3 were so panicked that as the boat was lowered, it capsized before reaching the water and they were all thrown into the sea.

By now the fire was raging and the metal plating on the sides of the ship glowed white-hot. Eighty women and children were trapped on the head of the ship. Some people attempted to run the gauntlet to the rear, where it was safer, and several of the crew risked their own lives to make a chain to pull them through, but the deck was so hot by then, the barefooted passengers ran back when their feet started blistering from the heat. The crew threw life rafts and lifebelts into the sea for those who had jumped or had fallen out of lifeboats.

The situation was dire when an aircraft carrier appeared on the horizon. However, moving the women and children from the *Empire Patrol* to HMS *Trouncer* proved very difficult. The refugees had to climb down to the sea and into life rafts, and then be brought up into the aircraft carrier. Several other ships came to assist, however, many passengers were already in the roiling sea.

By early morning of the next day, 488 of the 549 refugees had been accounted for and the search continued.

* * *

One of the most remarkable events that I discovered was the rescue of a small boy by a submarine. The morning that the HMS *Empire Patrol* left Alexandria, HMS *Spark* happened to be in port. Seeing scores of women at the rails as *Empire Patrol* pulled away, the submarine crew thought they were WRENS returning home, and waved to them, much to the delight of the Castellorizo women. Later that day, the *Spark*'s crew were told the ship was full of Greek women and children, and on fire. At 6 p.m. the *Spark* received news that an SOS had been transmitted and the refugees were taking to the lifeboats. HMS *Spark* raced towards the floundering ship, breaking its speed records to get to the refugees.

Four hours later, the burning ship came into view, glowing in the dark. They rigged up a searchlight, while a plane dropped flares. Someone shouted they could see a person in the water. There was a big swell, and it was pitch black, so everyone scanned the sea. There he was, a little boy on a small piece of wood, perhaps a hatch cover. He lay belly-down, paddling with his hands. One of the crew tied a rope around himself and went into the heaving sea to rescue him. The poor boy couldn't talk, or even stand, and was about eight years old. His burns were treated, then he was wrapped in blankets and fed. The submarine deposited him on the aircraft carrier, and after the captain had received a severe reprimand for acting without orders, the HMS *Spark* headed for home. On their way, they received a message from the aircraft carrier that the boy had been reunited with his jubilant mother.

Castellorizo in the Post-War Years

The wrangle over the future of Castellorizo was extraordinary. As Greece had never reclaimed Castellorizo, despite many appeals from its citizens, the foreign ministers from several countries agreed to cede the island to Turkey, but the Soviet Union asked for more time to study the island's circumstances. The island's future remained unresolved until the Council of Foreign Ministers met in April 1946 and heard a case put forward by Herbert Evatt. The Australian had helped write the UN charter and led the country's delegation to the assembly in 1946 and was an ardent spokesman for the rights of small nations.

The United States and Great Britain stressed that to sever Castellorizo from the Dodecanese islands would be harmful to a population that regarded itself as wholly Greek. The government of Greece finally agreed and when the peace treaty with Italy was signed the Dodecanese islands, including Castellorizo, were ceded to Greece on the 15th of February 1947.

Ironically, the long-awaited union with Greece came after most of the Castellorizon population had emigrated to other countries. The now nearly-deserted island bore little opportunity for earning a living, so its emigrants saw no reason to return. In 1946, the population was 655 and continued to fall.

Towards the late 1970s, tourism in Europe expanded. By 1985, ferries from Rhodes, and a small airport on the island, brought European backpackers. Descendants from Australia reclaimed their family homes and rebuilding began. This activity continues today as affluent expats from far and wide return to claim and renovate the homes of the ancestors.

Castellorizo is now a charming tourist destination. In the summer season, the population expands to almost two thousand. Consistent development is slowly restoring a permanent population.

The Story of Rosa

When somebody succeeds against all obstacles, one must shout about their persistence and tenacity. So, it was when I met with a Greek dancer on the island of Rhodes. From the age of three, Natasa Kosta loved to dance and started ballet lessons at the age of four. Despite many obstacles, she never gave up on her dream to become a professional dancer. An unusual career in Greece where most intelligent young people are pressured to pursue more traditional careers. Natasa won a scholarship to Bath Dance College in the UK, when she was just sixteen years old, and, at that tender age, went there to study ballet and modern dance. Two years later, she won a dance contract with Connecting Arts in Greece where I was lucky enough to see her perform.